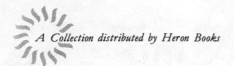
A Collection distributed by Heron Books

THE
GREATEST MASTERPIECES
OF
RUSSIAN LITERATURE

IVAN S. TURGENEV

FATHERS
AND SONS

———

LIZA

Translated from the Russian by
Avril Pyman, Ph.D., M.A., and by W.R.S. Ralston

Introduction by A.B. McMillin

Original Frontispiece by Marek Rudnicki

Original Illustrations by
Jacques Carelman for "Fathers and Sons"
and David Knight for "Liza"

Distributed by
HERON BOOKS

marek Rudzki

INTRODUCTION

Turgenev, the most poetic and yet one of the most realistic of Russian nineteenth century novelists, was also the first writer to make an impact in the West. His fame and popularity were established with English and French readers long before Tolstoy and Dostoevsky had gained any following outside their own country; it was the first time Western writers like Flaubert and Henry James, had met a Russian novelist whom they could regard as an equal, if not master. For the outside world "mute Russia" had found a voice, a voice at once powerful and poetic that is still listened to and admired today.

Ivan Sergeyevitch Turgenev was born at Orel, a provincial town in central Russia, on the 28th of October 1818. Son of a handsome ex-cavalry officer and a rich, unloved and cruelly despotic heiress (known locally as "the witch"), he spent most of his childhood on his mother's estate at Spasskoye (Orel province), where, no doubt, he witnessed many of the scenes of cruelty that were to make such a powerful effect when reproduced in his Sportsman's Sketches (1852). His mother's tyranny was complete, and the contrast between the cultured and civilised literary soirées often held at the manor house and, on the other hand, the sometimes bestial treatment of the serfs on the estate made a great impression on the young Ivan. His mother's domination in even the most intimate matters was so great as to be almost pathological, and throughout his life the writer's character reflected a certain weakness which may perhaps be traced back to this source.

INTRODUCTION

In the year 1833 he began to study in Moscow, but when a year later his mother moved to St. Petersburg he followed her and transferred to that university. Here he was able to make many valuable literary connections, such as Nikolai Gogol' and professor Pletnev, a friend of Pushkin's and editor of the influential liberal journal, The Contemporary Review. *On one occasion he was even able to meet Pushkin himself. After graduating he went to Berlin to continue his philosophical studies. Here he made the acquaintance of young Russian idealists, like Stankevich and Granovsky, and acquired a deep admiration for German culture and Western civilisation in general. He returned to Russia three years later a confirmed liberal and Westernizer, a position he maintained throughout his life. Indeed much of his life was to be spent in Europe, thanks to his infatuation for the Spanish prima donna, Mme Viardot (Paulina Garcia). Wife and husband alike found Turgenev's company pleasant and so it was often a curious ménage à trois that travelled between the musical centres of Europe. This attachment, which lasted all his life, was highly displeasing to his mother as was the decision to make "scribbling" his full-time occupation after only desultory attempts at joining the academic profession and the civil service. At her death in 1850 he received a very considerable fortune.*

Turgenev began his literary career as a poet and in the mid forties gained a considerable reputation, largely on the strength of a lengthy narrative poem, Parasha, *but it was not long before his true talent manifested itself in the* Sportsman's Sketches *which in 1847 began to appear in* The Contemporary Review *and finally came out in book form five years later. These "sketches" were simply scenes from Russian rural life, very quietly and poetically drawn, but almost all unobtrusively underlining something that was far from being a commonplace belief : that the peasants had individual characters and dignity no less and, indeed, often more so than the landowners who treated them so throughtlessly and cruelly. The cumulative effect of these restrained, humanitarian stories was extremely great : it is said that the future Alexander II was deeply impressed and that the book influenced his eventual decision to do away with the entire system of serfdom. (Emancipation came in 1861).* On the other hand the censor who had passed this Russian equivalent of Uncle Tom's Cabin *for publication was relieved of his post, whilst Turgenev himself, following what the authorities regarded as an excessively enthusiastic obituary for the "dangerous" Gogol', was soon banished to his estate. With political martyrdom—the crowning honour for a literary lion in Russia—he became established as the chief spokesman for liberal ideas and leading writer of the day—before even his first novel had appeared.*

Between 1856 and 1877 Turgenev wrote six novels as well as a number of long short stories and novellas. His novels are all faithful reflections of the ideas, moods and aspirations of the periods in which they are set. Turgenev's art was not so much one of imagination as of poetic representation of reality : in the forwards to an 1880 collected edition of his novels he wrote, "I have endeavoured ... conscientiously and impartially to depict and embody in suitable types both what Shakespeare calls the body and pressure of time *and that rapidly changing physiognomy of Russians of the cultured stratum which has been preeminently the object of my observations".* He *realised that his job was to record and he became something of a weathercock of ideas, read and respected (at any rate until the appearance of* Fathers and Sons) *by both liberals and conservatives, Westernizers and Slavophiles alike, so much so that the Russian critics, always inclined in this direction, wrote almost exclusively about the content of his work with little, if any, reference to its literary merits. A prime example of this was the radical critic Dobrolyubov's review of* On the Eve *entitled* When Will the Real Day Come ?. *Turgenev himself wrote in a letter to B. P. Botkin of 1855, "There are sometimes ages when*

INTRODUCTION

literature cannot be merely *art, for there are interests that are higher than poetic interests", and again three years later he wrote to Tolstoy : "our age has no time for birds singing their heads off in the branches". It is true also that, with the exception of* First Love *which will always be regarded as one of the finest of Turgenev's works, the novels are more successful than the novellas which are often about the same length as the novels proper but which eschew civic and topical themes. The reason for this is perhaps that although the political and social issues that are discussed and reflected in the novels have lost their immediacy and even interest for us, the novels are, as it were, fortified and given shape by the tension of the ideas pervading them. The first,* Rudin, *is not merely a portrait of a young and impractical liberal of the thirties (Turgenev must have met many such people at Moscow University, and, indeed, Rudin is thought to be a portrait of one of his friends, Michael Bakunin) but a masterpiece of gradual character portrayal and revelation. Likewise,* Fathers and Sons *retains its appeal and interest long after "nihilism" has become a word only found in histories of political thought, for the novel is not merely inspired topical journalism but treats the eternal problems of youth and age, radicalism and conservatism, theorizing and experience.*

Turgenev's novels have several features in common, apart from their concern with topical questions and contemporary types. They all share a remarkable delicacy of proportion in construction (compared with, for example, the works of Gogol' or Dostoevsky) ; in this respect Turgenev shows himself a follower of the tradition established by Pushkin, rather than the much more widely adopted Gogolian disregard for form found throughout most of the nineteenth century. He also showed himself an heir of Pushkin in the immensely poetic atmosphere of his novels, extending even to the characterisation. Like the great poet before him, but unlike most of this contemporaries Turgenev wrote evocatively rather than analytically. Perhaps the most poetical of all the novels is Liza, *although even here the author never lapses into sentimentality : his characters and the ideas and feeling that motivate their actions are too strong. This novel also presents a good example of Turgenev's impartiality and objectivity : the Slavophile Lavretsky is able to outpoint in argument the young and superficial Westernizer Panshin, despite the author's own lifelong adherence to the Westernizers.*

In 1850 Turgenev wrote a work that although of no exceptional literary merit was important in that it gave a name to a phenomenon which can be seen throughout Russian literature of the first part of the nineteenth century ; the book was, The Diary of a Superfluous Man. *The superfluous man was out of joint with his times and found his ideals frustrated ; often with considerable talents he seems to have been unable to take positive and effective action in whatever sphere he moved. Early examples of this type were Pushkin's Yevgeny Onegin, Lermontov's Pechorin and Griboyedov's Chatsky, whilst it found perhaps its purest embodiment in Goncharov's Oblomov. It was Turgenev, however, who, apart from providing a name (as he was also to do with the type of thinker exemplified by Bazarov), chronicled most thoroughly the thoughts and aspirations of these types, and this line of superfluous men is another link between his novels.*

In Rudin *(1856) the young and loquacious liberal idealist is shown to be quite incapable of coping with life's practical problems, his weakness being particularly evident in his dealings with Natal'ya, the girl he loves—one of the first in the remarkable gallery of characterful yet sensitive women appearing in Turgenev's work. In* Liza *too the heroine is a much stronger character than either of the men that love her. Critics and public alike accepted Turgenev's picture as reflecting reality, such was the authority he had built up, but when in his third novel,* On the Eve *(1860), the strongminded Yelena still had no real male counterpart the critics began to ask when there would be a true hero, or, in Dobrolyubov's words, when the real day would come. Even now the crtitics blamed the prevailing political and social atmosphere rather than the author of the novel.* On the Eve *had, in fact, a hero, Insarov, but he was a Bulgarian, whilst the Russians in the novel were too weak to claim the heroine's attentions. In such an atmosphere of expectation it was ironical that when, in* Fathers and Sons *(1862), Turgenev did finally present his readers with a hero not merely purposeful and effective but also Russian, the immediate reaction from both Left and Right was one of fierce hostility.*

Not that the book's reception was entirely unexpected : foreseeing controversy he spent the winter of 1861-2 in trying to retouch the novel to make it acceptable to both Right and Left. Relations with the Left had worsened considerably after some personal abuse from Dobrolyubov, leading Turgenev take On the Eve *to the conservative journal* The Russian Messenger *under Kathov, instead of to* The Contemporary Review, *now in the hands of the extremely left-wing Chernyshevsky and Dobrolyubov. The conservatives attacked the author for glorifying a boorish iconoclast and presenting a caricature of the older generation, whilst the radicals, as expected, abused him indignantly for "betraying the Left" and slandering and ridiculing the "nihilists". Later the young critic Pisemsky was to reverse the radical reaction, but the wound had been inflicted and Turgenev never really forgave the Left. In private correspondence the author several times referred to Bazarov as "the most sympathetic of all my characters", saying that he shared all the young nihilists's views except those on art. "If the reader does not like Bazarov", wrote Turgenev, "I am to blame". Bazarov is in character the exact opposite of the author, which perhaps explains some of this sympathy : the nihilist is as singleminded as his creator was impassive. But at the end of the book Bazarov is forced to conclude that he is as superfluous as all the idealists of the forties, that he has failed : is it simply as a loser that the author feels sympathy for him ? Many readers, however, unaware of Turgenev's statement that the entire work was aimed at attacking the nobility as a ruling class, may feel greater sympathy for the Kirsanovs than the harsh figure of Bazarov. Nikolai Kirsanov, in particular, seems a very close reflection of what we know of the author himself. The portrait of Bazarov was based on a casual acquaintance of Turgenev's, a certain country doctor called Dmitriyev, and indeed we are told that "without Dmitriyev there would have been no Bazarov". Fourteen years later, writing to Saltykov-Shchedrin, describing the creation of* Fathers and Sons, *he said that "the portrait seemed to be guided by some kind of* fate", *by "something stronger than the author himself". It was obviously not a malicious caricature any more than it was a politically-motivated panegyric. "For the first time", wrote Turgenev later, "I was seriously satisfied with my work", and yet it was for this portrait that he met a storm of abuse from representatives of all shades of political opinion. Such was the fate of one of the most impartial and objective writers Russia has ever known.*

Two more novels appeared after Father and Sons : Smoke *(1867) and* Virgin Soil *(1877), but neither enjoyed any real success. Turgenev was still read, but as a grand old man of letters rather than as the spokesman for the avant-garde. He was accused of being out of sympathy with youth, of losing touch with reality, and of living in an European ivory tower. What criticism could be more damning for a writer who believed that "to accurately and powerfully reproduce truth, the very reality of life, is the highest happiness for a writer, even if that truth does not coincide with his own sympathies" ?*

By the end of his life Turgenev enjoyed great prestige in Europe, and in 1880 he returned to Russia for the celebrations marking the fiftieth anniversary of Pushkin's death. The entire visit was a triumph for the old writer, now almost a stranger in his own land : old wounds had

INTRODUCTION

healed and honours were poured upon the head of this figure from the past. He died three years later at the small town of Bougival, near Paris.

In his heyday, the first years of Alexander II's reign, Turgenev was respected as both a leader of progressive thought and as a sensitive recorder of current moods, trends and ideas. His achievement was to avoid tendentiousness whilst dealing with topical and civic themes ; to provide a "golden mean". Nowadays he is read for the incomparable poetic atmosphere of his novels, for their grace and proportion, and for the wide range of delicate yet convincing portraits they contain. It is difficult to envisage a time when Liza and Fathers and Sons will cease to delight and fascinate Russian and Western readers alike.

London, March 1967.   A. B. McMillin

CONTENTS

FATHERS AND SONS

" WELL, Peter? Cannot you see them yet?" asked a
barin [1] of about forty who, hatless, and clad in a dusty
jacket over a pair of tweed breeches, stepped on to the
verandah of a posting-house on the 20th day of May,
1859. The person addressed was the *barin's* servant—
a round-cheeked young fellow with small, dull eyes and
a chin adorned with a tuft of pale-coloured down.

Glancing along the high road in a supercilious manner,
the servant (in whom everything, from the turquoise
ear-ring to the dyed, pomaded hair and the mincing
gait, revealed the modern, the rising generation) replied:
" No, *barin*, I cannot."

" Is that so?" queried the *barin*.

" Yes," the servant affirmed.

The *barin* sighed, and seated himself upon a bench.
While he is sitting there with his knees drawn under
him and his eyes moodily glancing to right and left, the
reader may care to become better acquainted with his
personality.

His name was Nikolai Petrovitch Kirsanov, and he
owned (some fifteen versts from the posting-house) a
respectable little property of about two hundred souls
(or, as, after that he had apportioned his peasantry
allotments, and set up a " farm," he himself expressed
it, a property " of two thousand *desiatini* " [2]). His

---

[1] Gentleman or squire.　　　[2] The *desiatin* = 2·86 acres.

father, one of the generals of 1812, had spent his life exclusively in military service as the commander, first of a brigade, and then of a division; and always he had been quartered in the provinces, where his rank had enabled him to cut a not inconspicuous figure. As for Nikolai Petrovitch himself, he was born in Southern Russia (as also was his elder brother, Paul—of whom presently), and, until his fourteenth year, received his education amid a circle of hard-up governors, free-and-easy aides-de-camp, and sundry staff and regimental officers. His mother came of the family of the Koliazins, and, known in maidenhood as Agathe, and subsequently as Agathoklea Kuzminishna Kirsanov, belonged to the type of " officer's lady." That is to say, she wore pompous mobcaps and rustling silk dresses, was always the first to approach the cross in church, talked volubly and in a loud tone, of set practice admitted her sons to kiss her hand in the morning, and never failed to bless them before retiring to rest at night. In short, she lived the life which suited her. As the son of a general, Nikolai Petrovitch was bound—though he evinced no particular bravery, and might even have seemed a coward—to follow his brother Paul's example by entering the army; but unfortunately, owing to the fact that, on the very day when there arrived the news of his commission, he happened to break his leg, it befell that, after two months in bed, he rose to his feet a permanently lamed man. When his father had finished wringing his hands over the mischance, he sent his son to acquire a civilian education; whence it came about that Nikolai, at eighteen, found himself a student at the University of St. Petersburg. At the same period his brother obtained a commission in one of the regiments of Guards; and, that being so, their father apportioned the two young men a joint establishment, and placed it under the more or less detached supervision of Ilya

Koliazin, their maternal uncle and a leading *tchinovnik*.[1]
That done, the father returned to his division and his
wife, and only at rare intervals sent his sons sheets of
grey foolscap (scrawled and re-scrawled in flamboyant
calligraphy) to which there was appended, amid a bower
of laborious flourishes, the signature " Piotr Kirsanov,
Major-General." In the year 1835 Nikolai Petrovitch
obtained his university degree; and in the same year
General Kirsanov was retired for incompetence at a
review, and decided to transfer his quarters to St.
Petersburg. Unfortunately, just as he was on the point
both of renting a house near the Tavritchesky Gardens
and of being enrolled as a member of the English Club,
a stroke put an end to his career, and Agathoklea
Kuzminishna followed him soon afterwards, since never
had she succeeded in taking to the dull life of the capital,
but always had hankered after the old provincial existence. Already during his parents' lifetime, and to their
no small vexation, Nikolai Petrovitch had contrived to
fall in love with the daughter of a certain *tchinovnik*
named Prepolovensky, the landlord of his flat; and
since the maiden was not only comely, but one of the
type known as " advanced " (that is to say, she perused
an occasional " Science " article in one newspaper or
another), he married her out of hand as soon as the
term of mourning was ended, and, abandoning the
Ministry of Provincial Affairs to which, through his
father's influence, he had been posted, embarked upon
connubial felicity in a villa adjoining the Institute of
Forestry. Thence, after a while, the couple removed to
a diminutive, but in every way respectable, flat which
could boast of a spotless vestibule and an icy-cold
drawing-room; and thence, again, they migrated to the
country, where they settled for good, and where, in due
time, they had born to them a son Arkady. The existence

[1] Civil servant.

of husband and wife was one of perfect comfort and tranquillity. Almost never were they parted from one another, they read together, they played the piano together, and they sang duets. Also, she would garden or superintend the poultry-yard, and he would set forth a-hunting, or see to the management of the estate. Meanwhile Arkady led an existence of equal calm and comfort, and grew, and waxed fat; until, in 1847, when ten years had been passed in this idyllic fashion, Kirsanov's wife breathed her last. The blow proved almost more than the husband could bear—so much so that his head turned grey in a few weeks. Yet, though he sought distraction for his thoughts by going abroad, he felt constrained, in the following year, to return home, where, after a prolonged period of inaction, he took up the subject of Industrial Reform. Next, in 1855, he sent his son to the University of St. Petersburg, and, for the same reason, spent the following three winters in the capital, where he seldom went out, but spent the greater part of his time in endeavouring to fraternise with his son's youthful acquaintances. The fourth winter, however, he was prevented by various circumstances from spending in St. Petersburg; and thus in the May of 1859 we see him—greyheaded, dusty, a trifle bent, and wholly middle-aged—awaiting his son's home-coming after the elevation of the latter (in Nikolai's own footsteps) to the dignity of a graduate.

Presently either a sense of decency or (more probably) a certain disinclination to remain immediately under his master's eye led the servant to withdraw to the entrance gates, and there to light a pipe. Nikolai Petrovitch, however, continued sitting with head bent, and his eyes contemplating the ancient steps of the verandah, up which a stout speckled hen was tap-tapping its way on a pair of splayed yellow legs, and thereby causing an untidy, but fastidious-looking, cat

4

to regard it from the balustrade with marked disapproval. Meanwhile the sun beat fiercely down, and from the darkened interior of a neighbouring granary came a smell as of hot rye straw. Nikolai Petrovitch sank into a reverie. " My son Arkady a graduate!"—the words kept passing and repassing through his mind. Again and again he tried to think of something else, but always the same thought returned to him. Until eventually he reverted to the memory of his dead wife. " Would that she were still with me!" was his yearning reflection. Presently a fat blue pigeon alighted upon the roadway, and fell to taking a hasty drink from a pool beside the well. And almost at the instant that the spectacle of the bird caught Nikolai Petrovitch's eye, his ear caught the sound of approaching wheels.

"They are coming, I think," hazarded the servant as he stepped forward through the gates.

Nikolai Petrovitch sprang to his feet, and strained his eyes along the road. Yes, coming into view there was a *tarantass*,[1] drawn by three stagehorses; and in the *tarantass* there could be seen the band of a student's cap and the outlines of a familiar, well-beloved face.

" Arkasha, Arkasha!" was Kirsanov's cry as, running forward, he waved his arms. A few moments later he was pressing his lips to the sun-tanned, dusty, hairless cheek of the newly-fledged graduate.

[1] A species of four-wheeled carriage.

5

II

" YES, but first give me a rub down, dearest Papa,"
said Arkady in a voice which, though a little hoarsened
with travelling, was yet clear and youthful. " See! I
am covering you with dust!" he added as joyously he
returned his father's caresses.

" Oh, but that will not matter," said Nikolai Petrovitch with a loving, reassuring smile as he gave the collar
of his son's blue cloak a couple of pats, and then did the
same by his own jacket. Thereafter, gently withdrawing from his son's embrace, and beginning to lead the
way towards the inn yard, he added: " Come this way,
come this way. The horses will soon be ready."

His excitement seemed even to outdo his son's, so
much did he stammer and stutter, and, at times, find
himself at a loss for a word. Arkady stopped him.

" Papa," he said, " first let me introduce my good
friend Bazarov, who is the comrade whom I have so
often mentioned in letters to you, and who has been
kind enough to come to us for a visit."

At once Nikolai Petrovitch wheeled round, and,
approaching a tall man who, clad in a long coat with a
tasselled belt, had just alighted from the *tarantass*,
pressed the bare red hand which, after a pause, the
stranger offered him.

" I am indeed glad to see you!" was Nikolai Petrovitch's greeting, " I am indeed grateful to you for
your kindness in paying us this visit! Alas, I hope that,
that—— But first might I inquire your name? "

" Evgenii Vasiliev," replied the other in slow, but
virile, accents as, turning down the collar of his coat,

6

he **revealed** his face more clearly. Long and thin, with a high forehead which looked flattened at the top and became sharpened towards the nose, the face had large, greenish eyes and long, sandy whiskers. The instant that the features brightened into a smile, however, they betokened self-assurance and intellect.

" My dearest Evgenii Vasiliev," Nikolai Petrovitch continued, " I trust that whilst you are with us you will not find time hang heavy upon your hands."

Bazarov gave his lips a slight twitch, but vouchsafed no reply beyond raising his cap—a movement which revealed the fact that the prominent convolutions of the skull were by no means concealed by the superincumbent mass of indeterminate-coloured hair.

" Now, Arkady," went on Nikolai Petrovitch as he turned to his son, " shall we have the horses harnessed at once, or should you prefer to rest a little ? "

" Let us rest at home, Papa. So pray have the horses put to."

" I will," his father agreed. " Peter! Bestir yourself, my good fellow! "

Being what is known as a " perfectly trained servant," Peter had neither approached nor shaken hands with the young *barin*, but contented himself with a distant bow. He now vanished through the yard gates.

" Though I have come in the *koliaska*," said Nikolai Petrovitch, " I have brought three fresh horses for the *tarantass*."

Arkady then drank some water from a yellow bowl proffered by the landlord, while Bazarov lighted a pipe, and approached the ostler, who was engaged in unharnessing the stagehorses.

" Only two can ride in the *koliaska*," continued Nikolai Petrovitch; " wherefore I am rather in a difficulty to know how your friend will——"

" Oh, he can travel in the *tarantass*," interrupted

7

Arkady. " Moreover, do not stand on any ceremony with him, for, wonderful though he is, he is also quite simple, as you will find for yourself."

Nikolai Petrovitch's coachman brought out the horses, and Bazarov remarked to the ostler:

" Come, bestir yourself, fat-beard ! "

" Did you hear that, Mitiusha ? " added another ostler who was standing with his hands thrust into the back slits of his blouse. " The *barin* has just called you a fat-beard. And a fat-beard you are."

For answer Mitiusha merely cocked his cap to one side and drew the reins from the back of the sweating shafts-horse.

" Quick now, my good fellows ! " cried Nikolai Petrovitch. " Bear a hand, all of you, and for each there will be a glassful of *vodka*."

Naturally, it was not long before the horses were harnessed, and then father and son seated themselves in the *koliaska*, Peter mounted the box of that vehicle, and Bazarov stepped into the *tarantass*, and lolled his head against the leather cushion at the back. Finally the cortège moved away.

III

" To think that you are now a graduate and home again!" said Nikolai Petrovitch as he tapped Arkady on the knee, and then on the shoulder. " There now, there now!"

" And how is Uncle? Is he quite well?" asked Arkady—the reason for the question being that though he felt filled with a genuine, an almost childish delight at his return, he also felt conscious of an instinct that the conversation were best diverted from the emotional to the prosaic.

" Yes, your uncle is quite well. As a matter of fact, he also had arranged to come and meet you, but at the last moment changed his mind."

" Did you have very long to wait?" continued Arkady.

" About five hours."

" Dearest Papa!" cried Arkady as, leaning over towards his father, he imprinted upon his cheek a fervent kiss. Nikolai Petrovitch smiled quietly.

" I have got a splendid horse for you," he next remarked. " Presently you shall see him. Also, your room has been entirely repapered."

" And have you a room for Bazarov as well?"

" One shall be found for him."

" Oh—and pray humour him in every way you can. I could not express to you how much I value his friendship."

" But you have not known him very long, have you?"

" No—not very long."

" I thought not, for I do not remember to have seen him in St. Petersburg last winter. In what does he most interest himself?"

"Principally in natural science. But, to tell the truth, he knows practically *everything*, and is to become a doctor next year."

"Oh! So he is in the Medical Faculty?" Nikolai Petrovitch remarked; after which there was silence for a moment.

"Peter," went on Nikolai, pointing with his hand, "are not those peasants there some of our own?"

Peter glanced in the direction indicated, and saw a few waggons proceeding along a narrow by-road. The teams were bridleless, and in each waggon were seated some two or three *muzhiks* with their blouses unbuttoned.

"Yes, they are some of our own," Peter responded.

"Then whither can they be going? To the town?"

"Yes—or to the tavern." This last was added contemptuously, and with a wink to the coachman that was designed to enlist that functionary's sympathy: but as the functionary in question was one of the old school which takes no share in the modern movement, he stirred not a muscle of his face.

"This year my peasants have been giving me a good deal of trouble," Nikolai Petrovitch continued to his son. "Persistently do they refuse to pay their tithes. What ought to be done with them?"

"And do you find your hired workmen satisfactory?"

"Not altogether," muttered Nikolai Petrovitch. "You see, they have become spoilt, more's the pity! Any real energy seems quite to have left them, and they not only ruin my implements, but also leave the land untilled. Does estate-management interest you?"

"The thing we most lack here is shade," remarked Arkady in evasion of the question.

"Ah, but I have had an awning added to the north balcony, so that we can take our meals in the open air."

"But that will give the place rather the look of a villa, will it not? Things of that sort never prove effectual.

10

But oh, the air here! How good it smells! Yes, in my opinion, things never smell elsewhere as they do here. And oh, the sky!"

Suddenly Arkady stopped, threw a glance of apprehension in the direction of the *tarantass*, and relapsed into silence.

" I quite agree with you," replied Nikolai Petrovitch. " You see, the reason is that you were born here, and that therefore the place is bound to have for you a special significance."

" But no significance can attach to the place of a man's birth, Papa."

" Indeed?"

" Oh no. None whatsoever."

Nikolai Petrovitch glanced at the speaker, and for fully half a verst let the vehicle proceed without the conversation between them being renewed. At length Nikolai Petrovitch observed:

" I cannot remember whether I wrote to tell you that your old nurse, Egorovna, is dead."

" Dead? Oh, the poor old woman! But Prokovitch— is *he* still alive?"

" He is so, and in no way changed—that is to say, he grumbles as much as ever. In fact, you will find that no *really* important alterations have taken place at Marino."

" And have you the same steward as before?"

" No; I have appointed a fresh one, for I came to the conclusion that I could not have any freed serfs about the place. That is to say, I did not feel as though I could trust such fellows with posts of responsibility." Arkady indicated Peter with his eyes, and Nikolai Petrovitch therefore subdued his voice a little. " He? Oh, *il est libre, en effet.* You see, he is my valet. But as regards a steward, I have appointed a *miestchanin*,[1] at a salary of

[1] A member of the trading or shopkeeping class.

250 roubles a year, and he seems at least capable. But "
—and here Nikolai Petrovitch rubbed his forehead,
which gesture with him always implied inward agitation
—" I ought to say that, though I have told you that you
will find no alterations of importance at Marino, the
statement is not strictly true, seeing that it is my duty
to warn you that, that——" Nikolai Petrovitch hesitated
again—then added in French: " Perhaps by a stern
moralist my frankness might be considered misplaced;
yet I will not conceal from you, nor can you fail to be
aware, that always I have had ideas of my own on the
subject of the relations which ought to subsist between a
father and his son. At the same time, this is not to say
that you have not the right to *judge* me. Rather, it is
that at my age—— Well, to put matters bluntly, the
girl whom you will have heard me speak of——"

" You mean Thenichka? " said Arkady.

Nikolai Petrovitch's face went red.

" Do not speak of her so loudly," he advised. " Yes,
she is living with us. I took her in because two of our
smaller rooms were available. But of course the arrangement must be changed."

" Why must it, Papa? "

" Because this friend of yours is coming, and also
because—well, it might make things awkward."

" Do not disturb yourself on Bazarov's account. He
is altogether superior to such things."

" Yes, so you say; but the mischief lies in the fact
that the wing is so small."

" Papa, Papa! " protested Arkady. " Almost one
would think that you considered yourself to blame
for something; whereas you have *nothing* to reproach
yourself with."

" Ah, but I have," responded Nikolai Petrovitch.
His face had turned redder than ever.

" No, you have *not*, Papa," repeated Arkady with a

12

loving smile, while adding to himself with a feeling of indulgent tenderness for his good, kind father, as well as with a certain sense of " superiority ": " Why is he making these excuses ? "

" I beg of you to say no more," he continued with an involuntary feeling of exultation in being " grown up " and " emancipated." As he did so Nikolai Petrovitch glanced at him from under the fingers of the hand which was still rubbing his brows. At the same moment something seemed to give his heart a stab. Mentally, as before, he blamed himself.

" Here our fields begin," he observed after a pause.

" I see," rejoined Arkady. " And that is our forest in front, I suppose ? "

" It is so. Only, only—I have sold it, and this year it is to be removed."

" Why have you sold it ? "

" Because I needed the money. Moreover, the land which it occupies must go to the peasants."

" What ? To the peasants who pay you no tithes ? "

" Possibly. But some day they will pay me."

" I regret the forest's loss," said Arkady, and then resumed his contemplation of the landscape.

The scenery which the party were traversing could not have been called picturesque, for, with slight undulations, only fields, fields, and again fields, stretched to the very horizon. True, a few patches of copse were visible, but the ditches, with their borderings of low, sparse brushwood, recalled the antique land-measurement of Katherine's day. Also, streams ran pent between abruptly sloping banks, hamlets with dwarfed huts (of which the blackened roofs were, for the most part, cracked in half) stood cheek by jowl with crazy grinding-byres of plaited willow, empty threshing-floors had their gates sagging, and from churches of wood or of brick which stood amid dilapidated graveyards the stucco was peeling,

13

and the crosses were threatening at any moment to fall.
As he gazed at the scene Arkady's heart contracted.
Moreover, the peasants encountered on the road looked
ragged, and were riding sorry nags, while the laburnum
trees which stood ranged like miserable beggars by the
roadside had their bark hanging in strips, and their
boughs shattered.   Lastly, the lean, mud-encrusted
cows which could be seen hungrily cropping the herbage
in the ditches were so "staring" of coat that the
animals might just have been rescued from the talons
of some terrible, death-dealing monster; and as one
gazed at those weak, pitiful beasts, almost one could
fancy that one saw uprisen from amid the beauty of
spring, the pale phantoms of Winter—its storms and
its frost and its snow.

"Evidently this is not a rich district," reflected
Arkady.   "Rather, it is a district which gives one the
impression neither of abundance nor of hard work. Yet
can it be left as it is? No! Education is what we need.
But how is that education to be administered, or, for
that matter, to be introduced?"

Thus Arkady. Yet, even as the thought passed through
his mind, Spring seemed once more to regain possession
of her kingdom, and everything around him grew golden-
green, and trees, shrubs, and herbage started to wave
and glimmer under the soft, warm breath of the vernal
zephyrs, and larks took to pouring out their souls in
endless, ringing strains, and siskins, circling high over
sunken ponds, uttered their cry, then skimmed the
hillocks in silence, and handsome black rooks stalked
among the tender green of the short corn-shoots, or
settled among the pale-white, smokelike ripples of the
young rye, whence at intervals they protruded their
heads.

Arkady gazed and gazed; and gradually, as he did so,
his late thoughts grew dimmer and disappeared, and,

throwing off his travelling-cloak, he peered so joyously, with such a boyish air, into his father's face that Nikolai Petrovitch bestowed upon him yet another embrace.

" We have but little further to go now," he remarked. " In fact, when once we have topped that rise the house will come into view. And what a time we are going to have together, Arkasha! For you will be able to help me with the estate (if you care to, that is to say?), and you and I will draw nearer to one another, and make one another's better acquaintance."

" We will! " cried Arkady. " And what splendid weather for us both! "

" Yes; specially for your home-coming is spring in all its glory. Yet I am not sure that I do not agree with Pushkin where he says, in *Eugène Onegin*:

> " How sad to me is your coming,
> O spring, spring, season of love! "

" Arkady," shouted Bazarov from the *tarantass*, " please send me a match or two, for I have nothing to light my pipe with."

Instantly Nikolai Petrovitch ceased quoting poetry, and Arkady (who had listened with considerable surprise, though also with a certain measure of sympathy, to his father) hastened to produce from his pocket a silver matchbox, and to dispatch the same by the hand of Peter.

" In return, would you care to have a cigar? " called Bazarov.

" I should," replied Arkady.

The result was that when Peter returned to the *koliaska* he handed Arkady not only the matchbox, but also a fat black cigar. This Arkady lit at leisure, and then proceeded to diffuse around him so strong and acrid an odour of tobacco that Nikolai Petrovitch (a non-smoker from birth) found himself forced to avert his nose (though he did this covertly, for fear of offending his son).

A quarter of an hour later the vehicles drew up at the steps of a new wooden mansion, painted grey, and roofed with red sheet-iron. The mansion was Marino, or Novaia Sloboda, or, to quote the peasants' name, " Bobili Chutor."

IV

THERE issued on to the verandah to greet the arrivals no throng of household serfs—only a solitary girl of twelve. Presently, however, she was joined by a young fellow much resembling Peter, but dressed in a grey livery coat to which embossed, silver-gilt buttons were attached. This was Paul Kirsanov's valet. In silence he opened the door of the *koliaska*, and unhooked the apron of the *tarantass*; whereupon the three gentlemen alighted, passed through a dark, bare hall (the face of a young woman peered at them for a moment from behind a door), and entered a drawing-room upholstered in the latest fashion.

" So here we are at home again! " exclaimed Nikolai Petrovitch, taking off his cap, and shaking back his hair. " Let us have supper, and then for bed, bed! "

" Yes, something to eat would undoubtedly be welcome," remarked Bazarov as, yawning, he seated himself upon a sofa.

" Quite so; I will have supper served at once." Nikolai Petrovitch, for no apparent reason, tripped over his own feet. " And here comes Prokofitch," he added.

As he spoke entered a man of about sixty who, white-haired, and of thin, swarthy features, was wearing a cinnamon-coloured tail-coat with brass buttons and a crimson collar. He smiled with delight as he approached and shook hands with Arkady. Then, with a bow to the guest, he retired to the doorway, and folded his hands behind his back.

" So here is the young master, Prokofitch! " said

17

Nikolai Petrovitch. " He is home at last. And how think you, is he looking? "

" Very well, very well," the old man said with another smile. The next moment, however, he knit his shaggy brows, and suggested: " Shall I lay the table? "

" If you please, if you please." Nikolai Petrovitch turned to Bazarov.

" Before supper," he said, " would you care to go to your room? "

" I thank you, no. But please have my trunk conveyed thither, and also this wrap." And Bazarov divested himself of his cloak.

" Certainly. Prokofitch, take the gentleman's cloak."

The old butler received the garment gingerly, held it well away from him with both hands, and left the room on tiptoe.

" And you, Arkady? " continued Nikolai Petrovitch. " Do you not wish to go to your room? "

" Yes; for a wash I should be thankful," was Arkady's reply as he moved towards the door. At that moment it opened to admit a man of medium height who was dressed in a dark English suit, a fashionably low collar, and a pair of patent leather boots. This was Paul Petrovitch Kirsanov. Although forty-five, he had close-cropped grey hair of the sheen of new silver, and his sallow, unwrinkled face was as clear-cut and regular of outline as though carved with a light, fine chisel. Still retaining traces of remarkable comeliness, his bright, black, oblong eyes had a peculiar attraction, and his every well-bred, refined feature showed that symmetry of youth, that air of superiority to the rest of the world which usually disappears when once the twenties have been passed.

Drawing from his trouser pocket a slender hand the long, pink nails of which looked all the slenderer for the snowy whiteness of the superimposed cuff and large opal sleeve-link, he offered it to his nephew; after which, this prefatory European " handshake " over, he thrice kissed Arkady in the Russian fashion—that is to say, touched his nephew's cheek with his perfumed moustache, and murmured: " I congratulate you."

Next Nikolai Petrovitch presented to him Bazarov. Inclining his supple figure with a faint smile, Paul Petrovitch this time did not offer his hand. On the contrary, he replaced it in his pocket.

" I was beginning to think that you never meant to arrive," he said with an amiable hoist of his shoulders and a display of some beautiful white teeth. " What happened to you? "

" Nothing," replied Arkady, " except that we lingered a little. For the same reason are we as hungry as wolves; so pray tell Prokofitch to be quick, Papa, and I shall be back in a moment."

" Wait; I will go with you," added Bazarov as he rose from the sofa; and the two young men left the room together.

" Who is your guest? " asked Paul Petrovitch.

" A friend of Arkady's, and, according to Arkady's showing, a man of intellect."

" He is going to stay here? "

" He is."

" A long-haired fellow like that? "

" Certainly."

In that particular direction Paul Petrovitch said no more, but, tapping the table with his finger-nails, added:

" *Je pense que notre Arkady s'est dégourdi.*[1] And in any case I am pleased to see him back again."

At supper little was said. In particular did Bazarov scarcely speak, though he ate heartily; and only Nikolai Petrovitch proved garrulous as he related various incidents in what he termed his " agricultural life," and

[1] " I think that our friend Arkady has acquired some polish."

gossiped of forthcoming administrative measures, committees, deputations, the need of introducing machinery, and other such topics.

For his part, Paul Petrovitch paced the room (he never took supper), and sipped a glassful of red wine, and occasionally interjected some such remark—rather, exclamation—as "Ah!" or "Oh, ho!" or "H'm!" Arkady's contribution consisted of a little St. Petersburg gossip, even though, throughout, he was conscious of a touch of that awkwardness which overtakes a young man when, just ceased to be a boy, he returns to the spot where hitherto he has ranked as a mere child. In other words, he drawled his phrases unnecessarily, carefully avoided the use of the term "Papasha,"[1] and, once, even went so far as to substitute for it the term "Otety"[2] —though, true, he pronounced it with some difficulty. Lastly, in his excessive desire to seem at his ease, he helped himself to more wine than was good for him, and tasted some of every brand. Meanwhile Prokofitch chewed his lips, and never removed his eyes from his young master.

Supper over, the company dispersed.

"A queer fellow is that uncle of yours," Bazarov said to Arkady as, clad in a dressing-gown, he seated himself by his friend's bed, and sucked at a short pipe. "To think of encountering such elegance in the country! He would take a prize with his finger-nails."

"You do not know him yet," said Arkady. "In his day he was a leading lion, and some time or another I will tell you his history. Yes, many and many a woman has lost her head over his good looks."

"Then I should think that he has nothing to live on save memories," observed Bazarov. "At all events, there is no one *here* for him to enslave. I looked him over to-night, and never in my life have beheld a collar of

[1] Dear Papa.   [2] Father.

20

such marvellous gloss, or a chin so perfectly shaven. Yet such things can come to look ridiculous, do not you think? "

" Yes—perhaps they can. But he is such an excellent fellow in himself! "

" Oh, certainly—a truly archangelic personage! Your father, too, is excellent; for though he may read foolish poetry, and though his ideas on the subject of industry may be few, his heart is in the right place."

" He is a man with a heart of gold."

" Nevertheless, did you notice his nervousness to-night? "

Arkady nodded as though to himself such a weakness was a perfect stranger.

" Curious indeed! " commented Bazarov. " Ah, you elderly Romanticists! You over-develop the nervous system until the balance is upset. Now, good-night. In my room there is an English washstand, yet the door will not shut! But such things (English washstands I mean) need to be encouraged: they represent ' progress.' "

And Bazarov departed, while Arkady surrendered himself to a sensation of comfort. How pleasant was it to be sinking to sleep in one's comfortable home, and in one's own familiar bed, and under a well-known coverlet worked by loving hands—perhaps those of his good, kind, tireless old nurse! And at the thought of Egorovna he sighed, and commended her soul to the Heavenly Powers. But for himself he did not pray.

Soon both he and Bazarov were asleep; but certain other members of the household there were who remained wakeful. In particular had Nikolai Petrovitch been greatly excited by his son's return; and though he went to bed, he left the candle burning, and, resting with his head on his hands, lay thinking deeply.

Also, his brother sat up in his study until nearly midnight. Seated in an ample armchair before a corner

21

where a marble stove was smouldering, he had effected no alteration in his costume beyond having exchanged his patent leather boots for a pair of heelless, red felt slippers. Lastly, he was holding, though not reading, the latest number of *Galignani,* and his eyes were fixed upon the stove, where a quivering blue spurt of flame kept alternately disappearing and bursting forth again. Whither his thoughts were wandering God only knows; but that they were not meandering through the past alone was proved by the fact that in his expression there was a concentrated gloom which is never in evidence when a man's mind is occupied with memories and no more.

Finally, seated on a chest in a small room at the back of the house, and wearing a blue dressing-jacket and. thrown over her dark hair, a white scarf, was the girl Thenichka. As she sat there she kept listening, and starting, and gazing towards an open door which at once afforded a glimpse of an infant's cot and admitted the sound of a sleeping child's respiration.

V

NEXT morning Bazarov was the first to awake and go out of doors.

"Ah," thought he to himself as he gazed about him, "this is *not* much of a place to look at."

When apportioning allotments to his peasantry, Nikolai Petrovitch had found himself forced to exclude from the new " farm " four *desiatins* of level, naked land, and upon this space had built himself a house, quarters for his servants, and a homestead. Also, he had laid out a garden, dug a pond, and sunk two wells. But the young trees had fared badly, very little water had risen in the pond, and the wells had developed a brackish taste. The only vegetation to attain robust growth was a clump of lilacs and acacias, under the shade of which the household was accustomed to take tea or to dine. Within a few minutes Bazarov had traversed all the paths in the garden, visited the stables and the cattlesheds, and made friends with two young household serfs whom he happened to encounter, and with whom he set forth to catch frogs in a marsh about a verst from the manor.

"For what do you want frogs, *barin*? " asked one of the lads.

"To make them useful," replied Bazarov (who possessed a peculiar gift for winning the confidence of his inferiors, even though he never cozened them, but, on the contrary, always treated them with asperity). " You see, I like to open them, and then to observe what their insides are doing. You and I are frogs too, except that

23

we walk upon our hind legs. Thus the operation helps
me to understand what is taking place in ourselves."

" And what good will that do you? "

" This. That if you should fall sick, and I should have
to treat you, I might avoid some mistakes."

" Then you are a doctor? "

" I am."

" Listen to that, Vasika! The *barin* says that you and
I too are frogs. My word! "

" I don't like frogs," remarked Vasika, a barefooted
boy of seven with a head as white as tow, and a costume
made up of a grey blouse and a stiff collar.

" *Why* don't you like them? " asked Bazarov. " Do
you think they will bite you? Nay! Into the water, my
young philosophers! "

Nikolai Petrovitch too had left his bed, and, on going
to visit Arkady, found him fully dressed; wherefore
father and son proceeded to repair to the terrace, and
there seated themselves under the shade of the awning.
Amid nosegays of lilac, a tea-urn was simmering on a
table by the balustrade, and presently there appeared
upon the scene also the damsel who, on the previous
night, had met the arrivals on the verandah. She
announced in shrill tones:

" Theodosia Nikolaevna is not very well this morning,
and cannot come to breakfast. So she has told me to ask
you whether you will pour out tea for yourselves, or
whether she is to send Duniasha? "

" I will pour it out myself," Nikolai Petrovitch replied
with some haste. " Will you have cream or lemon in your
tea, Arkady? "

" Cream," he replied. After a pause he continued:
" Papasha——"

Nikolai Petrovitch glanced confusedly in his direction.
" Yes? " said he.

Arkady lowered his eyes.

" Pardon me if my question should seem to you indiscreet," he began, " but, owing to your frankness of last
night, I am emboldened to return it. You will not take
offence, will you? "

" Oh no! Pray go on."

" Then I feel encouraged to ask you whether it—
whether it is because I am here that she—that is to say,
Thenichka—has not joined us at breakfast? "

Nikolai Petrovitch slightly averted his face.

" It may be so," he said at length. " At all events, I
presume that—that she prefers, she prefers—in fact,
that she is shy."

Arkady glanced at his father.

" But why should she be shy? " he inquired. " In the
first place, you know my views " (he uttered the words
with no little complacency), " and, in the second place,
surely you cannot suppose that I would by a hair's
breadth intrude upon your life and your habits? No;
sure am I that never could you make a bad choice; and
if you have asked this girl to reside under your roof, that
is tantamount to saying that she has well deserved it.
In any case, moreover, it is not for a son to summon his
father to judgment—least of all for me, who possess a
father like yourself, a father who has never restricted
his son's freedom of action."

At first Arkady's voice had trembled a little, since
not only did he feel that he was doing the " magnanimous," but also he knew that he was delivering something like a " lecture " to his father; but such an effect
does the sound of his own voice exercise upon a human
being that towards the end Arkady pronounced his words
firmly, and even with a certain degree of *empressement*.

" I thank you, Arkady," Nikolai Petrovitch said
faintly as his fingers began their customary perambula-

tion of his forehead. " Nor is your conjecture mistaken, for if this girl had not deserved the invitation, I should not, of course, have—in other words, as you imply, this is no frivolous whim on my part. Nor need I have spoken of the matter, were it not that I desired you to understand that she might possibly have felt embarrassed at meeting you on the very day after your arrival."

" Then let *me* go and meet *her*," exclaimed Arkady with another access of " magnanimity " as he sprang from his chair. " Yes, let *me* go and explain to her why she need not shun me."

Nikolai Petrovitch also rose.

" Arkady," he began, " pray do me a favour. Hitherto I had not warned you that——"

But, without listening to him, Arkady darted from the terrace. For a moment or two Nikolai Petrovitch gazed after him—then, overcome with confusion, relapsed into a chair. His heart was beating rapidly. Whether or not he was picturing to himself a strangeness of future relations with his son; whether he was imagining that, had his son refrained from interfering, the latter might have paid him more respect in future; whether he was reproaching himself for his own weakness—it is difficult to say what his thoughts were. Probably in them there was a combination of the feelings just indicated, if only in the form of apprehensions. Yet those apprehensions cannot have been deeply rooted, as was proved by the fact that, for all the beating of his heart, the colour had not left his face.

Soon hasty footsteps were heard approaching, and Arkady reappeared on the terrace.

" I have made her acquaintance! " he shouted with a kindly, good-humoured, triumphant expression. " That Theodosia Nikolaievna is not well to-day is a fact; but also it is a fact that she is going to appear later. And why did you not tell me that I had a little brother? Otherwise I should have gone and kissed him last night, even as I have done this moment."

Nikolai Petrovitch tried to say something—to rise and to make an explanation of some sort; but Arkady cut him short by falling upon his neck.

" What is this?   Again embracing? " said Paul Petrovitch behind them.

As a matter of fact, neither father nor son was ill-pleased to see him appear, for, however touching such situations may be, one may be equally glad to escape from them.

" At what are you surprised? " asked Nikolai Petrovitch gaily. " Remember that I have not seen Arkesha for several centuries—at all events, not since last night! "

" Oh, I am not surprised," said Paul Petrovitch. " On the contrary, I should not mind embracing him myself."

And Arkady, on approaching his uncle, felt once more upon his cheek the impression of a perfumed moustache. Paul Petrovitch then sat down to table. Clad in an elegant morning suit of English cut, he was flaunting on his head a diminutive fez which helped the carelessly folded tie to symbolise the freedom of a country life. At the same time, the stiff collar of the shirt (which was striped, not white, as best befitted a matutinal toilet) supported with its usual rigour an immaculately shaven chin.

" Well, Arkady? " said he.   " Where is your new friend? "

" Out somewhere. He seldom misses going for an early morning walk. But the great thing is to take no notice of him, for he detests all ceremony."

" So I have perceived." And with his usual deliberate-

27

ness Paul Petrovitch began to butter a piece of bread.
" Will he be staying here very long? "

" Well, as long as he may care to stay. As a matter of
fact, he is going on to his father's place."

" And where does his father live? "

" Some eighty versts from here, in the same province
as ourselves. I believe he has a small property, and used
to be an army doctor."

" H'm! Ever since last night I have been asking
myself where I can have heard the name before. Nikolai,
do you remember whether there was a doctor of that
name in our father's division? "

" Yes, there used to be."

" Then that doctor will be this fellow's father. H'm! "
And Paul Petrovitch twitched his moustache. " What
exactly is your Bazarov? " he enquired of Arkady.

" What *is* he? " Arkady repeated smiling. " Do you
really want me to tell you what he is, Uncle? "

" If you please, my nephew."

" He is a Nihilist."

" A what? " exclaimed Nikaloi Petrovitch, while
even Paul Petrovitch paused in the act of raising a knife
to the edge of which there was a morsel of butter
adhering.

" A Nihilist," repeated Arkady.

" A Nihilist? " queried Nikolai Petrovitch. " I imagine
that that must be a term derived from the Latin *nihil*
or ' nothing.' It denotes, I presume, a man who—a
man who—well, a man who declines to accept *anything*."

" Or a man who declines to *respect* anything,"
hazarded Paul Petrovitch as he re-applied himself to
the butter.

" No, a man who treats things solely from the critical
point of view," corrected Arkady.

28

" But the two things are one and the same, are they not? " queried Paul Petrovitch.

" Oh no. A Nihilist is a man who declines to bow to authority, or to accept any principle on trust, however sanctified it may be."

" And to what can that lead? " asked Paul Petrovitch.

" It depends upon the individual. In one man's case, it may lead to good; in that of another, to evil."

" I see. But we elders view things differently. We folk of the older generation believe that without principles " (Paul Petrovitch pronounced the word softly, and with a French accent, whereas Arkady had pronounced it with an emphasis on the leading syllable)— " without principles it is impossible to take a single step in life, or to draw a single breath. *Mais vous avez changé tout cela.* God send you health and a general's rank, Messieurs Nihil—how do you pronounce it? "

" Ni-hi-lists," said Arkady distinctly.

" Quite so (formerly we had Hegelists, and now they have become Nihilists)—God send you health and a general's rank, but also let us see how you will contrive to exist in an absolute void, an airless vacuum. Pray ring the bell, brother Nikolai, for it is time for me to take my cocoa."

Nikolai Petrovitch did as requested, and also shouted for Duniasha; but, instead of the latter, there issued on to the terrace Thenichka in person. A young woman of twenty-three, she was pale, and gentle-looking, with dark eyes and hair, a pair of childishly red, pouting lips, and delicate hands. Also, she was clad in a clean cotton gown, a new blue kerchief was thrown lightly over her rounded shoulders, and she was carrying in front of her a large cup of cocoa. Shyly she placed the latter before Paul Petrovitch, while a warm, rosy current of blood suffused the exquisite skin of her comely face, and then

29

she remained standing by the table, with lowered eyes and the tips of her fingers touching its surface. Yet, though she looked as though she were regretting having come, she looked as though she felt that she had a right to be there.

Paul Petrovitch frowned, and Nikolai Petrovitch looked confused.

" Good morning, Thenichka," the latter muttered.

" Good morning," she replied in a low, clear voice. Then she glanced askance at Arkady, and he smiled at her in friendly fashion. Finally she departed with a quiet step and slightly careless gait—the latter a peculiarity of hers.

Silence reigned on the terrace. For a while Paul Petrovitch drank his cocoa. Then he suddenly raised his head, and muttered:

" Monsieur Nihilist is about to give us the pleasure of his company."

True enough, Bazarov could be seen stepping across the flowerbeds. On his linen jacket and trousers was a thick coating of mud, to the crown of his ancient circular hat clung a piece of sticky marshweed, and in his hand he was holding a small bag. Also, something in the bag kept stirring as though it were alive. Approaching the terrace with rapid strides, he nodded to the company and said:

" Good morning, gentlemen! Pardon me for being so late. I shall be back presently, but first my captures must be stowed away."

" What are those captures?" Paul Petrovitch inquired. " Leeches?"

" No, frogs."

" Do you eat them? Or do you breed them?"

" I catch them for purposes of experiment," was Bazarov's only reply as carelessly he entered the house.

30

" In other words, he vivisects them," was Paul
Petrovitch's comment. " In other words, he believes in
frogs more than in principles."

Arkady threw his uncle a reproachful look, and even
Nikolai Petrovitch shrugged his shoulders, so that Paul
Petrovitch himself felt his *bon mot* to have been out of
place, and hastened to divert the subject to the estate
and the new steward.

VI

BAZAROV, returning, seated himself at the table, and fell to drinking tea. The brothers contemplated him in silence. Arkady glanced covertly from his father to his uncle, and back again.

" Have you walked far this morning? " at length Nikolai Petrovitch inquired.

" To a marsh beside an aspen coppice. By the way, Arkady, I flushed five head of woodcock. Perhaps you would like to go and shoot them? "

" Then you yourself are no sportsman? "

" No."

" That is to say, you prefer physics to anything else? " This from Paul Petrovitch.

" Yes, I prefer physics—in fact, the natural sciences in general—to anything else."

" Well, I am told that the *Germanics* have made great strides in that department? " (Paul Petrovitch used the term " Germanics " instead of " Germans " ironically, but no one noticed it.)

" True," was Bazarov's careless reply. " In fact, the Germans are, in the same respect, our masters."

" You think highly of the Germans? " Paul Petrovitch's tone was now studiously polite, for he was beginning to feel irritated with the man—his aristocratic nature could not altogether stomach Bazarov's absolute lack of ceremony, the fact that this doctor's son not only knew no diffidence, but actually returned snappish and reluctant answers, and infused a *brusquerie* akin to rudeness into his tone.

32

FATHERS AND SONS

" At least the savants of that part of the world have some energy in them," retorted Bazarov.

" Quite so. And your opinion of our Russian savants is —well, perhaps less flattering? "

" It is, with your leave."

" That constitutes a piece of laudable modesty on your part," Paul Petrovitch observed with a slight hitch of his figure and a toss of his head. " But how comes it about that Arkady has just told us that you recognise no authorities whatsoever? Do you not trust authorities? "

" Why should I? Is anything in the world trust-worthy? Certainly, should I be told a fact, I agree with it, but that is all."

" Oh! Then the Germans confine themselves solely to facts? " Paul Petrovitch's face had now assumed an expression of detachment, as though he had suddenly become withdrawn to the ultimate heights of the empyrean.

" No, not all Germans," replied Bazarov with a passing yawn. Clearly he had no mind to continue the contro-versy. Meanwhile Paul Petrovitch glanced at Arkady as much as to say: " Admit that your friend has beautiful manners! "

" For my own part," he continued, ostentatiously, and with an effort, " I, a fallible mortal, do *not* favour the Germans. Of course, I am not including in that category the *Russo*-Germans, who, as we know, are birds of passage. Rather, it is the Germans of Germany proper whom I cannot abide. Once upon a time they used to produce men like Schiller and like—what's his name?—Goethe: for both of which authors my brother has a marked predilection. But now the German nation has become a nation solely of chemists and materialists."

" A good chemist is worth a score of your poets," remarked Bazarov.

33

" Quite so." Paul Petrovitch hitched his eyebrows a little, as though he had come near to falling asleep. " Er —I take it then that you decline to recognise art, but believe only in science? "

" I have told you that I believe in nothing at all. What after all, is science—that is to say, science in the mass? A science may exist, even as a trade or a profession may exist; but with regard to science in the mass, there is no such thing."

" Very good. And, with regard to such other postulates as usually are granted in human affairs, the attitude which you adopt is negative in the same degree? "

" What is this? " suddenly countered Bazarov. " Is it an examination in tenets? "

Paul Petrovitch turned pale, and Nikolai Petrovitch thought it time to intervene in the dispute.

" Nay, we will debate the subject later," he said. " And then, while recognising your views, good Evgenii Vasilitch, we will state our own. Individually speaking, I am delighted that you should be interested in the natural sciences. For instance, I am told that recently Liebig[1] has made some surprising discoveries in the matter of the improvement of soils. Consequently you might be able to help me in my agricultural labours, and to give me much useful advice."

" Always I shall be at your service, Nikolai Petrovitch," replied Bazarov. " But what has Liebig to do with us? First the alphabet should be learnt before we try to read books. We have not even reached the letter A."

" You are a Nihilist—that is plain enough," reflected Nikolai Petrovitch; while aloud he added: " Yet allow me to seek your occasional assistance. Brother

[1] Justus Freiherr von Liebig (1803–1873), the great German chemist—in particular, the founder of agricultural chemistry.

Paul, I believe it is time that we interviewed our steward."

Paul Petrovitch rose from his chair.

" Yes," he said, without looking at any one in particular, " it is indeed a terrible thing to have lived five years in the country, and to have stood remote from superior intellects! If one is *ab origine* a fool, one becomes so more than ever, seeing that, however much one may try not to forget what one has learnt, there will dawn upon one, sooner or later, the revelation that one's knowledge is all rubbish, that sensible men have ceased to engage in such futilities, and that one has lagged far behind the times. But, in such a case, what is one to do? Evidently the younger generation know more than we do."

And, slowly turning on his heel, he moved away as slowly, with Nikolai Petrovitch following in his wake.

" Does Paul Petrovitch always reside here? " asked Bazarov when the door had closed upon the pair.

" Yes, he does. But look here, Evgenii. You adopted too sharp a tone with my uncle. You have offended him."

" What? Am I to fawn upon these rustic aristocrats, even though their attitude is one purely of conceit and subservience to custom? If such be Paul Petrovitch's bent, he had better have continued his career in St. Petersburg. Never mind him, however. Do you know, I have found a splendid specimen of the water beetle *dytiscus marginatus*. Are you acquainted with it? I will show it you."

" Did I not promise to tell you his history? " observed Arkady musingly.

" Whose history? The water beetle's? "

" No; my uncle's. At least you will see from it that he is not the man you take him for, but a man who deserves pity rather than ridicule."

" I am not prepared to dispute it. But how come you to be so devoted to him? "

" Always one ought to be fair."

" The connection I do not see."

" Then listen."

And Arkady related the story to be found in the following chapter.

VII

" LIKE his brother, Paul Petrovitch Kirsanov received his early education at home, and entered the Imperial Corps of Pages. Distinguished from boyhood for his good looks, he had, in addition, a nature of the self-confident, quizzical, amusingly sarcastic type which never fails to please. As soon, therefore, as he had received his officer's commission, he began to go everywhere in society, to set the pace, to amuse himself, to play the rake, and to squander his money. Yet these things somehow consorted well with his personality, and women went nearly mad over him, while men called him ' Fate,' and secretly detested him. Meanwhile he rented a flat with his brother, for whom, in spite of their dissimilarity, he had a genuine affection. The dissimilarity in question lay, among other things, in the fact that, while Nikolai Petrovitch halted, had small, kindly, rather melancholy features and narrow black eyes, and was of a disposition prone to reading omnivorously, to bestirring himself but little, and to feeling nervous when attending social functions, Paul Petrovitch never spent a single evening at home, but was renowned for his physical dexterity and daring (he it was who made gymnastics the rage among the gilded youth of his day), and read, at most, five or six French novels. Indeed, by the time that he reached his twenty-eighth year Paul had risen to be a captain, and before him there seemed to lie a brilliant career; but everything suddenly underwent a change, as shall be related forthwith.

" Among the society of St. Petersburg of that period

there was accustomed to appear, and to disappear, at irregular intervals a certain Princess R. whose memory survives to this day. Though wedded to a highly placed and very presentable (albeit slightly stupid) husband, she had no children, and spent her time between making unexpected visits abroad and unexpected returns to Russia. In short, she led a very curious life, and the world in general accounted her a coquette, in that she devoted herself to every sort of pleasure, and danced at balls until she could dance no more, and laughed and jested with young men whom she received before dinner in the half-light of a darkened drawing-room. Yet, strangely enough, as the night advanced she would fall to weeping and praying and wringing her hands, and, unable to rest, would pace her room until break of day, or sit huddled, pale and cold, over the Psalter. But no sooner would daylight have appeared than she would once more become a woman of the world, and drive, and laugh, and chatter, and fling herself upon anything which seemed to offer any sort of distraction. Also, her power to charm was extraordinary; for though no one could have called her a beauty (seeing that the one good feature of her face lay in her eyes—and even then it was not the small, grey eyes themselves which attracted, but the glance which they emitted), she had hair of the colour and weight of gold which reached to her knees. That glance!—it was a glance which could be careless to the point of daring or meditative to the point of melancholy; a glance so enigmatical that, even when her tongue was lisping fatuous nonsense, there gleamed in her aspect something intangible and out of the common. Finally, she dressed with exquisite taste.

" This woman Paul Petrovitch met at a ball; and at it he danced a mazurka with her. Yet, though, during the dance, she uttered not a single word of sense, he

38

straightway fell in love with her, and, being a man
accustomed to conquests, attained his end in this case
also. Yet, strangely enough, the facility of his triumph
in no way chilled him, but led him on to become more
and more resolutely, more and more painfully, attached,
and that though she was a woman in whom, even after
she had made the great surrender, there still remained
something as immutably veiled, as radically intangible,
as before—something which no one had yet succeeded in
penetrating. What was in that soul God alone knows.
Almost would it seem as though she were subservient
to a mysterious force of which the existence was absolutely unknown to her, but which sported with her as it
willed, and whose whims her mentality was powerless to
control. At all events, her conduct constituted a series
of inconsistencies, and even the few letters which she
wrote to Paul Petrovitch—missives which would undoubtedly have aroused her husband's suspicions had
he seen them—were written to a man who was practically
a stranger to her. And in time her love began to be succeeded by fits of despondency; she ceased to smile and
jest with the lover whom she had selected, and looked
at him, and listened to his voice, with reluctance. In
fact, there were moments—for the most part, unexpected moments—when this reluctance bordered upon
chill horror, and her face assumed a wild, corpse-like
expression, and she would shut herself up in her bedroom, whence her maid, with ear glued to the keyhole,
would hear issue sounds as of dull, hopeless sobbing.
Paul Petrovitch himself frequently found that, when returning home after one of these tender interviews, there
was naught within his breast save the bitter, galling
sensation which comes of final and irrevocable failure.
'What more could I want?' he would say to himself
in his bewilderment; yet always he spoke with an
aching heart.

39

" It happened that on one occasion he gave her a ring having a stone carved in the figure of the Sphinx.

" ' What? ' she exclaimed. ' Do you offer me the Sphinx? '

" ' I do,' he replied. ' The Sphinx is yourself.'

" ' I? ' she queried with a slow lift of her enigmatical eyes. ' You are indeed flattering! '

" With the words went the ghost of a smile, while her eyes looked stranger than ever.

" Even during the time that the Princess loved him things were difficult for Paul Petrovitch; but when she cooled in her affection for him (as soon happened) he came near to going out of his mind. Distracted with jealousy, he allowed her no rest, but followed her to such an extent that at length, worn out with his persistent overtures, she betook herself on a tour abroad. Yet even then Paul Petrovitch listened to neither the prayers of his friends nor the advice of his superior officers, but, resigning his commission, set out on the Princess's track. Thus four years were spent in hunting her down, and losing sight of her again: and though, throughout, he felt ashamed of his conduct, and disgusted with his lack of spirit, all was of no avail—her image, the baffling, bewitching, alluring image which ever flitted before his eyes, had implanted itself too deeply in his breast. At last—it was at Baden—the pair once more came together; and though it seemed that never had she loved him as she did now, before a month was over another rupture had occurred, and, this time, a final one, as, with a last flicker, the flame died down and went out. True, that the parting would come he had foreseen; yet still he sought to be friends with her (as though friendship with such a woman could have been possible!), and only the fact that she quietly withdrew from Baden, and thenceforth studiously avoided him, baffled his purpose.

Returning to Russia, he endeavoured to resume his former mode of life: but neither by hook nor crook could he regain the old rut. As a man with a poisoned system wanders hither and thither, so did he drive out, and retain all the customs of a society *habitué*. Nay, he could even have boasted of two or three new conquests. But no. What he wanted was obtainable neither through himself nor others, since his whole power of initiative was gone, and his head gradually growing grey. To sit at his club, to consume his soul in jaundice and *ennui*, to engage in bachelor disputes which failed to interest him —such was now become his sole occupation. And, as we know, it is an occupation which constitutes the worst of signs. Nor, for that matter, seems he to marriage to have given a thought.

" Thus ten years elapsed in colourless, fruitless pursuits. Yet Paul found time pass swiftly, indeed, with amazing swiftness, for nowhere in the world does it fly as it does in Russia (in prison only is its passage said to be still swifter); wherefore there came at length a night when, while dining at his club, he heard that the Princess was dead—that she had died in Paris in a state bordering upon insanity. Rising from the table, he fell to pacing the rooms of the club with a face like that of a corpse, and only at intervals halting to watch the tables of the card-players; until, his usual time for returning home having arrived, he departed. Soon after he had reached his flat there was delivered for him a package containing the ring which he had given to the Princess. The Sphinx on it was marked with a mark like the sign of the cross, and enclosed also was a message to say that through the cross had the enigma become solved.

" These things took place just at the time (early in '48) when Nikolai Petrovitch had lost his wife, and removed to St. Petersburg; and since, also, the period of Nikolai's

41

marriage had coincided with the earlier days of Paul's
acquaintance with the Princess, Paul had not seen his
brother since the day when the latter had settled in the
country. True, on returning from abroad, Paul had
paid Nikolai a visit with the intention of staying with
him for a couple of months, as a congratulatory compli-
ment on his happiness; but the visit had lasted a week
only, since the difference in the position of the two
brothers had been too great, and even now, though that
difference had diminished somewhat, owing to the fact
that Nikolai Petrovitch had lost his wife, and Paul
Petrovitch his memories (after the Princess's death he
made it his rule to try and forget her)—even now, I say,
there existed the difference that, whereas Nikolai Petrovitch could look back upon a life well spent, and had a
son rising to manhood, Paul Petrovitch was still a lonely
bachelor, and, moreover, entering upon that dim, murky
period when regrets come to resemble hopes, and hopes
are beginning to resemble regrets, and youth is fled, and
old age is fast approaching. To Paul Petrovitch that
period was particularly painful, in that, in losing his past,
he had lost his all.

" ' I shall not invite you to come to Marino,' were
Nikolai Petrovitch's words to his brother. ' Even when
my wife was alive, you found the place tedious; and
now it would kill you.'

" ' Ah, but in those days I was young and foolish and
full of vanity,' replied Paul Petrovitch. ' Even though I
may not have grown wiser, at least am I quieter. So,
if you should be willing, I will gladly come and make
your place my permanent home.'

" For answer Nikolai Petrovitch embraced him; and
though a year and a half elapsed before Paul Petrovitch
decided to carry out his intention, once setled on the
estate, he has never left it—no, not even during the three

winters spent by Nikolai Petrovitch with his son in St. Petersburg. Meanwhile he has taken to reading books— more especially English books, and, in general, to ordering his life on the English pattern. Rarely, also, does he call upon his neighbours, but confines his excursions, for the most part, to attending election meetings, where, as a rule, he holds his tongue, but occasionally amuses himself by angering and alarming the older generation of landowners with Liberal sallies. From the representatives of the younger generation he holds entirely aloof. Yet both parties, though they reckon him haughty, accord him respect. They do so because of his refined, aristocratic manners, and of what they have heard concerning his former conquests, and of the fact that he dresses with exquisite taste, that he always occupies the best suites in the best hotels, that he dines sumptuously every day, that once he took dinner with the Duke of Wellington at the Court of Louis Philippe, that invariably he takes about with him a silver *nécessaire* and a travelling bath, that he diffuses rare and agreeable perfumes, that he is a first-rate and universally successful whist-player, and that his honour is irreproachable. The ladies too look upon him as a man of charming melancholy: but with their sex he has long ceased to have anything to do.

" You see, then, Evgenii," wound up Arkady, " that you have judged my uncle very unfairly. Moreover, I have omitted to say that several times he has saved my father from ruin by making over to him the whole of his money (for they do not share the estate), and that he is always ready to help any one, and, in particular, that he stands up stoutly for the peasants, even though, when speaking to them, he pulls a wry face, and, before beginning the interview, scents himself well with eau-de-Cologne."

43

" We all know what nerves like his mean," remarked Bazarov.

" Perhaps so. Yet his heart is in the right place, nor is he in any way a fool. To myself especially has he given much useful advice, especially on the subject of women."

" Ah, ha! ' Scalded with milk, one blows to cool another's water.' That is a truism."

" Finally, and to put matters shortly," resumed Arkady, " he is a man desperately unhappy, not one who ought to be despised."

" *Who* is despising him? " exclaimed Bazarov. " All that I say is that a man who has staked his whole upon a woman's love, and, on losing the throw, has turned crusty, and let himself drift to such an extent as to become good for nothing—I say that such a man is not a man, a male creature, at all. He is unhappy, you say; and certainly you know him better than I do; but it is clear also that he has not yet cleansed himself of the fool. In other words, certain am I that, just because he occasionally reads *Galignani*, and because, once a month, he saves a peasant from distress for debt, he believes himself really to be a man of action."

" But think of his upbringing! " expostulated Arkady. " Think of the period in which he has lived his life! "

" His upbringing? " retorted Bazarov. " Why, a man ought to *bring himself* up, even as I had to do. And with regard to his period, why should I, or any other man, be dependent upon periods? Rather, we ought to make periods dependent upon *us*. No, no, friend! Sensuality and frivolity it is that are at fault. For of what do the so-called mysterious relations between a man and a woman consist? As physiologists, we know precisely of what they consist. And take the anatomy of the eye. What in it justifies the guesswork whereof you speak? Such talk is so much Romanticism and nonsense and unsoundness and artificiality. Let us go and inspect that beetle."

And the two friends departed to Bazarov's room, where he had already succeeded in creating a medical-surgical atmosphere which consorted well with the smell of cheap tobacco.

VIII

At his brother's interview with the steward (the latter was a tall, thin man of shifty eyes who to every remark of Nikolai's replied in an unctuous, mellifluous voice: " Very well, if so it please you ") Paul Petrovitch did not long remain present. Recently the system of estate-management had been reorganised on a new footing, and was creaking as loudly as an ungreased cartwheel or furniture which has been fashioned of unseasoned wood. For the same reason, though never actually giving way to melancholy, Nikolai Petrovitch often indulged in moodiness and sighing, for the reason that it was clear that his affairs would never prosper without money, and that the bulk of the latter had disappeared. As for Arkady's statement that frequently Paul Petrovitch had come to his brother's assistance, it had been perfectly true, for on more than one occasion had Paul been moved by the sight of his brother's perplexity to walk slowly to the window, to plunge a hand into his pocket, to mutter, " *Mais je puis vous donner de l'argent*," and, lastly, to suit the action to the word. But on the day of which we are speaking Paul had no spare cash himself; wherefore he preferred to remove himself elsewhere, and the more so in that the *minutiæ* of estate-management wearied him, and that he felt certain that, though powerless to suggest a better way of doing business than the present one, he knew at least that Nikolai's was at fault.

" He is not sufficiently practical," would be his

reflection. " He lets these fellows cheat him right and left."

On the other hand, Nikolai had a high opinion of Paul's practicality, and always sought his advice.

" I am a weak, easy-going fellow," he would say, " and have spent the whole of my life in retirement; whereas you cannot have lived in the world for nothing—you know it well, and have the eye of an eagle."

To this Paul Petrovitch would make no reply: he would merely turn away without attempting to undeceive his brother.

After leaving Nikolai Petrovitch's study, Paul traversed the corridor which separated the front portion of the house from the rear, and, on reaching a low doorway, halted in seeming indecision, tugged at his moustache for a moment, then tapped with his knuckles upon the panels.

" Who is there? " replied Thenichka from within. " Pray enter."

" It is I," said Paul Petrovitch as he opened the door.

Springing from the chair on which she had been seated with her baby, she handed the latter to the nurse-girl (who at once bore it from the room), and hastened to rearrange her bodice.

" Pardon me for having disturbed you," said Paul Petrovitch without looking at her, " but my object in coming here is to ask you (for I understand that you are sending in to the town to-day) if you would procure me a little green tea for my own personal use."

" I will," replied Thenichka. " How much ought I to have ordered? "

" I think that half a pound will suffice. But what a change! " he went on glancing around the room with an eye which included also in its purview Thenichka's features. " It is those curtains that I am referring to,"

FATHERS AND SONS

he explained on seeing that she had failed to grasp his meaning.

" Yes—those curtains. They were given me by Nikolai Petrovitch himself, and have been hung a long while."

" But it is a long time, remember, since last I paid you a visit. The room looks indeed comfortable, does it not?"

" Yes, thanks to Nikolai Petrovitch's kindness," whispered Thenichka.

" And you find things better here than in the wing?" continued Paul Petrovitch politely—also, without the least shadow of a smile.

" I do."

" And who is lodged in the wing in your place?"

" The laundry women."

" Ah!"

Paul Petrovitch relapsed into silence, while Thenichka thought to herself: " I suppose he will go presently." So far from doing so, however, he remained where he was, and she had to continue standing in front of him with her fingers nervelessly locking and unlocking themselves.

" Why have you had the little one taken away?" at length he inquired. " I love children. Pray show him to me."

Thenichka reddened with confusion and pleasure; and that though Paul Petrovitch was accustomed to make her nervous, so seldom did he address her.

" Duniasha!" she cried (Duniasha she addressed, as she did every one in the house, in the second person plural [1]). " Bring Mitia here, and be quick about it! But first put on his clothes." With that she moved towards the door.

[1] Used, as in French, in formal speech or that of a person addressing a social superior.

48

" Never mind, never mind," said Paul Petrovitch.

" But I shall soon be back." And she disappeared.

Left alone, Paul looked about him with keen attention. The small, low room in which he was waiting was clean and comfortable, and redolent of balm, camomile, and furniture polish. Against the walls stood straight-backed, lyre-shaped chairs which the late General had purchased during the period of the Polish campaign; in one corner stood a bedstead under a muslin coverlet, with, flanking it, a large, iron-clamped, convex-lidded chest; in the opposite corner burnt a lamp before a massive, smoke-blackened *ikon* of Saint Nikolai the Miracle Worker—the Saint's halo suspended by a red riband, and a tiny china egg resting on his breast; on the window-sills were ranged some carefully scaled jars of last year's jam, which filtered the light to green, and of which the parchment covers were inscribed, in Thenichka's large handwriting, " Gooseberry "—a jam of which Nikolai Petrovitch was particularly fond; from the ceiling hung, by a long cord, a cage containing a short-tailed siskin which kept up such a perpetual twittering and hopping that its cage rocked to and fro as it sang, and stray hemp seeds came pattering lightly to the floor; on the wall space above a small chest of drawers hung a few poorly executed photographs of Nikolai Petrovitch in various attitudes (the work of a travelling photographer); alongside these photographs hung a very unsuccessful one of Thenichka herself, since it revealed nothing but an eyeless face peering painfully from a dark frame; and, lastly, above the portrait of Thenichka hung a picture of Ermolov in a big cloak and a portentous frown—the latter directed principally towards a distant mountain range of the Caucasus, while over the forehead of the portrait dangled a silken pincushion in the shape of a shoe.

For five minutes or so there came from the adjoiniug room a sound as of rustling and whispering. From the chest of drawers Paul Petrovitch took up a greasy, dog's-eared volume of Masalsky's *The Strielitsi,* and turned over a few of its pages. Suddenly the door opened, and Thenichka entered with Mitia, whom she had now vested in a red robe and beaded collar, while his little head had been brushed, and also his face washed. Though he was breathing stertorously, and wriggling his whole body about, and twitching his tiny arms after the manner of all healthy children, the dainty robe had had its effect, and his face was puckered with delight. Also, Thenichka had tidied her own hair, and rearranged her bodice— well enough though she would have done as she was. For, in all the world, is there a more entrancing spectacle than that of a young, handsome mother with, in her arms, a healthy child?

" What a little beauty! " Paul Petrovitch exclaimed indulgently as he tickled Mitia's double chin with the tip of his forefinger. The baby fixed its eyes upon the siskin, and smiled.

" This is Uncle," said Thenichka as she bent over the boy and gave him a gentle shake. For fumigating purposes Duniasha deposited upon the window-sill a lighted candle, and, beneath it, a two-kopeck piece.

" How old is he? " asked Paul Petrovitch.

" Six months. On the eleventh of this month he will be seven."

" No, eight, will he not, Theodosia Nikolaievna? " timidly corrected Duniasha.

" No, seven."

Here the infant crowed, fixed his eyes upon the chest in the corner, and suddenly closed his five tiny fingers upon his mother's mouth and nose.

" The little rascal! " she said, without, however, freeing her features from his grasp.

" He is very like my brother," commented Paul Petrovitch.

" Whom else should he be like? " she thought.

" Yes," he continued, half to himself. " Undoubtedly I see the likeness." He gazed pensively, almost mournfully, at the young mother.

" This is Uncle," again she said to the child: but this time she said it under her breath.

" Oh, here you are, Paul! " cried Nikolai Petrovitch from behind them.

Paul Petrovitch faced about and knit his brows. But so joyously, and with such a grateful expression, was his brother regarding the trio that Paul could only respond with a smile.

" He is a fine little fellow, this baby of yours," the elder brother observed. Then, glancing at his watch, he added: " I came here merely to arrange about the purchase of some tea." With which he assumed an air of indifference, and left the room.

" He came here of his own accord, did he? " was Nikolai Petrovitch's first inquiry.

" Yes, of his own accord," the girl replied. " He just knocked at the door and entered."

" And what of Arkasha? Has he too been to see you? "

" No, Nikolai Petrovitch. By the way, might I return to the rooms in the wing of the house? "

" Why do you want to? "

" Because they suit me better than these."

" I think not," said Nikolai Petrovitch, rubbing his forehead with an air of indecision. " Before there was a reason for your being there, but that reason no longer exists."

" Good morning, little rascal! " was his next remark

as, with a sudden access of animation, he approached and kissed the baby's cheek. Then, bending a little, he pressed his lips to Thenichka's hand—a hand, against the red of Mitia's robe, as white as milk.

" Why have you done that, Nikolai Petrovitch? " she murmured with downcast eyes. Yet when she raised them, their expression, as she glanced from under her brows and smiled her caressing, but slightly vacant, smile, was charming indeed!

Of the circumstances of Nikolai Petrovitch's first meeting with Thenichka the following may be related. Three years ago it had fallen to his lot to spend a night at an inn in a remote country town; and, while doing so, he had been struck with the cleanliness of the room assigned him, and also with the freshness of the bed-linen. " Clearly," he had thought to himself, " the landlady must be a German." But, as it had turned out, she was not a German, but a Russian of about fifty, well-dressed, and possessed both of a comely, intelligent countenance and of a refined manner of speaking. When breakfast was over, he had had a long conversation with her, and conceived for her a great liking. Now, as fate would have it, he had just removed to his new house, and, owing to a reluctance to continue keeping bonded serfs, was on the look-out for hired domestics; while she, for her part, was in despair over the question of the hard times, which caused only a limited number of visitors to resort to the town. In the end, therefore, Nikolai Petrovitch proposed to her to come to his house as housekeeper; and to this proposal, (since her husband was dead, and her family consisted only of a young daughter named Thenichka) she eventually agreed. Accordingly, within two weeks Arina Savishna (such was the new housekeeper's name) arrived at Marino with her child, and took up her abode in the wing of the new manor-house; nor was it long before she had put the place to rights. To Thenichka, however, then a girl of sixteen, she never referred; and few people even caught a glimpse of the maiden, since she lived a life so modest and retired that only on Sundays could Nikolai Petrovitch contemplate the delicate profile of her face in an aisle of the parish church. More than a year thus elapsed.

But one morning Arina entered his study, bowed to him as usual, and requested him to be so good as to come and help her with her daughter, one of whose eyes had been injured with a spark from the stove. It so happened that, like most men of sedentary habit, Nikolai Petrovitch had picked up a smattering of medicine—nay, he had even compiled a list of homœopathic remedies for one and another emergency; wherefore he hastened to order Arina to produce the sufferer. As soon as she heard that the *barin* had sent for her, Thenichka turned very nervous, but followed her mother as in duty bound; whereupon Nikolai Petrovitch led her to the window, took her head in his hands, and, after an inspection of the red, inflamed eye, wrote out a prescription for a lotion, compounded the stuff himself, and, lastly, tore off a portion of his handkerchief, and showed her how best the eye could be bathed. Meanwhile Thenichka listened attentively, and then tried to leave the room. " But the idea of going away without kissing the *barin's* hand, foolish one! " cried Arina; whereupon, in lieu of offering the girl his hand, Nikolai Petrovitch felt so embarrassed that in the end he himself kissed her bent head at the spot where the hair lay parted. Soon Thenichka's eye healed, but the impression produced upon Nikolai Petrovitch did not pass away so quickly. Continually there flitted before him a pure, tender, timidly upturned face; continually he could feel between the palms of his hands soft coils of hair; continually appearing to his vision there would be a pair of innocent, half-parted lips between which a set of pearl-like teeth flashed back the sunlight. Consequently he began to observe the girl more in church, and to try to engage her in conversation. But shyness always overcame her, and, on one occasion when she happened to meet him on a narrow path through a rye field, she turned aside, and plunged into the mass of tall grain and undergrowth of cornflowers and wormwood. Yet, despite her endeavours to escape, his eye discerned her head amid the golden mesh of cornblades, and he called to her, as she gazed at him with wild eyes:

" Good morning, Thenichka! I shall not hurt you."

" Good morning, *barin*! " she whispered in reply, but did not leave her retreat.

As time went on, however, she grew more accustomed to his presence; and by the time that she was beginning really to get over her bashfulness, her mother died of cholera. Here was a dilemma indeed! For what was to be done with the young Thenichka, who had inherited her mother's love of orderliness, and also her mother's good sense and natural refinement? In the end, she was so young and lonely, and Nikolai Petrovitch was so good-hearted and modest, that the inevitable came about. The rest need not be related.

" So my brother has been to you? " he inquired again. " You say that he just knocked at the door and entered?

" Yes, he just knocked at the door and entered."

" Good! Now, hand me Mitia."

And Nikolai Petrovitch fell to tossing the baby up and down towards the ceiling—a proceeding which greatly delighted the little one, but as greatly disquieted the mother, who, at each upward flight, stretched her hands in the direction of the infant's naked toes.

Meanwhile Paul Petrovitch returned to his study, of

which the walls were lined with a paper of red wild roses, and hung with weapons; the floor was covered with a striped Persian carpet; and the furniture, consisting of a Renaissance bookcase in old black oak, a handsome writing-table, a few bronze statuettes, and a stove, was constructed, for the most part, of hazelwood, and upholstered in dark-green velvet. Stretching himself upon a sofa, he clasped his hands behind his head, and remained staring at the ceiling. Did presently the thoughts which were passing through his mind need to be concealed even from the walls, seeing that he rose, unhooked the heavy curtains from before the windows, and replaced himself upon the sofa?

IX

THE same day also saw Bazarov make Thenichka's acquaintance. This was when he was walking in the garden with Arkady, and discussing the question of why certain trees in the garden, especially oaks, had not prospered as they might have done. Said he:

"You ought to plant the place with as many silver poplars as you can, and also with Norwegian firs—limes too, if loam should first be added. For instance, the reason why this clump has done so well is that it is made up of lilacs and acacias, of which neither require much room. But hullo! There is some one sitting there!"

The persons seated in the arbour were Thenichka, Duniasha, and little Mitia. Bazarov halted, and Arkady nodded to Thenichka as to an old acquaintance. Then the pair passed on again, and Bazarov inquired of his companion:

"Who was she?"

"To whom are you referring?"

"You know to whom. My word, she *is* good-looking!"

Arkady explained, with a touch of embarrassment, the identity of Thenichka.

"Ah!" Bazarov remarked. "Then your father has not at all bad taste. Indeed, I commend it. But what a young dog he is! I too must be introduced."

And he turned back in the direction of the arbour.

"Evgenii!" exclaimed Arkady nervously as he followed his friend. "For God's sake be careful what you do!"

56

" You need not be alarmed. I know what is what. I am no rustic."

And, approaching Thenichka, he doffed his cap.

" Allow me to introduce myself," he said with a polite bow. " I am a friend of Arkady's, and a perfectly harmless individual."

Rising from her seat, Thenichka gazed at him in silence.

" Oh, and what a fine baby! " he continued. " Pray do not disturb yourself. Never yet have I cast upon a child an evil spell. But why are his cheeks so red? Is he cutting teeth? "

" Yes," replied Thenichka. " He has now cut four of them, and the gums are a little swelled."

" Then let me see them. Do not be afraid. I am a doctor."

With that he took the baby into his arms, and both Thenichka and Duniasha were astonished at the fact that it made no resistance, showed no fear.

" I see," he continued. " Well, everything is going right with him, and he will have plenty of teeth. Nevertheless, should he in any way ail, please let me know. Are you yourself well? "

" Yes, thank God! "

" ' Thank God,' say I too, for health on the part of the mother is the chief point of all. And you? " he added, turning to Duniasha. The latter, ultra-prim of demeanour in the drawing-room, and ultra-frivolous of behaviour in the kitchen, answered with a giggle.

" Well, you *look* all right. Here! Take your hero back again."

He replaced the baby in Thenichka's arms.

" How quiet he has been with you! " she exclaimed under her breath.

" Always children are quiet with me," he remarked. " You see, I know how to handle them."

57

"And *they* know when people are fond of them," put in Duniasha.

"True," assented Thenichka. "Though it is seldom that Mitia will go to any one's arms but mine."

"Would he come to me?" ventured Arkady, who, until now standing in the background, at this moment came forward towards the arbour. But on his attempting to wheedle Mitia to his arms, the infant threw back its head, and started to cry—a circumstance which greatly perturbed Thenichka.

"Another time—when he has come to be more used to me," said Arkady indulgently. And the two friends departed.

"What is her name?" asked Bazarov.

"Thenichka—Theodosia," replied Arkady.

"And her patronymic?"

"Nikolaievna."

"*Bene!* What I like about her is her total absence of shyness. True, that is a *trait* which some might have condemned in her, but I say, 'What rubbish!' For why need she be bashful? She is a mother, and therefore justified."

"I agree," said Arkady. "And my father——"

"Also is justified," concluded Bazarov.

"No, I do not agree in that respect."

"You do not altogether welcome a superfluous heir?"

"For shame, Evgenii!" cried Arkady heatedly. "How can you impute such motives? What I mean is that my father is not justified from *one* point of view. That is to say, he ought to marry her."

"Oh, ho!" said Bazarov quietly. "How high and mighty we are getting! So you still attribute importance to the marriage rite? This I should not have expected of you."

For some paces the friends walked on in silence. Then Bazarov continued:

"I have been inspecting your father's establishment. The cattle look poor, the horses seem broken-down, the buildings have a tipsy air, the workmen manifest a tendency to loaf, and I cannot yet determine whether the new steward is a fool or a rogue."

"You are censorious to-day?"

"I am; and the reason is that these good peasants are cheating your father—exemplifying the proverb that 'The Russian *muzhik* will break even the back of God.'"

"Soon I shall have to agree with my uncle in his opinion that you think but poorly of Russia."

"Rubbish! The Russian's very best point is that he holds a poor opinion of *himself*. Two and two make four. Nothing but that matters."

"And is nature also rubbish?" queried Arkady with a musing glance at the mottled fields where they lay basking in the soft, kindly rays of the morning sun.

"Nature *is* rubbish—at least in the sense in which *you* understand her. She is not a church, but a workshop wherein man is the labourer."

At this moment there came wafted to their ears the long-drawn strains of a violoncello, on which a sensitive, but inexperienced, hand was playing Schubert's *Erwartung*. Like honey did the voluptuous melody suffuse the air.

"Who is the musician?" asked Bazarov in astonishment.

"My father."

"What? Your father plays the 'cello?"

"He does."

"At his age?"

"Yes—he is only forty-four."

Bazarov burst out laughing.

"Why do you laugh?" asked Arkady.

"Pardon me, but the idea that your father—a man of

forty-four, a paterfamilias, and a notable in the county
—should play the 'cello! "

And he continued laughing, though Arkady, for all his
reverence for his mentor, failed to accomplish even a
smile.

X

DURING the next two weeks life at Marino pursued its normal course. Arkady took things easily, and Bazarov worked. In passing, it may be said that, for all his careless manner and abrupt, laconic speech, the latter had become an accepted phenomenon in the house. In particular had Thenichka so completely lost her shyness of him that one night she sent to awake him because Mitia had been seized with convulsions; whereupon Bazarov arrived, and, half-joking, half-yawning, according to his usual manner, helped her for two hours in the task of attending to the baby. Only Paul Petrovitch disliked the man with the whole strength of his soul, for he accounted him a proud, cynical, conceited plebeian, and suspected him not only of failing to respect, but even of holding in contempt, the personality of Paul Petrovitch Kirsanov. Also, Nikolai Petrovitch stood in slight awe of the young Nihilist, since he doubted the likelihood of any good accruing from Bazarov's influence over Arkady. Yet always he would listen with pleasure to Bazarov's discourses, and gladly attend the chemical or physical experiments with which the young doctor (who had brought a microscope with him) would occupy himself for hours at a stretch. On the other hand, in spite of Bazarov's domineering manner, all the servants had become attached to him, for they felt him to be less a *barin* than their brother; and in particular did Duniasha readily joke and talk with him, and throw him many meaning glances as she sped past in quail-like fashion, while Peter himself, though a man full of conceit and stupidity, with a forehead perpetually puckered, and a dignity which consisted of a deferential demeanour, a practice of reading journals syllable by syllable, and a habit of constantly brushing his coat; even Peter, I say, would brighten and strike an attitude when he was noticed by Bazarov. In fact, the only servant to disapprove of Bazarov was old Prokofitch, the butler, who looked sour whenever he handed the young doctor a dish, and called him a " sharper " and a " flaunter," and declared that, for all his whiskers, Bazarov was no better than " a dressed-up pig," whereas he, Prokofitch, was practically as good an aristocrat as Paul Petrovitch himself.

In the early days of June, the best season of the year, the weather became beautiful. True, from afar there came threatenings of cholera, but to the local inhabitants such visitations had become a commonplace. Each day Bazarov rose early to set forth upon a tramp of some two or three versts; nor were those tramps undertaken merely for the sake of the exercise (he could not abide aimless expeditions), but, rather, for the sake of collecting herbs and insects. Sometimes, too, he would succeed in inducing Arkady to accompany him; and whenever this was the case the pair would, on the way back, engage in some dispute which always left Arkady vanquished in spite of his superior profusion of argument.

One morning the pair lingered considerably by the way, and Nikolai Petrovitch set out across the garden to meet them. Just as he reached the arbour, he heard their voices and brisk footsteps approaching, though he himself was invisible to the returning friends.

" You do not understand my father," Arkady was saying.

Nikolai Petrovitch halted instead of revealing himself.

" Oh, he is a good fellow enough," replied Bazarov. " But also he is a man on the shelf, a man whose song has been sung."

Though Nikolai Petrovitch strained his ears, he failed

to catch Arkady's reply. So the " man on the shelf " lingered for a minute or two—then walked slowly back to the house.

" For the past three days I have noted him reading Pushkin," continued Bazarov. " You ought to explain to him that no good can come of that, for he is no longer a boy, and ought to have shaken himself free of such fiddlesticks. Who would desire to be a Romanticist? Give him something *practical*."

" For instance? "

" Let me consider. For a start, give him Büchner's [1] *Stoff und Kraft*."

" Good! " Arkady's tone was approving. " *Stoff und Kraft* is at least written in a popular style."

The same day Nikolai Petrovitch was sitting with his brother. At length he said:

" I find that you and I are men on the shelf that our songs have been sung. Eh? And perhaps Bazarov is right. Yet I confess that one thing hurts me: and that is that, though I had hoped to draw nearer to Arkady, I am being left in the rear, and he is for ever marching ahead. No longer do he and I understand one another."

" And why is he for ever marching ahead? " asked Paul Petrovitch indignantly. " How comes he to stand at such a distance from us? The reason is simply the ideas which that precious ' Nihilist ' is putting into his head. For myself, I detest the fellow, and think him a charlatan. Also, I am certain that, in spite of his frogs, he is making no real progress in physics."

" We ought not to say that, brother. For my own part, I look upon him as a man of culture and ability."

" If so, a detestably conceited one."

" Perhaps he *is* conceited," Nikolai Petrovitch allowed. " But then it would appear that nothing can be done

[1] Ludwig Büchner (1824 – 1899), German physician and materialist philosopher.

without something of the kind. What I cannot make out is the following. As you know, I have done everything possible to keep up with the times—I have organised my peasantry, I have set up such a farm that throughout the province I am known as ' Fine Kirsanov,' persistently I read and educate myself, in general I try to march abreast of the needs of the day. Yet, though I do all this, I am now given to understand that my day is past and gone! And, brother, I do not say that I am not partially inclined to accept that view."

" For what reason? "

" For the following. To-day, as I was reading Pushkin (I think it was ' The Gipsies ' that I had lighted upon), there suddenly entered the room Arkady. Silently, and with an air of kindly regret, and as gently as a child, he withdrew the book from my hand, and laid before me another book—a German production of some kind. That done, he gave me another smile, and departed with my volume of Pushkin under his arm."

" Good gracious! And what might be the book which he has given you? "

" This."

Nikolai Petrovitch extracted from the tail pocket of his frock-coat a copy (ninth edition) of Büchner's well-known work.

Paul Petrovitch turned it over in his hands.

" H'm! " he grunted. " Arkady does indeed seem solicitous for your education! Have you tried reading the book? "

" Yes."

" And how do you like it? "

" Well, either I am a fool or the thing is rubbish. Of the two views, the former seems to me the most probable."

" It is not because you have forgotten your German, I suppose? "

" Oh no. I understand the language perfectly."

Again Paul Petrovitch turned over the book, and again he glanced at his brother from under his brows. A moment's silence ensued.

" By the way," continued Nikolai Petrovitch with an evident desire to change the conversation, " I have received a letter from Koliazin."

" From Matvei Ilyitch ? "

" From the same. It seems that he has just arrived at ——, for the purpose of carrying out the Revision [1] of the province, and he writes very civilly that, as our kinsman, he would be glad to see Arkady and you and myself."

" Do you intend to accept his invitation ? " asked Paul Petrovitch.

" I do not. Do you ? "

" No. We have no need to drag ourselves fifty versts to eat blanc-mange. The good Mathieu wants to show off a little—that is all. He can do without us. But what an honour to be a Privy Councillor! Had I continued in the Service, continued hauling at the old tow-rope, I myself might have been Adjutant-General! As it is, I, like yourself, am on the shelf."

" Yes, brother. Clearly it is time that we ordered our tombstones, and folded our hands upon our breasts."

A sigh concluded Nikolai Petrovitch's speech.

" But *I* do not intend to give in so soon," muttered his brother. " There is first going to be a skirmish between that chirurgeon of Arkady's and myself. That I can see beyond a doubt."

And, sure enough, the " skirmish " occurred the same evening. Ready for battle as soon he repaired to the drawing-room for tea, Paul Petrovitch entered angrily, but firmly, and sat waiting for an excuse to advance upon the foe. Yet for a while that excuse hung fire, since

[1] *i.e.* the census-taking of the serf population.

Bazarov never said much in the presence of "the old Kirsanovs," and to-night was feeling out of spirits, and drank his tea in absolute silence. However, Paul Petrovitch was so charged with impatience that his wish was bound to attain fulfilment.

It happened that the conversation became turned upon a neighbouring landowner.

"He is just a petty aristocrat," Bazarov drily remarked (it seemed that he and the landowner had met in St. Petersburg).

"Allow me," put in Paul Petrovitch, his lips quivering. "In your view, do the terms ' good-for-nothing ' and ' aristocrat ' connote the same thing? "

"I said ' *petty* aristocrat,' " replied Bazarov as he lazily sipped his tea.

"Quite so. Then I take it that you hold the same opinion of aristocrats as of ' petty aristocrats ' ? Well, I may remark that your opinion is not mine. And to that I would add that, while I myself possess a reputation for Liberal and progressive views, I possess that reputation for the very reason that I can respect *real* aristocrats. For instance, my dear sir " (the latter term was so heatedly uttered that Bazarov raised his eyebrows), " for instance, my dear sir, take the aristocracy of England. While yielding upon their rights not an iota, they yet know how to respect the rights of others. While demanding fulfilment of obligations due to themselves, they yet fulfil their own obligations. And for those reasons it is to her aristocratic caste that England stands indebted for her freedom. It is because the English aristocratic caste itself supports that freedom."

"A tale which we have heard many times before! " commented Bazarov. "But what are you seeking to prove? "

"I am seeking to prove this," replied Paul Petrovitch. "That without a certain sense of personal dignity, without a sense of self-respect (both of which senses are inborn in the true aristocrat), the social edifice, the *bien public*, cannot rest upon a durable basis. It is *personality* that matters, my dear sir: and the human personality requires to be as firm as a rock, in that there rests upon it the entire structure of society. For example, I know that you ridicule my customs, my dress, my fastidious tastes. Yet do those very things proceed from that sense of duty—yes, of duty, I repeat—to which I have just alluded. In other words, I may live in the depths of the country, yet I do not let myself go. For I respect in myself the man."

" Allow me, Paul Petrovitch," said Bazarov. " You say that you respect yourself. Very good. Yet you can sit there with your hands folded! How will *that* benefit the *bien public*, seeing that inaction would scarcely seem to argue self-respect ? "

Paul Petrovitch blanched a little.

" That is another question altogether," he said. " However, I do not feel called upon to explain the reason why I sit with my hands folded (according to your own estimable term). It will suffice merely to remark that in the aristocratic idea there is contained a *principle*, and that nowadays men who live without principles are as destitute of morality as they are of moral substance. The same thing did I say to Arkady on the day after his arrival, and I say it now to you. You agree with me, Nikolai, do you not ? "

Nikolai Petrovitch nodded assent, while Bazarov exclaimed:

" The aristocratic idea, forsooth! Liberalism, progress, principles! Why, have you ever considered the vanity of those terms? The Russian of to-day does not need them."

" Then what, in your opinion, does he need? To listen to you, one would suppose that we stood wholly

67

divorced from humanity and humanity's laws; whereas, pardon me, the logic of history demands——"

" What has that logic to do with us? We can get on quite well without it."

" How can we do so? "

" Even as I have said. When you want to put a piece of bread into your mouth do you need logic for the purpose? What have these abstractions to do with ourselves? "

Paul Petrovitch waved his hand in disgust.

" I cannot understand you," he said. " You seem to me to be insulting the Russian people. How you or any one else can decline to recognise principles and precepts is a thing which passes my comprehension. For what other basis for action in life have we got? "

Arkady put in a word.

" Both I and Bazarov have told you," he said, " that we recognise no authority of any sort."

" Rather, that we recognise no basis for action save the useful," corrected Bazarov. " At present the course most useful is denial. Therefore we deny."

" Deny everything? "

" Deny everything."

" What? Both poetry and art and—I find it hard to express it?——"

" I repeat, *everything*," said Bazarov with an ineffable expression of *insouciance*.

Paul Petrovitch stared. He had not quite expected this. For his part, Arkady reddened with pleasure.

" Allow me," interposed Nikolai Petrovitch. " You say that you deny everything—rather, that you would consign everything to destruction. But also you ought to construct."

" That is not our business," said Bazarov. " First must the site be cleared."

"Yes; for the present condition of the people demands

it," affirmed Arkady. " And that demand we are bound to fulfil, seeing that no one has the right merely to devote himself to the satisfaction of his own personal egotism."

With this last Bazarov did not seem altogether pleased, since the phrase smacked too much of philosophy—rather, of " Romanticism," as Bazarov termed that science; but he did not trouble to confute his pupil.

" No, no! " Paul Petrovitch exclaimed with sudden heat. " I *cannot* believe that gentlemen of your type possess sufficient knowledge of the people to be rightful representatives of its demands and aspirations. For the Russian people is not what you think it to be. It holds traditions sacred, and is patriarchal, and cannot live without faith."

" I will not dispute that," observed Bazarov. " Nay, I will even agree that you are right."

" And, granting that I am right——"

" You have proved nothing."

" Yes, proved nothing," echoed Arkady with the assurance of a chess-player who, having foreseen a dangerous move on the part of his opponent, awaits the attack with expert composure.

" But how have I proved nothing? " muttered Paul Petrovitch, rather taken aback. " Do you mean to say that you are opposed to, not in favour of, the people? "

" Good gracious! Do not the common folk believe, when it thunders, that the Prophet Elijah is going up to Heaven in his chariot? You and I do not agree with that? The point is that the people is Russian, and that I am the same."

" Not after what you have just said! Henceforth must I decline to recognise you as any countryman of mine."

With a sort of indolent *hauteur* Bazarov replied:

" With his own hand did my grandfather guide the plough. Ask, therefore, of your favourite peasant which of us two—you or myself—he rates most truly as his countryman. Why, you do not know even how to speak to him ! "

" And you, while speaking to him, despise him."

" Should he merit contempt, yes. Reprobate, therefore, my views as much as you like, but who told you that they have come to me fortuitously rather than been derived from the very national spirit of which you are so ardent an upholder ? "

" Phaugh ! We need you Nihilists, do we not ? "

" Not ours is it to decide the need or otherwise, seeing that even a man like yourself considers that he has a use."

" Gentlemen, gentlemen ! " interposed Nikolai Petrovitch as he rose to his feet. " I beg of you to indulge in no personalities ! "

Paul Petrovitch smiled. Then, laying his hand upon his brother's shoulder, he forced him to resume his seat.

" Do not be alarmed," he said. " That very sense of dignity at which this gentleman pokes such bitter fun will keep me from forgetting myself."

And he turned to Bazarov again.

" Do you suppose your doctrine to be a new one ? " he continued. " If so, you are wasting your time. More than once has the Materialism which you preach been mooted; and each time it has been proved bankrupt."

" Another foreign term ! " muttered Bazarov. He was now beginning to lose his temper, and his face had turned a dull, copperish tint. " In the first place, we Nihilists preach nothing at all. For to preach is not our custom."

" What, then, is your custom ? "

" To proclaim facts such as that our civil servants

accept bribes, that we lack highways, commerce, and a single upright judge, and that——"

" Of course, of course! In other words, you and yours are to act as our ' censors ' (I believe that to be the correct term?). Well, I agree with many of your censures, but——"

" Other tenets which we hold are that to chatter, and to do nothing but chatter, concerning our differences is not worth the trouble, seeing that it is a pursuit which merely leads to pettiness and doctrinairism; that beyond question are our so-called leaders and censors not worth their salt, seeing that they engage in sheer futilities, and waste their breath on discussions on art and still life and Parliamentarism and legal points and the devil only knows what, when all the time it is the bread of sub-sistence alone that matters, and we are being stifled with gross superstition, and all our commercial enterprises are failing for want of honest directors, and the freedom of which the Government is for ever prating is destined never to become a reality, for the reason that, so long as the Russian peasant is allowed to go and drink himself to death in a dram-shop, he is ready to submit to any sort of despoilment."

" You have decided, then, you feel conscious, that your true *métier* is to apply yourselves seriously to nothing? "

" Even so," came the sullen reply, for Bazarov had suddenly become vexed with himself for having exposed his mind with such completeness to this *barin*.

" You have decided merely to deny everything? "

" We have decided merely to deny everything."

" And that you call Nihilism? "

" That we call Nihilism." In Bazarov's repetition of Paul Petrovitch's words there echoed, this time, a note of pride.

Paul Petrovitch knit his brows.

" So, so! " he said in a voice that was curiously calm.
" Nihilism is designed to combat our every ill, and you
alone are to act as our saviours and our heroes! Well,
well! But in what consider you yourselves and your
censorious friends to excel the rest of us? For you
chatter as much as does every one else."

" No, no! " muttered Bazarov. " At least we are
not guilty of *that*, however we may err in other ways."

" You do things, then? At all events, you are preparing to do things? "

Bazarov did not reply, although, in his excitement,
Paul Petrovitch had started up and then quickly
recovered his self-command.

" H'm! " continued Paul Petrovitch. " With you to act
is to demolish. But how is such demolition to benefit
when you do not even know its purpose? "

" We demolish because we are a force," interposed
Arkady.

Paul Petrovitch stared—then smiled.

" And a force need render account to no one," added
Arkady with a self-conscious straightening of his form.

" Fool! " gasped Paul Petrovitch. Evidently he could
contain himself no longer. " Have you ever considered
what you are maintaining with your miserable creed?
Even an angel would lose patience! ' A force,' forsooth!
You might as well say that the wild Kalmuck, or the
barbaric Mongol, represents a force. What boots such
a force? Civilisation and its fruits are what we value.
And do not tell me that those fruits are to be overlooked,
seeing that even the meanest *barbouilleur*,[1] the meanest
piano-player who ever earned five kopecks a night, is of
more use to society than you. For men of that kind at
least stand for culture rather than for some rude,
Mongolian propelling-power. Yes, you may look upon
yourselves as ' the coming race,' yet you are fit but to

[1] Scribbler.

sit in a Kalmuck shanty. ' A force,' foorsoth! Good
and ' forceful ' sirs, I beg to tell you that you number
but four men and a boy, whereas those others number
millions, and are folk of the kind who will not permit
such as *you* to trample upon their sacred beliefs, but will
first trample upon your worthy selves."

" Let them trample upon us," retorted Bazarov.
" We are more in number than you think."

" What ? You really believe that you will succeed in
inoculating the nation as a whole ? "

" From a little candle," replied Bazarov, " there arose,
as you know, the conflagration of Moscow." [1]

. " A pride almost Satanic in its nature, and then
banter! And thus you would seek to attract our youth,
thus you would attempt to win the inexperienced hearts
of our boys! For sitting beside you is one of those very
boys, and he is absolutely worshipping you! " (Upon
this Arkady knit his brows, and averted his head a little.)
" Yes, the canker has spread far already. For instance,
they tell me that in Rome our artists decline to enter
the Vatican, and look upon Raphael as next-door to a
fool, just because he is an ' authority '! Yet those very
artists are themselves so barren and impotent that their
fancy cannot rise above ' Girls at Fountains,' and so
forth, villainously executed! And such artists you
account fine fellows, I presume ? "

" Like those artists," said Bazarov, " I consider
Raphael to be worth not a copper groat. And as for the
artists themselves, I appraise them at about a similar
sum."

" Bravo, bravo! " cried Paul Petrovitch. " Listen,
O Arkady—listen to the way in which the young men of
the present day ought to express themselves! Surely our
youth will now rally to your side? For once upon a time
they had to go to school, since they did not like to be

73

taken for dunces, and therefore worked at their studies; but now they have but to say: ' Everything in the world is rubbish,' and, behold! the trick is done. They consider that delightful—and naturally! In other words, the blockheads of former days are become the Nihilists of the present."

" Your self-sufficiency—I mean, your self-respect— is carrying you away," Bazarov remarked nonchalantly (as for Arkady. his eyes had flashed, and his whole form was quivering with indignation). " But our dispute has gone far enough. Let us end it. Whenever you may feel that you can point out to me a single institution in our family or our public life which does not call for complete and unsparing rejection, I shall be pleased to accept your view."

" Of institutions of that kind I could cite you millions," exclaimed Paul Petrovitch. " For example, take the village commune."

Bazarov's lips twisted themselves into a contemptuous smile.

" The village commune," said he, " is a subject which you would do better to discuss with your brother, since he is learning by experience the meaning of that commune, and of its circular guarantee, and of its enforced sobriety and other contrivances."

" Take the family, then—yes, take the family, since at least among the peasantry it is still a surviving institution."

" And that question, too, I should imagine were best not dissected by you in detail. But see here, Paul Petrovitch. Allow yourself a minimum of two days to think over these things (you will need quite that amount of time to do so); and cite to yourself in succession our various social conditions, and give them your best attention. Meanwhile Arkady and myself will go and——"

" Go and make sport of everything, I presume? "

" No, go and dissect frogs. Come, Arkady! *Au revoir*, gentlemen."

And the two friends departed. Left alone, the brothers looked at one another.

" So," at last said Paul Petrovitch, " you see the young men of the day—you see our successors! "

" Our successors—yes," re-echoed Nikolai Petrovitch despondently. Throughout the conversation he had been sitting simply on pins and needles; throughout it he had dared do no more than throw an occasional pained glance at Arkady. " My brother, there came to me just now a curious reminiscence. It was of a quarrel which once I had with my mother. During the contest she raised a great outcry, and refused to listen to a single word I said; until at length I told her that for her to understand me was impossible, seeing that she and I came of different generations. Of course this angered her yet more, but I thought to myself: ' What else could I do? The pill must have been a bitter one, but it was necessary that she should swallow it.' And now *our* turn is come; now is it for *us* to be told by our heirs that we come of a different generation from theirs, and must kindly swallow the pill."

" You are too magnanimous and retiring," expostulated Paul Petrovitch. " For my part, I feel sure that we are more in the right than these two youngsters, even though we may express ourselves in old-fashioned terms, and lack their daring self-sufficiency. Indeed, what a puffed-up crowd is the youth of to-day! Should you ask one of them whether he will take white wine or red, he will reply, in a bass voice, and with a face as though the whole universe were looking at him: ' Red is my customary rule.' "

" Should you like some more tea? " interrupted Thenichka, who had been peeping through the doorway, but had not dared to enter during the progress of the dispute.

"No," was Nikolai Petrovitch's reply as he rose to meet her. "So you can order the *samovar* to be removed."

Meanwhile, with a brief "*Bon soir*," Paul Petrovitch betook himself to his study.

XI

HALF an hour later Nikolai Petrovitch sought his
favourite arbour. Despondent thoughts were thronging
through his brain, for the rift between himself and his
son was only too evident. Also, he knew that that rift
would widen from day to day. For nothing had he spent
whole days, during those winters in St. Petersburg, in
the perusal of modern works! For nothing had he listened
to the young men's discourses! For nothing had he been
delighted when he had been able to interpolate a word
into their tempestuous debates!

"My brother says that we are more in the right than
they," he reflected. "And certainly I too can say
without vanity that I believe these young fellows to
stand at a greater distance from the truth than ourselves.
Yet also I believe that they have in them something
which we lack—something which gives them an advantage over us. What is that something? Is it youth? No,
it is not youth alone. Is it that there hovers about them
less of the *barin* than hovers about ourselves? Possibly!"

Bending his head, he passed his hand over his face.

"Yet to reject poetry!" he muttered. "To fail to
sympathise with art and nature!"

And he gazed around as though he were trying to
understand how any one could be out of sympathy with
the natural world. Evening was just closing in, and the
sun sinking behind a small aspen copse which, situated
half a verst from the garden, was trailing long shadows
over the motionless fields. Along the narrow, dark track
beside the copse a peasant on a white pony was trotting;
and though the pair were overshadowed by the trees, the
rider was as clearly visible, even to a patch on his shoulder,

as the twinkling legs of his steed. Piercing the tangled
aspens, the sun's beams were bathing the trunks in so
brilliant a glow that trunks and beams were one bright
mass, and only the foliage on the boughs above formed
a dusky blur against the lighter tints of the flame-
coloured sky. Overhead bats were whirling; the wind
had sunk to rest; a few late-homing bees were buzzing
somnolently, sluggishly amid the lilac blossoms; and a
pillared swarm of gnats was dancing over a projecting
bough.

"O God, how fair!" was Nikolai's involuntary thought
as his lips breathed a favourite couplet.

Suddenly he remembered Arkady and *Stoff und Kraft*;
and though he continued to sit where he was, he quoted
poetry no more, but surrendered his mind wholly to the
play of his lonely, irregular, mournful thoughts. At all
times he was a man fond of dreaming; and to this
tendency his life in the country had added confirmation.
To think of what only a short while ago he had been
dreaming as he waited for his son on the post-house
verandah! For since that hour a change had come about,
and in the vague relations between himself and his son
there had dawned a more definite phase. Next, he saw
before him his dead wife. Yet he saw her, not as she had
appeared to him during the later years of her life—that is
to say, as a kindly, thrifty *châtelaine*—but as a young girl
slim of figure and innocently inquiring of eye. Yes, there
flitted before his vision a picture only of neatly plaited
tresses falling over a childish neck. And he thought of
his first meeting with her when, as a student, he had
encountered her on the staircase leading to his suite of
rooms. He remembered how, having accidentally brushed
against her, he had stopped to apologise, but had only
succeeded in muttering "Pardon, *monsieur*"; whereupon she had bowed, and smiled, and fled as in sudden
alarm—but only to turn, the next moment, at the bend

of the staircase, to look swiftly back, and then, as swiftly, to blush, and assume a more demure demeanour. Ah, those first timid meetings, those half-spoken words, those bashful smiles, those alternate fits of rapture and despair, that courtship that was destined to be crowned with swooning joy! Whither was it all fled? True, she had become his wife, and had conferred upon him such happiness as falls to the lot of few men on earth; but ever the thought recurred to him, and recurred again: "Why could those days of sweetness not have lasted for ever, so that we might have lived a life which should never have known death?"

He made no attempt to co-ordinate his thoughts. The predominant feeling in his mind was that he would give worlds to be able to connect himself with those blessed days by something stronger than the mere power of memory. He wanted to feel his Maria near him once more, to scent her dear breath. A curious mood had him in its grip.

"Nikolai Petrovitch!" came the voice of Thenichka from a spot somewhere in the vicinity. "Where are you?"

As he heard the call, a feeling that was neither vexation nor shame passed over him. No comparison between his dead wife and Thenichka was possible, yet he gave a start, and felt a passing regret that Thenichka had seized *that* moment to seek him. For in some way did the sound of her voice bring back to him his grey hairs, his old age, all that constituted the present. So for an instant the enchanted world which he had just entered, and which he had just seen emerge from the misty waves of the past, quivered—then disappeared.

"I am here, Thenichka," he called. "Please go away. I will come presently."

"Another reminder that I am a *barin*," he reflected. Thenichka retired, and suddenly he became aware of the fact that since the moment when he had sunk into a reverie nightfall had come. Yes, all around him there lay a motionless obscurity, with, gleaming amid it, as a small, pale blur, Thenichka's face. Rising, he started to return to the house, but his unstrung nerves could not calm themselves, and, glancing now at the ground, now towards the heavens where there swarmed myriads of twinkling stars, he fell to pacing the garden. He continued this pacing until he was almost worn out; for still did the vague, despondent, insistent sense of agitation refuse to leave his breast. Could Bazarov have divined his thoughts, how the Nihilist would have laughed! And even Arkady would have condemned him. For from the eyes of Nikolai Petrovitch—from the eyes of a man of forty-four who was the proprietor of an estate and a household—there were welling slow, uncalled-for tears. This was a hundred times worse than the 'cello-playing!

And still he continued his pacing, for he could not make up his mind to enter the peaceful, inviting retreat which beckoned to him so cheerfully with its lighted windows, and to leave the darkness of the garden, to forego the touch of fresh air upon his face, to throw off his present mood of sadness and emotion.

At a turn in the path he encountered Paul Petrovitch. "What is the matter with you?" Paul inquired. "You are looking as white as a ghost. Are you ill? Why not go to bed?"

Nikolai Petrovitch explained to him in a few words his frame of mind—then moved towards the house. Paul Petrovitch sauntered down towards the other end of the garden, and ever and anon, as he did so, indulged in wrapt contemplation of the heavens. Yet, save for the reflection of the starlight, there was nothing to be seen in his dark, handsome eyes; for he had not been born a Romanticist, and his drily fastidious, passionate,

Frenchified, misanthropic soul was incapable of castle-building.

"I tell you what," Bazarov said to Arkady the same night. "A splendid idea has come into my head. You know that to-day your father said that a certain eminent relation had sent him an invitation which he had no intention of accepting. Well, how would it be if you and I were to accept it, seeing that you too have been included in the honour? The weather has turned beautiful, and we might drive over and look at the town, and thus, incidentally, secure a few days' uninterrupted talk together."

"Should you then return here?"

"No. I should go on to my father's. You see, he lives thirty versts away only, and it is a long time since last I saw either him or my mother. Moreover, the old folk deserve to be humoured a little, seeing that they have been very good to me—especially my father—and that I am their only son."

"And shall you stay long?"

"No. Staying in that place is dull work."

"Then pay us a second visit on your way back?"

"I will if possible. We will go, then, eh?"

"At your pleasure," Arkady replied with a show of indifference. But, as a matter of fact, he was delighted with Bazarov's proposal; and only the thought that he must keep up his " Nihilism " prevented him from manifesting his feelings.

So, the next day, the pair set out for the town of —— ; while with one consent the youth of Marino broke into lamentations over their going, and Duniasha even went so far as to weep. Only their elders breathed more freely.

81

XII

THE town of ――― , whither our friends now proceeded,
lay under the dominion of one of those young, progressive, despotic provincial governors who afflict Russia
in an unending sequence. As early as the first year of his
rule this particular potentate had succeeded in quarrelling, not only with the President of the Provincial
Council (who was a retired staff officer, a horse breeder,
and an agriculturist), but also with his whole guber-
natorial staff of *tchinovniks*: with the result that at the
time of our story the commotion therefrom had attained
a pitch which had just necessitated the sending down of
a commissary empowered to hold an investigation. The
Government's choice for this purpose had fallen upon
Matvei Ilyitch Koliazin, the son of the Koliazin who
had once acted as guardian to the brothers Kirsanov,
and a man of the younger school—that is to say, a man
who, though a little over forty, still aimed at attaining
the dignity of a statesman, and having a breast covered
with stars (including at least one of a foreign minor
order), and who, also like the Governor whom he had
come to examine, was accounted a Progressive, and
held a high opinion of himself. Yet never did Matvei
allow his boundless vanity to prevent him from affecting
a stereotyped air of simplicity and good humour, or from
listening indulgently to anything that might be said to
him, or from cultivating so pleasant a laugh that everywhere he contrived to pass for " not a bad sort of a
fellow." True, he could on important occasions (if I
may quote the trite saying) " make dust fly " (" Energy
is indispensable for a State worker," was a frequent saw
of his—" *L'énergie est la première qualité d'un homme*

82

FATHERS AND SONS

d'état "); yet almost invariably did he end by being set down as a fool, while *tchinovniks* of more experience rode roughshod over him. Amongst other things, he had a custom of expressing a great respect for Guizot,[1] and also of striving to convince every one that he (Koliazin) was not one of " your men of routine, your retired bureaucrats," but, rather, a man who noted " every new and more important phenomenon of our social life." In fact, such phrases he had at his finger ends, and also he studied (though with a sort of careless pomposity only) the development of contemporary literature. Lastly, it not seldom befell that, on meeting a street procession of students, he would, though maturer of years than the majority of its members, add himself to its ranks. In short, only his circumstances and his epoch caused Matvei Ilyitch in any way to differ from those officials of the Alexandrine period who, before setting out to attend a reception at Madame Svietchin's [2] (then resident in St. Petersburg), would read a few pages of Condillac's [3] works. Yet, though an adroit courtier, Matvei was a mere glittering fraud, since, save that he knew how to hold his own against all comers (though, certainly, that is a great achievement in life), he was, in all matters of State, a complete stranger to common sense.

On the present occasion he welcomed Arkady with all the *bonhomie*, all the jocosity, of an " enlightened " bigwig. Nevertheless his face fell a little when he learned that the other relatives whom he had invited had preferred remaining in the country. " Your father always

[1] François Pierre Guillaume Guizot (1787-1874), the great French minister, ambassador, *litt·rateur*, and educationalist.
[2] Madame Svietchin (1782-1857), wife of the Russian General Svietchin. For more than forty years she maintained a famous salon.
[3] Etienne Bonnot de Mably de Condillac (1715-1780), a French philosopher who based knowledge solely upon the physical senses.

83

was a queer fish," he remarked as he parted the tails of a velvet " cutaway." And, having said this, he turned to a young *tchinovnik* in a tightly buttoned uniform, and asked him irritably what he wanted; at which onslaught the young *tchinovnik* (whose lips looked as though a confirmed habit of keeping their own counsel had gummed them permanently together) straightened himself with a sharp, apprehensive look at his superior. But, once Matvei had effected this " settling " of his subordinate, the great man paid the little one no further attention.

In passing, I may observe that to most of our bigwigs is this species of " settling " very dear, and that many are the expedients resorted to for its achievement. Particularly is the following method " quite a favourite," as the English say—in other words, much in request. Suddenly a given bigwig will cease to be able to grasp with his intelligence even the simplest sentence, and assume an air of abysmal density. For example, he will inquire what the day of the week may be, and be told (with great and stammering deference) that the day is, say, Friday.

" What ? " will roar the bigwig with an air of being forced to strain his ears to the utmost. " Eh ? what do you say ? "

" I-It is F-Friday, your E-E-Excellency."

" Eh, what ? Friday ? What mean you by Friday ? "

" Y-Your Excellency, F-Friday is, is— F-F-Friday is a day in the week."

" Come, come ! You need not have taken so much time to tell me *that*."

Matvei Ilyitch was just such a bigwig, although he called himself a Liberal.

" My good fellow," he now continued to Arkady, " I should advise you to go and leave your card upon the Governor. Of course you understand that my reason for counselling you to adopt this procedure is, not that I

in any way hold with any bygone ideas about kow-towing
to authority, but, rather, because the Governor is a good
fellow, and I know that you would like to see a little
society. For you too are not a bear, I hope? No? Well,
the Governor is giving a grand ball the day after to-
morrow."

" And shall you be there? " asked Arkady.

" I shall, of course, receive tickets for it," replied
Matvei Ilyitch with an assumed air of regret. " You
dance, I presume? "

" I do—though very badly."

" Never mind, never mind. There exists here plenty
of good society, and it would never do for a young fellow
like yourself to be a non-dancer. Again I say this, not
because I in any way revere antiquated notions, nor yet
because I think that intellect ought to go kicking its heels
about, but because Byronism has become absurd—*il a
fait son temps.*"

" But I belong to neither the Byronists nor——"

" Well, well! I will introduce you to some of our
ladies—I myself will take you under my wing." And
Matvei Ilyitch smiled in a self-satisfied way. " In fact,
you shall have a gay time here."

At this point a servant entered to announce the President of the Provincial Treasury. The latter, a mild-
eyed veteran with wrinkles around his lips and a great
love for nature, was accustomed to remark on summer
days that " of every little flower each little bee is now
taking its toll." So Arkady seized the occasion to depart.

He found Bazarov at the hotel where the pair were
putting up, and had great difficulty in persuading him
to join in the projected call upon the Governor.

" Well, well! " eventually said Bazarov. " I have laid
a hand upon the tow-rope, so it ill becomes me to complain of its weight. As we are here to inspect the local
lions, let us inspect them."

To the young men the Governor accorded a civil enough welcome, but neither bade them be seated nor set the example himself. A man in a perpetual hurry and ferment, he, on rising in the morning, was accustomed to don a tight uniform and stiff collar, and then to give himself up to such an orgy of orders-giving that he never finished a single meal. As the result, he was known throughout the province as " Bardeloue "—in reference, be it said, not to the great French preacher,[1] but to *burda*, fermented liquor. After inviting Arkady and Bazarov to the coming ball, the Governor, two minutes later, repeated the invitation as though he had never given it ; while likewise he mistook the pair for brothers, and addressed them throughout as " the Messieurs *Kaiserov*."

Subsequently, as the pair were proceeding homewards, a man of small stature, and dressed in a " Slavophil " costume, leapt from a passing *drozhki*, and, with a cry of " Evgenii Vasilitch ! " flung himself upon Bazarov.

" Is that you, Herr Sitnikov ? " remarked Bazarov without even checking his stride. " What chance brings you hither ? "

" A pure accident," was the other's reply as, turning to the *drozhki*, he signed to the coachman to follow at a foot's pace. " You see, I had business to do with my father, and he invited me to pay him a visit." Sitnikov hopped across a puddle. " Also, on learning of your arrival, I have been to call at your place." (True enough, on subsequently reaching the hotel, the two friends found awaiting them Sitnikov's visiting-card, with the corners turned down, and one side of it inscribed with his name in the French fashion, and the other with his name in Slavonic characters.)

" You are from the Governor's, I suppose ? " continued the little man. " I sincerely hope not, however."

[1] Louis Bourdaloue (1632–1704), a professor in the Jesuit College of Bourges

" Your hopes are vain."

" Then I too, alas, must pay him my *devoirs*. But first introduce me to your friend."

" Sitnikov—Kirsanov," responded Bazarov without halting.

" Delighted!" minced Sitnikov as he stepped back, struck an attitude, and hurriedly doffed his super-elegant gloves. " I have heard much of you, Monsieur Kirsanov. I too am an old acquaintance—I might even say, an old pupil—of Evgenii Vasilitch's. Through him it was that I came by my spiritual regeneration."

Arkady glanced at Bazarov's " old pupil," and saw that he had small, dull, pleasant, nervous features; also that his narrow, sunken eyes expressed a great restlessness, and that his lips were parted in a perpetual smile of a wooden and ingratiating order.

" Do you know," Sitnikov continued, " when Evgenii Vasilitch first told me that we ought to ignore every species of authority I experienced a sense of rapture, I felt as though I had suddenly ripened. ' Ah,' I thought, ' at last have I found my man!' By the way, Evgenii Vasilitch, you *must* come and see a certain lady of my acquaintance—one who, beyond all others, is the person to understand you, and to look upon your coming as a red-letter event. Perhaps you have heard of her already?"

" No. Who is she?" asked Bazarov reluctantly.

" A Madame Kukshin—a Madame, I should say, *Evdoksia* Kuvshin. And she is not merely a remarkable character and a woman of light and leading; she is also representative of the *émancipée*, in the best sense of the word. But look here. How would it be if all three of us were to go and see her? She lives only two steps away, and she would give us luncheon. You have not lunched already, I presume?"

" No, we have not."

87

" Then the arrangement would suit us all. By the way, she is independent, but a married woman."

" Good-looking? " queried Bazarov.

" N-No—one could not exactly say that."

" Then why ask us to go and see her? "

" Ah, ha! You *will* have your jest, I see. But remember that she will stand us a bottle of champagne."

" The practicality of the man! "

Sitnikov gave a shrill giggle.

" Shall we go? " he added.

" I cannot decide."

Here Arkady put in a word.

" We have come to inspect the local people," he remarked, " so let us inspect them."

" True enough," seconded Sitnikov. " And, of course, *you* must come, Monsieur Kirsanov. We could not go without you."

" What? Are all three of us to descend upon her? "

" What matter? She herself is an odd person."

" And you say that she will stand us a bottle of champagne."

" Yes; or even a bottle apiece," asserted Sitnikov. " I will go bail upon that."

" Go bail with what? "

" With my head."

" Your purse would have been better; but lead on."

XIII

THE villa in which Avdotia, or Evdoksia, Nikitishna Kukshin resided was one of the usual Moscow pattern, and stood in one of the recently consumed streets (for as we know, every fifth year sees each of our provincial capitals burnt to the ground) of the town of ——. Beside the front door there hung (over a cracked, crooked visiting-card) a bell-handle, while in the hall the visitors were met by a female who constituted, not exactly a maidservant, but a mob-capped "lady companion." And it need hardly be added that these two phenomena, the bell-handle and the "lady companion," constituted clear evidence of the "progressiveness" of the hostess's views.

On Sitnikov inquiring whether Avdotia Nikitishna were within, a shrill voice interrupted him from an adjoining room:

"Is that you, Victor? Pray enter."

The female in the mob-cap disappeared.

"I have not come alone," Sitnikov responded as, after an inquiring glance at Arkady and Bazarov, he divested himself of his greatcoat, and revealed thereunder a sort of sack jacket.

"Never mind," the voice replied. "*Entrez, s'il vous plaît.*"

The young men did as bidden, and found themselves in a room which resembled a workshop rather than a parlour. On tables were piled promiscuous papers, letters and Russian magazines (most of the latter uncut); everywhere on the floor were to be seen gleaming the fag-ends of cigarettes; and on a leather-padded sofa a lady—youngish, flaxen-haired, and clad in a *négligée* soiled silk gown—was lolling in a semi-recumbent position. About her stumpy wrists were clasped a large pair of bracelets, and over her head was thrown a lace mantilla. Rising, she draped her shoulders carelessly in a velvet tippet with faded ermine trimming, and, saying indolently, " Good day, Victor," pressed Sitnikov's hand.

" Bazarov—Kirsanov," he said in abrupt imitation of the former; whereupon she responded, " How do you do ? " and then added, as she fixed upon Bazarov a pair of large eyes between which glimmered a correspondingly small, pink, upturned nose: " I have met you before."

That said, she pressed his hand even as she had done Sitnikov's.

Bazarov frowned, for though the plain, insignificant features of the emancipated lady contained nothing actually to repel, there was something in their mien which produced upon the beholder the sort of unpleasant impression which might have inclined him to ask her: " Are you hungry, or bored, or afraid? At all events, what is it you want? " Also, like Sitnikov, she kept pawing the air as she spoke, and her every word, her every gesture, revealed such a lack of control as at times amounted to sheer awkwardness. In short, though she conceived herself to be just a simple, goodhearted creature, her bearing was of the kind to lead the beholder to reflect that, no matter what she did, it was not what she had intended to do, and that everything was done (to use the children's term) " on purpose "— that is to say, non-simply and non-naturally.

" Yes, I have met you before, Bazarov," she repeated (like many other contemporary females of Moscow and the provinces, she had adopted the fashion of calling men by their surnames alone on first introduction). " Will you have a cigar? "

"I thank you,"interposed Sitnikov (who had deposited his person in an armchair, and crossed his legs). " Also, pray give us some luncheon, for we are absolutely ravenous. Also, you might order us a bottle of champagne."

" You Sybarite! " exclaimed Evdoksia with a smile (a smile always brought her upper gum prominently into view). " Is he not, Bazarov? "

" No; it is merely that I love the comforts of life," protested Sitnikov pompously. " Nor need that in any way prevent me from being a Liberal."

" But it does, it does," cried Evdoksia. However, she gave orders to her servant to see both to the luncheon and to the champagne. " What is *your* opinion on the matter? " she added, turning to Bazarov. " I feel convinced that you share mine."

" No, I do not," he replied. " On the contrary, I think that, even from the chemical point of view, a piece of meat is better than a piece of bread."

" Then you study chemistry? " she exclaimed. " Chemistry is *my* passion also. In fact, I have invented a special liniment."

" A liniment? You? "

" Yes, I. And please guess its use. It is for making unbreakable dolls and pipe-bowls. You see that, like yourself, I am of a practical turn of mind. But, as yet, I have not completed my course of study. It still remains for me to read up my Liebig. *Apropos*, have you seen an article in the *Viedomosti* on Woman's Work—an article by Kisliakov? If not, you should read it (for I presume that you take an interest in the Feminine Question, and also in the Question of the Schools?). But what is your friend's line? *Apropos*, what is his name? "

These questions Madame Kukshin, as it were, mouthed, and did so with an affected carelessness which waited for no reply, even as a spoilt child propounds conundrums to its nurse.

" My name is Arkady Nikolaievitch Kirsanov,"

Arkady answered for himself. "And my particular line is doing nothing at all."

Evdoksia tittered.

"How nice!" she exclaimed. "Then you do not even smoke? Victor, I am furious with you!"

"Why?" enquired Sitnikov.

"Because I have just heard that you are again standing up for Georges Sand, that played-out woman. How is she even to be compared (that creature, who lacks a single idea on education or physiology or anything else) with Emerson? In fact, I believe that never in her life has she so much as *heard* of embryology—though in these days no one can get on without it." The speaker flung out her arms in an expressive gesture. "But what a splendid article was that of Elisievitch's! He is indeed a talented gentleman!" (This was another habit of Evdoksia's—the habit of persistently using the term "gentleman" for the ordinary word "man"). "Bazarov, pray come and sit beside me on the sofa. You may not know it, but I am dreadfully afraid of you."

"Why are you afraid of me (if you will forgive my curiosity)?"

"Because you are a dangerous gentleman—you are a critic so caustic that in your presence my confusion leads me to begin speaking like a lady-landowner of the Steppes. *Apropos*, I am a lady-landowner myself; for, though I employ a local steward named Erothei (a sort of Cooper's 'Pathfinder,' but compounded with a blend of independence in his composition), I retain the ultimate reins of management in my own hands. But how unbearable this town is!—yes, even though I have made it my permanent home, seeing that nothing else was to be done!"

"The town is what a town always is," remarked Bazarov indifferently.

"But its interests are so petty!" continued Evdoksia.

" *That* is what troubles me. Once upon a time I used to winter in Moscow, but now good Monsieur Kukshin has to dwell there alone. And Moscow itself is, is—well, not what it used to be. As a matter of fact, I contemplate going abroad. I have spent the whole year in making my preparations for the journey."

" You will go to Paris, I presume? "

" Yes, and to Heidelberg."

" Why to Heidelberg? "

" Because there the great Herr Bunsen [1] has his home."

Bazarov could not think of a suitable reply.

" Do you know Pierre Sapozhnikov? " continued she.

" No, I do not."

" He is always to be found at Lydia Khostatov's."

" Even with her I am not acquainted."

" Well, Sapozhnikov is going to escort me on my travels. For at least I am free—I have no children, thank God! Why I should have put in that ' Thank God! ' I scarcely know."

She rolled another cigarette between her nicotine-stained fingers, licked it, placed it between her lips, and struck a match. The servant entered with a tray.

" Ah! Here comes luncheon! Will you have some? Victor, pray uncork the bottle. It is your function to do so."

" Mine, yes, mine," he hummed; then gave another of his shrill giggles.

" Have you any good-looking ladies in this town? " Bazarov asked after a third glassful of champagne.

" Yes," replied Evdoksia. " But uniformly they are futile. For example, a friend of mine, a Madame Odintsov, is not bad-looking, and has nothing against her except a doubtful reputation (a thing of no consequence in

[1] Robert Wilhelm Bunsen (1811–1899), chemist and physicist; inventor of Bunsen's burner and magnesium light; and originator (with Kirchhov) of spectrum analysis.

itself); but, alas! she combines with it such a complete lack of freedom, or of breadth of view, or, in fact, of anything! The system of bringing up women needs a radical change. I myself have given much thought to the matter, and come to the conclusion that our women are ill-educated."

" Yes; the only thing to be done with them is to hold them in contempt," agreed Sitnikov. To him any opportunity of despising, of expressing scornful sentiments, was the most agreeable of sensations. Yet, though he thus chose women for his especial censure, he little suspected that before many months were over he himself would be grovelling at the feet of a wife—and doing so merely for the reason that she had been born a Princess Durdoleosov!

" No, to none of them would our conversation convey anything," he continued. " Nor is there a single one of them upon whom the attention of a serious-minded man would be anything but thrown away."

" Scarcely need they *desire* to have anything conveyed to them by our conversation," remarked Bazarov.

" Of whom are you speaking? " interposed Evdoksia.

" Of the smart women of the day."

" What? I suppose you agree with Proudhon's [1] opinion on the subject? "

Bazarov drew himself up.

" I agree with no man's opinions," he remarked. " I have some of my own."

" *A bas les autorités!* " cried Sitnikov, delighted at this unlooked-for opportunity of showing off in the presence of the man whom he worshipped.

" But even Macaulay——" began Madame Kukshin.

" *A bas* Macaulay! " roared Sitnikov. " How can you defend those dolls of ours? "

[1] Pierre Joseph Proudhon (1809–1865), a French doctrinaire who taught that anarchy is the culmination of all social progress

" I am not defending them at all," said Madame Kukshin. " I am merely standing up for the rights of women—rights which I have sworn to defend to the last drop of my blood."

" *A bas*——" began Sitnikov—then paused. " I do not reject them," he added in a lower tone.

" But you *do* reject them, for you are a Slavophil, as I can see very clearly."

" On the contrary, I am *not* a Slavophil; although, of course, I——"

" But you *are* a Slavophil: you believe in the principles of the *Domostroi*,[1] and would like always to be holding over women a scourge."

" A scourge is not a bad thing in its proper place," observed Bazarov. " But, seeing that we have reached the last drop of, of——"

" Of what ? " said Evdoksia.

" Of champagne, most respected Avdotia Nikitishna— not of your blood."

" Never when I hear my sex abused can I listen with indifference," resumed Evdoksia. " It is all too horrible, too horrible! Instead of attacking us, people ought to read Michel's [2] *De l'Amour*. What a wonderful work it is! Let us talk of love."

She posed her arm gracefully upon the tumbled cushions of the sofa.

There fell a sudden silence.

" What is there to say concerning love? " at length said Bazarov. " In passing, you mentioned a certain Madame Odintsov (I think that was the name?). Who is she? "

" A very charming woman," squeaked Sitnikov, " as

[1] A curious old sixteenth-century work which, usually attributed to the monk Sylvester, purports to be a " guide to household management," and, incidentally, gives a terrible picture of the power of the Russian husband over his wife.

[2] Louise Michel (1830–1906), a French anarchist long resident in London.

well as clever, rich, and a widow. Unfortunately, she is not sufficiently *developed*, and a closer acquaintance with our Evdoksia would do her a world of good. Evdoksia, I drink to your health! Let us sing the honours. ' Et toc, et toc, et tin, tin, tin! Et toc, et toc, et tin, tin, tin!' "

" You scamp, Victor! "

The luncheon proved a lengthy affair, for to the first bottle of champagne there succeeded a second, and to the latter a third, and to that a fourth. Meanwhile Evdoksia kept up an unceasing flow of chatter, and received effective assistance from Sitnikov. In particular did the pair discuss the nature of marriage (" the outcome of prejudice and vice "), the question whether people are born " single," and the consistency of " individuality." Then Evdoksia seated herself at the piano, and, red in the face with wine which she had drunk, clattered her flat finger-nails upon the keys, and essayed hoarsely to sing, first of all some gipsy ditties, and then the ballad, " Dreaming Granada lies asleep "; while, throwing a scarf over his head to represent the dying lover, Sitnikov joined her at the words " Your lips meet mine in a burning kiss."

At length Arkady could stand it no longer.

" Gentlemen," he exclaimed, " this is sheer Bedlam! "

As for Bazarov, he yawned, for he had done little more than interject a satirical word or two—his attention had been devoted, rather, to the champagne. At length he rose, and, accompanied by Arkady, left the house without so much as a word of farewell to the hostess. Sitnikov pursued the pair.

" Ah, ha! " he exclaimed as he skipped about the roadway. " Did I not tell you that she would prove a most remarkable personality? Would that more of our women were like her! In her way, she is a moral phenomenon."

" And your father's establishment? " remarked Bazarov as he pointed to a tavern which they happened to be passing. " Is that also a moral phenomenon? "

Sitnikov vented another of his shrill giggles. But, being also ashamed of his origin, he felt at a loss whether to plume himself upon, or to take offence at, Bazarov's unexpected pleasantry.

XIV

A FEW days later, the ball was held at the Governor's, and Matvei Ilyitch figured thereat as the guest of honour. For his part, the President of the Provincial Council (who was at loggerheads with the Governor) explained at large that only out of respect for Matvei had he deigned to be present, while the Governor continued, even when stationary, his usual process of orders-giving. With Matvei's suavity of demeanour nothing could be compared save his pomposity. Upon every man he smiled—upon some with a hint of superciliousness, upon others with a shade of deference; whilst to the ladies he bowed and scraped *en vrai chevalier français*, and laughed, throughout, the great, resonant, conspicuous laugh which a bigwig ought to do. Again, he clapped Arkady upon the back, addressed him loudly as " young nephew," and honoured Bazarov (who had been with difficulty coaxed into an ancient tail-coat) both with a distant, yet faintly condescending, glance which skimmed that individual's cheek, and with a vague, but affable, murmur in which there could be distinguished only the fragments " I," " Yes," and " 'xtremely." Lastly, he accorded Sitnikov a finger and a smile (in the very act, turning his head away), and bestowed upon Madame Kukshin (who had appeared minus a crinoline and in dirty gloves, but with a bird of paradise stuck in her hair) an " *Enchanté !* " The throng present was immense; nor was a sufficiency of cavaliers lacking. True, most of the civilian element crowded against the walls, but the military section danced with enthusiasm, especially an officer who, being fresh from six weeks in Paris, where he had become acquainted with daring cries of the

type of "Zut!" "Ah, fichtrrre!" "Pst, pst, mon
bibi!" and so forth, pronounced these quips to perfection, with true Parisian *chic*; while also he said " *Si
j'aurais* " for " *Si j'avais*," and " *absolument* " in the
sense of " certainly." In short, he employed that Franco-
Russian jargon which affords the French such intense
amusement whenever they do not think it more prudent
to assure their Russian friends that the latter speak the
tongue of France *comme des anges*.

As we know, Arkady was a poor dancer, and Bazarov
did not dance at all; wherefore the pair sought a corner,
and were there joined by Sitnikov. Summoning to his
visage his accustomed smile of contempt, and emitting
remarks mordantly sarcastic in their nature, the great
Sitnikov glanced haughtily about him, and appeared to
derive some genuine pleasure from thus striking an
attitude. But suddenly his face underwent a change.
Turning to Arkady, he said in a self-conscious way:
" Here is Madame Odintsov just entering."

Looking up, Arkady beheld, halted in the doorway, a
tall woman in a black gown. In particular was he struck
with the dignity of her carriage, and with the manner in
which her bare arms hung beside her upright figure.
From her gleaming hair to her sloping shoulders trailed
sprays of fuchsia flowers, while quietly, intelligently—I
say *quietly*, not dreamily—there gazed, with a barely
perceptible smile, from under a white and slightly
prominent forehead a pair of brilliant eyes. In general,
the countenance suggested latent, but gentle, kindly force.

" Do you know her? " Arkady inquired.

" I do—intimately," replied Sitnikov. " Shall I introduce you? "

" If you please; but only when this quadrille has come
to an end."

Bazarov's attention also had been caught by this
Madame Odintsov.

"What a face!" he exclaimed. "No other woman in the room has one anything like it."

As soon, therefore, as the quadrille was over, Sitnikov conducted Arkady to Madame Odintsov; and though at first—whether through the excessive "intimacy" of Sitnikov's acquaintance, or whether through the fact that he happened to stumble over his words—she gazed at him with a shade of astonishment, she no sooner heard Arkady's family name than her face brightened, and she inquired whether he was the son of Nikolai Petrovitch.

"I am," replied Arkady.

"Then I have twice had the pleasure of meeting your father. Also, I have heard much about him, and shall be most glad to know you."

At this point an aide-de-camp sidled up, and requested the honour of a quadrille: which request she granted.

"Then you dance?" exclaimed Arkady, but with great deference.

"I do. What made you think that I do not? Is it that I look too old?"

"Oh no, pardon me! By no means! Then perhaps I too might ask for a mazurka?"

Smiling indulgently, she replied, "If you wish," and then looked at him not so much in a "superior" manner as in that of a married sister who is regarding a very, very young brother. Though she was not greatly older than Arkady (she had just attained her twenty-ninth year), her presence made him feel the veriest schoolboy, and caused the difference of years to seem infinitely greater than it was. Next, Matvei Ilyitch approached her with a majestic air and a few obsequious words; whereupon Arkady moved away a little, while continuing to observe her. In fact, not until the quadrille was over did he find himself able to withdraw his eyes from her

100

bewitching person. Throughout, her conversation with her partner and the guest of honour was accompanied with small movements of the head and eyes, and twice she uttered a low laugh. True, her nose erred a little on the side of thickness (as do those of most Russian women), nor was the colour of her skin unimpeachable; yet Arkady came to the conclusion that never in his life had he encountered a woman so charming of personality. Continuously the sound of her voice murmured in his ears, and the very folds of her dress looked different from those of other women—they seemed to hang straighter and more symmetrically, and her every movement was smooth and natural.

Nevertheless, when the strains of the mazurka struck up, and, reseating himself beside his partner, he prepared to enter into conversation with her, he felt a distinct touch of diffidence. Nor, though he kept passing his hand over his hair, could he find a word to say. However, this timidity, this state of agitation, did not last long, for soon her calmness infected him, and within a quarter of an hour he was talking to her of his father, his uncle, and life in St. Petersburg and the country. For her part, she listened with kindly interest, while gently opening and closing her fan. Thus only at moments when other cavaliers came to ask her for dances (Sitnikov did this twice) did Arkady's chatter become interrupted; and whenever she returned to her place, to reseat herself with her bosom heaving not a whit more rapidly than it had done before, he would plunge into renewed conversation, so delighted was he at the fact that he had found some one to sympathise with him, to whom he could talk, at whose beautiful eyes and forehead and gentle, refined, intellectual features he could gaze at leisure. She herself said little, but her every word showed a knowledge of life which pointed to the fact that already this young woman had thought and felt much.

" Who was the man with you before Sitnikov brought you to me? " she inquired.

" So you noticed my friend? " exclaimed Arkady. " Has he not a splendid face? His name is Bazarov."

And, once launched upon the subject, Arkady descanted so fully, and with such enthusiasm, that Madame Odintsov turned to observe his friend more closely. But soon the mazurka began to draw to a close, and Arkady found himself regretting the prospect of losing the companion with whom he had spent such a pleasant hour. True, he had felt, throughout, that he was being treated with condescension, and ought to be grateful; but upon young hearts such an obligation does not press with any great weight.

The music stopped with a jerk.

" *Merci!* " said Madame Odintsov—then rose. " You have promised to come and see me. Also, bring with you your friend, for I am filled with curiosity to behold a man who has the temerity to believe in nothing."

Next, the Governor approached Madame with a distraught air and an intimation that supper was ready; whereupon she took his proffered arm, and, as she departed, turned with a last smile and nod to Arkady, who, in answer, bowed and stood following her with his eyes. How straight her figure looked under the sheen of her black gown!

" Already she will have forgotten my existence," he thought to himself, while an exquisite humility pervaded his soul. Then he rejoined Bazarov in their joint corner.

" Well? " his friend said. " Have you enjoyed yourself? Some man or other has just been telling me that the lady in question is—— But in all probability the man was a fool. What do *you* think of her? "

" The allusion escapes me," replied Arkady.

" Come, come, young innocence! "

" Or at all events your informant's meaning escapes

102

me. Madame is nice, but as cold and formal as, as——"

" As a stagnant pool," concluded Bazarov. " Yes, we all know the sort of thing. You say that she is cold, but that is purely a matter of taste. Perhaps you yourself like ice ? "

" Perhaps I do," the other muttered. " But of such things I am no judge; and in any case she wishes to make your acquaintance as well as mine, and has asked me to bring you with me to call."

" The description of me which you gave is easily imagined! On the other hand, you did rightly to offer her us both, for no matter who she may be—whether a provincial lioness or only an ' *émancipée* ' like the Kukshin woman, she has at least such a pair of shoulders as I have not seen this many a day."

Arkady recoiled from this cynicism, yet, as often happens in such cases, started to reproach his friend for something wholly unconnected with the utterance which had given umbrage.

" Why do you refuse women freedom of thought ? " he asked under his breath.

" For the reason, dear sir, that, according to my observation of life, no woman, unless she be a freak, thinks with freedom."

And here the conversation terminated, for supper had come to an end, and the friends departed. As they left the room Madame Kukshin followed them with a nervous and wrathful, yet slightly apprehensive, smile in her eyes. The reason of this was that she felt wounded in her conceit at the fact that neither of the young men had taken any notice of her. Nevertheless, she remained at the ball until most of the rest of the company had left; whereafter, it being four o'clock in the morning, she danced a polka-mazurka, *à la Parisienne*, with Sitnikov, and with this edifying spectacle brought the Governor's fête to a close.

103

XV

" Now let us see to what category of mortals to assign
this young person," said Bazarov to Arkady as, on the
following day, the pair mounted the staircase of the hotel
where Madame Odintsov was staying. " Somehow I
seem to scent impropriety in the air."

" You surprise me! " burst forth Arkady. " Do *you*,
Bazarov, do *you* hold with the narrow-minded morality
which——"

" Idiot! " exclaimed Bazarov contemptuously. " Do
you not know that both in our jargon and in the under
standing of the ordinary person the term ' improper
has now come to mean the same as ' proper ' ? In any
case I seem to scent money here. You yourself told me,
did you not, that Madame's marriage was a very strange
one?—though, for my part, I look upon marrying a rich
old man as anything but a strange proceeding—rather,
as a measure of prudence. True, I place little reliance
upon the gossip of townsfolk, but at least I prefer to
suppose that that gossip has, as our cultured Governor
would say, ' a basis in fact.' "

Arkady did not respond, but knocked at the door of
Madame's suite; and, the door having been opened, a
liveried man-servant ushered the visitors into a large,
hideously furnished room of the type which is always to
be found in Russian hotels—the only exception in the
present case being that the apartment was adorned with
flowers. Presently Madame herself entered, clad in a
plain morning gown, and looking even younger in the
spring sunlight than she had done in the ballroom.
Arkady duly presented Bazarov, and, as he did so,
remarked with surprise that his friend seemed confused,

while Madame was as imperturbable as ever. This *gaucherie* on his part Bazarov realised, and felt vexed at.

" Phaugh! " he thought to himself. " The idea that I should be afraid of a woman! "

Yet, like Sitnikov, he could only subside into a chair, and fall to talking with an exaggerated emphasis to the woman who sat with her brilliant eyes riveted with such attention upon him.

Anna Sergievna Odintsov had had for father one Sergei Nikolaievitch Loktev, a well-known gambler, speculator, and beau. After fifteen years of flaunting it in St. Petersburg and Moscow, and dissipating his whole substance, he had been forced to retire to the country, where soon afterwards he had died and left to his daughter Anna (aged twenty) and his daughter Katerina (aged twelve) only a small joint competence. As for the girls' mother (who had come of the impoverished house of the Princes X.), she had expired during the heyday of her husband's career in St. Petersburg. Anna's position after her father's death was therefore a very difficult one, for the brilliant education which she had received in the capital had in no way fitted her for the care of a household and an estate, nor yet for the endurance of a life in the country. Moreover, she possessed not a single acquaintance in that country neighbourhood, nor any one to whom to turn for advice, since her father had done his best to avoid associating with his neighbours, in that he had despised them as much as they, in their several ways, had despised him. Howbeit, Anna kept her head, and straightway sent for her mother's sister, the Princess Avdotia Stepanovna X., who, a malicious, presuming old woman, annexed, on the day of her arrival, all the best rooms in the house, raged and stormed from morning till night, and even declined to walk in the garden unless she could be accompanied by her only serf, a sullen-looking lacquey who wore a faded green livery, a blue collar, and a three-cornered hat. Nevertheless Anna put up with these tantrums of her aunt's, superintended the education of her sister, and resigned herself to the idea of living in seclusion for the rest of her life. But fate had ordained otherwise. That is to say, a certain Odintsov—a rich, bloated, unwieldy, soured, semi-imbecile hypochondriac of forty-six who was, nevertheless, neither stupid nor cruel—happened to see her, and became so enamoured that he offered her marriage: and to this proposal she consented. For six years the pair lived together, before the husband died, leaving her all his property. The following year she spent in the country; after which she went abroad with her sister—but only as far as Germany, since she quickly wearied of foreign parts, and was only too thankful to return to her beloved Nikolsköe, which lay some forty versts from the provincial town of ——. At Nikolsköe she had at her disposal a splendid, tastefully furnished mansion, a beautiful garden, and a range of orangeries (the late Odintsov having denied himself in nothing); but inasmuch as she made but rare appearances in the town, and then only on flying visits connected with business, the provincial gentry conceived a grudge against her, and took to gossiping of her marriage with Odintsov, and relating such impossible tales as that she had assisted her father in his nefarious schemes, that she had had her reasons for going abroad, and that certain unfortunate results of that tour had had to be concealed. " I tell you," the ardent retailer of such fables would say, " that she has been through the mill right enough." Eventually these rumours reached her ears, but she ignored them altogether, since her nature was at once bold and independent.

Seating herself at full length in an armchair, and crossing one hand over the other, she set herself to listen to Bazarov's harangue. Contrary to his usual custom, he spoke without restraint, for he was clearly anxious to interest his listener. Arkady again felt surprised at this, though he failed to detect whether or not Bazarov was succeeding in his aim, seeing that Anna Sergievna's face gave no clue to the effect produced, so fixedly did her features retain their faintly polite expression, so unvaryingly did her beautiful eyes reflect unruffled attention. True, at first Bazarov's vehemence gave her an unpleasant impression as of a bad smell or a jarring note; but in time she began to understand that it came of his being ill at ease, and she felt flattered at the fact. Only the paltry repelled her; and no one could well have accused Bazarov of that quality. Indeed wonders were never to cease for Arkady, since, though he had expected Bazarov to talk to Madame Odintsov as to a woman of intellect—to speak to her of his views and convictions (seeing that she had expressed a desire to behold a man who had " the temerity to believe in nothing "), he discoursed only on medicine, homœopathy, and botany. At the same time, Madame had not wasted her life of solitude, but had read a large number of standard works, and could express herself in the best of Russian; and though at one point she diverted the conversation to music, she no sooner perceived that he declined to recognise the existence of the art than she returned to botany, even though Arkady would gladly have continued the discussion of the importance of national melodies. In passing, her treatment of Arkady as a younger brother remained the same. What she valued in him was, evidently, the good humour and simplicity of youth—nothing more. Thus there was held; for three hours, an animated, but intermittent, discursive conversation.

At length the friends rose to say farewell. With a kindly glance Anna Sergievna offered them her beautiful white hand; then, after a moment's reflection, said irresolutely, but with a pleasant smile:

" If neither of you fear finding the time tedious, will you come and pay me a visit at Nikolsköe? "

" I should deem it the greatest pleasure! " cried Arkady.

" And you, Monsieur Bazarov? "

Bazarov merely bowed: which again surprised Arkady, while also he noticed that his friend's face looked flushed.

" Well? " the younger man said as the pair issued into the street. " Are you still of the opinion that she is, is——? "

" I cannot say. But what an icicle she has made of herself! " There was a pause. " At all events, she is an imposing personage, a *grande dame* who lacks but a train to her gown and a coronet to her head."

" But none of our *grandes dames* speak Russian as she does," remarked Arkady.

" No; for she has undergone a rebirth, and eaten of our bread."

" And what a charm is hers! "

" You mean, what a splendid body—the very thing for a dissecting theatre! "

" Stop, stop, for God's sake! Her body differs from all other women's."

" No need to lose your temper, young innocent. Have I not said that she stands in the front rank of women? Yes, we must pay her that visit."

" When? "

" The day after to-morrow. Nothing else is to be done here, for we need not stay to drink champagne with the Kukshin woman, and listen to the harangues of your kinsman, the Liberal bigwig. Not we! The day after to-morrow, therefore, let us give the whole thing the go-by. *Apropos*, my father's place lies near Nikolsköe. For Nikolsköe is on the —— road, is it not? "

" It is."

" *Optime !* Then we shall gain nothing by delay: only

108

fools and clever people procrastinate. Her anatomy, I repeat, is splendid."

Within three days, in bright, but not too warm, weather, the two friends were bowling along the road to Nikolsköe. With a will did the well-fed stage horses trot out, and lightly swish their flanks with their plaited, knotted tails; and as Arkady glanced along the road, he, for some unknown reason, smiled.

"Congratulate me!" cried Bazarov of a sudden. "To-day is the 22nd of June—the feast of my Patron Saint. Certainly he looks after me, does he not?" Then the speaker added in a lower tone: "But to-day, also, they are expecting me at home. . . . Well, let them expect me."

XVI

THE manor-house in which Anna Sergievna resided
stood on an open hillock, and close to a yellow stone
church with a green roof, white columns, and an entrance
surmounted by a fresco representative of Our Lord's
Resurrection—the latter executed in the " Italian "
style, and having as its most noticeable feature the
figure of a swarthy warrior whose rounded contours
filled the entire foreground. Behind the church, the
village extended into two long wings, and had thatched
roofs surmounted by a medley of chimneys ; while the
manor-house itself was built in a style homogeneous
with the design of the church—that is to say, in the
style commonly known as " Alexandrine," and embracing yellow-painted walls, a green roof, white columns,
and a front adorned with a coat-of-arms. In fact, both
buildings had been erected by a provincial architect to
the order of the late Odintsov, a man impatient (so he
himself always expressed it) of " vain and arbitrary
innovations." Lastly, to right and left of the house
there showed the trees of an antique garden, while
an avenue of clipped firs led the way to the principal
entrance.

The friends having been met in the hall by two strap-
ping lacqueys in livery, one of the latter immediately
ran for the butler; who (a stout man in a black tail-
coat) proceeded to usher the guests up a carpeted staircase, and into a room which contained a couple of beds
and the usual appurtenances of the toilet. Evidently
neatness was the order of the day in the establishment, for everything was both spotlessly clean and as
fragrant as the chamber wherein a Minister of State
holds his receptions.

110

" Anna Sergievna will be glad to see you in half an hour," the butler said. " Meanwhile, have you any orders for me? "

" No, worthy one," replied Bazarov. " Except that you might so far condescend as to bring me a small glassful of *vodka*."

" It shall be done, sir," said the butler with a shade of hesitation; whereafter he departed with creaking boots.

" What grandeur! " commented Bazarov. " In your opinion, how ought our hostess to be addressed? In the style of a duchess? "

" Yes, and of a very great duchess," replied Arkady. "The more so, seeing that she has invited such influential aristocrats as ourselves to visit her."

" I presume that you are referring to your humble servant—a future doctor, the son of a doctor, and the grandson of a sexton? By the way, are you aware that my grandparent was a sexton, even as was Speransky's? " [1] A smile curled his lips. " Thus you see that the lady is mistaken, woefully mistaken. We haven't such a thing as a tail-coat, have we? "

Arkady shrugged his shoulders bravely; but he too was feeling a little awe-stricken.

At the close of the half-hour the pair entered the drawing-room, which they found to be a large, lofty apartment of rich, but tasteless, appointments. Against the walls, in the usual affected style, stood heavy, expensive furniture, the walls themselves were hung with brown curtains to which were florid gilt borders (all these things the late Odintsov had ordered through a Muscovite friend who kept a wineshop), and above a divan in the centre of the room hung a portrait of a

[1] A " Westernist " statesman (1772–1839), who propounded various schemes of reform in connection with the Russian peasantry.

wrinkled, sandy-haired individual who seemed to be regarding the newcomers with extreme distaste.

" *He*," whispered Bazarov.

The hostess herself then entered. She was clad in a light dress, and had her hair dressed behind the ears— a style which communicated to her pure, fresh countenance an air of almost girlish juvenility.

" Thank you for having kept your promise," she said. " And now that you are come, I think that you will find the time not altogether dull. For one thing, I intend to introduce you to my sister, who is a skilful piano-player (of course, Monsieur Bazarov, to you such things are a matter of indifference, but you, Monsieur Kirsanov, I know, adore the art of music). Also, an elderly aunt lives with me as my companion, and at intervals a neighbour looks in for a game of cards. You see our home circle. Now let us seat ourselves."

Madame delivered this little speech with the precision of a lesson which she had learnt by heart, and then turned to converse with Arkady. On finding that her mother had known his, and that the latter had made the former her confidant during her love affair with Nikolai Petrovitch, the lad fell to speaking enthusiastically of his dead parent, while Bazarov applied himself to the inspection of some albums.

" What a domesticated individual I am! " thought he to himself.

Presently, with much pattering of paws, there burst into the room a splendid Russian greyhound with a blue collar; and it was followed by a young girl of eighteen with a dark complexion, dark hair, a round, but pleasant, face, and small, dark eyes. She was carrying a basket of flowers.

" My sister Katia," said Madame Odintsov, indicating the girl with her head.

Katia seated herself beside Madame, and fell to

112

arranging her flowers; while the greyhound (whose name was Fifi) approached each of the guests in turn, laid his cold nose in their hands, and wagged his tail.

" Have you gathered those flowers yourself? " asked Madame Odintsov.

" Yes, Anna Sergievna," the girl replied.

" And is your aunt going to join us at tea? "

" Yes."

These replies of Katia's were accompanied with a frank, but gentle and bashful, smile, and an upward glance half grave, half sportive. Everything in her betokened youth and freshness—her voice, the down on her cheeks, her little pink hands with their white, dimpled palms, and the slightly contracted shoulders. Also, she blushed without ceasing, and drew her breath with a fluttering respiration.

Presently Madame Odintsov turned to Bazarov.

" Surely it is only out of politeness that you are looking at those photographs?" she said. " They cannot possibly interest you. Pray move nearer to us, and let us engage in an argument."

Bazarov approached her.

" What shall we argue about? " he inquired.

" About anything you like. But first let me warn you that I am a redoubtable opponent."

" You? "

" Yes, certainly. You look surprised? Why so? "

" Because, so far as I can tell, your temperament is one of the cold and lethargic order, whereas argument needs impulsiveness."

" How have you contrived so quickly to appraise me? To begin with, I am both impatient and exacting. Ask Katia if I am not. Also, I am easily moved to impulse."

Bazarov darted a glance at her.

" Possibly," he said. " Certainly you ought to know best. But, since you desire to argue, let us argue. While

113

looking at those views of Saxon Switzerland, I heard you remark that they could not interest me. This you said, I presume, because you suppose me to be lacking in the artistic sense. Well, I am so. But might not those pictures be interesting to me solely from the geological point of view—from the standpoint of an observer, say, of the formation of mountains?"

" Pardon me, but, as a geologist, you would prefer to resort to some special work on that science, not to a few pictures."

" Oh, not necessarily. For a picture may instantly present what a book could set forth only in a hundred pages."

Anna Sergievna made no reply.

" Well," she resumed, leaning forward upon the table— a movement which brought her face closer to Bazarov's, " since you possess not a grain of the artistic instinct, how do you contrive to get on without it?"

"Rather, I would ask you: What is the artistic instinct able to effect?"

" It is able at least to help one to examine and to instruct one's fellow man."

Bazarov smiled.

" In the first place," he retorted, " the prime requisite in that connection is experience of life; and, in the second place, the study of detached personalities is scarcely worth the trouble. For all we human beings are alike, in body as in spirit. In each of us there is an identical brain, an identical spleen, an identical heart, an identical pair of lungs, an identical stock of the so-called moral qualities (trifling variations between which we need not take into account). Therefore from a single specimen of the human race may all the rest be judged. In fact, human beings are like trees in a forest. You never find a botanist studying its individual trunks."

Katia, who had been arranging her flowers, glanced

at Bazarov in amazement, and, in so doing, encountered his keen, contemptuous gaze, and blushed to her ears. Anna Sergievna shook her head.

" Trees in a forest! " she exclaimed. " Think you, then, that there is no difference between the wise man and the fool, the good and the bad? "

" No, I do not," replied Bazarov. " On the contrary, I believe that such differences do exist. The point is that they exist only as between the sound and the ailing. For instance, a consumptive's lungs are not as yours and mine; yet they have been fashioned precisely as our own have been. Also, whereas, to a certain extent, we know whence bodily disorders arise, *moral* disorders come of faulty education, the thousand and one follies with which the human brain is afflicted, in short, any irregular condition of the social body. Rectify that body, and moral sickness will soon cease to be."

Speaking as though he were saying to himself, " Believe me or not as you like, it is all one to me," Bazarov drew his long fingers through his whiskers, while his eyes glowed like coals.

" Then you think," pursued Anna Sergievna, " that, once the social body has been rectified, stupid and evil people will cease to exist? "

" At all events, once the social body is properly organised, the fact that a man be wise or stupid, good or bad, will cease to be of importance."

" Ah! I understand! That is because we all possess an identical spleen? "

" Precisely so, madam."

She turned to Arkady.

" And what is your opinion, Arkady Nikolaievitch? " she enquired.

" I agree with Evgenii," was his reply as, in his turn, he received a glance of astonishment from Katia.

" I am surprised, gentlemen," said Madame. " However, I can hear my aunt approaching, so let us spare her ears, and discuss this later."

Anna Sergievna's aunt—a small, spare woman with a mallet-shaped face, a pair of narrow, malicious eyes, and a grey false front—bestowed scarcely so much as a bow upon the guests, but at once relapsed into a huge velvet armchair which no one but herself was allowed to use. And even when Katia hastened to place for her a footstool, the old woman did not thank her, nor even look at her, but chafed her hands under the yellow shawl which covered the whole of her frail figure. Beyond all things was she fond of yellow; wherefore she had had her cap trimmed with ribands of the same hue.

" Have you slept well, Auntie?" Madame Odintsov inquired with a raising of her voice.

" That dog is here again!" the old woman muttered on noticing that Fifi was taking an irresolute step or two in her direction. " Turn the beast out, I say! Out with it!"

Calling Fifi, Katia opened the door for the animal to leave the room; whereupon, though it bounded out in joyous mood (under the impression that it was about to be taken for a walk), it no sooner found itself marooned outside than it fell to whining and scratching at the panels; which caused the Princess to frown, and necessitated Katia's exit to rectify matters.

" Tea is ready, I believe," Madame Odintsov continued. " Gentlemen, pray come. Will you have some tea, Auntie?"

The Princess rose from her chair in silence, and headed a procession to the dining-room, where a Cossack footman pulled a padded armchair from under the table (like the last, it was reserved for the Princess alone), and she subsided into its depths. Katia poured out tea, and handed her aunt the first cup—a cup adorned with a coat-of-arms; whereafter the old woman added some

116

honey to the beverage (she looked upon tea-drinking with sugar as a sin of extravagance, and the more so since never at any time would she consent to spend an unnecessary kopeck), and then asked hoarsely:

" What has Prince Ivan to say in his letter? "

No one answered, and in time Bazarov and Arkady apprised the fact that, though treated, certainly, with respect, the old woman attracted no one's serious attention.

" They keep her here for show," Bazarov reflected. " She is kept because she comes of a princely house."

Tea over, Anna Sergievna proposed a walk; but since at that moment a drop of rain came pattering down, the company (with the exception of the Princess) returned to the drawing-room. Presently the neighbour addicted to a game of cards came in, and proved to be one Porphyri Platonitch—a stout, grey-headed, affable, diverting individual who, in addition, could boast of a pair of legs as shapely as though turned with a lathe. Anna Sergievna then inquired of Bazarov (with whom she had again been in conversation) whether he would care to join them in the old-fashioned game of " Preferences "; and he consented on the ground that he could not too soon prepare himself for the post of a district physician.

" But take care," remarked his hostess. " Porphyri Platonitch and I are not unlikely to beat you. Meanwhile, do you, Katia, go and play something on the piano for the benefit of Arkady Nikolaievitch. I know that he loves music, and we too shall be glad to listen to you."

Reluctantly Katia approached the piano; nor, in spite of Arkady's fondness for music, did he follow her any more eagerly.

The truth of it was that he felt himself to be being " got rid of " by Madame Odintsov, and already there was simmering in his heart, as in the heart of any young

117

man of his age, that vague, oppressive feeling which is the harbinger of love.

Raising the lid of the piano, Katia murmured under her breath, and without looking at Arkady:

" What shall I play? "

" Anything you wish," he replied with indifference.

" But what sort of music do you *prefer*? " she persisted with unchanged attitude.

" Classical music," was the reply delivered with equal nonchalance.

" Mozart? "

" Certainly—Mozart."

So Katia produced the Viennese master's Sonata-Fantasia in C minor. She played it well, but coldly, and not with any excess of precision. Likewise, she kept her lips compressed, her eyes upon the keys, and her form erect and motionless. Only towards the close of the piece did her face kindle at all, while at the same moment a tiny curl detached itself from her loosely-bound hair, and fell over her dusky forehead.

Arkady also felt moved by the closing portion of the Sonata—the portion where the charming, careless gaiety of the melody gives place to sudden bursts of mournful, almost tragic lamentation. Yet the thoughts which Mozart's strains aroused in him bore no relation to Katia. He merely looked at her now and then, and reflected:

" She plays well; nor is she bad-looking."

The Sonata over, Katia inquired, without removing her hands from the keyboard: " Is that enough? " and Arkady replied that he would not think of troubling her further. Then he went on to talk of Mozart, and to ask her whether she herself had selected the Sonata, or whether it had been selected for her by some one. Katia answered in monosyllables, and from time to time went into hiding, retired into herself; and on each occasion

118

of this sort she made her reappearance but reluctantly, and with a face composed to a stubborn, almost a stupid, air. Yet she was not timid so much as diffident and a trifle overawed by the presence of the sister who had brought her up (not that the sister in question ever suspected it). Finally, she returned to her flowers, and Arkady found himself reduced to calling Fifi to his side, and stroking the dog's head with a kindly smile.

As for Bazarov, he had to pay forfeit after forfeit, for Anna Sergievna was fairly clever at cards, and Porphyri Platonitch was a player fully able to look after himself. Consequently the young doctor rose a loser, not by a considerable sum, but by one which, at all events, was sufficient to be scarcely agreeable. After supper Anna Sergievna started a discussion on botany.

" I wish you would take me for a walk to-morrow morning," she said. " I want you to teach me the Latin names of our field flowers, and also their characteristics."

" But how could the Latin names benefit you ? " he inquired.

" System is in all things necessary," she replied,

" A truly wonderful woman ! " Arkady commented the same evening, on finding himself alone with his friend in the bedroom.

" Yes," replied Bazarov. " She certainly possesses brains. Also, she has dreamed dreams."

" In what sense ? "

" In the best sense, my friend—in the very best sense, O Arkady Nikolaievitch. Certain also am I that she manages her property well. But the marvellous phenomenon is not she, but her sister."

" What ? That hoyden ? "

" Yes, that hoyden. The hoyden contains an element of freshness and virginity and timidity and reticence and anything else you like which makes her really an object worthy of interest. Of the one you could make

119

whatsoever you might desire, whereas of the other there is nothing to be said save that she represents a yesterday's loaf."

Arkady made no reply, and soon the two men were asleep and dreaming their own dreams.

The same night Anna Sergievna devoted much thought to her two guests. Bazarov she liked both for his total lack of affectation and for the piquancy of his criticisms; so that she seemed to divine in him something new, something which had hitherto remained unknown to her experience. All of which excited her curiosity.

And she too was a strange being. Free from all prejudice, and devoid of all strong beliefs, she rendered obeisance to nothing, and had in view no goal. Again, though much was open to her sight, and much interested her, nothing really satisfied her, and she had no wish for such satisfaction, since her intellect was at once inquiring and indifferent, and harboured doubts which never merged into insensibility, and aspirations which never swelled into unrest. True, if she had been dowered with less wealth and independence, she might have plunged into the fray, and learnt the nature of passion; but, as things stood, she took life unhastingly, and, though often finding it tedious, spent her days in a deliberate, rarely agitated manner. True, at times rainbow colours gleamed even before *her* eyes; yet no sooner had they faded than she would draw her breath as before, and in no way regret their disappearance. Again, though, at times, her imagination exceeded the bounds of what is considered permissible by conventional morality, her blood still coursed tranquilly through her lethargic and bewitchingly shaped frame; and only when she was issuing in a warm and tender glow from her comfortable bathroom would she fall to pondering upon the futility of life, its sorrow and toil and cruelty, and feel her soul swell to sudden temerity, and begin to seethe with noble aspirations. Yet even then, let but a draught happen to blow in her direction from an open window, and at once she would shrug her shoulders, commiserate herself, come very near to losing her temper, and become conscious of nothing but the thought that the one thing necessary was to ensure that by hook or by crook that abominable draught should be averted.

Again, like all women who have never known what it is to fall in love, she was sensible of a persistent yearning for something wholly undefined. There was nothing that she actually lacked, yet she seemed to lack everything. The late Odintsov she had merely tolerated (the marriage having been one *de convenance* only—though she would never have consented to become his wife had he not also been kindly of heart), and from the experience she had derived a certain aversion to the male sex in general, which she conceived to be composed exclusively of creatures slovenly, idle, wearisome, and weakly exacting in their habits. In fact, only once had she met (it was somewhere abroad) a man who had in any way attracted her. He had been a young Swede of a knightly countenance, honest blue eyes, and an open brow; but, for all the impression that he had made upon her, the impression in question had not prevented her from shortly afterwards returning to Russia.

" A strange man, that Bazarov," she thought to herself as she reposed in her magnificent bed with its lace-embroidered pillows and its light silken coverlet. It may be said, that, in addition to having inherited her late father's fastidious and luxurious tastes, she still cherished for that wayward, but kindhearted, parent a considerable affection, since during his lifetime he had not only adored her and cracked jokes with her on equal terms, but also accorded her his whole confidence,

121

and made it his invariable custom to seek her advice. Of her mother she had but the scantiest of remembrance.

"Yes, a strange man is that Bazarov," she repeated; after which she stretched her limbs, smiled, clasped her hands behind her head, ran an eye over the pages of two foolish French novels, let fall the second of these volumes from her hands, and relapsed into slumber— a cold, spotless figure in spotless, fragrant white.

When breakfast was over next morning, she set forth upon the botanising expedition with Bazarov; to return home just before luncheon time. Meanwhile Arkady did not leave the house, but spent an hour with Katia, nor found the time wearisome, seeing that of her own accord Katia volunteered to repeat the Sonata. Yet the instant that his eyes beheld Madame Odintsov returning his heart leapt within him. She was crossing the garden with a slightly tired step, but with her cheeks rosy of hue, her eyes shining under her round straw hat with even greater brilliancy than usual, and her fingers twirling between them the stalk of some field flower. Also, her light mantilla had slipped to her shoulders, and the broad ribands of her hat were floating over her bosom. Behind her walked Bazarov with his usual air of superciliousness and self-assurance, while on his face there was an expression cheerful, and even good-humoured. Yet somehow, Arkady did not like that expression.

Muttering "Good-morning," Bazarov passed towards his room, while Madame Odintsov accorded the young man a negligent handshake—then similarly continued her way.

"'Good morning!'" thought Arkady to himself. "One would think that she and I had made one another's acquaintance only to-day!"

122

XVII

As we know, time either flies like a bird or crawls like a snail. Thus a man is in best case when he fails to notice either the rapidity or the slowness of its flight. Similarly did Bazarov and Arkady spend their fortnight at Madame Odintsov's. Of this another contributory cause was the fact that alike in her household and in her daily life she maintained a *régime* to which she herself strictly adhered, and to which she constrained others to adhere; so that the daily domestic round accomplished itself according to a fixed programme. At eight o'clock the company would assemble for breakfast; whereafter, until luncheon time, individuals could do whatsoever they chose (the hostess herself devoting her attention to her steward—she administered her estate on the *obrok* or tithes system—her household servants, and her head housekeeper). Next, before dinner, the company would reassemble for conversation or for reading aloud; and the rest of the evening would be devoted to a walk, to cards, or to music. Lastly, at half-past ten Anna Sergievna would withdraw to her room, issue her orders for the following day, and retire to bed.

But to Bazarov this measured, slightly formal regularity was not wholly agreeable. " Somehow it reminds one of running on a pair of rails," he used to declare; while so much did the sight of liveried lacqueys and graded serfs offend his democratic instincts that once he averred that one might as well dine in the English fashion outright, and wear white ties and black tail-coats. These views he expressed to Anna Sergievna (something in her always led men to lay bare their opinions in her presence); and, after she had heard him out, she said:

"From your point of view, the matter is as you say, and perhaps I play the fine lady too much; but in the country one cannot live anyhow; such a course always leads one to grow slovenly."

So she continued her *régime* as before. Yet, though Bazarov grumbled, he and Arkady found that to that very formality they owed the fact that everything in the establishment "ran as on rails." In passing it may be mentioned that between the two young men there had taken place a change which dated from the day of their arrival at Nikolsköe, and manifested itself, as regards Bazarov (for whom Anna Sergievna evidently entertained a liking, though seldom did she agree with his *dicta*), in the form of an unwonted captiousness which led him easily to lose his temper, to speak always with reluctance, to glare about him, and to be as unable to sit still as though mines had been exploding beneath his seat. As for Arkady (now come finally to the conclusion that he was in love with Madame Odintsov), the change manifested itself, rather, in his falling a prey to a melancholy which in no way prevented him from making friends with Katia, and even helped him to maintain with her kindly and cordial relations.

"Whereas Madame cares nothing for me," he would reflect, "*this* good-hearted creature does not give me the cold shoulder."

And these reflections would cause his heart to taste once more the sensuous joy of "magnanimity." Dimly Katia herself divined that her society afforded him a sort of comfort; wherefore she saw no reason to deny either him or herself the pleasure of this innocent, half-diffident, half-trustful *camaraderie*. True, in the presence, and under the keen eye, of the elder sister (who always caused Katia to retire precipitately into her shell) the pair never exchanged a single word (indeed, as a man in love, Arkady could not well have paid attention to any one but the object of his adoration while in the latter's vicinity); but as soon as he found himself alone with Katia he began, to a certain degree, really to enjoy himself. That is to say, whereas he knew himself to be incompetent to interest Madame (seeing that whenever he found himself alone with her he blushed and lost his head, while she, on her side, did not know what to say to him, so jejune was his mind as compared with her own), in Katia's presence he felt perfectly at home, and could treat her with condescension, and let her expound to him the impressions which she derived from music and the reading of tales, poems, and other " trifles." Nor did he notice, nor would he have consented to recognise had he noticed, the fact that those same " trifles " interested him as much as they did Katia. At the same time, the latter in no way acted as a clog upon his melancholy; wherefore, just as Madame was at her ease with Bazarov, so the young man was at his with Katia, and, after a short period of joint converse, the two couples would usually diverge. This happened especially during walks, and the more readily in that, whereas Katia adored nature, and Arkady too loved it (though he would never have admitted the fact), to Madame and Bazarov the charms of the natural world represented more or less a matter of indifference. Hardly need I add that from this constant separation between Arkady and Bazarov there flowed inevitable results which brought about in the relations of the pair a gradual change. That is to say, Bazarov ceased to discourse on Madame Odintsov—he ceased even to censure her for her " aristocratic manners "; and while, with regard to Katia, he sang her praises as usual (at the same time advising the placing of a check upon her sentimental tendencies), he took to uttering these encomiums only in a half-hearted and a perfunctory way, and, in general, to lecturing his pupil less than he had formerly done.

Rather, he seemed to avoid him, to feel in some way uncomfortable in his presence.

These things Arkady duly noted, but kept his observations to himself.

The real cause of the innovation was the feeling which Madame Odintsov inspired in Bazarov's breast, and which he found to be a torture and a madness to him. Yet, had any one hinted to him, ever so distantly, that what was taking place in his soul could ever have been possible, he would have denied it with a contemptuous laugh and a cynical imprecation, seeing that, though a great devotee of feminine society and feminine beauty, he looked upon love in the ideal, the " romantic " (to use his own term) aspect as unpardonable folly, and upon the sentiment of chivalry as a sort of aberration or malady which moved him frequently to express his astonishment that Toggenburg and his Minnesingers and troubadours never ended by being clapped in a madhouse.

" Should a woman please you," he would say, " strive to attain your goal; but if you cannot attain that goal, waste no further trouble—just turn away. For the world does not rest upon a single keystone."

In similar fashion Madame Odintsov " pleased " Bazarov: yet, though the widespread reports in circulation about her might, with the freedom and independence of her views and the undoubted *penchant* which she entertained for himself, have been reckoned to tell in his favour, he soon discovered that, in her case, the " goal " was *not* to be attained. Also, he found to his surprise that he could not " turn away "—rather, that the mere thought of her made his blood boil. True, that symptom, if it had been the only one, might have been dealt with; but there became implanted in him something else—something which he had hitherto refused to admit, something of which he had hitherto made sport, but something which now aroused his pride. Therefore, although, when conversing with Anna Sergievna, he poured added scorn upon everything " romantic," he recognised, during his hours of solitude, that even in his own personality there lurked an element of " Romanticism." And at such times there was nothing for it but to rush out of doors into the woods, and to stride along at a pace which snapped off chance-met boughs, and found vent in curses at both them and himself. Or he would seek a hayloft or stable, and, stubbornly closing his eyes, strive to woo sleep, and almost invariably fail. Yet, as he sat there, there would come to him delusions that those proud lips *had* once responded to his kisses, that those chaste arms *had* embraced his neck, that those soulful eyes *had* gazed tenderly—yes, tenderly—into his: and at such times his head would whirl, and for a second or two, and until his discontent returned, he would relapse into a state of trance, and, as though urged by a demon, think thoughts of unavowable import. Again, there were times when he would conceive a change similar to his own to have taken place in *her*, and the expression of her face already to be charged with a special significance. Yet, this point reached, he would end merely by stamping his feet, grinding his teeth, and mentally shaking his fist at himself.

Once, when walking with her in the garden, he announced to her in curt, gruff tones that he intended soon to depart for his father's place; whereupon Anna Sergievna turned pale, as though something had pricked her heart, and pricked it in such a manner as to surprise even herself, and to leave her wondering what it could portend. Yet not for the sake of testing her, nor of seeing what might possibly come of it, had he mentioned his purposed departure (never at any time did he indulge in " scheming "). Rather, the reason was that, earlier

that morning, he had had an interview with his father's
steward, Timotheitch, a rough, but quick-witted, old
fellow who, in past days, had acted as his nurse, and
had now presented himself—with tousled, flaxen hair,
red, weather-beaten face, watery, sunken eyes, short,
stout jacket of grey-blue cloth, leathern girdle, and
tarred boots—at Nikolsköe.

" Good-day to you, ancient! " had been Bazarov's
greeting.

" Good-day to *you*, *batiushka*! " had responded the
old man with a gleeful smile which had covered his face
with wrinkles.

" And how is it that I see you here? " Bazarov had
continued. " Is it that they have sent you to fetch me? "

" By no means, pardon me, *batiushka*! " Timotheitch
had stammered out this denial for the reason that he had
suddenly recollected certain strict injunctions imposed
upon him before starting. " No, it is merely that I am
on my way to the town on affairs connected with the
estate, and turned aside a little to pay my respects to
your honour. No, not to disturb you at all—oh dear no! "

" Do not lie," Bazarov had said. " Is *this* the way to
the town? "

Timotheitch, cringing, had returned no reply.

" And how is my father? " Bazarov had continued.

" Quite well, thank God! "

" And my mother? "

" Your mother is the same, thank God! "

" And they are, I suppose, expecting me? "

The old man had cocked his head with a knowing air.

" Evgenii Vasilitch, why should they *not* be expecting
you? Yes, as God is my trust, I know that their hearts
are simply aching for a sight of you."

" Well, well! Do not make too long a stay of it, but tell
them that I will come presently."

" I will, *batiushka*."

Yet it had been with a sigh that Timotheitch had replaced his cap on his head with both hands, left the house, remounted the shabby *drozhki* which he had left waiting at the gates, and disappeared at a trot—though *not* in the direction of the town.

The same evening saw Madame sitting in her boudoir with Bazarov, and Arkady pacing the salon, and listening to Katia's music. As for the Princess, she had gone to bed, for she could not abide the presence of guests—least of all, of " those upstarts and good-for-nothings " as she termed our friends. In fact, though she confined herself, in the drawing-room or the dining-room, to sulking, she resorted, when alone with her maid in the bedroom, to abuse of Arkady and Bazarov which made her cap and her false front fairly dance on her head. These things, of course, Madame Odintsov knew.

" Why need you depart? " she said to Bazarov. " Have you forgotten your promise? "

Bazarov started.

" What promise? " he asked.

" Then you *have* forgotten it! I mean the promise to give me a few lessons in chemistry? "

" How can I fulfil it? My father is expecting me at home, and I ought not to stay a day longer. You had better read through *Notions Générales de Chimie*, by Pelouse and Frémy. It is an excellent work, and clearly written—the very thing you want."

" But you said that no book can adequately replace— I forget the exact phrase you used, but you know what I mean, do you not? "

" I cannot help myself," he muttered.

" Nevertheless, why go? " She lowered her voice as she spoke. Bazarov glanced at her as she leant back in her chair and crossed her arms (which were bare to the elbow), and saw that by the light of the lamp (softened with a shade of pleated paper) she was looking paler than

usual—also that the outlines of her figure were almost
buried in a soft white gown, from underneath which
there peeped forth the tips of her toes, posed crosswise.

" What reason should I have for remaining? " he
replied.

She gave her head the faintest toss.

" What reason should you have? " she re-echoed.
" Well, are you not happy here? Do you think that there
will be no one to regret your departure? "

" There will be no one. Of that I am certain."

" Then you are wrong," came the reply after a pause.
" But I do not believe you—I have an idea that you are
not speaking seriously."

Bazarov said nothing.

" Why do you not answer me? " she persisted.

" What is there to say? In general, to regret people's
absence is not worth while, and, least of all, the absence
of people like myself."

" Why, again? "

" Because I am a prosaic and eminently uninteresting
individual. Nor do I know how to talk."

" But you know how to play the esquire? "

" No, not even that. And, as you know, the softer
aspect of life, the aspect which you hold so dear, lies
altogether beyond me."

Madame Odintsov nibbled the corner of her handkerchief.

" Think what you like," she said, " but at least I shall
find things dull when you are gone."

" Arkady will remain," he hazarded.

She shrugged her shoulders.

" Nevertheless I shall find the time wearisome," she
repeated.

" Not for long."

" Why not? "

" Because, as you have very truly said, things never

seem dull to you save when your *régime* is infringed. In fact, with such faultless regularity have you ordered your life that there abides in it no room for dullness or depression or any other burdensome feeling."

" And I too am faultless, I suppose—I have ordered my life too regularly ever to err ? "

" I daresay. Take an example of it. In a few minutes it will be ten o'clock; when, as I know by experience, you will request me to leave your presence."

" Oh no, I shall not. You may remain. By the way, please open that window. The room is simply stifling."

Bazarov rose and unfastened the casement, which swung backwards with a snap, for the reason that he had not expected it to open so easily, and that his hands were trembling. Into the aperture glanced the soft, warm night with its vista of dark vault of heaven, faintly rustling trees, and pure, free, sweet-scented air.

"Also, please pull down the blind, and then resume your seat. I wish to have a little further talk with you before you go. Tell me something about yourself—a person to whom, by the way, you never refer."

" I would rather converse with you on more profitable subjects."

" What modesty! Nevertheless I wish to learn something of you, and of your family, and of the father for whose sake you are soon going to abandon me."

" Why the word ' abandon '? " reflected Bazarov. Then he added aloud: " Things of that kind interest no one—least of all you. I and my people are obscure folk."

" Whereas I, you imagine, am an aristocrat? "

Bazarov looked up.

" Yes," he replied with emphasis.

She smiled.

" Then I can see that your knowledge of me is small," she remarked. " But of course—you believe all human beings to be identical. and therefore not worth the

131

trouble of studying. Some day I will tell you my history. But first tell me yours."

"You say that my knowledge of you is small?" queried Bazarov. "You may be right. Possibly *every* human being is an enigma. Let us take an example of that. You have withdrawn from society, and find it irksome, and limit your visitors' list to a couple of students. Yet why, with your intellect and your beauty, do you live in the country?"

"Why?" came the sharp rejoinder. "But first be so good as to explain what you mean by my 'beauty.'"

Bazarov frowned.

"That lies beside the point," he muttered. "The point is that I cannot understand why you settle in a rural spot of this kind."

"You cannot understand it, you cannot explain it?"

"No. There is only one possible explanation: and that is that you remain here because you are a person of self-indulgence who love comfort and the amenities of life, and are indifferent to aught else."

Again Madame Odintsov smiled.

"Then you are still determined to believe that I am incapable of being moved.?" she said.

Bazarov glanced at her from under his brows.

"By curiosity, yes," he said. "But by nothing else."

"Indeed? Then I cease to wonder that you and I do not get on together. You are exactly like myself."

"That you and I do not get on together?" echoed Bazarov vaguely.

"Yes. But I had forgotten—you must be longing to retire?"

Bazarov rose. The lamp was casting a dim light, while into the fragrant, darkened, isolated room there came wafted at intervals, under the swinging blind, the sensuous freshness of the night, and the sounds of its mysterious whisperings. Madame Odintsov did not stir.

Over her was stealing the same strange agitation which had infected Bazarov. Suddenly he realised that he was alone with a young and beautiful woman.

" Need you go? " she asked slowly.

He made no reply—he merely resumed his seat.

" Then you think me a spoilt, pampered, indolent person? " she continued in the same slow tone as she fixed her eyes upon the window. " Yet this much I know about myself: that I am very unhappy."

" Unhappy? For what reason? Because you attach too much importance to petty slanders? "

She frowned. Somehow she felt vexed that he should have understood her thus.

" No: things of that kind do not disturb me," she said. " Never should I allow them to do so—I am too proud. The reason why I am unhappy is that I have no wish, no enthusiasm, to live. I daresay you will not believe me, and will think that a mere ' petty aristocrat,' a person who is lapped in lace and seated in an armchair, is saying all this (and I will not conceal from you that I love what you call ' the comforts of life '): yet all the while I feel as though I had no desire to continue my existence. Pray reconcile that contradiction if you can. But perhaps you consider what I say ' Romanticism '? "

Bazarov shook his head.

" You are yet young," he said. " Also, you are rich and independent. What more could you have? What more do you desire? "

" What more? " she re-echoed with a sigh. " I do not know. I only know that I feel tired, antiquated; I feel as though I had been living a long, long time. Yes, I am growing old," she continued as she drew the ends of her mantilla around her bare shoulders. In doing so, she glanced at Bazarov. Her eyes met his, and the faintest of blushes stole into her face. " Behind me lie many memories—memories of my life in St. Petersburg, of a

133

period of wealth followed by poverty, of my father's death, of my marriage, of my travels abroad—yes, many such memories there are. Yet none of them are worth cherishing. And before me lies only a weary road with no goal to it, along which I have no desire to travel."

" You are disenchanted," said Bazorov.

" No," she replied with a shiver. " Rather, I am dissatisfied. Oh that I could form a strong attachment of some kind ! "

" To fall in love *might* save you," remarked Bazarov. " But you are incapable of that. That is where your misfortune lies."

Madame dropped her eyes upon the sleeve of her mantilla.

" I am incapable of falling in love ? " she murmured.

" Not altogether. Moreover, I did wrong to call it a misfortune: for the person most to be pitied is the person who meets with that experience."

" What experience do you mean ? "

" The experience of falling in love."

" How come you to know that ? "

" By hearsay," he replied irritably, while to himself he added: " You are a mere coquette whom sheer idleness is leading to weary and madden me." And his heart swelled within him.

" On the other hand," he went on, " it may be that you are too exacting ? "

As he spoke he bent forward and fell to playing with the tassels of his chair.

" Possibly I am," she agreed. " But, you see, I conceive that it ought to be everything or nothing. ' A life for a life.' ' Take my all, give your all, and put a truce to regrets and any thought of return.' That is the best rule."

" Indeed ? " queried Bazarov. " Well, it is not a bad

rule, and I am surprised that you should have failed to attain your desire."

"Self-surrender, you think, is an easy thing?"

"Not if one considers matters first, and appraises oneself, and sets upon oneself a definite value. It is only surrender *without* consideration that is easy."

"But how could one not value oneself? If one had value, no one would desire one's surrender."

"That would not be your concern nor mine: some one else's business would it be to determine our respective values. The one thing that would immediately concern us would be to know *how* to surrender."

Madame Odintsov sat up sharply.

"I still believe you to be speaking from experience," she said.

"No; words, idle words—words not meant to be taken personally."

"Then you yourself might be capable of surrendering?"

"I might. But in any case I should not care to boast."

Both remained silent for a moment. From the drawing-room came the notes of the piano.

"How late Katia is playing!" remarked Anna Sergievna.

Bazarov raised his head.

"Yes, it *is* late," he said. "Time for you to go to rest."

"Wait a moment, however. Why should you hurry away? I have something more to say to you."

"What may it be?"

'Wait," she repeated. As she did so, her eyes gazed at him as though studying his personality. For a few moments he paced the room—then suddenly approached her, said "Good night," squeezed her hand until she could have shrieked with the pain, and departed.

135

FATHERS AND SONS

Raising her fingers to her lips, she blew after him a kiss. Then, rising with an abrupt, convulsive movement, she ran towards the door as though to call him back. But at that moment her maid entered with a decanter on a silver tray, and Madame halted, bid the maid begone, reseated herself, and sank into a reverie. Her hair, like a winding black snake, had broken loose from its fastenings. Dimly illumined by the lamp, she sat motionless, save that at intervals she chafed her hands, for the night air was beginning to grow chilly.

Two hours later Bazarov re-entered his bedroom in a state of dishevelment and despondency, and with his boots soaked with dew. Arkady was seated, fully dressed, at the writing-table, with a book in his hands.

" So you are not in bed yet ? " Bazarov remarked irritably.

Arkady's only reply was to ask the counter-question:

" You have been sitting with Anna Sergievna, have you not ? "

" I have," replied Bazarov. " I was sitting there while you and Katia were playing the piano."

" Oh, *I* was not playing," retorted Arkady. Then he stopped, for he felt the tears to be very near his eyes, and had no wish to let them fall in the presence of his satirical mentor.

XVIII

WHEN Madame Odintsov entered the breakfast-room next morning, Bazarov had been sitting over his cup for a considerable time. He glanced sharply at her as she opened the door, and she turned in his direction as inevitably as though he had signed to her to do so. Somehow her face looked pale, and it was not long before she returned to her boudoir, whence she issued again only at luncheon time. Since dawn the weather had been too rainy to admit of outdoor expeditions, and therefore the party adjourned to the drawing-room, where Arkady began to read aloud the latest number of some journal, while the Princess manifested her usual surprise at his conduct (as though it had been conduct of an indecent nature!), and fixed upon him a gaze which, though one of lasting malignancy, proved also to be one of which he took not the slightest notice.

"Pray come to my boudoir, Evgenii Vasilitch," said Anna Sergievna. "I have something to ask you. I think that last night you mentioned some textbook or another?"

Rising, she moved towards the door, whilst the Princess stared around the room as much as to say: "Dear, dear! This does surprise me!" Then she brought her eyes back to Arkady, who, raising his voice, and bending towards Katia (by whose side he was sitting), continued his reading as before.

Meanwhile Madame Odintsov walked hurriedly to her boudoir, and Bazarov followed with his eyes fixed upon the floor, and his ears open to no sound but the faint rustling of a silk dress. Arrived at her destination, Madame seated herself in the chair which she had

137

occupied overnight, and Bazarov also took a seat where he had sat on the occasion in question.

" What is the title of the book? " she asked after a brief pause.

" *Notions Générales*, by Pelouse and Frémy. " I can also recommend Ganot's *Traité Elémentaire de Physique Expérimentale*, which is more detailed in its plates than the other work, and, in general, is——"

But Madame Odintsov held up her hand.

" Pardon me," she interrupted. " I have not brought you here to discuss textbooks. I have brought you here to renew our conversation of last night, at the point where you left the room so abruptly. I hope that I shall not weary you? "

" I am entirely at your service. What was it we were discussing? "

She glanced at him.

" Happiness, I think," she said. " In fact, I was speaking to you of myself. The reason why I mention happiness is the following. Why is it that when one is enjoying, say, a piece of music, or a beautiful summer evening, or a conversation with a sympathetic companion, the occasion seems rather a hint at an infinite felicity existent elsewhere than a real felicity actually being experienced? Perhaps, however, you have never encountered such a phenomenon? "

" ' Where we are not, there do we wish to be,'—you know the proverb. Last night you said that you are dissatisfied. Such a thought never enters into my head."

" Is it that such thoughts seem to you ridiculous? "

" No—rather, that they never occur to me."

" Indeed? Well, to know what your thoughts *are* is a thing which I greatly wish to attain."

" I do not understand you."

" Then listen. For a long time past I have been wishing to have this out with you. Do not tell me—

you yourself know that it is useless to do so—that you are a man apart. As a matter of fact, you are a man still young, with all your life before you. I wish to know for what you are preparing, and what future awaits you, and what is the goal which you are seeking to reach, and whither you are travelling, and what you have in your mind—in short, who and what you are."

" I am surprised! Already you know that I dabble in natural science; while, as regards my future——"

" Yes? As regards your future? "

" I have told you that I purpose to become a district physician."

Anna Sergievna waved her hand impatiently.

" Why tell me that, when you yourself do not believe it? It is for Arkady to return me such answers, not you."

" And is Arkady in any way——? "

" Wait. Do you mean to tell me that such a modest rôle will really satisfy you, when you yourself have asserted that the science of medicine does not exist? No, no! You have given me that answer for the reason that you desire to keep me at arm's length, that you have no faith in me. Then let me tell you that I *am* capable of understanding you, that I too have known poverty and ambition, that I too have had my experiences."

" I daresay: yet pardon me when I intimate that I am not accustomed to bare my soul. Moreover, there is fixed between you and me such a gulf that——"

" A gulf? Do you again say that I am an aristocrat? Come, come, Evgenii Vasilitch! Have I not already told you that I——? "

" Can it avail anything to discuss the future when, for the most part, our futures are wholly independent of ourselves? Should the occasion arise to be up and doing, well and good: but, should the occasion *not* arise, at least let us leave ourselves room for thankfulness that we did not waste time in useless chatter."

139

"What? You call a friendly talk 'useless chatter'? Then do you deem me, as a woman, unworthy of your confidence, or do you despise all women?"

"You I do not despise: and that you know full well."

"I know nothing of the kind. Of course I can understand your reluctance to speak of your future career; but as to what is taking place within you at the present moment——"

"'Taking place within me at the present moment'?" Bazarov exclaimed. "One would think I was a state or a community! Nor is it a process which interests me; while, in addition, a man cannot always put into words 'what is taking place within him.'"

"I do not see it. Why should you hesitate to express what may be in your soul?"

"Could *you* do as much?" asked Bazarov.

"I could," came the reply after a brief hesitation.

Bazarov bowed in an ironical manner.

"Then you have the advantage of me," he said.

Her glance quickened into a note of interrogation.

"Very well," she said. "Yet I will venture to say that you and I have not met in vain, and that we shall always remain good friends. Moreover, I feel certain that in time your secretiveness and reserve will disappear."

"Then have you noticed in me much such 'secretiveness and reserve'?"

"I have."

Bazarov rose, and moved towards the window.

"Do you really want to know the cause of that 'secretiveness, and reserve'?" he asked. "Do you really want to know 'what is taking place within' me?"

"I do," she replied. Yet even as she spoke she felt run through her a tinge of apprehension for which she could not account.

"And you will not be angry with me if I tell you?"

140

" No."

" No? "

He approached her and halted behind her.

" Learn, then," he said, " that I love you with a blind, insensate passion. You have forced it from me at last! "

She stretched out her arms before her, while Bazarov, turning, pressed his forehead against the window-pane. His breath caught in his throat, and his whole body was quivering. Yet this was not the agitation born of the diffidence of youth, nor was it the awe inspired by a first confession of love. Rather, it was the beating of a strong and terrible emotion which resembled madness and was, perhaps, akin to it. As for Madame Odintsov, a great horror had come over her—also a great feeling of compassion for him.

" Evgenii Vasilitch! " she cried. In the words there rang an involuntary note of tenderness.

Wheeling about, he devoured her with his glance. Then he seized her hands in his, and pressed her to his bosom.

She did not free herself at once. Only after a moment did she withdraw to a corner, and stand looking at him. He rushed towards her again, but she whispered in hurried alarm:

" You have mistaken me! "

Had he taken another step, she would have screamed. Biting his lips, he left the room.

Half an hour later her maid brought her a note. It consisted of a single line only, and said: " Must I depart to-day, or may I remain until to-morrow? "

To it Anna Sergievna replied: " Why depart? I have failed to understand you, and you have failed to understand me—that is all."

But mentally she added: " Rather, I have failed to understand myself."

Until dinner time she remained secluded, and spent the hours in pacing her room with her hands clasped behind her. Occasionally she would halt before the window-panes or a mirror, to draw a handkerchief across a spot on her neck which seemed to be burning like fire. And every time that she did so she asked herself what had led her to force Bazarov's confidence; also, whether or not she had had any suspicion that such a thing might result.

" Yes, I *am* to blame," she finally decided. " Yet I could not have foreseen the whole *dénouement*."

Then she recalled Bazarov's almost animal face as he rushed to seize her in his arms. And at the thought she blushed.

" Or is it that——? " Here she stopped, and shook back her curls. The reason was that she had seen herself in a mirror, and, as in a flash, had learnt from that image of a head thrown back, with a mysterious smile lurking between a pair of half-parted lips and in a pair of half-closed eyes, something which confounded her.

" No, no! Again no! " she cried. " Only God knows what might come of it. Such things are not to be played with. Freedom from worry is the chief thing in the world."

Nor had her *sangfroid* really been shattered. Rather, she was a little agitated—so little that, when, for some unknown reason, she shed a tear or two, those tears owed their origin not to any deep emotion, to the fact that she was wounded, but to a sense of having involuntarily been at fault in permitting certain vague yearnings —a certain consciousness of the transience of life, a certain desire for novelty—to urge her towards the boundary line. And over that boundary line she had peeped. And in front of her she had beheld, not an abyss, but a waste, a sheer ugliness.

XIX

In spite of her self-command, in spite of her superiority to convention, Madame Odintsov could not but feel a little uncomfortable when she entered the dining-room for the evening meal. Nevertheless the meal passed off without incident, and after it Porphyri Platonitch came in, and related various anecdotes on the strength of a recent visit to the neighbouring town—among other things, a story to the effect that Governor "Bardeloue" had commanded his whole staff of officials to wear spurs, in order that, if need be, he could dispatch them on their errands on horseback! Meanwhile, Arkady talked in an undertone to Katia, and also paid diplomatic attention to the Princess; while Bazarov maintained such an obstinate, gloomy silence that Madame, glancing at him (as she did twice, and openly, not covertly), thought to herself, as she scanned his stern, forbidding face, downcast eyes, and all-pervading expression of rigid contempt: " No, no! Again, no! "

Dinner over, she conducted her guests into the garden, and, perceiving that Bazarov desired a word with her, walked aside a little, halted, and waited for him. Approaching with his eyes on the ground, he said in a dull way :

" I must beg your pardon, Anna Sergievna. Surely you must be feeling extremely angry with me? "

" No, not angry so much as grieved," she replied.

" So much the worse! But I have received sufficient punishment, have I not? My position now (I am sure that you will agree with me) is a very awkward one. True, you wrote in your message : ' Why need you depart?' but I cannot and will not remain. By to-morrow, therefore, I shall have departed."

" But why need you, need you——? "

" Why need I depart? "

" No, I was going to have said something quite different."

" We cannot recover the past," he continued, " and it was only a question of time before this should happen. I know only of one condition under which I could re-main. And that condition is never likely to arise. For (pardon my presumption) I suppose you neither love me now nor could ever do so? "

With the words there came a flash from under his dark brows.

She did not reply. Through her brain there flitted only the one thought: " I am afraid of this man! "

" Farewell," he continued, as though he had divined that thought. Then he moved away towards the house.

Entering the house a little later, Anna Sergievna called to Katia, and took the girl by the arm: nor throughout the rest of the evening did she once part from her. Also, instead of joining in a game of cards, she sat uttering laugh after laugh of a nature which ill consorted with her blanched and careworn face. Gazing at her perplexedly, as a young man will do, Arkady kept asking himself the question: " What can this mean? " As for Bazarov, he locked himself in his room, and only appeared to join the rest at tea. When he did so, Anna Sergievna yearned to say something kind to him, but could think of no words for the purpose. To her dilemma, however, an unexpected incident put an end. This was the entry of the butler to announce Sitnikov!

To describe the craven fashion in which the young Progressive entered the room would be impossible. Al-though, with characteristic importunity, he had decided

144

to repair to the residence of a lady with whom he was
barely acquainted, and who had not accorded him an
invitation (his pretext for such presumption being that,
according to information received, she happened to be
entertaining guests who were both intellectual and
" very intimate " with himself), he had since felt his
courage ebb to the marrow of his bones, and now,
instead of proffering all the excuses and compliments
which he had prepared in advance, blurted out some
ridiculous story to the effect that Evdoksia Kukshin had
sent him to inquire after the health of Anna Sergievna,
and that Arkady Nikolaievitch had always spoken of
him in terms of the highest respect. But at this point
he began to stammer, and so lost his head as to sit down
upon his own hat! No one bade him depart, however,
and Anna Sergievna even went so far as to present him
to her aunt and sister. Accordingly it was not long before
he recovered his equanimity, and shone forth with his
accustomed brilliancy. Often the appearance of the
paltry represents a convenient phenomenon in life, since
it relaxes over-taut strings, and sobers natures prone
to conceit and self-assurance by reminding them of
their kinship with the newcomer. Thus Sitnikov's
arrival caused everything to become duller and a trifle
more futile, but also rendered things simpler, and
enabled the company to partake of supper with a better
appetite, and to part for the night half an hour earlier
than usual.

" Let me recall to you some words of your own," said
Arkady when he had got into bed, and Bazarov was
still undressing. " I refer to the words: ' Why are you
downhearted? Have you just fulfilled a sacred duty? ' "

Between the two there had become established those
half-quizzical relations which are always a sign of tacit
distrust and a smouldering grudge.

" To-morrow I intend to set out for my father's place,"

remarked Bazarov, in disregard of what Arkady had said.

The latter raised himself on his elbow. Though surprised, he also, for some reason, felt glad.

" Ah! " he exclaimed. " Then *that* is why you are down-hearted? "

Bazarov yawned.

" When you are come to be a little older," he replied, " you will know more."

" And what of Anna Sergievna? " continued Arkady.

" Well? What of her? "

" Is it likely that she will let you go? "

" I am not her hireling."

Arkady relapsed into thought, and Bazarov sought his bed, and turned his face to the wall.

For a few moments silence reigned.

" Evgenii," said Arkady suddenly.

" Yes? "

" I too intend to leave to-morrow."

Bazarov made no reply.

" True, I shall be returning to Marino," continued Arkady, " but we might bear one another company as far as Khokhlovskie Viselki, and there you could hire horses of Thedot. Of course, I should have been delighted to make your family's acquaintance, but, were I to accompany you, I might act as a source of constraint upon them and yourself alike. You must pay us another visit at Marino later."

" I will. As a matter of fact, I have left some of my things there." Bazarov still had his face turned to the wall.

" Why does he not ask *me* the reason of *my* departure —a departure as sudden as his? " reflected Arkady. " Why is either of us departing, for that matter? "

As he continued to reflect he realised that, while unable to return a satisfactory answer to the question

146

propounded, he seemed to have got a heartache some-how, to be feeling that he would find it hard to part with the life at Nikolsköe to which he was grown so accustomed. Yet he could not remain there alone. That would be worse still.

" Between him and her there is something in the wind," he reflected. "That being so, what would my sticking here avail after he had gone? I should weary Anna Sergievna, and lose my last chance of pleasing her."

Then he began to draw a mental picture of the lady whom he had just named : until there cut across the fair presentment of the young widow another set of features.

" Katia too I shall miss," he whispered to his pillow (which had already received one of his tears). At length, raising his curly poll, he exclaimed :

" What, in the devil's name, brought that idiot Sitnikov here? "

He heard Bazarov stir under the bedclothes, then remark :

" You yourself are an idiot. We need the Sitnikovs of this world. Such donkeys are absolutely necessary to us, to *me*. The gods ought not to have to bake pots."

" Ah! " reflected Arkady. For, as in a flash, there had become revealed to him the bottomless profundity of Bazarov's conceit.

" Then you and I are the gods? " he said aloud. " Or are you a god, and I a donkey? "

" You are," came the gruff reply. " As yet, at all events, you are."

No particular astonishment was evinced by Madame Odintsov when, on the following day, Arkady informed her that it was his intention to accompany Bazarov. Rather, she looked distraught and weary. Katia glanced at him gravely and in silence, and the Princess went so far as to cross herself under her shawl—a precaution against the young men observing the gesture. Sitnikov too was dumbfounded at having just entered the break-fast-room in a new and most elegant suit (this time *not* of "Slavophil" cut, not to mention the fact that he had also had the pleasure of amazing his temporary valet with the multitude of his shirts), only to find himself confronted with the prospect of being deserted by his comrades! He shuffled and wriggled like a hare driven to the edge of a covert, and blurted out, almost in panic-stricken fashion, that he too had a great mind to depart. Nor did Madame Odintsov make any great effort to dissuade him.

" I have an exceedingly comfortable *koliaska*," the unfortunate young man said to Arkady, " and I could give you a lift in it, and leave Evgenii Vasilitch to use your *tarantass*, which would suit him better than the *koliaska*."

" But I should not like to take you so far out of your way, for the distance to my home is considerable."

" That would not matter, that would not matter. I have plenty of time to spare, and also some business to do in that direction."

" What? Leasehold business again? " inquired Arkady disparagingly. But Sitnikov was so distraught that he forbore to giggle in his usual fashion.

" I can guarantee that the *koliaska* is comfortable," he repeated. " Indeed, it could hold all three of us."

" Do not vex Monsieur Sitnikov by refusing," put in Madame Odintsov.

So, with a meaning glance at her, Arkady nodded assent to Sitnikov.

Breakfast over, the guests departed. Anna Sergievna offered Bazarov her hand.

" I hope we shall meet again? " she said.

" Only if you wish it," he replied.

" Then we *shall* meet again."

The first to issue upon the verandah and enter

Sitnikov's *koliaska* was Arkady. The butler assisted him obsequiously, although Arkady could with equal readiness have struck the man or burst into tears. As for Bazarov, he took possession of the *tarantass*.

Khokhlovskīe Viselki reached, Arkady waited until Thedot, the local posting-master, had harnessed fresh horses, and then, approaching the *tarantass*, said to Bazarov with his old smile:

" Evgenii, take me with you. I should like to come to your place, after all."

" Get in, then," muttered Bazarov.

This made Sitnikov, who had been walking up and down beside his conveyance, and whistling, fairly gasp. Nevertheless the heartless Arkady removed his luggage from the *koliaska*, seated himself beside Bazarov, and, according his late fellow-traveller a courteous bow, shouted: " Right away! " The *tarantass* started, and soon was lost to view. Much taken aback, Sitnikov gazed at his coachman. But the latter was flicking the flanks of the trace horse with his whip, and therefore Sitnikov had no choice but to leap into the vehicle, to shout to a couple of peasants: " Off with your caps, you rascals! " and be driven to the town, whither he arrived at a late hour, and where, on the following day, he declared to Madame Kukshin that he had had enough of " those odious churls and upstarts."

On Arkady seating himself beside Bazarov in the *tarantass*, he pressed his hand, and Bazarov seemed to divine the meaning of the silent hand-clasp, and to appreciate it. During the previous night the elder man had never once closed his eyes. Also, for several days past he had neither smoked a cigar nor eaten more than the merest scrap of food. Indeed, as he sat in the *tarantass*, his fine-drawn profile, under the overshadowing cap, looked sharper and grimmer than ever.

" Give me a cigar, will you? " he said. " Also,

149

pray look at my tongue, and tell me if it has a bilious appearance."

" Yes, it has," replied Arkady.

" I thought so, for this cigar seems tasteless. Moreover, the infernal thing has come unrolled."

" You have changed a good deal of late? " hazarded Arkady.

" I daresay. But I shall be myself again, soon. The only thing now troubling me is the fact that my mother is so good-naturedly fussy. Should one's paunch not be projecting, or should one not eat at least ten meals a day, she relapses into despair. My father, of course, is different, for he has been all over the world, and knows what is what. This cigar is simply unsmokable." And Bazarov consigned it to the dust of the roadway.

" The distance to your place is twenty-five versts, I suppose? " queried Arkady.

" It is so. But inquire of that sage there." And Bazarov pointed to the peasant (an *employé* of Thedot's) who was seated on the box.

The " sage " in question replied that he " could not say exactly," since the verst-posts in those parts had not been measured out; after which he went on to swear at the shaft horse for " kicking " its " jowl about "— that is to say, jerking its head up and down.

" Aye, aye," commented Bazarov. " Take warning from me, my young friend. An instructive example sits before you—an example of the vanity of this world. By a single thread does the destiny of every man hang, and at any moment there may open before him an abyss into which he and his may plunge. For always he is laying up for himself misfortune."

" At what are you hinting? " asked Arkady.

" At nothing. I am merely saying outright that you and I have behaved very foolishly. However, why talk of it? I have noticed that in surgical operations it is

150

the patient who fights against his hurt who soonest gets well."

"I do not understand you," Arkady said. "So far as I can see, you have nothing whatsoever to complain of."

"You cannot understand me? Well, mark this: that you had far better go and break stones by the roadside than allow a woman to obtain even the least hold over you. Such a thing is sheer " (he nearly said " Romanticism," but changed his mind) " rubbish."

"Perhaps you do not believe me?" he went on. " Nevertheless, I tell you that, though you and I have been cultivating feminine society, and enjoying it, the sense of relief when such society is abandoned is like taking a cold bath on a summer's day. Never ought a man to touch such follies. Always he ought, as the excellent Spanish saying has it, ' to remain as the beasts of the field.' Look here," he added to the peasant on the box. "Do you, my man of wisdom, possess a wife?"

The peasant turned a portion of a flat, near-sighted visage in the friends' direction.

" A wife?" he repeated. " Yes, I do. Why shouldn't I?"

"Never mind that. Do you ever beat her?"

"My wife? Sometimes. But never without good cause."

" Excellent! And does she ever beat *you*?"

The peasant gave his reins a jerk.

" What a thing, *barin*!" he exclaimed. " Surely you must be joking?" Evidently the question had offended him.

"You hear that, Arkady Nikolaievitch?" said Bazarov. "You and I have been similarly beaten. That is what comes of being gentry."

Arkady laughed in spite of himself, but Bazarov

151

turned away, and did not speak again until the end of the journey.

To Arkady the twenty-five versts seemed like fifty; but at length there came into view, on the slope of a low hill, the homestead of the manor where Bazarov's parents resided. On one side of it, amid a clump of young birch trees, there could be seen the servants' quarters under their thatched roofs; while at the door of the nearest hut a couple of fur-capped peasants were engaged in a contest of mutual abuse.

" You are an old pig! " one of them said to the other. " And that is worse than being a young one."

" Your wife is a witch," retorted the other.

" From the lack of restraint in their bearing," commented Bazarov, " as well as from the playfulness of their terms of speech, you will gather that my father's peasantry are not downtrodden. But here is my father himself. I can see him stepping out on to the verandah. He will have heard the sound of our collar-bells. Yes, it *is* he! I recognise his figure. But how grey he looks, poor old fellow! "

XX

BAZAROV leant forward from the *tarantass*, and Arkady, peering over his friend's shoulder, beheld, on the entrance steps of the manor-house, a tall, thin man with dishevelled hair and a narrow, aquiline nose. Clad in an old military tunic of which the front was flying open, he was standing with legs apart, a long pipe in his mouth, and eyes blinking in the glare of the sunlight.

The horses pulled up.

"So you have come at last!" exclaimed Bazarov's father, still continuing to smoke (though, as he did so, the stem of the pipe was rattling and shaking between his fingers). "Now, jump out, jump out!"

Again and again he embraced his son.

"Eniusha, Eniusha!"[1] the tremulous voice of an old woman also cried as the door of the house opened and there appeared on the threshold a short, rotund old dame in a white cap and a short striped blouse. Gasping and staggering, she would have fallen had not Bazarov hastened to support her. As he did so her fat old arms clasped him around the neck, and her head sank upon his bosom. All then was still for a moment. Only her convulsive sobs broke the silence. Meanwhile Bazarov Senior breathed hard, and blinked more vigorously than ever.

"Enough, enough, Arisha!" he said at length with a glance at Arkady, who had remained standing beside the *tarantass* (and even the peasant on the box-seat had turned away his head). "Pray cease, I tell you. This is not necessary. I beg of you to cease."

"Ah, Vasili Ivanitch!" whimpered the poor old

[1] An endearing diminutive of Evgenii.

153

woman. "To think of the long while since last I saw
my Eniusha, my own, my darling boy!" Still keeping
her arms clasped around Bazarov, she withdrew her
ruffled, convulsed, tear-stained face from his breast,
looked at him for a moment with blissful, yet comical,
eyes, and glued herself again to his bosom.

"Yes, yes," said Vasili Ivanitch. "Such is in the
nature of things. But had we not better go indoors? See!
Evgenii has brought a guest!"

With a slight scrape and a bow, he added to Arkady:

"Pray pardon us, sir, but you will understand the
situation. A woman's weakness—ahem!—and a mother's
heart."

His lips, chin, and eyebrows too were working.
Evidently he was striving to master himself, and to
appear totally indifferent. Arkady responded to his
bow with a like salutation.

"Yes, yes, dear mother; let us go indoors," said
Bazarov. Leading the shaking old lady into the house,
he seated her in a cosy chair, bestowed upon his father
another hurried embrace, and then presented Arkady.

"I am glad indeed to make your acquaintance!"
said Vasili Ivanitch. "I am glad indeed! But do not
expect too much of us, my dear sir. My establishment
is organised on simple lines; it is placed on what I
might call 'a war footing.' Come, come, Arina! Pray
calm yourself, and attend to your duties as a hostess.
Oh, fie, to give way in such a manner! What will our
guest think of you?"

"My dear, I do not know the gentleman's name,"
the old lady sobbed through her tears.

"Arkady Nikolaievitch," prompted Vasili Ivanitch
in an undertone, but with great ceremony.

"Then pray pardon a foolish old woman, sir." Arina
Vlasievna blew her nose, inclined her head to right and
left, and wiped each eye in turn as she did so. "Yes,

pray pardon me, but I had thought never again to see my darling boy before I died."

" But, you see, we *have* seen him again," said Vasili Ivanitch. " Here, Taniushka! "—this to a barefooted serf girl of thirteen who, clad in a bright red cotton frock, had been an interested, but timid, observer in the doorway. " Bring your mistress a glass of water on a salver. Do you hear? And you, gentlemen," he continued with old-fashioned sprightliness, " will you be so good as to step into the study of a retired veteran ? "

" First another kiss, Eniusha," gasped Arina Vlasievna. Then, as Bazarov bent over her form, she added : " How handsome you have grown ! "

" Handsome or not, he is human," said Vasili Ivanitch. " Wherefore, now that you have satisfied your mother's heart, I look to you to see also to the satisfaction of our honoured guests. For than yourself no one knows better that nightingales cannot be fed on air."

This caused the old lady to rise from her chair, and to exclaim :

" Yes, yes: in one moment, Vasili Ivanitch. The table shall be laid, and I myself will hurry to the kitchen, and see that the *samovar* be got ready. Everything shall be done. Why, it must be three years since last I gave Eniusha a meal."

" Yes, three years, dear wife. But now bustle about, and do not let yourself get flurried. Gentlemen, accompany me, I beg of you. But here is Timotheitch coming to pay you his respects. How delighted he looks, the old rascal ! Now, pray favour me with your company."

And he strode fussily ahead with much shuffling and creaking of flat-soled slippers.

The Bazarovian establishment consisted of six small rooms, of which one—the room to which Vasili Ivanitch was now conducting our friends—was looked upon as the study. Between its two windows there stood a fat-legged table, strewn with dusty, fusty papers; on the walls hung a number of Turkish weapons, *nagaiki*,[1] and swords, a couple of landscapes, a few anatomical plates, a portrait of Hufeland,[2] a black-framed monogram done in hair, and a diploma protected with a glass front; between two large birchwood cupboards stood a ragged, battered leathern sofa; on shelves lay huddled a miscellany of books, boxes, stuffed birds, jars, and bladders; and, lastly, in a corner reposed a broken electric battery.

" Already I have warned you," said Vasili Ivanitch to Arkady, " that we live here, so to speak, *en bivouac*."

" Make no excuses," put in Bazarov. " Kirsanov knows that you and I are not Crœsuses, and that no butler is kept. But where can we find Arkady a bed? That is the question."

" We have an excellent room in the wing, where he would be most comfortable."

" You have added a wing, then? "

" Yes, Evgenii Vasilitch," Timotheitch interposed. " At least, a bathroom."

" But it is to a room *next* the bathroom that I am referring," Vasili Ivanitch hastened to explain. " However, that will not matter, since it is now summer time. I will run up there at once, and see that it is put in order. Meanwhile, Timotheitch, fetch in the luggage. To you, Evgenii, I will allot the study. *Cuique suum*." [3]

" There! " said Bazarov to Arkady as soon as his father had left the room. " Is he not just such a jolly, good-hearted, queer old fellow as your own father, though in a different way? He chatters just as he always used to do."

[1] Cossack whips.
[2] Christoph Wilhelm Hufeland (1762–1836), a well-known German physicist whose treatise *Makrobiotik*, or *The Art of Prolonging Life*, has been translated into almost every European language.
[3] " To each his own."

" Yes; and your mother seems an excellent woman."

" She is. Moreover, you can see that she does not attempt to hide her feelings. Only wait and see what a dinner she will give us! "

" But as you were not expected to-day," put in Timotheitch, who had just re-entered with Bazarov's portmanteau, " no beef has been got into the house."

" Never mind. Let us dine *without* beef—or, for that matter, without anything at all. ' Poverty is no crime.' "

" How many souls [1] are there on your father's property? " asked Arkady.

" It is not his property; it is my mother's. The number of souls on it is, I think, fifteen."

" No, twenty-two," corrected Timotheitch with an air of pride. The next moment the sound of shuffling slippers was heard once more, and Vasili Ivanitch re-entered.

" Your room will be ready for you in a few minutes," he announced grandiloquently to Arkady. " Meanwhile, here is your servant." He pointed to a close-cropped urchin who, clad in an out-at-elbows blue *kaftan* and an odd pair of shoes, had also made his appearance. " His name is Thedika, and, for all my son's injunction, I had better repeat to you not to expect too much of him—though certainly he will be able to fill your pipe for you. I presume that you smoke? "

" I do, but only cigars."

" A commendable rule! I too prefer cigars, but find them extremely difficult to procure in this isolated part of the country."

" Have done with bewailing your poverty," Bazarov goodnaturedly interrupted. " Rather, seat yourself on this sofa, and take a rest."

Vasili Ivanitch smilingly did as he was bidden. Extremely like his son in features (save that his forehead

[1] *i.e.* serfs.

157

was lower and narrower, and his mouth a trifle wider), he was for ever on the move—now shrugging his shoulders as though his coat cut him under the armpits, now blinking, now coughing, now twitching his fingers. In this he was sharply differentiated from his son, whose most distinguishing characteristic was his absolute immobility.

" Have done with bewailing my poverty? " repeated the old man. " Why, you cannot surely think that I would weary our guest with complaints concerning our isolation? As a matter of fact, a man of brains need *never* be isolated, and I myself do everything in my power to avoid becoming moss-grown, and falling behind the times."

Extracting from his pocket a new yellow handkerchief which he had contrived to lay hands upon while proceeding to Arkady's room, he continued, as he flourished the handkerchief in the air:

" Of the fact that, at some cost to myself, I have organised my peasantry on the *obrok* system, and apportioned them one-half, even more, of my land, I will not speak, since I conceive that to have been my duty, as well as a measure dictated by prudence (though no other landowner in the neighbourhood would have done as much). Rather, I am referring to scholarships and to science."

" I see that you have here *The Friend of Health* for 1855," remarked Bazarov.

" Yes, a friend sent it me," Vasili Ivanitch hastened to explain. " Phrenology too we take into account " (he addressed this last to Arkady rather than to Bazarov, while accompanying it with a nod towards a small plaster bust of which the cranial surface was divided into a series of numbered squares). " Yes indeed! Nor are we ignorant of Schönlein [1] and Rademacher."

[1] Johann Lukas Schönlein (1793–1864), a noted German physician.

" In the province of —— you still believe in Rademacher ? " queried Bazarov.

Vasili Ivanitch laughed.

" In the province of —— we still believe in——? Ah, gentlemen! Hardly could you expect us to move as fast as you do. You find us in a state of transition. In my day, the humoralist Hoffmann and the vitalist Braun had already come to be looked upon with ridicule (and their fulminations undoubtedly seem absurd); but now you have replaced Rademacher with a new authority, and are making obeisance to that authority exactly as though in twenty years' time he too will not have fallen into contempt."

" Let me tell you, for your comforting," said Bazarov, " that we ridicule all medicine, and render obeisance to no one."

" What? Do you not wish to become a doctor? "

" Yes; but the one thing does not preclude the other."

Vasili Ivanitch raked out his pipe until only a glowing morsel of ash remained.

" Perhaps so, perhaps so," he said. " That point I will not dispute. For who am I that I should dispute such things—I who am a mere retired army doctor, *et voilà tout*—an army doctor who has taken to agriculture? "

With that he turned to Arkady.

" Do you know, I served under your grandfather," he said. " He was then in command of a brigade. Many and many a review have I seen. And the society in which I mixed, the men whom I had as comrades! Yes, this humble individual has felt the pulses of Prince Vitzentschein and Zhukovsky, and also known all the leaders of the Southern Army of '14." He pursed his lips impressively. " At the same time, of course, my department was a separate one from theirs. It was the department of the lancet, you understand. Your

159

grandfather stood high in the esteem of every one, and was a true soldier."

" We will agree that he was a decent old curmudgeon," drawled Bazarov.

" To think of speaking so, Evgenii! " exclaimed the old man. " General Kirsanov was not one of those who——"

" Never mind him. As we were driving hither I greatly admired your birch plantation. It is doing splendidly."

Vasili Ivanitch's face brightened instantly.

" Yes, and see what a garden I have made! " he exclaimed. "Every tree in it has been planted with my own hands—orchard trees, and bush fruit trees, and every sort of medicinal herb. Ah, young sirs, though you may be wise in your generation, many a truth did old Paracelsus [1] discover *in herbis et verbis et lapidibus.* For myself, I have now retired from practice; yet twice a week am I given a chance to refurbish my ancient store of knowledge, since folk come to me for advice, and I cannot well turn them away. In particular do the poor seek my help, since there is no other doctor hereabouts. Yet stay! A certain retired major dabbles in the art. Once I asked him whether he had ever *studied* medicine, and he replied that he had not, that all that he did he did ' out of philanthropy'! 'Out of philanthropy'! Ha, ha, ha! What think you of that, eh? Ha, ha, ha! "

" Fill me a pipe, Thedika," said Bazarov curtly.

" And there was another doctor who came to visit a patient in this neighbourhood," continued Vasili Ivanitch in a tone of mock despair. " But by the time he arrived the patient had already joined his forefathers, and the servant of the house would not admit the doctor, saying that the latter's services were no longer required. This

---

[1] Theophrastus Bombastus von Hohenheim (1493–1541), most commonly known by his self-coined name of Paracelsus, and a German-Swiss traveller and physician.

the doctor had scarcely expected, and he was rather taken aback. 'Did the *barin* gasp before he died ?' he inquired. 'He did, sir,' was the reply. 'Very much?' 'Yes, very much.' 'Good!' And the doctor returned home. Ha, ha, ha!"

Yet no one laughed except the old man himself. True, Arkady contrived to summon up a smile, but Bazarov only stretched himself and yawned. The conversation lasted about an hour, and then Arkady managed to get away to his room, which he found to consist of the vestibule to the bathroom, but at the same time to be clean and inviting. Soon afterwards Taniushka arrived to announce dinner.

The meal, though hastily prepared, was excellent, and even sumptuous. Only the wine proved to be rather of the " gooseberry " order—the dark-coloured sherry procured by Timotheitch from a certain wine merchant in the town smacking in equal parts of resin and of honey. Also, in addition, the flies made themselves a nuisance, owing to the fact that the page boy whose duty it was to keep them at bay with a green whisk had, for the nonce, been banished, lest he should excite too much comment on the part of the up-to-date visitors. Lastly, Arina Vlasievna had robed herself in gala attire—that is to say, in a high-peaked cap with yellow ribands and a blue, embroidered shawl. She burst into renewed weeping on beholding her beloved Eniusha, but, this time, gave her husband no occasion to chide her, so speedily did her own fear of staining her shawl cause her to wipe away the tears. None but the two young men ate anything, for the host and hostess had long ago dined; while as waiters there officiated Thedika (much burdened with the novelty of wearing shoes) and a woman of a masculine type of face, and with a hump on her back, who was also accustomed to execute the functions of housekeeper, keeper of the poultry, and sempstress. During the meal

Vasili Ivanitch paced to and fro, and discussed, in cheerful, and even rapturous, terms, the grave fears which
Napoleon's [1] policy and the intricacy of the Italian
question inspired in his breast. Arina Vlasievna, for her
part, quite disregarded Arkady, and offered him not a
single dish, but, seated with her hand supporting her
face (to which a pair of puffy, cherry-coloured lips and a
few moles communicated a kindly expression), kept her
eyes fixed upon her son, while her breath came in a succession of pants. Her great desire was to ask her son how
long he was going to stay, but she dared not do so for fear
he should reply: " Only for two days," or something of
the kind—which was a prospect of a nature to make her
heart die within her. On the roast being served, Vasili
Ivanitch disappeared, and returned, the next moment,
with an uncorked bottle of champagne.

" See here," he exclaimed. " Rustic though we may
be, we still keep something to make merry with on state
occasions."

That said, he filled three tumblers and a wine-glass,
proposed a health to " our inestimable guests," heel-
tapped his glass in the military fashion, and forced his
wife to drain hers to the dregs. Presently the pastry
course supervened; during which, though Arkady could
not bear anything sweet, he deemed it his duty to partake
of no less than four out of the many confections which
had been prepared for his benefit. And this obligation
he felt to be the more binding in that Bazarov bluntly
declined all, and lit a cigar. Lastly there appeared tea,
cream, biscuits, and butter; after which Vasili Ivanitch
conducted the party into the garden, in order that the
guests might admire the beauty of the evening. As he
passed a certain bench he whispered in Arkady's ear:

" This is where I love to sit and meditate as I watch
the sun sinking. It is just the spot for a hermit like

[1] Napoleon III.

162

myself. And, further on, I have planted a few of Horace's favourite trees."

" What trees? " asked Bazarov, who had partially overheard.

" Acacia trees."

The other yawned, and, on observing this, Vasili Ivanitch hastened to say:

" I expect that you travellers would like now to seek the arms of Morpheus? "

" We should," Bazarov assented. " Yes, that is a true saying."

Upon which the son said " Good night " to his mother, and kissed her on the forehead, while she bestowed upon him a threefold embrace and (covertly) a blessing; while Vasili Ivanitch conducted Arkady to his room, and wished him " such God-given rest as I myself used to enjoy during the happier years of my life."

And certainly Arkady slept splendidly in the mint-scented annexe to the bathroom, where the only sound to be heard was that of a cricket chirping lustily against a rival from behind the stove.

Meanwhile, on leaving Arkady, Vasili Ivanitch re-paired to the study, where, squatting at the foot of the sofa, he was about to enter into a discursive conversation with his son when the latter dismissed him, on the plea that he desired, rather, to go to sleep. Yet never once did Bazarov close his eyes that night, but lay staring into the darkness, since his memories of childhood had less power to move him than had the remembrance of the bitter experience through which he had recently passed.

For her part, Arina Vlasievna said her prayers with an overflowing heart, and then indulged in a long talk with Anfisushka; who, planted like a block before her mistress, with her solitary eye fixed upon the latter, communicated in a mysterious whisper her opinions and prognostications on the subject of Evgenii Vasilitch.

Finally Arina Vlasievna's pleasurable emotion, coupled with the wine and the tobacco smoke, so caused the old lady's head to start whirling that, when her husband came to bed, he found himself obliged to moderate her exuberance with a gesture.

Arina Vlasievna was a true Russian housewife of the old school. That is to say, she ought to have lived a couple of hundred years earlier, during the period when the ancient Muscovite Empire was in being. At once pious and extremely nervous, she believed in every species of portent, divination, proverb, and vision; also in such things as *urodivie*,[1] household demons, wood spirits, unlucky encounters, spells, popular medicines, Thursday salt, and an ever-imminent end to the world. Again, she placed much faith in such ideas as that, if a lighted candle lasts through the night preceding Easter Day, the buckwheat crops will come up well; that, should a human eye chance to fall upon a mushroom during the process of its growth, such growth will terminate forthwith; that the devil loves to be wheresoever there is water; and that all Jews bear on their breasts a blood-red stain. Again, she stood in great awe of mice, adders, frogs, sparrows, leeches, thunder, cold water, draughts, horses, billy-goats, fair men, and black cats, and also looked upon crickets and dogs as unclean creatures. Again, she never ate veal, pigeons, crabs, cheese, asparagus, artichokes, hare, or water melons (the last-named for the reason that, when split open, they reminded her of the head of John the Baptist!). Nor could she ever speak of oysters without a shudder. Again, though she loved eating, she observed every fast; though she slept ten hours out of the twenty-four, she

[1] *Urodivie*, or " sacred imbeciles," were persons who, deficient of intellect in the ordinary sense, were yet believed by ancient Russia to enjoy particularly intimate communication with the divine and the unseen.

never even went to bed if Vasili Ivanitch had got a headache; she read no books beyond *Alexis* or *Siskins of the
Forest*; she wrote, at most, two letters a year; she knew
every wrinkle as regards the departments of housekeeping, boiling, and baking (and that even though she herself never laid a finger upon anything, and hated even
to have to stir from her place); she was aware that there
were certain folk in the world who must command, and
others who must serve—wherefore she loved servility
and genuflexions; she treated all her subordinates with
kindness and consideration; she sent never a beggar
away empty; and she condemned no one for a fault,
although at times she had a tendency to talk scandal.
Likewise, in her youth she had been comely, and a player
of the clavichord, and able to speak a little French; but,
owing to long residence with a husband whom she had
married purely for love, she had grown rusty in those
accomplishments, and forgotten alike her French and her
music; she loved and feared her son to a degree almost
beyond expression; she deputed the management of her
property entirely to Vasili Ivanitch, and never interfered with it, but would fall to gasping, and waving her
handkerchief about, and affrightedly raising her eyebrows, whenever her helpmeet happened to broach some
new plan or some necessary reform which he had in his
mind's eye; and, lastly, she was of so apprehensive a
temperament that she lived in constant fear of some
unknown misfortune, and would burst into tears should
any one mention anything of a mournful character.

Such women are now extinct; and only God knows
whether we ought to be glad of the fact.

XXI

WHEN, in the morning, Arkady rose and opened the
window, the first object to greet his eyes was Vasili
Ivanitch. Clad in a smock-frock, and belted with a handkerchief, the old man was busily digging in his vegetable
garden. As soon as he noticed his young guest, he
leaned upon his spade, and cried:

"Good morning! How have you slept?"

"Splendidly," replied Arkady.

"And I, as you see, am imitating Cincinnatus, and
preparing a bed of late turnips. By the mercy of God
do the times compel every man to win his bread with
his own hands. At all times, indeed, is it useless to
rely upon others: it is best to work oneself. Thus Jean
Jacques Rousseau was right. Half an hour ago, however,
you would have seen me in a very different rôle—first
of all, injecting opium into a woman who had come
to me with what the peasants call 'the goad,' and we
dysentery, and then pulling out some teeth for a second
woman. And, would you believe it, when I proposed ad-
ministering ether to the second woman she would have
none of it! These things I do gratis, you know, and as
an amateur. Yet, let that not surprise you, for, after all,
I am but a plebeian, but a *homo novus*. Come downstairs
to sit in the shade and enjoy the freshness of the morning
until breakfast shall be ready."

Arkady did as invited.

"You confer a favour upon me," said Vasili Ivanitch,
raising his hand in military fashion to the battered
skull-cap which adorned his head. "You see, I know

166

you to be used to luxury and ease. Yet even the folk of the great world need not disdain to snatch a brief respite under the roof of a cottage."

" I neither belong to the great world nor am used to luxury," protested Arkady.

"Come now !" Vasili Ivanitch indulged in an amiable affectation of incredulity. " I myself, though I am now on the shelf, have rubbed about in my time, and can tell a bird by its flight. Also, I dabble a little in physiognomy and psychology. For that matter, I will not hesitate to say that, had I *not* enjoyed those advantages, I should long ago have come to rack and ruin, for the reason that, being one of the small fry, I should soon have been jostled out of the way by the crowd. Also, without flattery, I may say that the friendship which I discern to be existing between you and my son affords me the greatest pleasure. Only this moment I was speaking to him; for (as probably you know) he jumps out of bed at a very early hour, and goes careering all over the countryside. M-might I make so bold as to ask you whether you have known him long? "

" Only since last winter."

" Indeed? Also, might I make so bold as to ask whether—But sit you down, will you not?—might I also, as his father, venture to ask your frank opinion of him? "

" Your son is the most remarkable man that I have ever met," came the enthusiastic reply.

Vasili Ivanitch's eyes closed suddenly, while his cheeks quivered, and the spade slipped from his hand.

" Then you think——? " he began.

" I do not *think*—I am certain that there lies before your son a future which will make your name famous. I have felt certain of this since the first moment I met him."

" Indeed? Indeed? " Vasili Ivanitch could scarcely

167

articulate the words, but on his capacious lips there had dawned, and become fixed, a smile of triumph.

" Would you like to hear how our first meeting came about? "

" Indeed I should! And any other details you like."

Arkady therefore plunged into a discourse on Bazarov of the same ardour and the same enthusiasm as he had displayed on the night of the mazurka with Madame Odintsov. As Vasili Ivanitch listened, he blew his nose, rolled his handkerchief into a ball, coughed, and ruffled his hair; until, no longer able to contain himself, he reached over in Arkady's direction, and pressed his lips to the young man's shoulder.

" You have indeed cheered my heart! " he exclaimed, still smiling. "I simply idolise my son! But while my dear old wife is able to stand on rather a different footing with Evgenii—she is his mother, you know—I myself dare not express my whole feelings in his presence, for the reason that he dislikes such things, and is opposed to any manifestations of emotion. For the same reason some folk accuse him of hardness of heart and pride and insensibility; but men like Evgenii cannot be measured by ordinary standards, can they? For example, any one but he would have gone on acting as a drag upon his parents; but, would you believe it? never once since his birth has he asked us for a *kopeck* more than he absolutely needed! There, by God! "

" Yes, your son is a sincere, single-minded man," agreed Arkady.

" Yes, single-minded," affirmed Vasili Ivanitch. "And not only do I idolise him—I am proud of him, and have as my one conceit the hope that some day there may stand in his biography the following words: ' He was the son of a plain military doctor who, nevertheless, had the wit to divine the merits of the subject of this book, and to spare no pains in his education.' "

The old man's voice faltered for a moment, but presently resumed:

" What think you? Will the field of medicine bring him the fame which you have foretold? "

" Not the field of medicine alone—though in it, as elsewhere, he will become a leader."

" What field, then, Arkady Nikolaievitch? "

" I could not say. But in any case he will rise to fame."

"'He will rise to fame'!" The old man relapsed into a state of ecstatic contemplation.

Presently Anfisushka arrived with a large plate of raspberries and the message:

" Arina Vlasievna has sent me to say that breakfast is ready."

Vasili Ivanitch started from his reverie.

" Bring us also some nice cool plums," he said.

" I will, sir."

" Yes, mind that they are cool. Arkady Nikolaievitch, do not stand on ceremony, but help yourself. Is Evgenii Vasilitch yet back, Anfisushka? "

" I am," called Bazarov from Arkady's room.

Vasili Ivanitch wheeled about.

" Aha! " he cried. " So you have gone to pay your friend a visit? But you are too late, *amice*: he and I have been having a long conversation together, and it is now breakfast time, and your mother is calling us. By the way, Evgenii, a word or two with you."

" Concerning what? "

" Concerning a peasant who is suffering from jaundice."

" Jaundice? "

" Yes, of a very chronic and stubborn kind. I have prescribed scurvy grass and St. John's wort, and ordered the man to eat carrots, and given him a dose of soda; but such things are mere palliatives—I want something of a more drastic nature. That you laugh at medicine

169

I am, of course, aware; but none the less I feel certain that you could give me some good, practical advice. But that you can do later. At the present moment, let us go in to breakfast."

And he leapt from the bench on which he had been seated, trolling gaily the couplet:

> "Let us take for our rule, for our rule let us take it,
> To live but for pleasure, and never forsake it!"

"What high spirits!" Bazarov remarked as he retired from the window.

Later, when the noontide sun was glowing from behind a thin canopy of dense, pale vapour, and all was still save that the chirping of a few birds in the trees lulled the hearer to a curious, drowsy lethargy, and the incessant call of a young hawk on a topmost bough made the air ring with its strident note, Arkady and Bazarov made for themselves pillows of sweet, dry, fragrant, crackling hay, and stretched themselves in the shadow of a rick.

"Do you see that aspen tree?" remarked Bazarov. "I mean the one growing at the edge of a depression, where a brick kiln used to stand? Well, when I was a boy I used to believe that, together, the depression and the aspen tree constituted a special talisman, in that, when near them, I never found time hang heavy upon my hands. Of course, the explanation is that in those days I failed to understand that that immunity from *ennui* was due to the very fact of my being a boy. But, now that I am grown up, the talisman seems to have lost its power."

"How long were you here in those days?"

"Only two years. After that we moved elsewhere. In fact, we led a wandering life, and spent it mostly in towns."

"Is the house an old one?"

170

" It is. My maternal grandfather built it."

" Who was he? "

" The devil only knows! I think a major of some sort, a man who had served under Suvorov,[1] and could tell all manner of tales about crossing the Alps—though I daresay he told plenty of lies too."

" Ah! I noticed a portrait of Suvorov in the drawing-room. Cheerful-looking old houses like this I simply love. Somehow they seem to have a smell of their own."

" Yes—a smell of lamp-oil mingled with trefoil," agreed Bazarov with a yawn. " But what flies they contain as well! "

There was a pause. Then Arkady resumed:

" Were you strictly kept when you were a boy? "

" You have seen for yourself what my parents are like. Surely they do not seem very severe folk."

" And do you love them very much? "

" I do."

" Certainly they seem to love *you*."

Bazarov was silent. Presently, however, clasping his hands behind his head, he asked:

" Do you know what is in my mind? "

" No. What? "

" I am thinking of the pleasant life that my parents must lead. To think that at sixty my father can still fuss about, and talk of ' palliatives,' and doctor people, and do the bountiful to the peasants, and, in short, enjoy himself, and that my mother has her days so crammed full of occupations (including sighing and groaning) that she does not know which to begin upon first! On the other hand, *I*——"

" Yes, you? "

[1] Alexander Vasilievitch Suvorov (1729 – 1800), the great Russian general who, after defeating Napoleon in Italy, crossed the Alps to join hands with Korsakov, but found the latter to have been routed by Masséna.

171

Am doing what you see—lying under a rick. The
space occupied by my body is small indeed compared
with the surrounding immensity in which it has neither
part nor lot, and the portion of time allotted to me here
on earth is insignificant indeed compared with the
eternity which I have never known, and shall never
enter! Yet in this same atom, in this same mathematical
point which I call my body, the blood circulates, and the
brain operates at will. A fine discrepancy for you—a
fine futility!"

" I would remark that what you have just said applies
to every human being in creation."

" True. What I mean is that my parents know not a
single tedious moment, nor are in the least distressed
with the thought of their insignificance—it is a thought
which never stinks in their nostrils; whereas *I*—well, I
feel nothing but weariness and rancour in my breast."

" Rancour? Why rancour?"

" How can you ask? Have you forgotten the recent
past?"

"No: only, I do not recognise your right to be *angry*:
unhappy, perhaps, but not——"

" I perceive you to understand love as it is understood by all our modern young men. That is to say,
chirping ' Tsip, tsip, tsip!' like pullets, you take to
your heels as soon as ever you see love approaching. I,
however, am different.—But enough of this. What is
past help is best not talked about." Bazarov rolled over
on to his elbow. " Ah! Here is a young ant towing in its
wake a half-dead fly. Pull, brother, pull! Never mind
that the fly hangs back, but avail yourself of your
animal right to abjure all sympathy, seeing that our
friend has only himself to thank for his trouble."

" Do not speak like that," expostulated Arkady.
" How are you yourself to thank for your trouble?"

Bazarov raised his head.

172

" Nay," he said, " I was but jesting. Never have I got myself into trouble, and never shall any woman do it for me. Amen! I have spoken. Never will you hear from me another word on the subject."

For a while the two friends lay without speaking.

" Yes," continued Bazarov, " man is a strange being. Contemplating from a distance the dull life led by my parents, one would almost feel inclined to say to one-self: ' What could be better than that, seeing that in that existence one merely eats and drinks and knows oneself to be acting in a sane and regular manner?' Yet a man will still become depressed, and yearn for company, even though he may curse it when he has got it."

" One ought so to order one's life that every moment in it shall be of significance," said Arkady sententiously.

" Of course; but while the significant, and even the pseudo-significant—yes, the absolutely insignificant as well—may be bearable, it is trifles, trifles that matter."

" Unless a man recognise their existence, they do not exist."

" H'm! A contra-platitude."

" What is that ? "

" This—that, should you say that education is useful, you will be uttering a platitude; but, should you say that education is harmful, you will be uttering a contra-platitude. The one is identical with the other, except that they differ a little in elegance of expression."

" And which has right on its side? "

" ' Which has right on its side? ' I can only re-echo: ' Which? ' "

" Come! You are out of spirits to-day."

" Am I? Then the sun must have touched me a little, or else I must have eaten too many raspberries to be good for me."

" Then you would do well to have a sleep."

173

" I think you are right. Only, do not look at me while I sleep, for a man cuts his very worst figure at such a time."

" Surely *you* do not care for people's opinion? "

" I do, even though a man in the best sense of the term ought never to trouble his head about such things, seeing that such a man is either above criticism or too feared and hated for critics to wish to tackle him."

" Curious! For I myself never hate any one."

" And I hate a great many people. You, you see, are a tender soul, you are so much pap, and therefore hatred could never come within your purview. People as retiring, as devoid of self-confidence as you are——"

" What about your own self-confidence? " interrupted Arkady. " What about your own opinion of yourself? "

Bazarov paused—then replied:

" As we were passing the hut of your *starosta* to-day (what a neat, pretty little place it looked!) you said to me: ' Not until every peasant shall have come to own such a place as this, and every one of us shall have contributed his mite to that end, will Russia attain perfection.' But, for my part, I abominate the scurvy churl for whom I am supposed to jump out of my skin, even though never a ' thank you ' should I get from him for doing so. For why should he thank me? His *métier* happens to be living in a white hut, and mine to be——"

" Come, come, Evgenii! One is almost forced to agree with those who accuse us of being unprincipled."

" You talk like your uncle. No such thing as principle exists. That you seem never to have divined. Instincts only exist, and upon them everything depends."

" How so? "

" Thus. We will take myself as an example. Owing to the nature of my instincts, I am prone to deny—I am prone to deny because my brain is so constituted. In the same way, if you were to ask me why I am interested in chemistry, and why you like apples, I should reply that the same reason holds good in each case—that our respective instincts are what they are. In other words, there exists between your instincts and mine a certain affinity. Deeper it is not given us to probe."

" Then is honour an instinct? "

" It is."

" Oh, Evgenii! " cried Arkady sorrowfully.

" Do you dislike the conversation? Then let us philosophise no more, but ' permit nature to waft upon us the silence of sleep,' to quote Pushkin."

" Pushkin never said any such thing," objected Arkady.

" Then, if he did not, he ought, being a poet, to have done so. Perhaps he had served in the army? "

" Never did he serve in the army."

" Indeed? Why, in his every line we come across ' To battle, to battle, for the honour of Russia! ' "

" That is a mere invention on your part. The statement is an absolute calumny."

" A calumny? What matters a calumny? What is there in the term to be afraid of? Slander a man as much as you like, yet for himself he will hear things twenty times worse."

" Suppose we sleep," said Arkady irritably.

" With pleasure," Bazarov replied.

Nevertheless neither succeeded in the effort, for almost every sleep-destroying sentiment happened to be in the ascendant. So, after five minutes of such ineffectual striving, both opened their eyes, and lay mutely gazing about them.

" Look! " cried Arkady after a pause. " Do you see that withered maple leaf fluttering to the ground? Are not its movements exactly like those of a butterfly?

175

Strange that an object so joyous and full of life should be able so to counterfeit an object mournful and dead!"

"My friend," protested Bazarov, "let me make at least *this* request of you: that you do not talk in ' beautiful language.' "

"I talk as I am able. I decline to be domineered over. Should a thought chance to enter my head, why should I not express it? "

"Similarly am I at liberty to express the thought that to talk in 'beautiful language' is sheerly indecent."

"Indecent? Then swearing is *not* indecent? "

"Aha! I perceive you still to be minded to follow in your uncle's footsteps. How the idiot would have rejoiced if he could have heard you! "

"*What* did you call Paul Petrovitch? "

"I called him merely what he is—merely an idiot."

"Have done!" shouted Arkady.

"Therein I detect the tie of blood," said Bazarov calmly. "It is a very stubborn factor, I have noticed, in some people. A man may abjure everything else, and cut himself adrift from every other prejudice, yet still remain powerless to confess that the brother who habitually steals his shirts is a thief. You see, the difficulty lies in the word 'my.' Is not that so? "

"No. It was from a sense of justice, rather than from a sense of kinship, that I spoke. But since you have no understanding of the former, as an instinct which you simply do not possess, you are not in a position to pass judgment upon such a feeling."

"In other words, 'I, Arkady Kirsanov, am altogether above your comprehension.' Well, I make mute obeisance to that."

"Come, come, Evgenii! We shall end by quarrelling."

"Oh that you *would* do me the favour to quarrel! We

176

could have a real set-to *à outrance*, and with our coats off."

" To the end that——? "

" To the end that we might rend one another in pieces. Why not? Here, amid the hay, in this idyllic setting, far from the madding crowd and every human eye, it would be not at all a bad thing. No, you shall *not* make it up with me! Rather will I seize you by the throat! "

As he extended his long, sharp fingers, Arkady rolled over and prepared jestingly to grapple with his assailant. But the next moment the sight of Bazarov's face, with its expression of malice and the non-jesting menace which lurked in the twisted smile and the flashing eyes, gave him a shock, and filled him with involuntary awe.

" *This*, then, is where you have got to! " cried Vasili Ivanitch from behind them as, vested in a home-made cotton pea-jacket and a home-made straw hat, the old military doctor suddenly confronted the pair. " I have been searching for you everywhere, and certainly you have chosen a capital spot, and are engaged also in a capital occupation—in the occupation of lying on the earth and gazing at the heavens. For my part, I believe that such an occupation can have its uses."

" I gaze at the heavens only when I am going to sneeze," said Bazarov. Then, turning to Arkady, he added in an undertone: " Forgive me if I hurt you."

" Do not mention it," was Arkady's rejoinder in a similar undertone, as covertly he pressed his friend's hand.

Shocks of such a kind, however, were bound, in time, to react upon their friendship.

" As I look at you, young gentlemen," Vasili Ivanitch continued as, nodding his head, he rested his hands upon a crooked stick, his own manufacture, which had a Turk's head for a handle, " I cannot sufficiently admire you. What strength you embody! How you speak of the flower of youth, of capacity, and of talent! You resemble Castor and Pollux themselves."

"To think of your flaunting your mythology like that!" said Bazarov. "At the same time, you must have been a fine Latin scholar in your day. In fact, did not you once receive a silver medal for an essay?"

"The Dioscuri, the Dioscuri themselves!" continued the old man ecstatically.

"Come, come, father! Do not play the fool."

"Ah, well! No, I have not sought you out to pay you compliments: I have come to inform the pair of you that dinner is nearly ready, and also to give you, Evgenii, a warning. I know that, as a man of sense, as well as a man well versed in the world, you will be charitable. The case is this. This morning your mother took it into her head to organise a thanksgiving ceremony on the occasion of your return.—No, do not think that I am inviting you to the ceremony: on the contrary, it is over. All that I am going to say is that Father Alexis——"

"The priest?"

"Yes, and our private confessor. Well, this Father Alexis is going to dine with us, even though I had not expected it, and it was not my suggestion, but merely an arrangement which has come about somehow—probably through his having failed to understand me aright. Not that we look upon him as anything but a man of rectitude and good sense."

"Surely you do not mean to imply that he is likely to devour my portion of the food, do you?"

Vasili Ivanitch burst out laughing.

"Ha, ha, ha!" he cried.

"I feel easy, then," continued Bazarov. "In fact, never do I mind with whom I sit at table."

Vasili Ivanitch's face brightened at once.

" I felt sure of that in advance," he said. " Yes, I knew that you, a young man, are as superior to prejudice as I am at sixty-two " (Vasili had none the less shrunk from confessing that he had wished for the thanksgiving ceremony as much as his wife had, since his piety was fully equal to hers). " In any case Father Alexis would like to make your acquaintance; while you, for your part, will very likely take to him, seeing that he not only plays cards, but also (though this is quite between ourselves) smokes a pipe! "

" Indeed? After dinner, then, we will have a game, and I will despoil him utterly."

" Ha, ha, ha! We shall see, we shall see."

" Then at times you hark back to old days? " Bazarov asked with a tinge of surprise.

Vasili Ivanitch's bronzed cheeks took on a faint flush.

" For shame, Evgenii! " he muttered. " Remember that the past is the past. Nevertheless, even in this gentleman's presence I am ready to confess that in my youth I had my addictions, and that, since, I have paid for them. But how hot the weather is! Let me seat myself beside you; though I hope that, in doing so, I shall not interrupt your conversation? "

" By no means," replied Arkady with alacrity.

Vasili Ivanitch subsided with a grunt and the remark:

" Your *logement* reminds me of my military bivouacking days—this rick being a dressing-station." There followed a sigh. " Aye, many and many an experience have I had in my time. For instance, let me tell you a curious story about the black death in Bessarabia."

" When you received the order of St. Vladimir? " said Bazarov. " Yes, I know the story. But why do you never wear the badge of the order? "

" As I have told you, I care not a jot for appearances," protested Vasili Ivanitch (though only on the previous day had he had the red riband of the order removed from his coat). He then embarked upon the story.

" Evgenii has gone to sleep," presently he whispered to Arkady with a good-humoured wink and a pointing finger. " Come, come, Evgenii! " he added in a louder tone. " It is time to get up! Time for dinner! "

Father Alexis—a stout, good-looking man with thick, well-combed hair and an embroidered girdle over a lilac cassock—proved a clever, resourceful guest who, taking the initiative as regards shaking hands with Arkady and Bazarov (somehow he seemed to divine that they did not require his blessing), bore himself, in general, with complete absence of restraint, and, while neither demeaning himself nor imposing general constraint, made merry over scholastic Latin, defended his archbishop, quaffed a couple of glasses of wine (refusing a third), and accepted one of Arkady's cigars, though, instead of smoking it, he put it into his pocket to take home with him. The only thing that was at all unpleasant was the fact that every now and then, on raising a stealthy hand to brush from his face a fly, he, in lieu of doing so, crushed the insect flat!

Dinner over, he seated himself with modest zest at the card-table, and ended by despoiling Bazarov of two-and-a-half roubles in paper money (this rural establishment took no account of the system of computing cash in silver). During the game the hostess sat beside her son with her cheek resting on her hand as usual, and only rose from the table when it became necessary to order further relays of refreshment. Yet to caress Bazarov was more than she dared do; nor did he give her the least encouragement in that direction; in addition to which Vasili Ivanitch further restrained her ardour by whispering at intervals: " Do not worry our Evgenii. Young men do not like that sort of thing." Also, hardly need it be said that the dinner of which the company had just partaken had been of the usual sumptuousness, seeing that at break of day Timotheitch had set out for Circassian beef, and that the *starosta* also had galloped in quest of trout, eels, and crabs, while a sum of forty-two kopecks had been paid to peasant women for mushrooms. Arina Vlasievna's eyes, fixed immovably upon Bazarov, had in them something more than tenderness and affection. In them there were also sadness, curiosity, a touch of apprehension, and a kind of painful deference. Yet never did he mark their expression, since never did he turn in her direction, save to put to her the curtest of questions, and, once, to ask her to lay her hand in his, " for luck." On the latter occasion she slipped her plump fingers into his hard, capacious palm, waited a little, and then asked him:

" Has that helped you at all in your play? "

" It has not," he replied with a contemptuous grimace. " On the contrary, things are even worse than they were before."

" Yes, the cards seem to be against you," remarked Father Alexis with an assumed air of sympathy as he stroked his handsome beard.

" But beware of the Code Napoléon, my father," observed Vasili Ivanitch as he played an ace. " Beware of the Code Napoléon."

" Which, in the end, brought Napoleon to St. Helena," retorted the father as he trumped the ace.

" A glass of currant wine, Eniushka dear? " asked Arina Vlasievna.

Bazarov replied with a shrug of his shoulders.

Next day he said to Arkady:

" To-morrow I must depart. The place wearies me, for I wish to work, and it is impossible to do so here. I will come to your place, I think, for all my chemical preparations are there. Moreover, one can at least lock

181

one's door at your place; whereas here, though my father keeps saying, ' My study is entirely at your disposal, and no one shall disturb you,' he himself is never absent for a moment. And, for that matter, I should be ashamed to lock him outside, or my mother either. Sometimes I can hear her groaning in the next room. Yet no sooner do I go out to her than I find that I have not a word to say."

" She will be much distressed at your departure," said Arkady. " And so will he."

" But I intend to return."

" Exactly when? "

" When I am on my way back to St. Petersburg."

" I am particularly sorry for your mother."

" Why so? Has she been stuffing you with fruit? "

Arkady lowered his eyes.

" You do not know her," he said. " She is not only a good woman, but also a very wise one. This morning I had half an hour's very practical and interesting talk with her."

" A talk in which she told you all about me? "

" We spoke of other topics besides yourself."

" Possibly. Possibly, too, you, as an outsider, may see things clearer than I do. Yet when a woman can talk for half an hour it is a good sign, and I will depart as I have said."

" But you will not find it easy to break the news to her, for her plans for us extend over a couple of weeks."

" No, it may not prove easy, as you say; and the less so since the devil led me to vex my father this morning. It was like this. A few days ago he had one of his serfs flogged, and therein did rightly. No, you need not look at me with such indignation. I say my father did rightly for the reason that the peasant in question had proved himself to be an arrant thief and drunkard. Unfortunately, my father had not expected me to get to hear of the occurrence; wherefore he was the more put out when he found that I had done so. Well, now his vexation will be twofold! However, no matter. He will get over it before long."

Yet, though Bazarov had said " No matter," he let the whole of the rest of the day elapse before he could make up his mind to acquaint Vasili Ivanitch with his intention. Finally, just as he was saying good-night to his father in the study, he observed with a prolonged yawn:

" By the way, I had almost forgotten to request you to have our horses sent forward to Thedot's."

Vasili Ivanitch looked thunderstruck.

"Then is Monsieur Kirsanov leaving us?" he inquired.

" Yes, and I am going with him."

Vasili Ivanitch fidgeted for a moment or two.

" You say that you are going with him?" he murmured.

" Yes. I *must* go. So pray have the horses sent forward as requested."

" I—I will, I will," the old man stuttered. " So they are to go to Thedot's? Yes, yes, very well. Only, only —is there any particular reason for this change of plan? "

" There is. I am engaged to pay Arkady a short visit. That done, I will return to you."

" Only to be a *short* visit? Good! " And Vasili Ivanitch pulled out his pocket-handkerchief, and blew his nose. In doing so, he bent his head very low—almost to the ground. " Well, well! Things shall be as you desire. Yet we had hoped that you would have stayed with us a little longer. Three days only! Three days after three years of absence! Ah, that is not much, Evgenii—it is not much! "

" But I tell you I intend to return soon. You see, I *must* go."

" You have no choice, eh? Very well, very well. Of course engagements must be kept. Yes, yes; of course they must be kept. And I am to send the horses forward? Very good. Naturally, Arina and I had not altogether looked for this. Only to-day she has been to a neighbour to beg flowers for your room."

Nor of the fact that, each morning, he had gone downstairs in his slippers to confer with Timotheitch; nor of the fact that, producing, with tremulous fingers, one ragged banknote after another, he had commissioned his henchman to make various purchases with special reference to the question of eatables (in particular, of a certain red wine which he had noticed the young men to like); no, of none of these facts did Vasili Ivanitch make any mention.

"The greatest thing in the world is one's freedom," he went on. "I, too, make it my rule. Never should one let oneself be hampered or——"

A sudden break occurred in his voice, and he made for the door.

"I promise you that we will return soon, my father. I give you my word of honour upon that."

But Vasili Ivanitch did not look round—he just waved his hand and departed. Mounting to the bedroom, he found Arina asleep, so started to say his prayers in an undertone, for fear of awaking her. But at once she opened her eyes.

"In that you, Vasili Ivanitch?" she asked.

"Yes, mother."

"Have you just left Eniusha? Do you know, I am anxious about him. Does he sleep comfortably on the sofa? To-day I told Anfisushka to lay him out your travelling mattress and the new pillows. Also, I would have given him our feather bed had he not disliked soft lying."

"Do not fret, mother dear. He is quite comfortable. 'Lord, pardon us sinners!'" And Vasili Ivanitch went on with his prayers. Yet his heart was full of an aching

184

compassion for his old companion; nor did he want to tell her overnight of the sorrow which was awaiting her on the morrow.

Next day, therefore, Arkady and Bazarov departed. From earliest morn an air of woe pervaded the household. Anfisushka let fall some crockery, and Thedika's perturbation ended in his taking off his shoes. As for Vasili Ivanitch, he fussed about, and made a brave show—he talked in loud tones, and stamped his feet upon the floor as he walked; but his face had suddenly fallen in, and his glance could not meet that of his son. Meanwhile Arina Vlasievna indulged in quiet weeping. Indeed, but for the fact that her husband had spent two hours that morning in comforting her, she would have broken down completely, and lost all self-control.

But at last, when, after reiterated promises to return within, at most, a month, Bazarov had freed himself from the arms which sought to detain him, and entered the *tarantass*; when the horses had started, and their collar-bow had begun to tinkle, and the wheels to revolve; when to gaze after the vehicle any longer had become useless, and the dust had subsided, and Timotheitch, bent and tottering, had crawled back into his pantry; when the old couple found themselves alone in a house which seemed suddenly to have grown as dishevelled and as decrepit as they—then, ah, then did Vasili Ivanitch desist from his brief show of waving his handkerchief in the verandah, and sink into a chair, and drop his head upon his breast.

" He has gone for ever, he has gone for ever," he muttered. " He has gone because he found the life here tedious, and once more I am as lonely as the sand of the desert ! "

These words he kept repeating again and again; and, each time that he did so, he raised his hand, and pointed into the distance.

185

But presently Arina Vlasievna approached him, and, pressing her grey head to his, said:

" Never mind, my Vasia. True, our son has broken away from us; he is like a falcon—he has flown hither, he has flown thither, as he willed: but you and I, like lichen in a hollow tree, are still side by side, we are not parted. . . . And ever I shall be the same to you, as you will be the same to me."

Taking his hands from his face, Vasili Ivanitch embraced his old comrade, his wife, as never—no, not even during the days of his courtship—he had done before. And thus she comforted him.

XXII

In silence, or merely exchanging a few unimportant words, the travellers made their way to Thedot's posting-house. Arkady felt anything but pleased with Bazarov, and Bazarov felt anything but pleased with himself. Moreover, the younger man's heart was heavy with the sort of unreasoning depression which is known only to youth.

The driver hitched his horses, and then, mounting to the box, inquired whether he was to drive to the right or to the left.

Arkady started. The road to the right led to the town, and thence to his father's house; while the road to the left led to Madame Odintsov's establishment.

He glanced at Bazarov.

" To the left, Evgenii? " he queried.

Bazarov turned away his head.

" Why that folly again? " he muttered.

" Folly, I know," said Arkady, " but what does that matter? We need but call in passing."

Bazarov pulled his cap over his eyes.

" Do as you like," he said.

" To the left, then," cried Arkady to the coachman; and the *tarantass* started in the direction of Nikolsköe. Nevertheless, for all that the friends had decided upon this foolish course, they remained as silent and downcast as ever.

Indeed, Madame Odintsov's butler had not even made his appearance upon the verandah before the pair divined that they had done unwisely to yield to such an impulse. The fact that no one in the house had expected them was emphasised by the circumstance that when Madame entered the drawing-room they had already

187

spent a considerable time there in awkward silence. However, she accorded them her usual suave welcome, though she seemed a little surprised at their speedy return, and, at heart, not over-pleased at it. For this reason they hastened to explain that theirs was a mere passing call, and that in about four hours they would be continuing their journey to the town. In reply she said nothing beyond that she requested Arkady to convey her greetings to his father, and then sent for her aunt; and inasmuch as the Princess entered in a state of having just overslept herself, her wrinkled old face betokened even greater malignity than usual. Katia was not well, and did not leave her room at all: and this caused Arkady suddenly to realise that he would have been as glad to see her as Anna Sergievna. The four hours were filled with a desultory conversation which Anna Sergievna carried on without a single smile: nor until the very moment of parting did her usual friendliness seem to stir within her soul.

" I am out of humour to-day," she said, " but that you must not mind. Come again soon. I address the invitation to you both."

Bazarov and Arkady responded with silent bows, re-entered the *tarantass*, and drove forward to Marino, whither they arrived, without incident, on the following evening. *En route*, neither of the pair mentioned Madame Odintsov, and Barazov in particular scarcely opened his mouth, but gazed towards the horizon with a hard look in his eyes.

But at Marino every one was delighted to see them, for Nikolai Petrovitch had begun to feel uneasy at the prolonged absence of his son, and now leapt from the sofa with a cry of joy when Thenichka ran to announce that " the young gentlemen " were arriving. Yes, even Paul Petrovitch felt conscious of a touch of pleasant excitement, and smiled indulgently as he shook hands with the wanderers. Ensued then much talking and questioning, in which Arkady took the leading part, and more especially during supper, which lasted far into the night, since Nikolai Petrovitch ordered up several bottles of porter which had just arrived from Moscow, and made so merry that his cheeks assumed a raspberry tint, and he fell to venting half-boyish, half-hysterical laughs. Moreover, the general enlivenment extended even to the kitchen, where Duniasha kept breathlessly banging doors, and at three o'clock in the morning Peter essayed to execute on the guitar a Cossack waltz which would have sounded sweet and plaintive amid the stillness of the night had not the performance broken down after the opening cadenza, owing to the fact that nature had denied the cultured underling a talent either for music or for anything else.

Indeed, of late, life at Marino had been far from comfortable. In particular had poor Nikolai Petrovitch been in a bad way, for his troubles in connection with the estate—troubles of an exclusively futile and hopeless order—were growing greater from day to day. The worst of them came of the system of hired labour, which enabled some of the workmen to keep demanding either their discharge or an increase of wages, and others to depart as soon as ever they had received their earnest-money. Also, some of the horses had fallen sick, certain implements had been burnt, all hands were performing their tasks in a slovenly manner, a milling machine ordered from Moscow had turned out to be useless owing to its weight, a second such machine had broken down on its first being used, half the cattle sheds had disappeared in a conflagration caused by a blind old serf woman " smoking " her cow with a firestick during blustery weather (though she herself asserted that the trouble had come of the *barin's* manufacturing new-fangled cheeses and lacteal products in general), and, lastly, the

189

steward had grown so fat and lazy (as do all Russians who
fall upon " easy times "), and permitted his dislike of
Nikolai Petrovitch so to limit his activities, that he had
come to doing no more than bestowing an occasional
prod upon a passing pig, or threatening some half-naked
serf boy, while spending the rest of the time in bed.
Again, such of the peasants as had received allotments
under the *obrok* system had failed to pay their dues, as
well as applied themselves to stealing timber to such an
extent that, almost every night, the watchman had to
apprehend a culprit or two, as well as to impound horses
which peasants had turned out to graze in the meadows
attached to the manor. For illicit grazing of this sort
Nikolai Petrovitch had decreed forfeiture of the horses;
but usually the matter ended in the animals being kept
for a day or two at the *barin's* expense, and then restored
to their owners. Lastly, the peasants had taken to
quarrelling among themselves, through brothers con-
ceiving the idea of demanding a share of each other's
earnings, and through their wives suddenly finding themselves unable to get on in the same hut; wherefore feuds
had arisen which had caused whole households to spring
to their feet as at a word of command, and to flock to the
portico of the estate office, where, breaking in upon the
barin's privacy (very often with bruised faces and
drunken gait), they demanded justice and an immediate
settlement, while female sobs and whimperings mingled
with the curses of the male portion of the throng. Whenever this had happened Nikolai Petrovitch had had to
part the hostile factions from one another, and to shout
himself hoarse, even though he had known in advance
that no equitable decision was feasible. Finally, there
had been a deficiency of hands for the harvest, since a
neighbouring *odnovorzty*[1] of benign aspect who had under-

[1] A freeholder, a member of the class which, in the days of
this story, stood midway between the *pomiestchik*, or landowner,
and the *Krestianin*, or serf.

taken to provide harvesters at two roubles per *desiatin* had cheated without compunction, and supplied women workers who also demanded extortionate wages. Meanwhile the grain had rotted in the fields, and, later on, the women had not got through the mowing before the Board of Overseers had begun to press for immediate payment of percentage dues and arrears.

" I can do nothing," would be Nikolai Petrovitch's despairing exclamation " My principles forbid me either to contend with these people or to send for the *stanovoi*: [1] yet, without the power to threaten punishment, one can make no headway with such folk."

" *Du calme, du calme*," Paul Petrovitch would advise. Then he would growl, frown, and twist his moustache.

From these brawls Bazarov kept entirely aloof: nor, as a guest, was he called upon to interfere in them, but was free, from the day of his arrival, to apply himself solely to his frogs, infusoria, and chemical compositions. On the other hand, Arkady considered himself bound, if not to help his father, at all events to offer to help him; wherefore he listened to Nikolai's complaints with patience, and on one occasion even tendered him advice (though not advice meant to be taken, but advice designed to manifest the interest felt by him, Arkady, in current affairs). As a matter of fact, estate-management was not wholly distasteful to him, and he could find pleasure in thinking out agricultural problems; but his mind was filled with other preoccupations. For one thing, he discovered to his surprise that his thoughts were constantly turning in the direction of Nikolsköe; and though there had been a time when he would have shrugged his shoulders upon being told that he would ever come to find residence under the same roof as Bazarov—least of all, when that roof was his father's—a dull affair, he found time hang heavy on his hands, and his attention easily

[1] Magistrate.

191

stray elsewhere. So he tried the expedient of walking until thoroughly worn out, but even this did not help him; until eventually he learnt, in conversation with his father, that recently some letters of great interest had been chanced upon—letters which Arkady's mother had indited to the mother of Madame Odintsov. And from that moment onwards he never rested until he had induced Nikolai Petrovitch to re-discover the said letters, and to turn out, during the search, a score of boxes and drawers. Then only, when the half-mouldy documents had been dragged to light, did the young man feel easier in his soul, and bear himself as though now he saw before him the goal of his existence.

" ' I address the invitation to both of you,' " he kept whispering to himself. " Yes, that is what she said. Damn it, I will go."

But next there would recur to his memory the recent visit and its cold reception; until once more he would be seized with his old timidity and awkwardness. In the end, however, the spirit of adventurous youth, aided by a secret desire to try his luck, to test his strength unaided, and without a protector, contrived to win the day.

Ten days later, therefore, he invented a pretext, in the shape of a desire to study the working of Sunday schools, to drive to the town, and thence to Nikolsköe. As he drove, the manner in which he encouraged his postilion communicated to his progress the character, rather, of a young officer's trip to fight his first duel, for diffidence, impatience, and delight were well-nigh choking him.

" Above all things," he kept reflecting, " I must not think too much of myself." And though the postilion who had fallen to his lot was of the type of rascal who pulls up at every tavern door, there hove in sight, before long, the familiar, high-pitched roof of the mansion.

" But what am I doing ? " now occurred to him the thought. " Indeed, would it not be better to go back ? "

FATHERS AND SONS

Unfortunately, to the sound of the postilion's whist-
lings and tongue-clickings the *troika* of horses trotted
bravely forward, and presently the bridge thundered
under the combined weight of the hooves and wheels. Ah,
there was the avenue of clipped firs! Yes, and *there* was
a glimpse of a pink dress amid some dark foliage! Yes,
and *there* a glimpse of a young face peering from the
shade of a silken parasol! Yes, yes—it *was* Katia! He
had recognised her in an instant, as she him! Bidding
the postilion pull up, Arkady leapt from the carriage,
and approached the maiden.

" So it is you? " she exclaimed. And at the same
moment a blush overspread her face. " Let us go and
look for my sister. She is in the garden, and will be
delighted to see you."

So she conducted him thither. How lucky that he had
met her as he had done! More pleased he could not have
felt if she had been his own sister. Yes, things were
indeed fortunate! Now there would have to be no butler,
and no formal announcement of his arrival.

Of Anna Sergievna he caught sight at a turn in the
path. She had her back to him, but presently, on hearing
the sound of approaching footsteps, faced about.

Once more confusion seized Arkady in its grip. Yet
no sooner had she spoken than he felt his courage return.

" How do you do? " she said in her even, kindly way
as she advanced to meet him with a smile that was
slightly tempered with the sun and wind. " Where did
you find him, Katia? "

" I have brought with me something which you are
unlikely to have been expecting," he said. " For I——·'

" But you have brought me yourself," she rejoined.
" And that is the best bringing of all."

XXIII

AFTER speeding Arkady on his way with satirical expressions of regret (as well as giving him to understand that the satirist laboured under no delusions as to the object of the young man's journey), Bazarov withdrew into complete seclusion, since a perfect fever for work had come upon him. Nor did he quarrel any longer with Paul Petrovitch, and the less so since the latter had now come to adopt an exclusively aristocratic attitude, and to express his sentiments only in monosyllables, not in words. Once, and once only, did he allow himself to engage in a controversy with Bazarov over the then current question of the rights of the *dvoriané*. But suddenly he checked himself, and said with an air of cold politeness:

"It is clear that we shall never understand one another. At all events *I* have not the honour to understand *you*."

"True," agreed Bazarov. "For a man may understand the precipitation of ether, and be *au fait* with what is taking place in the sun, yet, confront him with the fact that another man blows his nose differently from the manner in which he blows his own, and at once that man will become lost in perplexity."

At the same time, there were occasions when Paul Petrovitch requested permission to attend the other's experiments; and once he went so far as to apply his perfumed, clean-shaven features to the microscope, for the purpose of observing how a transparent infusorium could swallow a greenish-looking particle, and then masticate the same with fang-like protuberances which grew in its throat. Still more frequently was Nikolai Petrovitch present in Bazarov's room. Indeed, but for

194

the counter-distraction of estate-management, he would have spent his whole time in the process of what he called "self-improvement." Yet he never hampered the young naturalist: on the contrary, he would seat himself in a remote corner of the room, and, but for a guarded question or two, confine himself solely to silently and absorbedly watching the experiments. Also, at meal times he always endeavoured to turn the conversation in the direction of physics or geology or chemistry, for the reason that he divined in any other direction (that of industry, or, still more, that of politics) there lay a greater danger of collisions, or, at all events, of mutual soreness. For rightly did he divine that his brother's enmity towards Bazarov had by no means abated. And to this conclusion an incident which occurred at a juncture when cholera had just made its appearance in the neighbourhood, and carried off two victims from Marino itself, lent additional colour. One night Paul Petrovitch happened to be seized with a fainting fit, yet refused to apply to Bazarov for assistance; and when Bazarov, on meeting him on the following day, inquired why such a course had not been adopted, Paul Petrovitch—still pale, but as carefully brushed and combed as ever—retorted: " Did not you yourself tell me that you have no belief in medicine? "

Thus day followed day. Yet, though Bazarov devoted himself wholly to work, there was one person in the house whom he did not hold at arm's length, but was always willing to talk to. That person was Thenichka. Mostly he encountered her in the early mornings, when she was walking in the garden or the courtyard; but never did he enter her room, nor did she ever come to his door, save once, for the purpose of asking him to help her with Mitia's bath. And she not only trusted Bazarov; she also held him in no awe, and allowed herself more freedom in his presence than she did in

195

that of Nikolai Petrovitch himself. The reason is difficult to determine. Perhaps it was the fact that unconsciously she detected in Bazarov none of the *dvorianin* element, none of that superiority which at once attracts and repels; the young Nihilist, to her, was just a clever doctor, and no more. At all events, she was so free from shyness in his presence that she would dandle her child unabashed, and, on one occasion, when seized with a headache, went so far as to accept at his hands a spoonful of medicine. True, in Nikolai Petrovitch's presence she seemed to shun Bazarov; but this was done more out of a sense of decorum than through subtlety. As for Paul Petrovitch, she feared him as much as ever, for he had taken to watching her with a keen, steady eye, and to making his appearance behind her as though his figure, clad in its inevitable English suit, and posed in its usual attitude of hands in trousers pockets, had suddenly sprung from the floor. " Whenever I see him I feel cold all over," once she complained to Duniasha; whereupon that maiden's thoughts reverted longingly to another " unfeeling " individual who had, all unwittingly, come to be " the cruel tyrant " of her. heart.

Thenichka, therefore, liked Bazarov, and Bazarov liked Thenichka. Indeed, no sooner did he speak to her than his face would undergo a change, and, assuming a bright, almost a good-humoured, expression, exchange its habitual superciliousness for something like playful solicitude. Meanwhile she grew more beautiful daily. In the lives of young women there is a season when they begin to unfold and bloom like the roses in summer: and to that period Thenichka had just come. Everything, even the July heat then prevalent, contributed to it. Dressed in a gown of some light white material, she looked even lighter and whiter than it; and though she escaped actual sunburn, the heated air imparted to her cheeks and ears a faint tan, and, permeating her frame with gentle indolence, imbued her exquisite eyes with dreamy languor. No longer could she do any work; she could only let her hands sink upon her lap, and there remain. Seldom going even for a stroll, she spent the most of her time in a state of gently querulous and panting, but not distasteful, inertia.

" You should go and bathe as often as you can," Nikolai Petrovitch said to her one day (he had had a large, canopied bathing-place constructed in one of the last few ponds on the estate).

" Ah! " she gasped. " Even to walk to the pond half-kills me: and to walk back from it half-kills me again. There is no shade in the garden, you see."

" True," he agreed, wiping his forehead.

At seven o'clock one morning, when Bazarov was returning from a walk, he encountered Thenichka in the midst of a lilac clump which, though past the season of flowering, was still green and leafy. As usual, she had a white scarf thrown over her head, and beside the bench on which she was sitting there was a bunch of red and white roses with the dew yet glistening on their petals. He bade her good morning.

" It is you, then, Evgenii Vasilitch! " she exclaimed as she put aside a corner of her scarf to look at him— a movement which bared her arm to the elbow.

" What are you doing? " he asked as he seated himself beside her. " Is it a nosegay you are making? "

" Yes, for the breakfast table. Nikolai Petrovitch is so fond of such things."

" But breakfast is not yet. What a waste of flowers! "

" I know, but I gather them now because later the weather becomes too hot for walking. This is the only time when it is possible even to breathe. The heat makes me faint, and I am afraid of falling ill with it."

" Mere fancy. Let me feel your pulse."

He took her hand in his, and found the pulse to be

197

beating with such regularity that he did not trouble even to count its throbs.

" You will live to be a hundred," he said as he relinquished her wrist.

" God preserve me from that! " exclaimed she.

" Why so? Surely you would like to live a long time? "

" Yes—I should; but not for a hundred years. You see, my grandmother lived to be eighty-five, but suffered terribly. Long before she died she had a constant cough, and was also blind and deaf and crooked, and had become a burden to herself. What would be the use of a life like that? "

" You think that it is better to be young? "

" I do. And why not? "

" How is it better? Tell me that."

" How is it better? Oh, as long as one is young one can do what one wants to do—one can walk about, and carry things, and not be dependent upon other folk. Is not that the best way? "

" I do not know. At all events *I* care not whether I be young or old."

" What makes you say that? Surely you cannot mean it? "

" No? Well, think of what my youth means to me. I am a lonely man, a man without home or——"

" But all depends upon yourself."

" No, it does not. I only wish that some one would take pity upon my loneliness! "

She glanced at him, but said nothing. After a pause she resumed:

" What is that book of yours? "

" This? It is a learned, scholarly work."

" How you study! Do you never grow tired of it? By this time, I should think, you must know everything."

" Indeed I do not. . . . But try reading a few lines of the book."

" I should never understand them. Is it a Russian book? " (She took the heavily bound volume into her hands.)

" What a large book! " she continued.

" Yes. Also, it is a Russian book."

" Nevertheless I should not be able to understand it."

" I do not want you to understand it. I merely want to be able to watch you as you read. For when you read you twitch your little nose most charmingly! "

She began to read aloud a page " on Creosote," but soon burst out laughing, and replaced the book upon the bench, whence it slipped to the ground.

" I love to see you laugh," said Bazarov.

" Say no more," she interrupted.

" Also, I love to hear you speak. Your voice is like the bubbling of a brook."

She turned away her head, and fell to sorting her flowers. Presently she resumed:

" Why do you love to hear me speak? You must have talked to many much finer and cleverer ladies? "

" I assure you, nevertheless, that all the ' fine and clever ladies ' in the world are worth less than your little finger."

" Oh, come! " And she crossed her hands.

Bazarov picked up the book.

" It is a work on medicine," he observed. " Why did you throw it away? "

" It is a work on medicine? " she re-echoed, and turned to him again. " Do you know, ever since you gave me those capsules—you remember them, do you not?—Mitia has slept splendidly! I can never suffi- ciently thank you. You are indeed good! "

" But the physician ought to be paid his fee," remarked

he with a smile. " Doctors never do their work for nothing."

Upon this she raised her eyes. They looked all the darker for the brilliant glare which was beating upon the upper portion of her face. As a matter of fact, she was trying to divine whether he was speaking in earnest or in jest.

" Of course I should be delighted to pay you! " she said. " But first I must mention the matter to Nikolai Petrovitch."

" What? " he exclaimed. " You really think it is *money* I want? No, I do not require of you money."

" What, then? " she queried.

" What? Well, guess."

" How can I guess? "

" Then I must tell you. I want, I want—I want one of those roses."

She burst into a peal of laughter, and clapped her hands with delight at the request. Yet the laughter was accompanied with a certain sense of relief. Bazarov eyed her.

" Ah, you must excuse my laughing, Evgenii Vasilitch," she said (bending over the seat of the bench, she fumbled among the roses). " Which sort should you prefer? A red rose or a white one? "

" A red one, and not too large."

" Then take this one," she said, sitting up again. Yet even as she spoke she drew back her outstretched hand, and, biting her lips, glanced in the direction of the entrance to the arbour, and listened intently.

" What is it? " asked Bazarov. " Do you hear Nikolai Petrovitch coming? "

" No. Besides, every one has gone out to the fields. Nor do I fear any one except Paul Petrovitch. I merely thought that, that——"

" You thought what? "

200

" That some one *might* be coming this way. It seems I was wrong. Take this rose."

She handed Bazarov the gift.

" *Why* do you fear Paul Petrovitch? " he asked.

" I do so because he frightens me—when I speak to him he returns me no answer; he just stares at me in a meaning sort of way. You, too, do not like him, I believe? It was with him that you had such a quarrel, was it not? What it was all about I do not know, but at least I know that you worsted him like, like——"

With a gesture she signified the manner in which she considered Bazarov to have routed Paul Petrovitch.

" And, had *he* worsted *me*," he inquired, " would you have taken my part? "

" How could I? We should have agreed no better than you and he."

" You think so? Then let me tell you that a certain little hand could twist me around its little finger."

" Whose hand is that? "

" I expect you can guess. But smell this rose which you have just given me."

She bent forward in the direction of the flower, and as she did so her scarf slipped from her head to her shoulders, and revealed a mass of dark, soft, fluffy, glossy hair.

" Wait," said Bazarov. " I, too, will smell the rose."

And, reaching forward, he kissed her full on her parted lips.

She started back, and pressed her hands against his breast as though to repel him; but so weak was the act of repulsion that he found it possible to renew and to prolong his kiss.

Suddenly there sounded from among the lilac bushes a dry cough, and just as Thenichka darted to the other end of the bench Paul Petrovitch appeared, bowed slightly to the pair, said with a sort of melancholy acidity in his tone: " It is you, then? " and turned on his heel and departed. The next moment Thenichka picked up her roses and rushed from the arbour. As she passed Bazarov she whispered in his ear: "That was indeed wrong of you, Evgenii Vasilitch!" And the words voiced a note of reproach that was palpably genuine and unfeigned.

Instantly Bazarov's thoughts recurred to another scene in which he had recently taken part, and he became conscience-stricken, as also contemptuous of himself, and vexed. He shook his head, congratulated himself ironically on his folly, and departed to his room.

As for Paul Petrovitch, he left the garden and walked slowly into the forest. He remained there a considerable time; and, on returning to breakfast, looked so dark of mien that Nikolai Petrovitch inquired anxiously whether he were not ill.

" As you know," replied the other quietly, " I suffer habitually from biliousness."

XXIV

Two hours later he knocked at Bazarov's door.

" I feel that I must apologise for disturbing you in your pursuits," he said as he seated himself near the window and rested both hands upon a fine ivory-headed cane which he had brought with him (as a rule he did not carry one). " But the fact is that circumstances compel me to request five minutes of your time."

" The *whole* of my time is at your disposal," replied Bazarov, across whose features, as Paul Petrovitch had crossed the threshold, there had flitted a curious expression.

" No; five minutes will be sufficient. I have come to ask you a simple question."

" And what might that question be? "

" Listen. When first you came to stay in my brother's house, and I had not yet been forced to deny myself the pleasure of conversing with you, it fell to my lot to hear you hold forth on many different subjects. But, unless my memory deceives me, never once did the conversation between you and myself, or in my presence, happen to fall upon the subject of the duel or single combat. Would you, therefore, mind putting yourself out to the extent of giving me the benefit of your views on the subject mentioned? "

Bazarov, who had risen to receive his visitor, now reseated himself upon the edge of the table, and folded his arms upon his breast.

" My views are as follows," he replied. " From the theoretical standpoint, the duel is a sheer absurdity. From the practical standpoint, it is another matter altogether."

" You intend to convey (if I have understood you aright ?) that, apart from your theoretical views on the duel, you would not, in practice, allow yourself to be insulted without subsequently demanding satisfaction ? "

" You have guessed my meaning precisely."

" Good! It is a view which I am indeed glad to hear you express, in that it delivers me from a dilemma."

" You mean, from a state of indecision ? "

" They are one and the same thing. I express myself in this manner to the end that you may understand me. I am not one of your college rats. Consequently I repeat that through your words I am relieved of the necessity of resorting to what would have been a painful expedient. To speak plainly, I have made up my mind to fight you."

Bazarov raised his eyebrows a little.

" To fight me ? " he said.

" Yes, to fight you."

" And for what reason—if you do not mind telling me ? "

" For a reason which I might explain, but concerning which I prefer to remain silent. Suffice it for me to intimate that your presence offends me, that I detest and despise your person, and (should the foregoing be insufficient) that I——"

" Enough! " interrupted Bazarov. His eyes had flashed even as Paul's had done. " Further explanations would be superfluous. You have presumed to whet upon me your chivalrous spirit; wherefore, though I might have refused it, I will afford you satisfaction to the top of your bent."

" I have to express to you my sincere obligation. From the first did I feel encouraged to hope that you would accept my challenge without constraining me to resort to more forcible measures."

" In other words, and speaking without metaphor, to that cane ? " said Bazarov in a tone of supreme indifference. " Well, that is fair enough. Further insults are not needed—nor would you have found the offering of them altogether free from danger. Pray, therefore, remain a gentleman. It is as one that I accept your challenge."

" Good! " replied Paul Petrovitch; and he laid aside his cane. " Next, a few words on the subject of the conditions of our duel. First, pray be so good as to inform me whether or not you deem it necessary to resort to the formality of some such small difference of opinion as might serve as an ostensible excuse for my challenge? "

" I think that unnecessary. Such things are best done without formalities of any kind."

" I agree—that is to say, I, like you, consider that to go into the true reasons for our antagonism would be inexpedient. Let us therefore allege to the world that we could not abide one another. What need would there be to say more? "

" What indeed? " echoed Bazarov in a tone decidedly ironical.

" Also, with regard to the actual conditions of the duel. Inasmuch as we have no seconds—for where could we find them?——"

" Quite so. Where indeed? "

" I have the honour to propose to you the following. Let us fight to-morrow morning—say, at six o'clock: the rendezvous to be behind the copse, the weapons to be pistols, and the distance ten paces."

" Ten paces. Quite so! You and I abhor each other even at ten paces."

" Eight, then, if you wish? "

" The same applies to eight."

" And the number of shots to be two apiece. Also, in case either of us should fall, let each of us previously place in his pocket a letter laying upon himself the entire blame for his demise."

" To that condition I wholly demur," said Bazarov.

" I think that you are straying into the pages of a French novel, and away from reality."

" Possibly I am. But, also, you will agree that to incur an unmerited suspicion of murder is a prospect not pleasant to contemplate ? "

" I do. Yet still there remains another method of avoiding such an awkward imputation. That is to say, though we shall have no seconds, we can have a witness."

" Whom precisely, if I might ask ? "

" Peter."

" Peter ? What Peter ? "

" Peter the valet, a man who stands at the apex of contemporary culture, and could therefore play the rôle, and perform the functions, proper to such an occasion pre-eminently *comme il faut.*"

" I think that you are jesting, my good sir ? "

" No, I am not. If you will deign to give my proposal consideration you will speedily arrive at the conviction that it is as simple as it is charged with good sense. Schiller it would be impossible to hide in a bag, but I will undertake to prepare Peter for the part, and to bring him to the rendezvous."

" Still you are pleased to jest," said Paul Petrovitch as he rose. " But as you have so kindly met me, I have not the right to make further claims upon your time. All is arranged, then ? In passing, have you any pistols ? "

" How should I have any pistols ? I am not a man of war."

" Then perhaps you will allow me to offer you some of mine ? Rest assured that they have not been fired by me for five years."

" A very comforting assurance ! "

" Lastly," said Paul Petrovitch as he reached for his cane, " it only remains for me to thank you, and to leave you to your pursuits. I have the honour to bid you good-day."

" And I to say farewell until our pleasant meeting."
With which Bazarov escorted his visitor to the door.

Paul Petrovitch gone, Bazarov stood awhile in
thought. Then he exclaimed:

" Splendid indeed! Yet also unutterably stupid!
What a comedy to play! Talk of educated dogs dancing
on their hind legs! . . . However, I could not have
refused him, for, otherwise, he would have struck me
and *then* "—Bazarov turned pale, for his pride had been
aroused—" well, *then* I should have strangled him like
a kitten! "

He returned to his microscope, but found his heart
to be still beating, and the coolness necessary to scientific
observation to have disappeared.

" I suppose he saw us this morning," he continued to
himself. " Yet surely he is not doing this on his brother's
behalf? For what is there in a kiss? No; something
else is in the background. Bah! What if it should be that
he himself is in love with her? Yes, that is it. It is as
clear as day. What a mess! Truly a horrible mess, however it be viewed! For first of all I am to have my brains
blown out, and then I am to be made to leave this place!
And there is Arkady to consider, and that old heifer
Nikolai Petrovitch. Awkward! Awkward indeed! "

However, the day dragged its slow length along.
Thenichka remained practically non-existent (in other
words, she kept to her room as closely as a mouse to its
hole), Nikolai Petrovitch walked about with a careworn
air (it had been reported to him that mildew had begun
to attack the wheat), and Paul Petrovitch's mien of icy
urbanity succeeded in damping the spirits of Prokofitch
himself.

Presently Bazarov sat down to write a letter to his
father, but tore it up, and threw the pieces under the
table.

" Should I be killed," he reflected, " my parents will

207

hear of it soon enough. But I shall *not* be killed—I have yet far to wander about the world."

Next he ordered Peter to call him at dawn; and inasmuch as the order was accompanied with a mention of important business, Peter jumped to the conclusion that it was Bazarov's intention to take him to St. Petersburg. Bazarov then retired to rest. Yet, late though he had done so, he was troubled with fantastic visions. Ever before him there flitted Madame Odintsov, who was also his mother. And ever behind her there walked a black cat, which was also Thenichka. For his part, Paul Petrovitch figured as a forest which the dreamer was engaged to fight.

At length, when four o'clock arrived, Peter came to rouse him. Hastily dressing himself, he left the house with the valet. The morning was fine and fresh, and though a few wisps of cloud were trailing across the pale-blue transparency of the zenith, a light dew had coated the grass and foliage with drops, and was shining like silver on spiders' webs. The steaming earth seemed still to be seeking to detain the roseate traces of dawn in her embrace; but presently every quarter of the sky became lit up, and resounded again to the songs of larks.

Bazarov walked straight ahead until he reached the copse—then seated himself at the shadowy edge of the trees, and explained to Peter the services which he looked to the latter to perform; upon which the " cultured " menial came near to fainting, and was calmed only with an assurance that he would but have to stand at a distance, as a looker-on, and that in no case would responsibility attach to his person.

" And think," Bazarov concluded, " in what an important rôle you are about to figure ! "

But Peter, extending his hands deprecatingly, only turned up his eyes, became green in the face, and went and leant against a birch tree.

The copse was skirted by the road from Marino, and the light coating of dust bore no mark of having been disturbed since the previous evening, whether by wheel or by foot. Involuntarily Bazarov kept glancing along this road as, plucking and chewing stems of grass, he repeated again and again to himself: " What a piece of folly! " More than once, too, the morning air made him shiver, and Peter gaze plaintively in his direction; but Bazarov only laughed, for *he* at least was no coward.

At length hoofs sounded along the road, and there came into sight from behind the trees a peasant driving two horses with traces attached. As the man passed Bazarov he looked at him inquisitively, but failed to doff his cap; and this circumstance impressed Peter unfavourably, since the valet considered it a bad omen.

" Like ourselves, that peasant has risen early," thought Bazarov. " But whereas *he* has risen to work, *we*——! "

" Some one else is coming, I believe," whispered Peter.

Bazarov raised his head, and saw Paul Petrovitch, in a light check jacket and a pair of snow-white trousers, walking briskly along the road. Under his arm was a green, baize-covered box.

" Pardon me for having kept you waiting," he said with a bow to Bazarov, and then one to Peter (for even to the latter he, for the nonce, seemed to accord something of the respect due to a second). " As a matter of fact, I was loth to arouse my valet."

" I beg that you will not mention it," replied Bazarov. " We ourselves have only just arrived."

" So much the better! " And Paul Petrovitch glanced about him. " There will be no one to see us or disturb us. Are you agreeable to proceeding? "

" Quite."

" And I presume that you require no further explanations? '

" None whatsoever."

" Then kindly load these." Paul Petrovitch took from the box a brace of pistols.

" No. Do you load, while I measure the distance—my legs are longer than yours." This last Bazarov added with a dry smile. " Now, one, two, three——"

" I beg your pardon, sir," gasped Peter, who was trembling as with ague. " I beg your pardon, but might I move further away ? "

" Four, five—— Certainly, my good fellow! Pray do so. You can go and stand behind that tree there, and stop your ears—provided that you do not also stop your eyes. Lastly, should either Monsieur Kirsanov or myself fall, you are to run and pick up the fallen. Six, seven, eight——" Bazarov halted. "That will do, I suppose ? " he added to Paul Petrovitch. " Or would you prefer me to add another couple of paces ? "

" Do as you please," the other replied as he rammed home the second of the two bullets.

" Then I will add those two paces." And Bazarov scratched a line in the soil with his toe. " Here is the mark. *Apropos*, how many paces is each of us to retire from our respective marks ? "

" Ten, I presume," said Paul Petrovitch as he proffered Bazarov a brace of pistols. " Will you kindly make choice of these ? "

" I will. Nevertheless you will agree that our duel is singular, even to the point of absurdity? For pray observe the countenance of our second! "

" It is still your pleasure to jest," Paul Petrovitch responded coldly. " Of the singularity of our contest I make no denial. I merely consider it my duty to warn you that I intend to fight you in grim earnest. So, *à bon entendeur, salut !* "

" Yet, even though we intend to exterminate one another, why should we not enjoy our jest, and thus

210

combine *utile* with *dulce* ? You have spoken to me in French. I reply in Latin."

" I repeat that I intend to fight you in grim earnest," said Paul Petrovitch; with which he moved to his place, and Bazarov, after counting ten paces from his mark, turned, and halted.

" Are you ready? " inquired Paul Petrovitch.

" I am."

" Then engage."

Bazarov started to advance, and Paul Petrovitch did the same, with his left hand thrust into his coat pocket, and his right gradually elevating the muzzle of his pistol.

" The fellow is aiming straight for my nose," thought Bazarov to himself. " And how the rascal is screwing up his eyes as he marches! This is not a wholly pleasing sensation. I had better keep my eyes fixed upon his watch-chain."

Past Bazarov's ear something suddenly whistled, while almost at the same moment there came the sound of a report.

" I seemed to hear something, but no matter," was the thought which flashed through Bazarov's brain. Then he advanced another step, and, without aiming, pulled the trigger.

As he did so Paul Petrovitch gave a faint start, and clapped his hand to his thigh, down the white trouser-leg of which there began to trickle a thin stream of blood.

Bazarov threw aside his pistol and approached his antagonist.

" Are you wounded? " he inquired.

" Pray recall me to the mark," said Paul Petrovitch. " You have the right so to do, and we are merely wasting time. The conditions of the contest allow of a second shot apiece."

" Pardon me, that can be deferred," said Bazarov,

catching hold of Paul Petrovitch, who was beginning to
turn pale in the face. " I am no longer a duellist, but a
doctor, and must examine your wound. Peter! Here!
Where the devil has the man got to? "

" This is sheer folly," gasped Paul Petrovitch. " I
need no help. Let us——" Yet, even as he tried to
twirl his moustache, his arm fell to his side, his eyes
closed, and he collapsed in a swoon.

" Something new! " involuntarily cried Bazarov as he
laid his antagonist upon the grass. " A swoon! Let us
see what is the matter with him."

Taking out his pocket-handkerchief, he wiped away
the blood, and probed the neighbourhood of the wound.

" The bone is intact," he muttered. " Yes, and the
bullet has merely pierced the flesh a little below the
surface. Nothing but the *musculus vastus externus* is so
much as touched. In three weeks' time we shall have
him trotting about again. A swoon! Oh these men of
nerves! What thin skins, to be sure! "

" Is—is he dead? " came in Peter's tremulous voice
from behind.

Bazarov looked up.

" No," he said. " Run for a little water, and he will
outlive us both."

Unfortunately the " perfect servant " did not understand what was said to him, but remained stock still.
In fact, even when, the next moment, Paul Petrovitch
opened his eyes Peter went on crossing himself and
repeating: " He is dying! "

" Monsieur Bazarov," the wounded man said with a
twisted smile, " you were perfectly in the right when
you said that the face of that man was the face of a fool."

" It is so," agreed Bazarov. " Damn you, will you
fetch some water! " (The latter to the valet.)

" There is no need," put in Paul Petrovitch. " It was
only a passing vertigo. Kindly assist me to sit up. That

212

is it. A scratch like this will require only to be bandaged for me to walk home again. There will be no necessity to have the *drozhki* sent. For that matter, the duel need not be renewed unless you wish it. At least to-day you have acted like a gentleman. Kindly note that I have said so."

" To the past we have no need to refer," said Bazarov. " And, as regards the future, it calls for equally little remark, seeing that I intend to leave here at once. Allow me to bind your leg. The wound is not dangerous, but one of a nature which will make it as well to have the blood staunched. But first I must restore that stuck pig to life."

Shaking Peter vigorously by the collar, he dispatched him in search of the *drozhki*.

" But see that you do not alarm my brother," was Paul Petrovitch's injunction also to the man. " You are not to breathe a word of what has happened."

Peter set off at full speed. During the time that he was hastening for the *drozhki*, the two antagonists sat silently side by side on the ground, while Paul Petrovitch tried his best not to look at Bazarov, for the reason that he did not feel inclined to become reconciled with him, while at the same time he felt ashamed alike of his impulsiveness, his failure, and the scheme which had had this ending, though he realised that it might have been worse.

" At least will the fellow swagger here no more," he thought to himself by way of consolation. " And, for that, much thanks! "

The silence was a heavy, awkward silence, for neither of the pair felt comfortable—each of them recognised that the other had taken his measure. To friends, such a recognition may be very agreeable, but to foes it is far from welcome—least of all, when neither explana-tions nor a parting are feasible.

213

" I hope that I have not bound your leg too tightly? " said Bazarov at last.

" Oh no," replied Paul Petrovitch. " As a matter of fact, it is doing splendidly." After a pause he added: " But we cannot deceive my brother. How would it be if we were to tell him that we fell out over politics? "

" Capital! " agreed Bazarov. " Tell him, for instance, that I started cursing Anglomaniacs."

" A good idea! But what can that man be thinking of us? I cannot imagine." The speaker pointed to the same peasant who, shortly before the duel, had driven a pair of loose horses past Bazarov, and was now shuffling homewards, while doffing his cap at the sight of the gentlemen.

" Who can say? " replied Bazarov. " Probably he is thinking of nothing at all. As Madame Radcliffe [1] frequently reminds us, the Russian *muzhik* is an unknown quantity. Does *any* one understand him? He does not even understand himself."

" There you go again! " began Paul Petrovitch, but suddenly broke off to say in a still louder tone: " See what that fool Peter has done! Here comes my brother himself! "

Sure enough, on turning his head, Bazarov saw Nikolai Petrovitch's pale face peering from the *drozhki*. Nor had the vehicle come to a halt before Nikolai had sprung from the step, and rushed towards his brother.

" What is this? " he cried in agitated accents. " Evgenii Vasilitch, I beg of you to tell me what has happened."

" Nothing has happened," replied Paul Petrovitch in Bazarov's stead. " You are disturbing yourself to no purpose. I had a small quarrel with Monsieur Bazarov, and have paid a penalty as small."

[1] Ann Radcliffe, *née* Ward (1764-1823), an English novelist who wrote *The Mysteries of Udolpho* and other tales, and travelled extensively.

214

" But whence did it arise? For God's sake tell me! "

" What is there to say? It arose from the fact that Monsieur Bazarov spoke in disrespectful terms of Sir Robert Peel. I would hasten to add that, throughout, I alone was at fault, and that Monsieur Bazarov bore himself admirably—I being the challenger."

" But look at the blood! "

" Pshaw! Did you suppose my veins to run with water? As a matter of fact, the blood-letting will do me good. Is not that so, doctor? Help me to mount the *drozhki*, and away with melancholy! By to-morrow I shall be recovered. Splendid! That is the way to do it. Right away, coachman! "

When on the point of starting homewards in the wake of the *drozhki*, Nikolai Petrovitch perceived Bazarov to be for remaining behind.

" Evgenii Vasilitch," he said, " I would beg of you to attend my brother until a doctor can be procured from the town."

Bazarov nodded in silence.

An hour later Paul Petrovitch was reposing in bed with his leg neatly and artistically bandaged. The whole house was in a turmoil, Thenichka greatly upset, and Nikolai able to do nothing but wring his hands. The sick man, on the contrary, laughed and jested, especially with Bazarov, and, to meet the occasion, had donned a fine linen shirt, an elegant morning jacket, and a Turkish fez. Lastly, he forbade any one to close the shutters, and kept venting humorous protests against the necessity of abstaining from food.

Towards nightfall, however, fever supervened, and his head began to ache; with the result that when the doctor arrived from the town (Nikolai Petrovitch had disobeyed his brother in this respect, and Bazarov also had consented to his doing so, in that, after paying the patient a single visit, and that a very brief one, and being put

215

to the mortification of having to avoid Thenichka on two occasions when he met her, he had felt that he preferred to spend the rest of the day in loneliness, bitterness, and rancour)—when the doctor arrived from the town he advised a cooling draught, but at the same time confirmed Bazarov's opinion that no danger was to be apprehended. In passing, it may also be mentioned that, on being informed by Nikolai Petrovitch that Paul Petrovitch's wound had been self-inflicted through an accident, the said doctor replied " H'm! "; to which, on receiving into his hand a fee of twenty-five roubles, he added that of course things of the kind often occurred.

No one in the house, that night, retired to bed, or even undressed, but at intervals Nikolai Petrovitch would tiptoe into his brother's room, and as silently withdraw. At intervals, too, Paul Petrovitch would awake from a doze, sigh faintly, and say to Nikolai either " *Couchez-vous* " or " Please give me a drink." But once it happened that Nikolai sent the invalid a glass of lemonade by the hand of Thenichka; and this time Paul Petrovitch scanned her long and searchingly before draining the tumbler to the dregs. Towards morning the fever increased a little, and a trace of lightheadedness made its appearance which for a while caused the patient only to utter disconnected words. But suddenly he opened his eyes, and, on seeing his brother bending solicitously over the bed, murmured:

" Nikolai, do not you think that Thenichka slightly resembles Nelly? "

" What Nelly, Paul? Who is Nelly? "

" How can you ask? The Princess R., of course. In the upper portion of the face especially Thenichka resembles her. *C'est de la même famille.*"

Nikolai Petrovitch made no reply. He could only remain lost in wonder that bygone fancies could so survive in the human consciousness.

" That *this* should have cropped up again! " he reflected.

On another occasion Paul Petrovitch muttered as he clasped his hands behind his head: " How I love this idle existence! " And again, a few minutes later, he whispered: " I will not allow a single rascal to touch me! "

Nikolai Petrovitch sighed. To whom the words referred he had not a notion.

At eight o'clock next morning Bazarov entered Nikolai's room. His stock of insects, birds, and frogs had either been packed up or liberated.

Rising to meet him, Nikolai said:

" So you have come to say good-bye? "

" I have."

" I understand your feelings, and I commend them. I know that my poor brother alone was to blame, and is now paying the penalty. Also, I gather from what he says that your position was such that you could not possibly have acted otherwise than as you did— that for you to have avoided this duel would have been impossible. That being so, we must attribute the mischance to the—er—standing antagonism of your views " (here Nikolai Petrovitch tripped over his words a little). " My brother is one of the old school, a man of hot temper and great persistency. Consequently we have God to thank that things have turned out no worse. Finally I may say that every possible precaution against publicity has been taken."

" Quite so," said Bazarov carelessly. " But I will leave my address with you, in case of anything occurring."

" I hope that nothing *will* occur. Indeed, my one regret is that your stay in my house should have—should have terminated in such a fashion. And I am the more grieved in that Arkady——"

217

"I expect to be seeing him very soon," interrupted Bazarov, whom "explanations" or "speeches" of any kind always roused to fever pitch. "On the other hand, should I *not* do so, pray convey to him my greetings and my regrets."

"I will," said Nikolai Petrovitch with a bow; but even before he had finished Bazarov had left the room.

Paul Petrovitch, too, as soon as he heard that Bazarov was on the point of departing, expressed a desire to see him, and to shake hands with him. Yet Bazarov remained as cold as ice, for well he knew that Paul Petrovitch's only aim was to make a show of "magnanimity," while to Thenichka he did not say good-bye at all—he merely exchanged with her a glance as she peeped from one of the windows. Her face looked to him careworn.

"Before long she will either trip or elope," he reflected.

On the other hand, Peter was so moved at the prospect of parting with his patron that he wept on the latter's shoulder until his transports were cooled with the question: "Surely your eyes are not made of water?" while Duniasha's emotion was such that she had to take refuge in a thicket. Meanwhile the cause of all this grief mounted the travelling-cart, and lit a cigar; and even when he had travelled four versts, and reached a spot where a turn in the road brought the Kirsanov farm into line with the new manor-house, he merely expectorated some tobacco juice, and muttered, as he wrapped himself closer in his cloak: "The cursed tomnoddies!"

Thenceforth Paul Petrovitch began to mend, but still was ordered to keep his bed for another week. What he called his "imprisonment" he bore with very fair patience, although he remained fussy in the matter of his toilet, and constantly had himself sprinkled with eau-de-Cologne. Meanwhile Nikolai Petrovitch read aloud to him the newspapers, and Thenichka served him with soup, lemonade, scrambled eggs, and tea. Yet she never entered the room without feeling a mysterious nervousness come over her. Paul Petrovitch's unexpected behaviour had frightened every one in the house, but her it had frightened most of all. Only old Prokofitch seemed undismayed at the occurrence, and kept asserting that, in his day, " the gentry used to bore holes in one another right enough, but only the gentry. Jackanapes like that Bazarov would have been ducked in the gutter for their pains."

Thenichka felt little pricking of conscience, but there were times when the thought of the true cause of the quarrel rendered her at least uneasy, and the more so because Paul Petrovitch's way of looking at her was now so strange that, even when she turned her back to him, she could still feel his eyes upon her. In combination, therefore, her worries led to her growing thinner, and also (as often happens in such circumstances) to her adding to her beauty.

At length, one morning, Paul Petrovitch felt so much better that he left his bed, and removed to the sofa; while Nikolai Petrovitch, after seeing that he had all he wanted, betook himself to the farm. Also, it fell to Thenichka's lot to take the invalid a cup of tea; and when she had placed it on the table, she was about to withdraw, when Paul Petrovitch requested her to remain.

" Why should you hurry away? " he said. " Is it that you have other things to do? "

" No—yes. That is to say, I have to go and pour out tea for the servants."

" Duniasha can do that. Surely you will stay awhile with a sick man who has something of great importance to say to you? "

Silently she seated herself on the edge of a chair.

" Listen," he continued, as he tugged at his moustache.

219

" For some time past I have been wanting to ask you why you are so afraid of me? "

" Afraid of you? "

" Yes; for you never look at me. In fact, one would think that your conscience was uneasy."

Her face reddened, but she looked Paul Petrovitch straight in the eyes. Somehow his aspect struck her as peculiar, and her heart began to throb.

" Is your conscience clear? " he asked.

" Yes, Why should it not be? " she responded in a whisper.

" I do not know. Certainly I can recall no one against whom you can have committed a fault. Against me? It is scarcely probable. Against others in this house? That is as improbable. Against my brother? But him you love, do you not? "

" I do."

" With your whole heart and soul? "

" With my whole heart and soul."

" Really and truly, Thenichka? " (never before had he addressed her thus). " Look me in the eyes. To lie is a terrible sin. You know that, of course? "

" But I am *not* lying, Paul Petrovitch. Did I not love Nikolai Petrovitch, I should not want to live."

" And you would exchange him for no one else? "

" *Whom* should I exchange him for? "

" I do not know. Surely not for the gentlemen who has just left us? "

Thenichka rose to her feet.

" Why should you torment me in this way? " she cried. " What have I done that you should speak to me so? "

" Thenichka," came the mournful reply, " I speak to you in this manner for the reason that I saw——"

" You saw what? "

" I saw *you*—in the lilac arbour."

220

She blushed to her ears, to the very roots of her hair.

" But how was I to blame? " at length she contrived to say.

Paul Petrovitch raised himself on the sofa.

" You swear, do you, that you were *not* to blame? " he said. " That you were not in the slightest degree to blame? Not at all? "

" I love Nikolai Petrovitch," came the reply, delivered with sudden energy and a rising sob, " and never shall I love any other man. As for what you saw, before the Throne of Judgment I swear that I am innocent, that I have always been so, and that I would rather die than be suspected of having deceived Nikolai Petrovitch, my benefactor."

Her voice failed her. Then, behold! she felt Paul seize and press her hand! Turning her head, she looked down at him—and stood almost petrified. For his face was even paler than usual, his eyes were glistening, and —most surprising thing of all!—a great tear was trickling down his cheek!

" Thenichka," he whispered in a voice which hardly seemed his own, " I beg of you always to love, and never to cease loving, my brother. He is such a good, kind fellow as has not his equal in the world. Never desert him for another; never listen to any tales which you may hear of him, but reflect how terrible it would be for him to love and not to be loved ! Yes, think well, Thenichka, before ever you forsake him."

Thenichka's amazement caused her eyes almost to start from her head, and her nervousness completely to vanish. Judge, also, of her surprise when, though he did not draw her to himself, nor kiss her, Paul Petrovitch raised her hand to his lips, and then burst into a convulsive fit of sobbing!

" God in Heaven! " she thought to herself. " What if this should make him have another fainting fit ? "

221

Meanwhile, in that one moment Paul Petrovitch was living over again a past phase of his ruined life.

Presently hurried footsteps were heard causing the staircase to creak; and just as Paul pushed Thenichka away from him and replaced his head upon the pillow, the door opened, and Nikolai Petrovitch—fresh, ruddy, and smiling—entered with little Mitia. The latter, equally fresh and ruddy, was leaping in Nikolai's arms, and pressing his tiny, naked feet against the buttons of his father's rural smock.

Running to father and child, Thenichka threw her arms around both alike, and sank her head upon the former's shoulder. This caused him to halt in amazement, for never before had the bashful, reserved Thenichka shown him any endearment in the presence of a third person.

"What is the matter?" he exclaimed, Then he glanced at Paul, handed Mitia to Thenichka, and, approaching the bedside, inquired if his brother were worse.

Paul's face was buried in his handkerchief, but he replied:

"Oh dear no. Not at all. If anything, I am better— yes, very much better."

"Nevertheless you have been over-hasty in removing to the sofa," said Nikolai Petrovitch; after which he turned to ask Thenichka why she was leaving the room, but she departed abruptly, and closed the door behind her.

"I had come to show you my little rascal," Nikolai continued. "He had been pining for a sight of his uncle. But she has carried him away for some reason. What is the matter? Has something occurred?"

"My brother," replied Paul Petrovitch—and as he uttered the words Nikolai Petrovitch gave a start, and felt ill at ease, he knew not why. "My brother, pray

222

give me your word of honour that you will fulfil the request which I am going to make."

" What request, Paul? I beg of you to continue."

" A request of the first importance. Upon it, I believe, your entire happiness depends. Also, what I am going to say represents the fruit of much thought. My brother, the request is that you will do your duty, the duty of a good and honourable man. In other words, I beseech you to put an end to this scandal and bad example, which is unworthy of you, unworthy of a man who is the best of souls."

" To what do you refer, Paul? "

" To this. You ought to *marry* Thenichka. She loves you, and is the mother of your child."

Stepping back, Nikolai Petrovitch clasped his hands together.

" Do *you* say this? " he exclaimed. " Do *you* say this —*you* whom I have always understood to be opposed to such unions? Do *you* say this? Surely you know that solely out of respect for yourself have I hitherto refrained from doing what rightfully you call my duty? "

" Wrongfully, then, have you respected me," said Paul Petrovitch with a sad smile. " In fact, almost I am beginning to think that Bazarov was right when he accused me of only feigning the aristocratic instinct. For it is not enough for you and me to trouble ourselves about worldly matters alone. We are old men past our prime, who ought to lay aside all pettinesses, and to fulfil strictly our obligations. Nor forget that, should we thus act, we shall receive an added measure of happiness as our reward."

Nikolai Petrovitch flung himself upon his brother, and embraced him again and again.

" You have opened my eyes," he cried. " When I described you as the best man in the world I was not wrong: and now I perceive your wisdom to be equal to your magnanimity."

" Quieter, quieter! " advised Paul. " Do not further inflame the leg of an old fool who, at fifty, has fought a duel like a young ensign. Then the matter is settled, and Thenichka is to become my *belle-sœur* ? "

" Yes, my dearest Paul. But what will Arkady say ? "

" Arkady ? He will be delighted. True, marriage does not come within his purview or principles, but at least his sense of social equality will be tickled. And, in the nineteenth century, what does caste matter ? "

" Paul, Paul, let me embrace you once more. You need not be afraid. I will do it very carefully." And the two brothers flung their arms around one another.

" Well ? " continued Paul Petrovitch. " What think you ? Shall we tell her at once ? "

" No, we need not be in too much of a hurry," replied Nikolai Petrovitch. " As a matter of fact, you have been having a talk with her, have you not ? "

" I have been having a talk with her ? *Quelle idée !* "

"However, your first business is to recover. Thenichka will not run away, and in the meanwhile the affair must be carefully considered."

" Then you have decided upon it ? "

" Certainly I have! And I thank you with all my heart. But I must leave you for a while now, for you ought to have some rest, and any excitement is bad for you. Matters can be discussed later. Go to sleep, dearest of brothers, and may God restore you to health! "

" Why did he thank *me* ? " thought Paul Petrovitch to himself after Nikolai had gone. " Does not the affair depend upon him alone, seeing that, after the marriage, I myself shall have to depart elsewhere—to Dresden or to Florence, and to abide there until I die? "

He bathed his forehead with eau-de-Cologne, and then closed his eyes. As he lay with his handsome, refined head resting on the pillow, he looked, in the clear light of the sun, like a corpse.

224

XXV

In the shade of a tall ash tree in the garden at Nikolsköe Katia and Arkady were seated on a bench. Beside them, on the ground, lay Fifi—his lengthy body twisted into the curve known to sporting folk as " the hare's crouch." Neither from Arkady nor from Katia was a word proceeding. Arkady was holding in his hands a half-opened book, and she was picking a few crumbs from a basket, and throwing them to a small family of sparrows which, with the timid temerity of their tribe, were chirping and hopping at her very feet. A faint breeze was stirring the leaves of the ash tree, and dappling Fifi's tawny back and the dark line of the pathway with a number of wavering circles of pale golden light; but Arkady and Katia were wholly in shade, save that an occasional streak glanced upon, and gleamed in, her hair. Just for the reason that the pair were silent and side by side was there present to their consciousness a *camaraderie* which, while causing neither to have the other definitely in mind, pleased each with the sense of the other's propinquity. The expression of both is changed since last we saw them. Arkady's face wears a staider air, and Katia looks more animated and less retiring.

At length, however, Arkady spoke.

" Do you not think," he said, " that our Russian term *yasen* is particularly suitable to the ash tree? For no other tree cleaves the air with such airy brightness."[1]

Katia looked up.

" I agree," she replied, while Arkady proudly reflected: " At all events *she* does not reprove me for talking in ' beautiful language.' "

[1] *Yasen* is derived from the adjective *yasni*, meaning clear or bright.

" By the way," Katia continued with a glance at the book in his hands, " I cannot say that I always approve of Heine. I like him neither when he is laughing nor when he is in tears—I like him only when he is meditative and languid."

" Well, *I* like him when he is laughing," Arkady remarked.

" Then still there survives in you a trace of your old satirical tendency. Still your reformation needs to be completed."

" Indeed? " thought Arkady. " My satirical tendency? Oh, that Bazarov could have heard that! "

While aloud he said:

" Who is ' we '? Yourself? "

" Oh dear no! My sister, and Porfiri Platonitch, with whom you no longer quarrel, and my aunt, whom, three days ago, you escorted to church."

" I did so only because I could not refuse. And as regards Anna Sergievna, kindly remember that, in many things, she agrees with Bazarov."

" Yes, she used to be greatly under his influence, and so did you."

" And so did I? Then am I now emancipated from that influence? "

Katia returned no reply.

" I know that you never liked him," Arkady continued.

" Did I not? It was not for me to judge him."

" Never do I hear that reply without declining to believe it. There is not a person living whom *all* of us have not the right to judge. A disclaimer of that kind always represents an excuse."

" To tell the truth, I disliked him less than I felt him to be a stranger to me—as complete a one as I to him— or you either, for that matter."

" What do you mean? "

" I mean that—well, how can I express it? That,

whereas he was a wild bird, you and I are tame ones."

" *I* am a tame one? "

Katia nodded assent. Arkady scratched his ear.

" Look here," he said. " I may tell you that that constitutes, in essence, an insult."

" Why so? Do you *want* to be a wild bird? "

" Not necessarily a wild one, but at least one strong and energetic."

" You need wish no such thing. Your friend was both, yet he would rather have been otherwise.

" H'm! You believe that he used to exercise a considerable influence over Anna Sergievna? "

" Yes. But no one can hold a rein over her for long " Katia added this last *sotto voce*.

" What makes you think that? "

" The fact that she is very proud—rather, that she values her independence."

" Who does not? " queried Arkady, while there flashed through his mind the thought: " Why this mention of her? " Curiously enough, the same thought occurred to Katia too. But this was not so curious as might have been supposed, seeing that when young people meet in frequent and amicable converse, identical thoughts are apt to enter their brains.

Arkady smiled, edged nearer to Katia, and said in a whisper: " Confess that you are a little afraid of her."

" Of whom? "

" Of *her*," repeated Arkady meaningly.

" Are *you* afraid of her? " countered Katia.

" I am. Please note that I believe you to be the same." Katia raised a menacing finger.

" I am surprised at you! " she exclaimed. " Never at any time has my sister been better disposed towards you than she is now. She likes you considerably more than when you first came."

" Really? "

" Yes. And have you not noticed it? You ought to be pleased at the notion."

Arkady reflected.

" How I have contrived to win Anna Sergievna's good graces I do not know," at length he said. " Surely it cannot be because I brought her those letters which were written by your mother? "

" It is, though, and because of other reasons as well —reasons which I will forbear to mention."

" Why will you? "

" Because I will."

" Oh, I know your faculty for obstinacy."

" It is one which I possess."

" Also, your faculty for observing things."

Katia glanced at him. Then she inquired:

" Why lose your temper? What are you thinking of? "

" This: that I cannot understand how you come to possess those powers of observation which undoubtedly are yours. I understand it the less because you are so nervous and distrustful and shy of everybody and——"

" It is because I have lived such a lonely life. A life of that kind leads one to reflect in spite of oneself. Am I shy of *every* one, though? "

Arkady bestowed upon her an appreciative glance.

" Never mind," he said. " At all events it is not often that people in your position—I mean, people of your wealth—possess such a gift. To them, as to the Tsars, truth penetrates hardly."

" But I am *not* wealthy."

Arkady failed at first to follow her meaning, but reflected: " Certainly the property belongs to her sister, not to her." Nor was the thought wholly unpleasing— so little so that presently he added:

" You said that very prettily."

" I said what? "

228

" That you are not wealthy. You said it so simply, so without any false shame, so without the least *arrière pensée*. *Apropos*, the consciousness of the ordinary person who both knows and confesses that he or she is poor always seems to me to contain more than the mere words imply—it harbours also a touch of vanity."

" I have, thanks to my sister, had no experience of poverty. And as for my possessions, I mentioned them only because the words came of themselves to my lips."

" Quite so. Yet confess that you too harbour a grain of the vanity to which I have alluded."

" Give me an example of my doing so."

" An example? Well, may I ask why you have not married a rich man? "

" Were I to love such a one very much, I—— But no man of that sort has come my way: wherefore I have made no such marriage."

" There, now! " cried Arkady. " But why should you not do so in the future? "

" Because even the poets deprecate *mésalliances*."

" You mean that you wish either to rule or——? "

" Oh no! What good would that be? On the contrary, I am prepared to be ruled, even though I believe that inequality in any form works badly. A union of self-respect with submission—that is what I best understand, that is what spells true happiness. A mere subordinate existence is—well, something which I do not fancy."

" ' Something which I do not fancy,' " commented Arkady. " Yes, you are of the same blood as Anna Sergievna: you are as independent as she, and you are even more secretive. In fact, however deep-rooted and sacred a stock of sentiments you might hold, you would never, of your own accord, give them utterance."

" Of course! How could you suppose anything else? "

"Also, you are clever, and have a measure of character equal to, if not greater than, hers."

"I dislike being compared with my sister. You seem to have forgotten that she is both 'beautiful' and 'intellectual' and—— Moreover, you, above all people, ought not to say anything to her disparagement, and still less to say it seriously."

"Why 'you, above all people'? Do you think that I am jesting?"

"I am certain of it."

"Indeed? But what if I were to say that I really mean my words? What if I were to say that, if anything, I have under-expressed what is in my mind?"

"I fail to follow you."

"Do you? Your quickness of perception has been overrated."

"Why has it?"

Averting his head, Arkady returned no reply, while Katia fell to searching for the last crumbs in her basket, and throwing them to the sparrows. Unfortunately, the throw of her arm proved too strong, and the birds flew away without even touching the food offered them.

"Katia," said Arkady, "it may be that you look upon these things as matters of no moment. Kindly note, therefore, that neither for your sister nor for any other person would I exchange Mademoiselle Katerina Sergievna."

Rising, he walked away as though in sudden alarm at having allowed the words to escape his lips. Meanwhile Katia, with her hands resting upon the basket and her head bent, gazed after him. Gradually there crept into her cheeks a rosy tint; and though her lips were not smiling, and her dark eyes contained a hint of perplexity, there lurked also in her expression another unexpressed feeling.

"Are you alone?" said Anna Sergievna's voice from

230

behind her. " I thought that Arkady came with you into the garden? "

Katia slowly raised her eyes to her sister (tastefully, and even showily, dressed, the latter was standing on the path, and engaged in stirring Fifi's ears with the point of an open parasol), and as slowly replied:

" Yes—I am alone."

" So I see," commented Madame with a smile. " He has gone indoors, I suppose? "

" Probably."

" And you have been reading with him? "

" I have."

Anna Sergievna took Katia under the chin, and raised her face towards her own.

" You have not quarrelled, I hope? " she said.

" Oh no," said Katia, and quietly put away her sister's hand.

" What solemn replies! Well, I came here to propose a walk, since he is always asking me to go one. But, to pass to another subject, some shoes have arrived for you from the town, so you had better go and try them on. Only yesterday I was noticing how shabby your old ones are. In general, you do not take sufficient pains in such matters, for you have charming feet, and also not ugly hands, even though a trifle too large. You ought to take care of your feet. When you are here you do not do so sufficiently."

Madame passed onwards with a light rustle of her handsome gown, while Katia rose from the bench, and, taking the volume of Heine, departed in another direction—though *not* to try on the boots.

" ' You have charming feet,' " she repeated to herself as she tripped up the sun-baked steps of the terrace. " ' You have charming feet.' Well, before long some one shall be at them."

Confusion then overcame her, and she took the remaining steps at a bound.

231

Meanwhile Arkady made for his room. As he was passing through the hall he was overtaken by the butler, and informed that Monsieur Bazarov was awaiting him above.

"Evgenii Vasilitch?" exclaimed Arkady in a tone very much as of alarm. "Has he been here long?"

"A few minutes only. He instructed me not to announce him to Madame but to take him straight to your room."

"I hope that nothing unfortunate has occurred at home," reflected Arkady as he ran up the stairs and opened the door of the bedroom. But the first sight of Bazarov's face reassured him, even though a more experienced eye might have detected in the features of the unlooked-for guest certain signs that inward turmoil underlay their usual rigidity. Clad in a dust cloak and a travelling cap, he was seated on the window-sill, and did not rise even when, rushing towards him with exclamations of astonishment, and fussing to and fro like a man who believes himself to be overjoyed, as well as desires other people to believe it, Arkady cried:

"What a surprise! What has brought you here? Surely everything at home is well, and all are in good health?"

"Everything at your home is well," said Bazarov; "but all are not in good health. However, if your brains are not hopelessly wandering, first tell them to bring me some *kvass*, and then sit down and listen to my few but, I hope, well-chosen words."

This quieted Arkady, and upon that Bazarov told him of the duel with Paul Petrovitch. The recital finished, Arkady stood amazed, as well as distressed. But this he did not think it necessary to state—he merely inquired whether his uncle's wound were really a harmless one, and, on receiving the reply that it was of a nature uninteresting from every but the medical

232

point of view, forced a smile. Yet all the while he felt secretly hurt, and also secretly ashamed. This Bazarov seemed to divine.

" See," he said, " what comes of consorting with feudal folk! Should one's lot be cast among them, inevitably one gets drawn into their knightly tourneys. Being on my way to my parents' place, I have turned aside to——But no; I will not be guilty of a foolish and useless lie. The real reason why I have turned aside is that—oh, the devil only knows why! Times there are when a man ought to take himself by the scruff of the neck, and uproot himself like a radish from a garden border. That is what *I* did when I was last here. But, since, a longing has come upon me to take just another peep at all that I then forsook—to view once more the border where I used to grow."

" By the words ' all that I then forsook ' I hope that you do not mean myself as well? " cried Arkady anxiously. " Do not say that you intend to sever me also from your friendship? "

Bazarov looked at him. He did so fixedly, almost sharply.

" Would the eventuality distress you? " he inquired. " Rather, it is you who have forsaken me, O verdant and transparent soul. *Inter alia*, I hope that your affair with Anna Sergievna is progressing? "

" My ' affair with Anna Sergievna '? "

" For her sake, was it not, you came hither from the town? Ah, tender young chicken of mine, what about those Sunday Schools? Come, come! Do not tell me that you are not in love with her. Or have you at last learnt to be secretive? "

" Always I have been frank with you, as you know; wherefore pray believe me when I say—I call God to witness that it is true—that your surmises are mistaken."

" Truly a new song! " remarked Bazarov *sotto voce.*

233

" But do not disturb yourself: it is all one to me. Certainly, a Romanticist would have said: ' Our roads are beginning to diverge '; but *I* say no more than that clearly we have no further use for one another."

" Oh, Evgenii! "

" Dear lad, it is no misfortune. At all times is something in the world finding out that it has no use for something else. So we must say good-bye. Ever since I arrived in this place I have been feeling as uncomfortable as a Governor's lady when she hears a work of Gogol's read aloud. In fact, I did not order my horses to be unharnessed."

" But you cannot act like this! "

" Why not ? "

" Because, apart from my own feelings, such a speedy departure would be the height of rudeness to Anna Sergievna. I know that she would like to see you."

" No, she would not."

" I am positive that she would. Why pretend like this ? Are you going to say that it is not for her sake alone that you are here ? "

" You have grounds for that surmise, yet I say that you are wrong."

But Arkady proved to be right, for Anna Sergievna really desired to see Bazarov, and, through the butler, sent him word to that effect. After tidying his costume, therefore, and tucking his new great-coat under his arm (in readiness to depart as soon as the interview should be concluded), he went downstairs, and was received, not in the room where he had unexpectedly disclosed his passion, but in the drawing-room. Anna Sergievna's manner, as she offered him the tips of her fingers, was pleasant enough, yet her face betrayed involuntary tension.

" To begin with," Bazarov hastened to say, " allow me to reassure you. You see before you a corpse which

has long returned to its senses, and is also not destitute
of hope that others have forgotten its folly. I am unlikely to see you again for an extended period, but,
though (as you know) I am not given to sentiment, I feel
that I should like to bear away with me the thought that
my image still fills your mind with aversion."

She caught at her breath like a person who has just
arrived at the summit of a lofty mountain. Then her face
lightened into a smile, and, offering Bazarov her hand a
second time, she allowed it to respond to the pressure of
his.

" When sorrow is asleep, do not wake it," she said.
" And the less so since my conscience convicts me, if not
of coquetry on that occasion, at all events of something
else. One word more. Let us be friends again. For it was
all a dream, was it not? And who remembers dreams?"

" Who indeed? And love—well, love is a mere
empirical sentiment."

" I am glad to hear you say so."

Thus Anna Sergievna, and thus Bazarov. And both
conceived themselves to be speaking the truth. But was
it the truth?—at all events, the whole truth? The
speakers themselves did not know, and therefore the
author does not. Nevertheless both the man and the
woman framed their words to create an atmosphere of
mutual confidence.

Next Anna Sergievna asked Bazarov how he had spent
his time at the Kirsanovs'; and though he came within
an ace of telling her of the duel with Paul Petrovitch, he
checked himself in time, and replied that he had been
engaged in work.

" And I," she said, " have been, for some unknown
reason, out of humour, and meditating going abroad;
but the fit is passing now (thanks to the arrival of your
friend Arkady Nikolaievitch), and already I find myself
relapsing into my old rut, and resuming my true rôle."

" And what is your true rôle? "

" The rôle of acting as aunt or preceptress or mother—call it what you like—to my sister. In passing, I wonder if you are aware that once upon a time I did not altogether understand your close friendship with Arkady Nikolaievitch? Somehow he seemed too insignificant for you. But now, I know him better, and have convinced myself that in his head there is a brain. Above all things, he is young, young—not like you and myself, Evgenii Vasilitch."

" But he is still shy in your presence? " queried Bazarov.

" He——" began Anna Sergievna; then, checking herself, continued: " No; he is gaining confidence, and has taken to talking to me quite freely; whereas once upon a time, though I did not seek his company, he used to flee whenever I came near him. By the way, he is great friends with Katia."

Somehow this irritated Bazarov.

" Never can a woman forbear dissembling," was his reflection. Aloud he said with a frigid smile: " Then you say that he used to flee from you? But surely it cannot be a secret that formerly he cherished for you *une grande passion*? "

" What? He too? "

" Yes, he too," affirmed Bazarov with a nod. " But I think that you knew that? It was not a piece of news that I have just told you? "

Her eyes became fixed upon the floor.

" I believe you to be wrong," she observed.

" So do not I. But perhaps I ought not to have mentioned it? " To himself he added: " And perhaps you will not, in future, play the hypocrite with me."

" Why should you not have mentioned it? " she queried. " As a matter of fact, I believe you to be attaching importance to a mere passing impression, and shall soon think that you have a tendency to exaggerate."

"Suppose we talk of something else?" he suggested.

"For what reason?"

However, of her own accord she diverted the conversation into another channel. True, she had assured him, and she herself believed, that everything was buried in the past; yet she felt ill at ease, and conscious that, even while jesting or exchanging the merest of *bagatelles*, she had weighing upon her a nervous oppression. In fact, it was akin to the case of passengers afloat. Though such folk will laugh and talk with the same apparent indifference as on land, let but the machinery stop, or the least sign of anything unusual appear, and at once every face will display that peculiar expression of anxiety which comes only of constant knowledge of ever-present danger.

Of similar sort was Anna Sergievna's interview with Bazarov; nor was it prolonged, in that soon she began to feel so absent-minded, and to answer with such vagueness, that she proposed a move to the hall, where there were found Katia and the Princess.

"And where is Arkady Nikolaievitch?" inquired the hostess; and, on being told that he had not been seen for over an hour, she sent messengers to summon him. But this proved a lengthy task, seeing that he had withdrawn to the remotest corner of the garden, and, sitting with chin upon hands, was plunged in thought. Those thoughts were important and profound, but not sad; and though he knew that Anna Sergievna was alone with Bazarov, he felt none of his old jealousy, but, rather, gazed before him with quiet cheerfulness—with an air as though something had pleased and surprised him, and led him to arrive at a certain decision.

XXVI

ALTHOUOH the late Monsieur Odintsov had disliked "innovations," he had not been opposed to the indulgence of "a certain play of refined taste," and had erected, in a space between the hothouses and the lake, a building modelled in the style of a Greek temple, but consisting of undeniable Russian bricks. Also, he had caused to be inserted in the massive rear wall of this temple or gallery six niches for six statues which were designed to represent Solitude, Silence, Thought, Melancholy, Modesty, and Sensibility, and which he had purposed to import from abroad; but only one of these, the statue of the Goddess of Silence, with a finger to her lips, had actually been delivered and erected; and even of that the household underlings had knocked off the nose on the very day of the statue's arrival. True, a neighbouring sculptor had offered to furnish the goddess with a nose "twice as good as the last one," but Odintsov had none the less ordered her removal to a corner of the millhouse, where for several years past she had acted as a source of superstitious awe to the peasant women of the district. Likewise, the front wall of the temple had become so overgrown with bushes that only the capitals of the supporting columns remained visible above the mass of verdure, and even at midday the interior of the building was cool and pleasant; and though Anna Sergievna had never really liked the place since the day when she had discovered an adder there, Katia paid it frequent visits, and, seating herself on a great stone bench which was fixed under one of the niches, would read or work, or surrender herself to the influence of that perfect restfulness which, known, probably, to every one, comes of a silent, half-unconscious contemplation of the great waves of life as they break for ever around and against us.

On the morning after Bazarov's arrival Katia was in her usual position on the bench, and beside her was Arkady—he having specially asked her to accompany him thither.

Though an hour was still wanting to luncheon time, the dew and the freshness of the morning had already given place to the sultriness and the aridity of noontide. Arkady's face yet bore the expression of yesterday, but Katia's features were stamped with one, rather, of depression. This was because after breakfast her sister had called her into the boudoir, and to some of those blandishments which always alarmed the girl had added a word of advice that Katia should observe more caution in her converse with Arkady, and, above all things, avoid such solitary *tête-à-têtes* with him as appeared to have aroused the attention of the household in general, and of the Princess in particular. Since the previous evening Anna Sergievna had been out of humour; and inasmuch as Katia's conscience was not wholly clear of responsibility in the matter, she had intimated, when yielding to Arkady's request, that it must be for the last time.

" Katia," he began with a sort of easy uneasiness, " since the day when I had the good fortune to reside under the same roof as yourself I have talked to you on many different subjects. But one particular question has for me a paramount importance: nor upon that question have I yet touched. Yesterday you said that during my stay here I have undergone a process of reformation "—he neither sought nor avoided Katia's eye — " and, to be frank, such a reformation has, in part at least, come about. Better than any one else do you know that this is so—you to whom, above all others, that remaking is due."

" To me ? " she re-echoed.

" Yes, to you," Arkady repeated. " No longer am I
the presumptuous lad who came here a short while ago:
not for nothing have I attained my twenty-third year.
And though I still wish to be of use in life, though I still
wish to consecrate the whole of my faculties to the service of Truth, I no longer seek my ideals where I was
wont to do—they appear to me to stand much nearer
home. Hitherto I have been in ignorance of myself,
hitherto I have set myself tasks beyond my powers;
but now, through a certain feeling which is within me,
my eyes have become opened. By the way, the manner
in which I express myself may be lacking in clarity, yet
I venture to hope that I have made myself understood ? "

Katia said nothing; but she ceased to look at the
speaker.

" In my opinion," he went on in a tone of rising emotion, while in a birch tree overhead a chaffinch started
pouring forth a flood of unstudied song, "in my opinion,
it is the duty of an honourable man to be frank with
those who, with those who—in short, with those who
stand nearest to him in life. Consequently I, I am
minded to—to——"

Here Arkady's eloquence failed him. He stumbled
and stuttered and had to pause for a moment. Meanwhile
Katia's eyes remained lowered. One would have thought
that she did not in the least understand this preamble,
but was expecting to hear something quite of a different
nature.

" That I shall surprise you I know in advance," continued Arkady, once more spurring his faculties. " And
that surprise will be the greater when I tell you that the
feeling to which I have alluded concerns, to a certain
extent—yes, to a certain extent, yourself. For yesterday, you will remember, you imputed to me a lack of
gravity "—he was speaking much like a man who,
having blundered into a bog, feels that at each step he

sinks deeper and deeper, yet struggles on in the hope of eventually extricating himself—" and such a reproach is all too often levelled against, all too often falls upon, young people who have ceased to deserve it. Were I but possessed of more self-confidence " ("God help me! God help me! " he thought despairingly, but Katia did not even turn her head)—" had I but the right to hope that——"

" Did I but feel sure that you really mean what you say," broke in, at this moment, the clear accents of Anna Sergievna.

Arkady became dumb, and Katia turned pale; for along a little path which skirted the bushes screening the temple there were advancing Bazarov and Madame! Katia and Arkady could not actually see the pair, yet they could hear every word uttered, and even catch the sound of their breathing, and the rustle of Anna Sergievna's dress. Advancing a few more steps, the couple halted, and remained standing in front of the building.

" It is like this," Anna Sergievna continued. " You and I have blundered into an error. That is to say, while neither of us is in the heyday of youth—I so least of the two—and both of us have lived our lives and are weary, we are also (for I need not stand on ceremony) individuals of intellect. Consequently, though, at first, we interested one another, and felt our mutual curiosity aroused, it happened that subsequently——"

" That subsequently I grew stale in your eyes," hazarded Bazarov.

" Oh no! That that was not the cause of the situation you are well aware. But, whatever the cause, you and I have not a *compelling need* of one another. Therein lies the point. In other words, both of us have in us—how shall I express it?—both of us are too mutually *akin*. We were slow to grasp that fact. Now, Arkady——"

" Have you a ' compelling need ' of him? " put in Bazarov.

" For shame, Evgenii Vasilitch! You yourself have averred that he is not wholly indifferent to me; and I too have long suspected that he cherishes for me at least a measure of admiration. As we are on the subject, I will not attempt to conceal from you that of late the fact that I am old enough to be his aunt has not prevented me from devoting to him more of my thoughts than I used to do. In his fresh young sentimentality there is a certain charm."

" The term ' fascination ' comes handier in such cases," said Bazarov in the deep, quiet tone which, with him, always signified sarcasm. " As a matter of fact, I found Arkady secretive yesterday—he made but the scantiest of references either to you or your sister. That constitutes an important symptom."

" Katia and he are brother and sister to one another," said Madame. " Indeed I am pleased to see it—though perhaps I ought not to connive at so much familiarity."

" I presume that the element speaking in you is the sister? " drawled Bazarov.

" Of course! But need we stand here? Let us move on. We hold curious conversations, do we not? Indeed, to think of all the things which I now say to you! Yet I still fear you a little, even though I trust you as being, at heart, a good man."

" I am far from good; and you only call me so because I have lost all significance in your eyes. Ill boots it to weave chaplets for the head of a corpse."

" Evgenii Vasilitch, we cannot always command ourselves," came the sound of Anna Sergievna's next words; but the next moment the wind soughed, the leaves rustled, and the rest of what she was saying was carried away into the distance. Nothing beyond it save (after a pause) " You are free, are you not? " on

242

FATHERS AND SONS

the part of Bazarov could be distinguished. Then the sound of their footsteps died away, and once more complete silence reigned.

Turning to Katia, Arkady saw that she was sitting as before, but with her head more bent.

" Katerina Sergievna," he said tremulously, and with his hands clasped, " I shall love you always, and beyond recall; nor shall I ever love another woman. This is what I have been trying to say to you this morning, in the hope that I might ascertain your views, and then beg for your hand. I am not a rich man, but I would make any sacrifice for your sake. Come, then! Will you answer me? Will you trust me? Surely you do not think that I am speaking out of frivolity? Recall the past few days : may you not rest assured now that my remaining self (you know what I mean) is gone for ever? Come, look at me—look at me and speak but a word, a single word. I love you, I love you! Do not refuse to believe that I mean what I say."

Gravely, yet with a radiant look in her eyes, Katia raised her head, and, after a moment's thought, said with the trace of a smile: " *Yes.*"

Arkady leapt up.

" ' Yes'? You have said ' Yes,' Katia! But what do mean by that word? Do you mean that you believe in my love, or do you mean that——? No, no; I dare not finish the sentence."

Katia repeated only the word " Yes," but this time she left no room for misunderstanding. Arkady seized her large, but not unshapely, hands in his, and, panting with rapture, strained her to his breast. He could scarcely stand upon his feet—he could only keep repeating again and again: " Katia! Katia! " Meanwhile she shed a few innocent tears at which she smiled as they fell. The man who has not seen such tears in the eyes of his beloved does not know the height of

243

happiness to which, with mingled joy and gratitude and modesty, a woman can attain.

Next morning Anna Sergievna sent for Bazarov to her boudoir; and when he arrived she, with a forced smile, handed him a folded sheet of notepaper. That sheet represented a letter from Arkady, a letter in which he begged for her sister's hand.

Bazarov skimmed the epistle—then scarcely could forbear venting the rancour which blazed for a moment in his breast.

" It is as I said, you see," he commented. " Only yesterday you were telling me that his feeling for Katerina Sergievna was that of a brother for a sister! And what are you going to do? "

" What would you advise me to do? " she said, still smiling.

" I presume "—he also was smiling, although he was feeling as wholly out of spirits, as little inclined towards gaiety, as she was—" I presume that we have no choice but to bestow our blessing upon the young couple. In every respect it would be a good match, for his father has a nice little property, Arkady is the only son, and the father is too easy-going to be likely to raise any difficulty "

Madame Odintsov rose and paced the room for a moment or two — her face alternately flushing and turning pale.

" So that is what you think? " she said. " Well, I too see no impediment. Indeed, the affair rejoices me both for Katia's sake and for—yes, for his. But first I must await his father's consent; and for that purpose I will send Arkady himself to interview Nikolai Petro-vitch. . . . So I was right yesterday, was I not? I was right when I said that you and I are become elderly? How did I fail to foresee this? I am indeed surprised at it! "

244

Again she smiled, but, in the very act of smiling, turned away.

"Our young folk are indeed cunning," remarked Bazarov. After a pause he added:

"Good-bye now. I hope that the affair may develop well. From a distance I, too, shall rejoice."

She turned and faced him.

"Need you really go?" she asked. "Why not stay a little longer? Pray stay, for I find talking to you a stimulant—it is like walking on the edge of a precipice: at first one is afraid, then one gathers courage. Do not go."

"I thank you for the proposal, as also for your flattering estimate of my conversational powers," said Bazarov. "Nevertheless, I have tarried overlong in a sphere which is alien to my personality. Only for a while can flying fish support themselves in the air. Then they relapse into their natural element. Allow me to flop back into mine."

Yet a bitter laugh was twisting his pale features. She saw it, and felt sorry for him.

"The man still loves me," was her thought, and she extended a sympathetic hand.

He understood her, however.

"No, no!" he exclaimed as he withdrew a step or two. "Though poor, I have never yet accepted alms. Good-bye, and may your lot always be happy."

"Yet we shall meet again," she replied with an involuntary gesture. "Of that I am certain."

"Anything may occur in this world," he remarked—then bowed and was gone.

That afternoon he said to Arkady as he knelt down to pack his trunk:

"I hear that you are going to make a nest for yourself? And why should you not? It is an excellent course to take. But for you to dissemble is useless,

245

and I had scarcely expected that you would do so. Has the preoccupation of it all deprived you of your tongue?"

"When I left you at Marino I had no thought of this," said Arkady. "You are the dissembler, though, are you not? For when you say 'It is an excellent course to take,' you dissemble, as well as waste your time, seeing that I am well aware of your views on marriage."

"Merely my way of expressing myself. You see what I am doing at this moment. In my trunk is a vacant space. I am packing it with straw. And the same with life's trunk. To avoid leaving empty spaces therein we pad the interstices. You need not be offended. You cannot fail to remember what I really think of Katerina Sergievna. While some maidens earn cheap reputations by merely smiling at right moments, your *inamorata* can show more—indeed, so much more that soon you will be (and very properly) under her thumb."

Slapping down the lid of the trunk, Bazarov rose from the floor.

"Now, farewell," he said. "No, I will not deceive you: we are parting for ever, and you know it. In my opinion you have acted wisely, for you were not meant to live the hard, bitter, reckless life of Nihilism—you lack at once the necessary coolness and the necessary venom. But this is not to say that in you there is not a due measure of youthful spirit. What I mean is that that asset alone is not sufficient for the work. The *dvorianin* is powerless to progress beyond either well-bred effervescence or well-bred humility: and both sentiments are futile. For example, you have not yet been blooded, yet already you think yourself a man: whereas the two chief conditions of our existence are battle and bloodshed. Yes, the dust from our heels hurts your eyes, and the grime on our bodies makes you

246

feel dirty. In other words, although you derive a certain gratification from indulging in self-criticism, and think no small beer of yourself, you have failed to grow to our stature. To us such things are vanities. Tools of an altogether different kind are what we need for the task. Consequently I repeat that, though a fine young fellow enough, you are also just a little-minded, so-called ' liberal-minded ' *baritch* [1]—what my father calls a ' product of evolution.' "

" Evgenii," was Arkady's sad reply, " we are parting for ever, yet this is all that you have to say to me! "

Bazarov scratched his head.

" Something else I could say, Arkady," he replied. " But I will not say that something—it would savour too much of Romanticism. Get married as soon as you can, line your nest, and beget plenty of offspring. Nor will those offspring be altogether fools, seeing that they will be born in due season, and not when you and I were. . . . My horses are ready and I must depart. Of the rest of the household I have taken leave already. Shall we embrace once more, eh ? "

The tears gushed in torrents from Arkady's eyes as he flung himself upon his old friend and mentor.

" Ah, youth, youth! " commented Bazarov. " See what comes of being young! But before long, I know, Katerina Sergievna will have set things right. Yes, she will console you."

With a last good-bye he mounted the travelling cart, and, in the act of doing so, pointed to a pair of jackdaws which were sitting perched upon the stable roof.

" See! " he cried. " *There's* an instructive lesson for you! "

" What do you mean? " queried Arkady.

" What ? " was Bazarov's ejaculation. " Are you so ignorant of, or so forgetful of, natural history as not to

[1] A small squire.

know that the jackdaw is the most respected of family birds? Mark the good example before you. Farewell, señor! "

And with a clatter the cart started on its way

Nor was Bazarov mistaken, for, even before nightfall, Arkady, deep in conversation with Katia, had completely forgotten his vanished instructor. Moreover, already the young fellow was beginning to play second fiddle to his *fiancée* : which circumstance the girl, on realising, in no way felt surprised at. So it was arranged that on the following day he should depart for Marino to interview his father; and in the meanwhile, Anna Sergievna, having no desire to hamper the young couple, merely observed such a show of propriety as involved her not leaving them together for long, but at the same time keeping at a distance the Princess, who, since the tidings of the impending union, had been in a state of lachrymose rancour. For herself, Anna Sergievna had at first feared that the spectacle of the young people's happiness would prove too much for her; but now the contrary proved to be the case, and she not only failed to feel hurt at the spectacle, but even found that it interested her and eventually softened her—a consummation which brought both relief and regret.

" Bazarov was right," she reflected. " It was mere curiosity, mere love of ease, mere egoism, mere——"

" Children, is love an empirical sentiment? " once she asked of Arkady and Katia: but neither of the pair understood her meaning. Moreover, they were fighting a little shy of her, since they could not altogether forget the conversation which they had involuntarily overheard; but in time Anna Sergievna succeeded in overcoming also this timidity, and found the task the more easy to perform in that she had succeeded also in overcoming her disappointment.

XXVII

THE old Bazarovs' delight at their son's return was the greater in that the event was so unexpected. To such an extent did Anna Vlasievna fuss and flounce about the house that Vasili Ivanitch likened her to a hen partridge (no doubt the short tail of her blouse *did* impart to her rather a bird-like aspect); while, as regards Vasili himself, he grunted, and sucked the amber mouthpiece of his pipe, and, grasping the shank, inverted the bowl as though to make sure that it was secure, and, finally, parted his capacious lips, and gave vent to a noiseless chuckle.

" I am going to spend with you six whole weeks," said Bazarov. "But I desire to work, and therefore must not be disturbed."

" Before we will disturb you, you shall forget what my face looks like," replied Vasili Ivanitch.

And he kept his word; for, after allotting his son the study, he not only remained completely out of sight, but even prevented his wife from manifesting the least sign of tenderness.

" When Evgenii last visited us," he said to her, " you and I proved a little wearisome; so this time we must be more discreet."

Anna Vlasievna agreed, much as she lost by the arrangement, seeing that now she beheld her son only at meal times, and feared, even then, to speak to him.

" Eniushenka," she would begin—then, before he had had time to raise his eyes, pluck nervously at the strings of her cap, and whisper: " Oh no; it was nothing," and address herself, instead, to Vasili Ivanitch; saying, for instance (with cheek on hand as usual): " My dear,

249

which would our darling Eniusha prefer for dinner— cabbage soup or beef with horse-radish ? " And when Vasili Ivanitch would reply: " Why should you not ask him yourself ? " she would exclaim: " Oh no, for that might vex him."

But eventually Bazarov ceased to closet himself, in that there came an abatement of the work fever, and to it succeeded fits of depression, *ennui*, and an inordin- ate restlessness. In his every movement there began to loom a strange discontent, from his gait there dis- appeared its old firm, active self-confidence, and, ceasing to indulge in solitary rambles, he took to cultivating society, to attending tea in the drawing-room, to pacing the kitchen garden, and to joining Vasili Ivanitch in a silent smoking of pipes. Nay, on one occasion he even paid Father Alexis a visit!

At first the new order of things rejoiced Vasili Ivanitch's heart: but that joy proved short-lived.

" Though I could not say why, Eniusha makes me anxious," he confided to his spouse. " Not that he is discontented or ill-tempered—such things would not have mattered: rather, it is that he is sad and brooding, and never opens his lips. Would that he would curse you and me, for instance! Also, he is thinner; nor do I like the colour of his face."

" O God! " whispered the old woman. " Yet I may not even put my arms around his neck! "

From that time onwards Vasili Ivanitch began to make cautious attempts to question Bazarov concern- ing his work, his health, and his friend Arkady; but always Bazarov returned reluctant, indifferent replies, and once, when his father was for introducing the foregoing topics, said irritably:

" Why are you for ever tiptoeing around me? Your present manner is even worse than your former one."

" There, there—I did not mean anything," was poor Vasili Ivanitch's reply.

Political allusions proved equally fruitless. For instance, when Vasili Ivanitch was seeking to engage his son's interest on the score of the impending emancipation of the serfs and progress in general, the other muttered carelessly:

" Yesterday, when passing through the courtyard, I heard some peasant lads singing, not one of the good old songs, but ' The age of truth is coming in, when hearts shall glow with love.' There's progress for you! "

Occasionally Bazarov would repair to the village, and, in his usual bantering fashion, enter into conversation with some peasant.

" Well," he said to a *muzhik*, " pray expound to me your views on life. For they tell me that in you lie the whole strength and the whole future of Russia—that you are going to begin a new epoch in our history, and to give us both a real language and new laws."

The peasant made no reply at the moment. Then he said:

" We might do all that if first we had a new chapel here."

" Tell me something, though, about the world in general," Bazarov interrupted. " The world stands on three fishes, does it not? "

" It does that, *batiushka*," the peasant replied with the quiet, good-humoured sweetness of the patriarchal age. " But above it stands the will of the masters. The *baré* are our fathers, and the harder the *barin* drives, the better for the *muzhik*."

Shrugging his shoulders contemptuously at this statement, Bazarov turned away, while the peasant slunk off homewards.

" What did he say? " asked a sullen-looking, middle-aged peasant who had been standing at the door of his

251

hut during the course of the foregoing colloquy. " Was he talking of arrears of taxes? "

" Of arrears of taxes! " retorted the first peasant, his tone now containing not a trace of its late patriarchal sweetness, but, rather, a note of purely dry contempt. " He was chattering just for chattering's sake—he likes to hear his own tongue wag. Do not all of us know what a *barin* and the likes of him are good for? "

" Aye," agreed the second peasant; whereafter, with much nodding of caps and gesticulating of fists, they fell to discussing their own affairs and requirements. So alas for Bazarov's scornful shrug of the shoulders! And alas for that knowledge of the way in which the peasant should be talked to whereof the young Nihilist had made such boast when disputing with Paul Petrovitch! In fact, never had it dawned upon the mind of the self-confident Bazarov that, in the eyes of the *muzhik*, he was no better than a pease-pudding.

However, he succeeded in discovering for himself an occupation. This was when, in bandaging a peasant's leg, Vasili Ivanitch's hands shook a little through senility, and his son hastened to his assistance: and from that time forth Bazarov acted as Vasili Ivanitch's partner, even though he maintained unabated his ridicule both of the remedies which he himself advised and of the father who hastened to put them into practice. Yet in no way did his son's raillery annoy Vasili Ivanitch: rather, it heartened the old man. Smoking his pipe, and drawing his dirty overall in to his waist with both thumbs, he would listen delightedly to the scoffer, and chuckle, and show his blackened teeth the more in proportion as the sallies contained a greater measure of venom. Nay, stupid or simply senseless as many of these witticisms were, he would frequently catch them up, and repeat them. To take one instance, he, for several days in succession, kept assuring every one in

the village and in the town that " we call this the nine
o'clock office " — the sole basis being the fact that
once, on learning of his (Vasili Ivanitch's) habit of
attending Matins, Bazarov had made use of the phrase
in question.

" Thank God, Evgenii has ceased to mope," he confided in a whisper to his wife. " In fact, you should
have heard him rating me to-day! "

Also, the thought that he had such an assistant in his
labours filled the old man with pride.

" Yes, yes," he would say as he handed some peasant
woman in a man's jacket a phial of medicinal water or
a pot of cold cream, " you ought daily to thank God
that my son happens to be staying with me, since otherwise you could not possibly have been treated according to the latest and most scientific methods. Do you
understand? I say that even Napoleon, the Emperor
of the French, has not at his disposal a better physician
than my son."

And the peasant woman (who had come, it may be,
to complain of " a lifting with the gripes "—an expression which probably she herself could not have explained) would bow, then proffer the three or four eggs
which would be tied up in a corner of her neckcloth.

Also, when Bazarov extracted a tooth from the jaw
of a travelling pedlar, Vasili Ivanitch could not allow
even the very ordinary character of the tooth to prevent
him from preserving it as a rarity, and showing it to
Father Alexis.

" See what a fang! " he said. " And to think of the
strength which Evgenii must possess! He lifted the
pedlar clean from the ground! It was like uprooting
an oak tree! "

" Splendid! " was Father Alexis' comment—he knew
not what else to say, nor, for that matter, how else to
get rid of the enthusiastic veteran.

Lastly, there was an occasion when a peasant from a neighbouring village brought his brother to be treated. Suffering from typhus, the patient was lying face downwards on the straw in the cart, and had reached the last stage, since already his body was covered with spots of a hectic nature, and he had long lost consciousness. To an expression of regret that resort had not sooner been had to medical aid, Vasili Ivanitch could add no more than an intimation that no hope was left: nor was he wrong, seeing that even before the peasant succeeded in conveying his brother back to the village, the sick man had breathed his last.

Three days later Bazarov entered his father's room with an inquiry for some hell-stone.

" I have some," said Vasili Ivanitch; " but what do you want it for? "

" For the cauterisation of a wound."

" A wound on whom? "

" A wound on myself."

" On yourself? Let me see the place. Where is it? "

" There—on that finger. To-day I went to the village whence they brought the typhus patient the other day; and though they tried to conceal the body, I succeeded in discovering it. Not for a long time had I had a chance of doing that sort of work."

" Yes? "

" And the sequel was that I cut myself, and, on repairing to the district physician, found that he did not possess what I wanted."

Vasili Ivanitch went white to the lips. Hurrying, without a word, into his study, he returned thence with some hell-stone. Bazarov was for carrying it away forthwith.

" No, no! " cried Vasili Ivanitch. " For God's sake allow me to see to this in person."

Bazarov smiled.

254

" You are indeed a keen practitioner," he commented.

" Do not jest, I beg of you. Show me the finger. No, it is not a large wound. Am I hurting it at all ? "

" Not in the least. Have no fear. You can press it harder still if you like."

Vasili Ivanitch paused.

" Do you not think," he said, " that it would be better to cauterise the finger with an iron ? "

" No, I do not. Moreover, that ought, in any case, to have been done sooner; whereas by now even the hell-stone is unlikely to prove effectual, seeing that, as you know, once absorbed into the system, the germ renders all remedies too late."

" How ' too late '? " gasped Vasili Ivanitch.

" What I say. Four hours have elapsed since the injury."

Vasili Ivanitch gave the wound a further cauterisation.

" So the district physician had no hell-stone ? " he queried.

" None."

" God in heaven! To think of that man calling himself a doctor, yet being without such an indispensable remedy! "

" You should have seen his lancets! " remarked Bazarov. Then he left the room.

Throughout that evening and the next few days Vasili Ivanitch kept making every possible excuse to enter his son's room; and though he never actually referred to the wound—he even strove to confine his conversation to purely extraneous subjects—his observation of his son remained so persistent, his solicitude so marked, that at length Bazarov, losing patience, bade him begone. Of course Vasili Ivanitch promised not to repeat the intrusion; and as a matter of fact he kept this promise the more religiously in that Arina Vlasievna (who had had the matter carefully concealed from her) was beginning to scent something in the wind, and to press for reasons why, during the previous night, her husband had never once closed his eyes. Accordingly, for the next two days Vasili Ivanitch faithfully observed the undertaking he had given; and that although the covert observation of his son's looks which he maintained showed them to be growing by no means to his liking: but on the third day, during dinner, Vasili Ivanitch could bear it no more, for Bazarov was sitting with his eyes lowered and his plate empty.

" You are eating nothing, Evgenii? " he said with his face composed to express absolute indifference. " In my opinion, the dinner is well cooked."

" The only reason why I am eating nothing," replied Bazarov, " is that I am not hungry."

" You have no appetite? " the old man queried timidly. " Also, is—is your head aching at all? "

" Yes. Why should it not ache? "

Arina Vlasievna began to prick up her ears.

" Do not be angry, Evgenii," Vasili Ivanitch continued, " b-but might I feel your pulse and examine you? "

Bazarov looked at him.

" You need not feel my pulse," he said. " Without that, I can tell that I have a touch of fever."

" You feel shivery, eh? "

" Yes. I think I will go and lie down. Pray make me a little lime-juice tea, for I seem to have caught a chill."

" Yes," Arina Vlasievna put in, " I heard you coughing last night."

" But it is only a chill," added Bazarov, and left the room.

So Arina Vlasievna set to work to make the lime-juice tea, and Vasili Ivanitch went into an adjoining room and tore his hair.

Bazarov did not get up again that day, but passed the

night in a state of heavy coma. At one o'clock he opened his eyes with an effort, and, on seeing his father's pale face in the lamp-light, bade him depart. At once the other excused himself for the intrusion, but nevertheless returned on tiptoe, and, concealing himself behind the open doors of a cupboard, remained there to watch his son. Nor did Arina Vlasievna go to bed, but at intervals set the study door ajar, in order that she might " see how our Eniusha was sleeping " and look at Vasili Ivanitch: for though nothing of the latter was to be discerned except a bowed, motionless back, even that much afforded her a little comfort.

In the morning Bazarov attempted to rise, but his head swam, and blood gushed from his nose, so he desisted from the attempt. In silence Vasili Ivanitch tended him, and Arina Vlasievna came to ask him how he felt. He replied " Better," then turned his face to the wall. Instantly Vasili Ivanitch fell to gesticulating violently at his wife with both hands: which proceeding proved so far successful that, by dint of biting her lips, Arina Vlasievna contrived to force back the tears, and leave the room. Of a sudden everything in the house had seemed to turn dark. Everywhere faces looked drawn, and everywhere there was to be observed a curious stillness of which one cause, among others, was the fact that there had hastily been removed from the courtyard of the village a vociferous cock which no reasoning had been able to convince of the necessity of silence.

So Bazarov continued lying with his face to the wall. Once or twice Vasili Ivanitch essayed a tentative question or two, but the attempt only wearied Bazarov, and the old man at length subsided into an armchair, and sat nervously twitching his fingers. Next, Vasili repaired to the garden for a few minutes, and looked, as he stood there, like a statue which has been struck with immeasurable astonishment (never at any time was the

257

expression of surprise absent from his features); where-after he returned to his son's room, in the hope of evading questions on the part of his wife, but she took him by the hand, and grimly, almost threateningly asked· " What is the matter with our Eniusha ? " and when Vasili strove to pull himself together, and to force a smile, there issued, to his horror, not a smile at all, but a sort of irresponsible laugh.

Earlier in the morning he had sent for a doctor to assist him; wherefore he now considered that it would be well to advise his son of the fact, lest Bazarov should lose his temper on discovering the fact in question for himself.

Vasili Ivanitch explained the situation, and then Bazarov turned himself about on the sofa, gazed at his father for a moment or two, and asked to be given some-thing to drink. Vasili Ivanitch handed him some water, and seized the opportunity also to feel his son's forehead. It seemed to be on fire.

" My father," said Bazarov in a hoarse, dragging voice, " I fear that my course is run. The infection has caught me, and in a few days you will be laying me in my grave."

Some one might have thrust Vasili Ivanitch violently backwards, so sharply did he stagger.

" Evgenii," he gasped, " why say that ? God have you in his keeping! It is merely that you have caught a chill."

" Come, come! " interrupted Bazarov, but in the same dragging tone as before. " It is useless to talk like that to a doctor. All the signs of infection are present. That you know for yourself."

" But—but where are the signs of—of infection ? "

Look at these. What do they mean ? "

And Bazarov pulled up the sleeve of his shirt. What he showed his father was a number of red, angry-looking patches that were coming into view.

258

FATHERS AND SONS

Vasili Ivanitch started and turned cold with fear. At length he contrived to stammer out:

"Yet—even supposing that, that there should be anything in the nature of infection——"

"Of pyæmia, you mean," the son prompted.

"Anything in the nature of epidemic infec——"

"Of pyæmia, I repeat," grimly, insistently corrected Bazarov. "Have you forgotten your textbooks?"

"Yes—well, have it your own way. But we will cure you, all the same."

"Fiddlesticks! But, apart from that question, I had scarcely looked to die so soon. To be frank, I think it hard upon me. And now you and my mother must fall back upon the fund of religious strength which lies within you. The hour to put it to the test has arrived." He drank some more water. "One particular request I desire to make while my brain is yet clear, for, by to-morrow, or the day after, it will, as you know, have failed, and even now I am not sure whether I am expressing myself sensibly, seeing that, as I was lying here just now, I seemed to see a pack of red dogs leaping around me, and yourself making a point at me as a dog does at a partridge. Yes, it was like being drunk. Can you understand what I say?"

"Yes, yes, Evgenii; you are talking quite sensibly."

"Very well. Now, I believe that you have sent for a doctor; and if the fact will give you any comfort, I too shall be pleased. But also I beg that you will send word to, to——"

"To Arkady Nikolaievitch?" the old man suggested.

"To whom? To Arkady Nikolaievitch?" re-echoed Bazarov bewilderedly. "Oh, you mean that young cockerel of ours? No, no—do not disturb him, for he has just joined the company of the jackdaws. You need not be surprised at these words—they do not mean that delirium is setting in; they are merely a metaphor.

259

Well, it is to Madame Odintsov, the lady landowner of this neighbourhood, that I desire a messenger to be sent. I suppose you have heard of her? " (Vasili Ivanitch nodded assent.) "All that the messenger need say is that Evgenii Vasilitch sends his compliments, and is dying. Will you do this? "

" Of course I will, Evgenii! But why think that you are going to die? Come, come! Were such a thing to happen, where would be the justice of the world? "

" I could not say. I only know that I desire the messenger to be sent."

" He shall start at once, and I myself will write the letter."

" No, no: that will not be necessary. Merely let the messenger deliver my greeting. That, and nothing more. Now I will return to my red dogs. How curious it is that, though I strive to concentrate my thoughts upon death, there results from them nothing—I see before me only a great blur! "

And he turned his face wearily to the wall, while Vasili Ivanitch left the room, ascended to the bedroom above, and fell upon his knees before the sacred *ikons*.

" Pray, Arina, pray! " he moaned. " Our son is dying! "

On the doctor arriving, the latter proved to be the district physician who had failed to produce hell-stone when required. After an examination of the patient he prescribed a watching course, and also added a few words as to a possible recovery.

"Have you ever known people in my condition *not* set out for the Elysian Fields? " asked Bazarov sharply as he caught hold of the leg of a table which stood beside his sofa, and shook it until the table actually altered its position. " See my strength! " he continued. " All of it is still there, yet I must go hence! To think that, whereas an old man has lost touch with life, I should—— ! Ah,

however much you may deny death, it never will deny *you.* . . . I hear some one weeping. Who is it ? " There was a pause. " Is it my mother ? Poor soul! No one will be left for her to stuff with her marvellous *borstchi.*[1] And you, Vasili Ivanitch—are you too whimpering? Come, come! If Christianity cannot help you, try to become a Stoic philosopher. You have often enough boasted of being one."

" Aye, a fine philosopher I, to be sure! " sobbed poor old Vasili with the tears hopping down his cheeks.

Thereafter Bazarov grew hourly worse, for the disease was taking the rapid course inevitable under the circumstances. Yet his powers of memory were unimpaired, and he understood everything that was said to him, for as yet he was making a brave fight to retain his faculties.

" No, I must not let my senses fail," he kept whispering to himself as he clenched his fists. " But oh, the folly of it all! " And then he would repeat to himself, over and over again, some such formula as " Eight and ten—what do they make ? "

Meanwhile Vasili Ivanitch wandered about in a state bordering upon distraction—proposing first one remedy, and then another, and constantly covering up his son's feet.

" Suppose we wrap him in an ice-sheet ? " he suggested once in a tone of agony. " How, too, about an emetic, or a mustard plaster on his stomach, or a little blood-letting? "

But to each and all of these remedies the doctor (whom Vasili Ivanitch had begged to remain in the house) demurred. Likewise the doctor drank the patient's lemonade, and then requested to be given a pipe and " something warm and strengthening "—to wit, a glassful of *vodka.* Meanwhile Arina Vlasievna sat on a chair by the door, and only at intervals retired to pray. It seemed

[1] Roast beef with horse radish.

261

that a few days earlier she had let fall, and broken, a toilet mirror, and that all her life long she had looked upon such an occurrence as an evil omen. With her, in silence, sat Anfisushka; while, as for Timotheitch, he had departed with the message to Madame Odintsov.

That night Bazarov did not improve, for he was racked with high fever; but as morning approached, the fever grew a little easier, and after he had asked Arina Vlasievna to perform his toilet, and had kissed her hand, he managed to swallow a little tea: which circumstance caused Vasili Ivanitch to pluck up courage, and to exclaim:

" Thank God, the crisis has both come and gone!"

" Do not be too sure of that," rejoined Bazarov. " For what does the term ' crisis ' signify? Some one once invented it, shouted 'Crisis!' and congratulated himself ever after. Extraordinary how the human race continues to attach credence to mere words! For example, tell a man that he is a fool, yet refrain from assaulting him, and he will be downcast; but tell him that he is a man of wisdom, yet give him no money, and he will be overjoyed."

So reminiscent of Bazarov's former sallies was this little speech that Vasili Ivanitch's heart fairly overflowed.

" Bravo!" he cried, clapping his hands in dumb show. " Well said!"

Bazarov smiled a sad smile.

" Then you think," said he, " that the ' crisis ' is either approaching or retiring? "

" I know that you are better. That I can see for myself. And the fact rejoices me."

" Well, it is not always a bad thing to rejoice. But have you sent word to, to—to *her*? You know whom I mean? "

" Of course I have, Evgenii."

262

The improvement did not long continue, for to it there succeeded attacks of pain. Vasili Ivanitch sat by the bed: and as he did so it seemed as though something in particular were worrying the old man. Several times he tried to speak, and each time he failed. But at length he contrived to gasp out:

"Evgenii! Son! My dearest son! My own beloved son!"

Even Bazarov could not remain wholly indifferent to such an unwonted appeal. Turning his head a little, and making an evident effort to shake off the unconsciousness that was weighing him down, he murmured:

"What is it, my father?"

"This, Evgenii." And all of a sudden the old man fell upon his knees beside the bed. "Evgenii, you are better now, and with God's help will recover; but do, in any case, seize this hour to comfort me and your mother by fulfilling all the duties of a Christian. Yes, though to say this is painful for me, how much more terribly would it hurt me if—if this chance were to pass for ever, Evgenii! Think, oh think of what——"

The old man could say no more, while over the son's face and closed eyes there passed a curious expression. A pause followed. Then Bazarov said:

"To comfort you, I will not altogether refuse your request; but, since you yourself have said that I am better, surely there can be no need for hurry?"

"Yes, you *are* better, Evgenii—you *are* better; but who can say what may lie in the dispensation of God? Whereas, once this duty shall have been fulfilled——"

"Yet I will wait a little," interrupted Bazarov. "This much, however, I will concede: that, should you prove to be wrong in your surmise as to my recovery, I will allow the Last Sacrament to be administered."

"And, Evgenii, I beg of you to——"

"I will wait a little, I repeat. And now let me go to sleep. Do not disturb me."

And he replaced his head in its former position, while the old man rose from his knees, reseated himself in the chair, rested his chin upon his hands, and fell to biting his fingers.

Presently Vasili's ear caught the rumble of a light carriage—the sound which is always so distinguishable in a quiet country spot. Nearer and nearer came the sound of the wheels; nearer and nearer came the hard breathing of horses. Springing from his chair, he rushed to the window. Into the courtyard of the mansion there was turning a two-seated, four-horsed buggy! Without stopping to think what this could mean, he darted forward to the front door, where, transported with joy, he was just in time to see a liveried footman open the door of the vehicle, and assist thence a lady in a black cloak, with a veil of the same hue.

" I am Madame Odintsov," she said. " Is Evgenii Vasilitch still alive? I presume you are his father? I have brought with me a doctor."

Even as she spoke the doctor in question—a German-looking little individual in spectacles—descended in a slow and dignified manner from the buggy.

" O angel of mercy! " cried Vasili Ivanitch as, seizing her hand, he pressed it convulsively to his lips. " Yes, our Evgenii is still alive! And now he will be saved! Wife! Wife! There is an angel come to us from Heaven! "

" What? " responded the old woman with a gasp as she came running out of the hall. So lost in bewilderment was she that, falling at Anna Sergievna's feet, she actually began madly to kiss the hem of the visitor's cloak.

" Come, come! " Madame exclaimed. " What does all this mean? "

But Arina Vlasievna was deaf to everything, and Vasili Ivanitch too could only continue repeating:

" There is an angel come to us from Heaven! There is an angel come to us from Heaven! There is an angel come to us from Heaven! "

" *Wo ist der Kranke?* (Where is the patient)? " asked the doctor with a touch of impatience.

This restored Vasili Ivanitch to his senses.

" Come this way, come this way," he said. " Yes, pray follow me, *Werthester Herr Kollega*" (titles based upon the strength of bygone memories).

For answer the German exclaimed "Eh?", and pulled a not very gracious smirk.

Vasili Ivanitch led the way to the study.

" Here is the doctor brought by Madame Anna Sergievna Odintsov," he said as he bent over his son. " She herself too is here."

Bazarov opened his eyes with a start.

" What do you say? " he asked.

" I say that Madame Anna Sergievna Odintsov is here, and that she has brought with her this good doctor."

Bazarov peered around.

" Where is Anna Sergievna? " he murmured. " Do you say that she is here? Then I wish to see her."

" You shall see her, Evgenii; but first of all I must have a chat with this gentleman, and tell him the story of your illness: for Sidor Sidorovitch " (that was the name of the district physician) " has gone home, and a short consultation must be held."

Bazarov eyed the German.

" All right," he said. " Hold your consultation as soon as you like. Only, do not speak in Latin, for I know the meaning of the words *Jam moritur*."

" *Der Herr scheint des Deutschen mächtig zu sein*," the newly-arrived disciple of Æsculapius remarked to Vasili Ivanitch.

" *Ich habe——*" the old man began; then added: " But perhaps we had better speak in Russian, my dear sir? "

FATHERS AND SONS

And the consultation followed.

Half an hour later Vasili Ivanitch conducted Anna Sergievna into the study. As the doctor passed out he whispered to her that recovery was hopeless.

She glanced at Bazarov, and halted as though petrified, so striking was the bloodshot, deathlike face, with the dim eyes turned so yearningly in her direction. Nevertheless her feeling was one merely of chill, oppressive terror, while at the same moment there flashed through her brain the thought that, if she had loved him, no such feeling could now have been present.

" I thank you," he said with an effort. " I had not expected this, and you have done a kind act in coming. So we meet once more, even as you foretold! "

" Has not Madame Anna Sergievna indeed been kind ? " put in Vasili Ivanitch.

" Father, pray leave us," said Bazarov. "I know, Anna Sergievna, that you will excuse him. For at such a time as this——" And he nodded towards his weak, prostrate form.

Vasili Ivanitch left the room.

" A second time I thank you," continued Bazarov. " To have acted so is worthy of the Tsars. For they say that even the Sovereign visits a deathbed when requested."

' Evgenii Vasilitch, I hope that——"

" Let us speak plainly. My course is run. I am under the wheel, and we need not think of the future. Yet how curious it is that to each individual human being death, old though it is as an institution, comes as a novelty! . . . Nevertheless, it shall not make me quail: and then there will fall the curtain, and then—well, then they will write *Fuit*." There followed a feeble gesture. " But what did I want to say to you? That I have loved you? There was a time when the phrase ' I love ' had for me no meaning; and now it will have less than ever, seeing

266

that love is a form, and that my particular embodiment of it is fast lapsing towards dissolution. It——
Ah, how perfect you are! You stand there as beautiful as——"

There passed over Anna Sergievna an involuntary shudder.

" Nay," he said. " You need not be afraid. But will you not sit down? Seat yourself near me, but not too near, for my malady is infectious."

She crossed the room with a rapid step, and seated herself beside the sofa on which he was lying.

" O woman of kind heart! " he whispered. " And to think that you are beside me once more! To think that you, so pure and fresh and young, are in this sorry room! Well, good-bye, and may you live long, and enjoy your time while you may. Of all things in this world long 'life is the most desirable: yet you can see for yourself what an ugly spectacle I, a half-crushed, but still wriggling, worm, am now become. There was a time when I used to say: ' I will do many things in life, and refuse to die before I have completed those tasks, for I am a giant ': but now I have indeed a giant's task in hand—the task of dying as though death were nothing to me. . . . No matter. I am not going to put my tail between my legs."

He broke off, and groped for his tumbler. She handed it him without drawing off her glove. Her breath was coming in jerks.

" It will not be long before you will have forgotten me," he went on. " For a dead mortal is no companion for a living one. I daresay that my father will tell you what a man is being lost to Russia; but that is all rubbish. Nevertheless, do not undeceive him, for he is old, old. Rather, comfort him as you would comfort a child, and also be kind to my mother. Two such mortals as them you will not find in all *your* great world—

no, not though you search for them with a candle by daylight. . . . Russia needs me, indeed! Evidently she does *not* need me. Whom, then, does she need? She needs shoemakers, tailors, butchers. . . . What does a butcher sell? He sells meat, does he not? . . . I think that I am wandering—I seem to see before me a forest. . . ."

He pressed his hand to his forehead, and Anna Sergievna bent over him.

" Evgenii Vasilitch," she said, " I am here."

With a combined movement he took her hand and raised himself a little.

" Good-bye," he said with a sudden spasm of energy and a last flash of his eyes. " Good-bye. . . . I kissed you that time, did I not, when, when——? . . . Ah, breathe now upon the expiring lamp, that it may go out in peace."

She pressed her lips gently to his forehead.

" Enough," he murmured as he sank back upon the pillow. " Now let there come—darkness."

She left the room quietly.

" Well? " whispered Vasili Ivanitch.

" He has gone to sleep," she replied in a voice that was scarcely audible.

But Bazarov was not fated to go to sleep. Rather, as night approached he sank into a state of coma, and, on the following day, expired. Father Alexis performed over him the last rites of religion, and at the moment when Extreme Unction was being administered, and the holy oil touched his breast, one of the dying man's eyelids raised itself, and over the face there seemed to flit something like an expression of distaste at the sight of the priest in his vestments, the smoking censer, and the candles before the *ikon*.

Finally, when Bazarov's last breath had been drawn, and there had arisen in the house the sound of " the

general lamentation," something akin to frenzy came
upon Vasili Ivanitch.

" I declare that I protest!" he cried with his face
blazing and quivering with fury, and his fist beating
the air as in menace of some one. " I declare that I
protest, that I protest, that I protest!"

Upon that old Arina Vlasievna, suffused in tears, laid
her arms around his neck, and the two sank forward
upon the floor. Said Anfisushka later, when relating
the story in the servants' quarters: " There they knelt
together—side by side, their heads drooping like those
of two sheep at midday."

.   .   .   .

Ah, but in time the heat of noontide passes, and to it
there succeed nightfall and dusk, with a return to the
quiet fold where for the weary and the heavy-laden
there waits sleep, sweet sleep.

XXVIII

SINCE that time six months have passed, and there has fallen upon the country a " white " winter—a winter of clear, keen, motionless frosts, of deep, crackling snow, of pink-rimed trees, of pale-emerald heavens, of smoke-capped chimneys, of puffs of vapour from momentarily opened doors, of faces fresh and hard-bitten, of horses galloping headlong to thaw their frozen limbs. It is now the close of a January day, and the increasing chill of evening is nipping the still air in an ever-tightening vice as the sun sinks downward into a sea of red.

But in the windows of Marino there are lights burning, and Prokofitch, vested in a black tail-coat, a pair of white gloves, and a peculiar atmosphere of solemnity, is laying the table with seven covers. This is because a week ago there were solemnised in the tiny church of the parish—solemnised quietly, almost without a wit-ness—two sets of nuptials: the nuptials of Arkady and Katia and those of Nikolai Petrovitch and Thenichka. And to-day Nikolai Petrovitch is offering his brother a farewell dinner, for the reason that Paul is on the point of departing for Moscow, whither Anna Sergievna has already removed after bestowing upon the younger of the two couples a handsome dowry.

At three o'clock precisely the company gathers around the board. Mitia too is present with his *niania* (in nurse's cap), while Paul Petrovitch is seated between Katia and Thenichka, and the bridegrooms are ranged one on either side of their newly-wedded spouses. A change has taken place in our old acquaintances since last we saw them—they have improved, as regards the younger ones, both in appearance and in sedateness of demeanour. Only Paul Petrovitch looks thinner; though the circumstance imparts, if anything, an added touch of refinement and "grand - seignorishness" to his always expressive features. Thenichka, in particular, is a different person from what she was. Clad in a brand-new silken gown, and wearing a broad velvet band over her hair and a necklace around her throat, she holds herself with an immovable dignity, yet also with an immovable deference towards her surroundings. And meanwhile she smiles, as much as to say: "Pardon me, but *I* am not responsible for this"; while the others respond with similar smiles, as though they too would be glad to excuse themselves for their share in the proceedings. Yet the fact that on every one present sits a touch of gravity and embarrassment becomes the company no less than do their other characteristics. Everywhere, too, there is to be seen such an anxious solicitude for mutual wants that the company could seem unanimously to be playing some simple-minded comedy; and though, of the guests, the quietest is Katia, it is plain, from her confidence of bearing, that, as a daughter-in-law, she has found favour in the eyes of Nikaiai Petrovitch.

At length the meal comes to an end, and Nikolai, rising and grasping a wine-glass, addresses Paul Petrovitch:

"Dearest brother, you are about to leave us. Yes, you are about to leave us. But not for long must you be absent, since I, for one, could never express to you how much I, how much I—that is to say, how much we—— But, to tell you the truth, I am not good at making a speech. Arkady, to you I depute the task."

"But I am not ready, Papa."

"Neither am I. However, Paul, I embrace you, and wish you every joy, and beg of you to return to us soon."

Whereupon Paul Petrovitch exchanges greetings all

271

round (not excluding little Mitia), and, in particular, kisses Thenichka's hand (which she has not learnt to offer in the right way), drinks a twice-filled glass to the company at large, and says with a profound sigh: " May you all be happy, my friends! Farewell![1]" And though the English terminal flourish passes unnoticed, every one is touched with the benediction which has preceded it.

" Yes, and I drink to the memory of Bazarov," whispers Katia to her husband as she clinks glasses with him: but though, in response, he squeezes her hand, he decides not to propose the toast in public.

And here, apparently, there ought to follow the word *Finis*; but since some of my readers may care to know how each of the characters in the book is faring at the present day, I will satisfy that curiosity.

To take Anna Sergievna first, she has married—not for love, nor yet out of a sense of duty—a rising young statesman who is an intelligent legislator, a severely practical thinker, a man of strong will and eloquence, and a lover with a temperament as cold as ice. Nevertheless the pair reside on amicable terms, and may, in time, attain to happiness—nay, even to love.

As for the Princess, she is dead, and her memory perished with her.

The Kirsanovs, father and son, are settled at Marino, and appear to be righting their industrial affairs, in that Arkady has developed into a capable manager, and the estate now brings in a fair income. Nikolai Petrovitch, too, is constant in his endeavours to make peace on the property, and, riding systematically round it, delivers long speeches in the belief that only need the peasantry be " reasoned with "—that is to say, plied with the same words over and over again—for the *muzhik* gradually

[1] In the text this word is given in English.

272

to become a tractable animal. Yet Nikolai earns the approval neither of the educated gentry, who speak with affected jauntiness of the coming " 'mancipation "[1] (they invariably give the syllable "an" a nasal inflection), nor of those uneducated landowners who roundly curse what they term " that —— 'muncipation." In other words, for both classes Nikolai Petrovitch is too "mild."

Katerina Sergievna has had a son born to her, and named him Kolia; Mitia is now a big, active, volubly lisping boy; and Thenichka (rather, Theodosia Niko-laievna) adores her daughter-in-law only less than her husband and Mitia. In fact, that adoration reaches the point that, should Katia sit down to the piano, Thenichka cannot leave her though the playing continue all day.

Then a word concerning Peter the valet. As much a lump of mingled stupidity and conceit as ever, he still pronounces his e's as u's, but has taken unto himself a wife, and, with her, a respectable dowry. The daughter of a market gardener of the neighbouring town, she had already refused two eligible *partis* solely on the ground that they did not possess watches! But Peter possesses not only a watch, but also a pair of patent leather pumps.

Again, any day on the Brühl Terrace, in Dresden, you may meet, between two and four o'clock in the afternoon (the fashionable hour for a promenade), a man of about fifty. Grey-headed, and afflicted with gout, yet still hand-some, he is elegantly dressed, and stamped with that air of good breeding which comes only of long association with elevated strata of society. That man is Paul Petro-vitch. Having left Moscow for foreign parts for his health's sake, he has settled in Dresden for the reason that there he possesses the largest number of English and nomad-Russian acquaintances. Towards the former he

[1] *i.e.* the emancipation of the serfs, which was carried out in 1861.

273

bears himself with simplicity, and almost with modesty, but with a touch of *hauteur*; and, in return, the English look upon him as a trifle tedious, but respect him on the score of his being " quite a gentleman." In the presence of the Russian element, however, Paul Petrovitch is more free and easy—he gives rein unstintedly to his sarcasm, and rallies both his compatriots and himself. Yet from *him* such things come pleasantly, and with a gay *insouciance*, and in a becoming manner; while, in addition, he holds Slavophil views—views which (as we all know) invariably induce the great world to rate their holder a person *très distingué*. True, never by any chance does Paul read a Russian book; yet by way of compensation, there stands on his writing-table a silver ash-tray shaped like a *muzhik's* clog. Moreover, from some of our Russian tourists he receives considerable attention when they happen to be passing through the town; and even our old friend Matvei Ilyitch Koliazin, on finding himself " in temporary opposition," has paid him a visit while *en route* to Bohemia for a course of the waters. In fact, the only persons who show Paul no deference at all are the native Germans, whose society he does not greatly cultivate. Yet even they agree that, in the matter of obtaining tickets for the Court Chapel or the theatre and so forth, none is so clever, so dexterous, as " der Herr Baron von Kirsanov." In fact, always does he do " the right thing " so far as he is able; and even yet he can create some stir, owing to the fact that he has once, and to good purpose, been a social lion. Yet life presses upon him not a little heavily—more heavily than he himself is aware. Merely need one look at him as, huddled against the aisle wall of the Russian church, he sits plunged in thought, with his lips bitterly compressed, and continues sitting there until, remembering his surroundings, he makes, almost imperceptibly, the sign of the cross.

In similar fashion, Madame Kukshin has gone abroad

—in her case, to Heidelberg, where she is engaged in studying, not natural science, but architecture—a branch wherein she has, according to herself, "discovered several new laws." Also, still she is hail-fellow-well-met with students, more especially with some of those Russian physicists and chemists who swarm in Heidelberg, and who, though at first flabbergasting the simple-minded German professors with the moderation of their views, subsequently proceed to flabbergast those professors with the wholeheartedness of their sloth. In fact, it is of two or three of those chemistry students who, though unable to distinguish even oxygen from azote, are yet charged to the brim with conceit and the spirit of "denial," that Madame Kukshin's circle is chiefly composed.

Similarly, friend Sitnikov is preparing to become a great man. For which purpose he is flaunting it in St. Petersburg, and (to quote his own expression) "carrying on the work of the late Bazarov." True, rumour declares that some one has recently given him a second thrashing; as also that he (Sitnikov) has declined to face the music—rather, that he has preferred to hint in an obscure article in an equally obscure newspaper that his assailant is the coward; but to this report Sitnikov merely attaches the epithet "ironical." For the rest, his father continues to send him remittances, while his wife accounts him equally a *littérateur* and a fool.

Lastly, in a remote corner of Russia there lies a little country cemetery. Like most cemeteries of the kind, it is depressing of aspect. Over its fences dense masses of weed have grown, its drab wooden crosses are rickety and turning mouldy under their blistered, painted canopies, its stone paths have lost their alignment, and look as though some one has displaced them from below, its two or three ragged trees diffuse only the scantiest of shade, and sheep wander unhindered over its tombs. But among

275

those tombs there lies a grave which no man molests and no animal tramples upon: only the birds perch upon it and sing as evening falls. For around that grave stands an iron railing, and at its head and foot are planted two young fir trees. It is the grave of Evgenii Vasilitch Bazarov. Occasionally from the neighbouring manor-house there come two aged and decrepit folk, a man and his wife. Supporting one another with a step which ever grows heavier, they approach the railing, sink upon their knees, and weep long, bitter tears as they gaze at the dumb headstone where their son lies sleeping. Then they exchange a word or two, dust the stone with assiduous care, lay upon it a sprig of fir, and offer a last petition. Yet even then they can scarce bear to tear themselves from the spot where they can draw nearest to their son, and to their memories of him.

But are those tears, those prayers, all fruitless? Is that love, that hallowed, selfless love, of theirs to be wholly unavailing? No, no, and a thousand times no! For, though the heart which lies within that tomb may have been passionate and wild and erring, the flowers which bloom in that spot contemplate us with eyes of naught but peace and innocence, and speak to us of naught but the eternal, mighty calm of " unheeding " nature, as an image of the Eternal Reconciliation, and of the Life which shall have no End.

LIZA

I

A BEAUTIFUL spring day was drawing to a close. High aloft in the clear sky floated small rosy clouds, which seemed never to drift past, but to be slowly absorbed into the blue depths beyond.

At an open window, in a handsome mansion situated in one of the outlying streets of O., the chief town of the government of that name—it was in the year 1842—there were sitting two ladies, the one about fifty years old, the other an old woman of seventy.

The name of the first was Maria Dmitrievna Kalitine. Her husband, who had formerly occupied the post of Provincial Procurator, and who was well known in his day as a good man of business—a man of bilious temperament, confident, resolute, and enterprising—had been dead ten years. He had received a good education, and had studied at the university, but as the family from which he sprang was a poor one, he had early recognised the necessity of making a career for himself and of gaining money.

Maria Dmitrievna married him for love. He was good-looking, he had plenty of sense, and, when he liked, he could be very agreeable. Maria Dmitrievna, whose maiden name was Pestof, lost her parents while she was still a child. She spent several years in an Institute at Moscow, and then went to live with her brother and one of her aunts at Pokrovskoe, a family estate situated fifteen versts from O. Soon afterwards her brother was called away on duty to St. Petersburg, and, until a sudden death put an end to his career, he kept his aunt and sister with only just enough for them to live upon. Maria Dmitrievna inherited Pokrovskoe, but she did not long reside there. In the second year of her marriage with Kalitine, who had succeeded at the end of a few days in gaining her affections, Pokrovskoe was exchanged for another estate—one of much greater intrinsic value, but unattractive in appearance, and not provided with a mansion. At the same time Kalitine purchased a house in the town of O., and there he and his wife permanently established themselves. A large garden was attached to it, extending in one direction to the fields outside the town, " so that," Kalitine, who was by no means an admirer of rural tranquillity, used to say, " there is no reason why we should go dragging ourselves off into the country." Maria Dmitrievna often secretly regretted her beautiful Pokrovskoe, with its joyous brook, its sweeping meadows, and its verdant woods, but she never opposed her husband in anything, having the highest respect for his judgment and his knowledge of the world. And when he died, after fifteen years of married life, leaving behind him a son and two daughters, Maria Dmitrievna had grown so accustomed to her house and to a town life, that she had no inclination to change her residence.

In her youth Maria Dmitrievna had enjoyed the reputation of being a pretty blonde, and even in her fiftieth year her features were not unattractive, though they had lost somewhat of their fineness and delicacy. She was naturally sensitive and impressionable, rather than actually good-hearted, and even in her years of maturity she continued to behave in the manner peculiar to " Institute girls "; she denied herself no indulgence, she was easily put out of temper, and she would even burst into tears if her habits were interfered with. On the other hand, she was gracious and affable when all her wishes were fulfilled, and when nobody opposed her in anything. Her house was the pleasantest in the town; and she had a handsome income, the greater part of which was derived from her late husband's earnings, and the rest from her own property. Her two daughters lived with her; her son was being edu-

LIZA

cated in one of the best of the crown establishments at
St. Petersburg.

The old lady who was sitting at the window with
Maria Dmitrievna was her father's sister, the aunt with
whom she had formerly spent so many lonely years at
Pokrovskoe. Her name was Marfa Timofeevna Pestof.
She was looked upon as an original, being a woman of
an independent character, who bluntly told the truth
to every one, and who, although her means were very
small, behaved in society just as she would have done
had she been rolling in wealth. She never could abide
the late Kalitine, and as soon as her niece married him
she retired to her own modest little property, where she
spent ten whole years in a peasant's smoky hut. Maria
Dmitrievna was rather afraid of her. Small in stature,
with black hair, a sharp nose, and eyes which even in old
age were still keen, Marfa Timofeevna walked briskly,
held herself bolt upright, and spoke quickly but distinctly, and with a loud, high-pitched voice. She
always wore a white cap, and a white *kofta* [1] always
formed part of her dress.

" What is the matter? " she suddenly asked. " What
are you sighing about? "

" Nothing," replied Maria Dmitrievna. " What
lovely clouds! "

" You are sorry for them, I suppose? "

Maria Dmitrievna made no reply.

" Why doesn't Gedeonovsky come? " continued Marfa
Timofeevna, rapidly plying her knitting needles. (She
was making a long worsted scarf.) " He would have
sighed with you. Perhaps he would have uttered some
platitude or other."

" How unkindly you always speak of him! Sergius
Petrovich is—a most respectable man."

" Respectable! " echoed the old lady reproachfully.

" And then," continued Maria Dmitrievna, " how
devoted he was to my dear husband! Why, he can
never think of him without emotion."

[1] A sort of jacket.

281

" He might well be that, considering that your husband pulled him out of the mud by the ears," growled Marfa Timofeevna, the needles moving quicker than ever under her fingers. " He looks so humble," she began anew after a time. " His head is quite grey, and yet he never opens his mouth but to lie or to slander. And, forsooth, he is a councillor of state! Ah, well, to be sure, he is a priest's son." [1]

" Who is there who is faultless, aunt? It is true that he has this weakness. Sergius Petrovich has not had a good education, I admit—he cannot speak French—but I beg leave to say that I think him exceedingly agreeable."

" Oh, yes, he fawns on you like a dog. As to his not speaking French, that's no great fault. I am not very strong in the French ' dialect ' myself. It would be better if he spoke no language at all; he wouldn't tell lies then. But of course, here he is, in the very nick of time," continued Marfa Timofeevna, looking down the street. " Here comes your agreeable man, striding along. How spindle-shanked he is, to be sure—just like a stork! "

Maria Dmitrievna arranged her curls. Marfa Timofeevna looked at her with a quiet smile.

" Isn't that a grey hair I see, my dear? You should scold Pelagia. Where can her eyes be? "

" That's just like you, aunt," muttered Maria Dmitrievna, in a tone of vexation, and thrumming with her fingers on the arm of her chair.

" Sergius Petrovich Gedeonovsky! " shrilly announced a rosy-cheeked little Cossack,[2] who suddenly appeared at the door.

[1] *Popovich*, or son of a pope: a not over respectful designation in Russia.

[2] A page attired in a sort of Cossack dress.

II

A TALL man came into the room, wearing a good enough coat, rather short trousers, thick grey gloves, and two cravats—a black one outside, a white one underneath. Everything belonging to him was suggestive of propriety and decorum, from his well-proportioned face, with locks carefully smoothed down over the temples, to his heelless and never-creaking boots. He bowed first to the mistress of the house, then to Marfa Timofeevna, and afterwards, having slowly taken off his gloves, he approached Maria Dmitrievna and respectfully kissed her hand twice. After that he leisurely subsided into an easy-chair, and asked, as he smilingly rubbed together the tips of his fingers—

" Is Elizaveta Mikhailovna quite well? "

" Yes," replied Maria Dmitrievna, " she is in the garden."

" And Elena Mikhailovna? "

" Lenochka is in the garden also. Have you any news? "

" Rather! " replied the visitor, slowly screwing up his eyes, and protruding his lips. " Hm! here is a piece of news, if you please, and a very startling one, too. Fedor Ivanovich Lavretsky has arrived."

" Fedia! " exclaimed Marfa Timofeevna. " You're inventing, are you not? "

" Not at all. I have seen him with my own eyes."

" That doesn't prove anything."

" He's grown much more robust," continued Gedeonovsky, looking as if he had not heard Marfa Timofeevna's remark; " his shoulders have broadened, and his cheeks are quite rosy."

" Grown more robust," slowly repeated Maria Dmitrievna. "One would think he hadn't met with much to make him robust."

"That is true indeed," said Gedeonovsky. "Any one else, in his place, would have scrupled to show himself in the world."

"And why, I should like to know?" broke in Marfa Timofeevna. "What nonsense you are talking! A man comes back to his home. Where else would you have him betake himself? And, pray, in what has he been to blame?"

"A husband is always to blame, madam, if you will allow me to say so, when his wife behaves ill."

"You only say that, *batyushka*,[1] because you have never been married."

Gedeonovsky's only reply was a forced smile. For a short time he remained silent, but presently he said, "May I be allowed to be so inquisitive as to ask for whom this pretty scarf is intended?"

Marfa Timofeevna looked up at him quickly.

"For whom is it intended?" she said. "For a man who never slanders, who does not intrigue, and who makes up no falsehoods—if, indeed, such a man is to be found in the world. I know Fedia thoroughly well; the only thing for which he is to blame is that he spoilt his wife. To be sure he married for love; and from such love-matches no good ever comes," added the old lady, casting a side glance at Maria Dmitrievna. Then, standing up, she added: "But now you can whet your teeth on whom you will; on me, if you like. I'm off. I won't hinder you any longer." And with these words she disappeared.

"She is always like that," said Maria Dmitrievna, following her aunt with her eyes—"always."

"What else can be expected of her at her time of life?" replied Gedeonovsky. "Just see now! Who does not intrigue,' she was pleased to say. But who is there nowadays who doesn't intrigue? It is the custom of the present age. A friend of mine—a most respect-

[1] Father.

able man, and one, I may as well observe, of no slight
rank—used to say, ' Nowadays, it seems, if a hen wants
a grain of corn she approaches it cunningly, watches
anxiously for an opportunity of sidling up to it.' But
when I look at you, dear lady, I recognise in you a truly
angelic nature. May I be allowed to kiss your snow-
white hand? "

Maria Dmitrievna slightly smiled, and held out her
plump hand to Gedeonovsky, keeping the little finger
gracefully separated from the rest; and then, after he
had raised her hand to his lips, she drew her chair closer
to his, bent a little towards him, and asked, in a low
voice—

" So you have seen him? And is he really well and in
good spirits? "

" In excellent spirits," replied Gedeonovsky in a
whisper.

" You haven't heard where his wife is now? "

" A short time ago she was in Paris; but she is gone
away, they say, and is now in Italy."

" Really it is shocking—Fedia's position. I can't
think how he manages to bear it. Every one, of course,
has his misfortunes; but his affairs, one may say, have
become known all over Europe."

Gedeonovsky sighed.

" Quite so, quite so! They say she has made friends
with artists and pianists; or, as they call them there,
with lions and other wild beasts. She has completely
lost all sense of shame——"

" It's very very sad," said Maria Dmitrievna; " especially for a relation. You know, don't you, Sergius
Petrovich, that he is a far-away cousin of mine? "

" To be sure, to be sure! You surely don't suppose
I could be ignorant of anything that concerns your
family."

" Will he come to see us? What do you think? "

" One would suppose so; but afterwards, I am told,
he will go and live on his estate in the country."

Maria Dmitrievna lifted her eyes towards heaven.

" Oh, Sergius Petrovich, Sergius Petrovich!   how often I think how necessary it is for us women to behave circumspectly! "

" There are women and women, Maria Dmitrievna. There are, unfortunately, some who are—of an unstable character; and then there is a certain time of life—— and, besides, good principles have not been instilled into them when they were young."

Here Sergius Petrovich drew from his pocket a blue handkerchief, of a check pattern, and began to unfold it.

" Such women, in fact, do exist."

Here Sergius Petrovich applied a corner of the hand-kerchief to each of his eyes in turn.

" But, generally speaking, if one reflects—that is to say——   The dust in the streets is something extra-ordinary," he ended by saying.

" *Maman, maman*," exclaimed a pretty little girl of eleven, who came running into the room,   " Vladimir Nikolaevich is coming here on horseback."

Maria Dmitrievna rose from her chair.   Sergius Petrovich also got up and bowed.

" My respects to Elena Mikhailovna," he said; and discreetly retiring to a corner, he betook himself to blowing his long straight nose.

" What a lovely horse he has! " continued the little girl.   " He was at the garden gate just now, and he told me and Liza that he would come up to the front door."

The sound of hoofs was heard, and a well-appointed cavalier, mounted on a handsome bay horse, rode up to the house, and stopped in front of the open window.

III

"GOOD evening, Maria Dmitrievna!" exclaimed the rider's clear and pleasant voice. "How do you like my new purchase?"

Maria Dmitrievna went to the window.

"Good evening, Woldemar! Ah, what a splendid horse! From whom did you buy it?"

"From our remount-officer. He made me pay dear for it, the rascal."

"What is its name?"

"Orlando. But that's a stupid name. I want to change it. *Eh bien, eh bien, mon garçon.* What a restless creature it is!"

The horse neighed, pawed the air, and tossed the foam from its nostrils.

"Come and stroke it, Lenochka; don't be afraid."

Lenochka stretched out her hand from the window, but Orlando suddenly reared and shied. But its rider, who took its proceedings very quietly, gripped the saddle firmly with his knees, laid his whip across the horse's neck, and forced it, in spite of its resistance, to return to the window. "*Prenez garde, prenez garde,*" Maria Dmitrievna kept calling out.

"Now then, stroke him, Lenochka," repeated the horseman; "I don't mean to let him have his own way."

Lenochka stretched out her hand a second time, and timidly touched the quivering nostrils of Orlando, who champed his bit, and kept incessantly fidgeting.

"Bravo!" exclaimed Maria Dmitrievna; "but now get off, and come in."

The rider wheeled his horse sharply round, drove the spurs into its sides, rode down the street at a hand gallop, and turned into the court-yard. In another minute he had crossed the hall and entered the drawing-room, flourishing his whip in the air.

At the same moment there appeared on the threshold of another doorway a tall, well-made, dark-haired girl of nineteen—Maria Dmitrievna's elder daughter, Liza.

IV

THE young man whom we have just introduced to our readers was called Vladimir Nikolaevich Panshine. He occupied a post at St. Petersburg—one devoted to business of a special character—in the Ministry of the Interior. He had come to O. about certain affairs of a temporary nature, and was placed there at the disposal of the governor, General Zonnenberg, to whom he was distantly related.

Panshine's father, a retired cavalry officer,[1] who used to be well known among card-players, was a man of a worn face, with weak eyes, and a nervous contraction about the lips. Throughout his life he always revolved in a distinguished circle, frequenting the English clubs [2] of both capitals, and being generally considered a man of ability and a pleasant companion, though not a person to be confidently depended upon. In spite of all his ability, he was almost always just on the verge of ruin, and he ultimately left but a small and embarrassed property to his only son. About that son's education, however, he had, after his own fashion, taken great pains.

The young Vladimir Nikolaevich spoke excellent French, good English, and bad German. That is just as it should be. Properly brought-up people should of course be ashamed to speak German really well; but to throw out a German word now and then, and generally on facetious topics—that is allowable; " *c'est même très chic,*" as the Petersburg Parisians say. Moreover, by the time Vladimir Nikolaevich was fifteen, he already knew how to enter any drawing-room whatsoever

[1] A *Shtabs-Rotmistr*, the second captain in a cavalry regiment.
[2] Fashionable clubs having nothing English about them but their name.

without becoming nervous, how to move about it in an agreeable manner, and how to take his leave exactly at the right moment.

The elder Panshine made a number of useful connections for his son; while shuffling the cards between two rubbers, or after a lucky " Great Schlemm," [1] he never lost the opportunity of saying a word about his young " Volodka " to some important personage, a lover of games of skill.   On his part, Vladimir Nikolaevich, during the period of his stay at the university, which he left with the rank of " effective student," [2] made acquaintance with several young people of distinction, and gained access into the best houses.   He was cordially received everywhere, for he was very good looking, easy in manner, amusing, always in good health, and ready for everything.   Where he was obliged, he was respectful; where he could, he was overbearing. Altogether, an excellent companion, *un charmant garçon*. The Promised Land lay before him.   Panshine soon fathomed the secret of worldly wisdom, and succeeded in inspiring himself with a genuine respect for its laws. He knew how to invest trifles with a half-ironical importance, and to behave with the air of one who treats all serious matters as trifles.   He danced admirably; he dressed like an Englishman.   In a short time he had gained the reputation of being one of the pleasantest and most adroit young men in St. Petersburg.

Panshine really was very adroit—not less so than his father had been.   And besides this, he was endowed with no small talent; nothing was too difficult for him. He sang pleasantly, drew confidently, could write poetry, and acted remarkably well.

He was now only in his twenty-eighth year, but he was already a chamberlain, and he had arrived at a highly respectable rank in the service.   He had thorough confidence in himself, in his intellect, and in his sagacity. He went onwards under full sail, boldly and cheerfully;

[1] " A bumper."
[2] A degree a little inferior to that of Bachelor of Arts.

the stream of his life flowed smoothly along. He was accustomed to please every one, old and young alike; and he imagined that he thoroughly understood his fellow-creatures, especially women—that he was intimately acquainted with all their ordinary weaknesses.

As one who was no stranger to art, he felt within him a certain enthusiasm, a glow, a rapture, in consequence of which he claimed for himself various exemptions from ordinary rules. He led a somewhat irregular life, he made acquaintance with people who were not received into society, and in general he behaved in an unconventional and unceremonious manner. But in his heart of hearts he was cold and astute; and even in the midst of his most extravagant rioting, his keen hazel eye watched and took note of everything. It was impossible for this daring and unconventional youth ever quite to forget himself, or to be thoroughly carried away. It should be mentioned to his credit, by the way, that he never boasted of his victories. To Maria Dmitrievna's house he had obtained access as soon as he arrived in O., and he soon made himself thoroughly at home in it. As to Maria Dmitrievna herself, she thought there was nobody in the world to be compared with him.

Panshine bowed in an engaging manner to all the occupants of the room, shook hands with Maria Dmitrievna and Elizaveta Mikhailovna, lightly tapped Gedeonovsky on the shoulder, and, turning on his heels, took Lenochka's head between his hands and kissed her on the forehead.

" Are not you afraid to ride such a vicious horse? " asked Maria Dmitrievna.

" I beg your pardon, it is perfectly quiet. No, but I will tell you what I really am afraid of. I am afraid of playing at preference with Sergius Petrovich. Yesterday, at the Bielenitsines', he won all the money I had with me."

Gedeonovsky laughed a thin and cringing laugh; he wanted to gain the good graces of the brilliant young official from St. Petersburg, the governor's favourite.

291

In his conversations with Maria Dmitrievna he frequently spoke of Panshine's remarkable faculties. "Why, really now, how can one help praising him?" he used to reason. "The young man is a success in the highest circles of society, and at the same time he does his work in the most perfect manner, and he isn't the least bit proud." And indeed, even at St. Petersburg, Panshine was looked upon as an efficient public servant; the work "burnt under his hands;" he spoke of it jestingly, as a man of the world should, who does not attach any special importance to his employment; but he was a "doer." Heads of departments like such subordinates; he himself never doubted that in time, supposing he really wished it, he would be a Minister.

"You are so good as to say that I won your money," said Gedeonovsky; "but who won fifteen roubles from me last week? And besides——"

"Ah, rogue, rogue!" interrupted Panshine, in a pleasant tone, but with an air of indifference bordering on contempt, and then, without paying him any further attention, he accosted Liza.

"I cannot get the overture to Oberon here," he began. "Madame Bielenitsine boasted that she had a complete collection of classical music; but in reality she has nothing but polkas and waltzes. However, I have already written to Moscow, and you shall have the overture in a week."

"By the way," he continued, "I wrote a new romance yesterday; the words are mine as well as the music. Would you like me to sing it to you? Madame Bielenitsine thought it very pretty, but her judgment is not worth much. But, after all, I think I had better sing it by-and-by."

"Why by-and-by?" exclaimed Maria Dmitrievna, "why not now?"

"To hear is to obey," answered Panshine, with a sweet and serene smile, which came and went quickly; and then, having pushed a chair up to the piano, he sat down, struck a few chords, and began to sing the following romance, pronouncing the words very distinctly:—

> Amid pale clouds, above the earth,
>   The moon rides high,
> And o'er the sea a magic light
>   Pours from the sky.
>
> My spirit's waves, as towards the moon,
>   Towards thee, love, flow:
> Its waters stirred by thee alone
>   In weal or woe.
>
> My heart replete with love that grieves
>   But yields no cry,
> I suffer——cold as yonder moon
>   Thou passest by.

Panshine sang the second stanza with more than usual expression and feeling; in the stormy accompaniment might be heard the rolling of the waves. After the words, " I suffer! " he breathed a light sigh, and with downcast eyes let his voice die gradually away. When he had finished, Liza praised the air, Maria Dmitrievna said, " Charming! " and Gedeonovsky exclaimed, " Enchanting!—the words and the music are equally enchanting! " Lenochka kept her eyes fixed on the singer with childish reverence. In a word, the composition of the young *dilettante* delighted all who were in the room. But outside the drawing-room door, in the vestibule, there stood looking on the floor an old man who had just come into the house, to whom, judging from the expression of his face and the movements of his shoulders, Panshine's romance, though really pretty, did not afford much pleasure. After waiting a little, and having dusted his boots with a coarse handkerchief, he suddenly squeezed up his eyes, morosely compressed his lips, gave his already curved back an extra bend, and slowly entered the drawing-room.

" Ah! Christophor Fedorovich, how do you do? " Panshine was the first to exclaim, as he jumped up quickly from his chair. " I didn't suspect you were there. I wouldn't for anything have ventured to sing my romance before you. I know you are no admirer of the light style in music."

" I didn't hear it," said the new-comer, in imperfect Russian. Then, having bowed to all the party, he stood still in an awkward attitude in the middle of the room.

" I suppose, Monsieur Lemm," said Maria Dmitrievna, " you have come to give Liza a music lesson."

" No; not Lizaveta Mikhailovna, but Elena Mikhailovna."

" Oh, indeed! very good. Lenochka, go upstairs with Monsieur Lemm."

The old man was about to follow the little girl, when Panshine stopped him.

" Don't go away when the lesson is over, Christophor Fedorovich," he said. " Lizaveta Mikhailovna and I are going to play a duet—one of Beethoven's sonatas."

The old man muttered something to himself, but Panshine continued in German, pronouncing the words very badly—

" Lizaveta Mikhailovna has shown me the sacred cantata which you have dedicated to her—a very beautiful piece! I beg you will not suppose I am unable to appreciate serious music. Quite the reverse. It is sometimes tedious; but, on the other hand, it is extremely edifying."

The old man blushed to the ears, cast a side glance at Liza, and went hastily out of the room.

Maria Dmitrievna asked Panshine to repeat his romance; but he declared that he did not like to offend the ears of the scientific German, and proposed to Liza to begin Beethoven's sonata. On this, Maria Dmitrievna sighed, and, on her part, proposed a stroll in the garden to Gedeonovsky.

" I want to have a little more chat with you," she said, " about our poor Fedia, and to ask for your advice."

Gedeonovsky smiled and bowed, took up with two fingers his hat, on the brim of which his gloves were neatly laid out, and retired with Maria Dmitrievna.

Panshine and Liza remained in the room. She fetched the sonata, and spread it out. Both sat down to the piano in silence. From upstairs there came the feeble sound of scales, played by Lenochka's uncertain fingers.

Note to p. 21.—It is possible that M. Panshine may have been inspired by Heine's verses:—

> Wie des Mondes Abbild zittert
>   In den wilden Meereswogen,
> Und er selber still und sicher
>   Wandelt an dem Himmelsbogen.
>
> Also wandelst du, Geliebte,
>   Still und sicher, und es zittert
> Nur dein Abbild mir im Herzen,
>   Weil mein eignes Herz erschüttert.

V

CHRISTOPH THEODOR GOTTLIEB LEMM was born in 1786, in the kingdom of Saxony, in the town of Chemnitz. His parents, who were very poor, were both of them musicians, his father playing the hautboy, his mother the harp. He himself, by the time he was five years old, was already practising on three different instruments. At the age of eight, he was left an orphan, and at ten he began to earn a living by his art. For a long time he led a wandering life, playing in all sorts of places—in taverns, at fairs, at peasants' marriages, and at balls. At last he gained access to an orchestra, and there, steadily rising higher and higher, he attained to the position of conductor. As a performer he had no great merit, but he understood music thoroughly. In his twenty-eighth year, he migrated to Russia. He was invited there by a great seigneur, who, although he could not abide music himself, maintained an orchestra from a love of display. In his house Lemm spent seven years as musical director, and then left him with empty hands. The seigneur, who had squandered all his means, first offered Lemm a bill of exchange for the amount due to him; then refused to give him even that; and ultimately never paid him a single farthing. Lemm was advised to leave the country, but he did not like to go home penniless from Russia—from the great Russia, that golden land of artists. So he determined to remain and seek his fortune there.

During the course of ten years, the poor German continued to seek his fortune. He found various employers, he lived in Moscow and in several county towns, he patiently suffered much, he made acquaintance with poverty, he struggled hard.[1] All this time, amidst all the troubles to which he was exposed, the idea of ultimately returning home never quitted him. It was the only thing that supported him. But Fate did not choose to bless him with this supreme and final piece of good fortune.

At fifty years of age, in bad health and prematurely decrepit, he happened to come to the town of O., and there he took up his permanent abode, managing somehow to obtain a poor livelihood by giving lessons. He had by this time entirely lost all hope of quitting the hated soil of Russia.

Lemm's outward appearance was not in his favour. He was short and high-shouldered, his shoulder-blades stuck out awry, his feet were large and flat, and his red hands, marked by swollen veins, had hard, stiff fingers tipped with nails of a pale blue colour. His face was covered with wrinkles, his cheeks were hollow, and he had pursed-up lips which he was always moving with a kind of chewing action—one which, joined with his habitual silence, gave him an almost malignant expression. His grey hair hung in tufts over a low forehead. His very small and immobile eyes glowed dully, like coals in which the flame has just been extinguished by water. He walked heavily, jerking his clumsy frame at every step. Some of his movements called to mind the awkward shuffling of an owl in a cage, when it feels that it is being stared at, but can scarcely see anything itself out of its large yellow eyes, blinking between sleep and fear. An ancient and inexorable misery had fixed its ineffaceable stamp on the poor musician, and had wrenched and distorted his figure—one which, even without that, would have had but little to recommend it; but in spite of all that, something good and honest, something out of the common run, revealed itself in that half-ruined being, to any one who was able to get over his first impressions.

[1] Literally, " like a fish out of ice: " as a fish, taken out of a river which has been frozen over, struggles on the ice.

LIZA

A devoted admirer of Bach and Handel, thoroughly well up to his work, gifted with a lively imagination, and that audacity of idea which belongs only to the Teutonic race, Lemm might in time—who can tell?—have been reckoned among the great composers of his country, if only his life had been of a different nature. But he was not born under a lucky star. He had written much in his time, and yet he had never been fortunate enough to see any of his compositions published. He did not know how to set to work, how to cringe at the right moment, how to proffer a request at the fitting time. Once, it is true, a very long time ago, one of his friends and admirers, also a German, and also poor, published at his own expense two of Lemm's sonatas. But they remained untouched on the shelves of the music shops; silently they disappeared and left no trace behind, just as if they had been dropped into a river by night.

At last Lemm bade farewell to everything. Old age gained upon him, and he hardened, he grew stiff in mind, just as his fingers had stiffened. He had never married, and now he lived alone in O., in a little house not far from that of the Kalitines, looked after by an old woman-servant whom he had taken out of an almshouse. He walked a great deal, and he read the Bible, also a collection of Protestant hymns, and Shakespeare in Schlegel's translation. For a long time he had composed nothing; but apparently Liza, his best pupil, had been able to arouse him. It was for her that he had written the cantata to which Panshine alluded. The words of this cantata were borrowed by him from his collection of hymns, with the exception of a few verses which he composed himself. It was written for two choruses: one of the happy, one of the unhappy. At the end the two united and sang together, "Merciful Lord, have pity upon us, poor sinners, and keep us from all evil thoughts and worldly desires." On the title-page, very carefully and even artistically written, were the words, "Only the Righteous are in the Right. A

Sacred Cantata. Composed, and dedicated to Elizaveta Kalitine, his dear pupil, by her teacher, C. T. G. Lemm." The words " Only the Righteous are in the Right " and " To Elizaveta Kalitine " were surrounded by a circle of rays. Underneath was written, " For you only. Für Sie allein." This was why Lemm grew red and looked askance at Liza; he felt greatly hurt when Panshine began to talk to him about his cantata.

VI

PANSHINE struck the first chords of the sonata, in which he played the bass, loudly and with decision, but Liza did not begin her part. He stopped and looked at her— Liza's eyes, which were looking straight at him, expressed dissatisfaction; her lips did not smile, all her countenance was severe, almost sad.

" What is the matter? " he asked.

" Why have not you kept your word? " she said. " I showed you Christophor Fedorovich's cantata only on condition that you would not speak to him about it."

" I was wrong, Lizaveta Mikhailovna—I spoke without thinking."

" You have wounded him and me too. In future he will distrust me as well as others."

" What could I do, Lizaveta Mikhailovna? From my earliest youth I have never been able to see a German without feeling tempted to tease him."

" What are you saying, Vladimir Nikolaevich? This German is a poor, lonely, broken man; and you feel no pity for him! you feel tempted to tease him! "

Panshine seemed a little disconcerted.

" You are right, Lizaveta Mikhailovna," he said. " The fault is entirely due to my perpetual thoughtlessness. No, do not contradict me. I know myself well. My thoughtlessness has done me no slight harm. It makes people suppose that I am an egotist."

Panshine made a brief pause. From whatever point he started a conversation, he generally ended by speaking about himself, and then his words seemed almost to escape from him involuntarily, so softly and pleasantly did he speak, and with such an air of sincerity.

" It is so, even in your house," he continued. " Your mamma, it is true, is most kind to me. She is so good.

300

You—but no, I don't know what you think of me. But
decidedly your aunt cannot abide me. I have vexed
her by some thoughtless, stupid speech. It is true that
she does not like me, is it not? "

" Yes," replied Liza, after a moment's hesitation.
" You do not please her."

Panshine let his fingers run rapidly over the keys; a
scarcely perceptible smile glided over his lips.

" Well, but you," he continued, " do you also think
me an egotist? "

" I know so little about you," replied Liza; " but I
should not call you an egotist. On the contrary, I
ought to feel grateful to you——"

" I know, I know what you are going to say," interrupted Panshine, again running his fingers over the keys,
" for the music, for the books, which I bring you, for the
bad drawings with which I ornament your album, and
so on, and so on. I may do all that, and yet be an
egotist. I venture to think that I do not bore you, and
that you do not think me a bad man; but yet you
suppose that I—how shall I say it?—for the sake of an
epigram would not spare my friend, my father himself."

" You are absent and forgetful, like all men of the
world," said Liza, " that is all."

Panshine slightly frowned.

" Listen," he said; " don't let's talk any more about
me; let us begin our sonata. Only there is one thing
I will ask of you," he added, as he smoothed the sheets
which lay on the music-desk with his hand; " think of
me what you will, call me egotist even, I don't object to
that; but don't call me a man of the world, that name
is insufferable. *Anch'io sono pittore.* I too am an
artist, though but a poor one, and that—namely, that
I am a poor artist—I am going to prove to you on the
spot. Let us begin."

" Very good, let us begin," said Liza.

The first adagio went off with tolerable success,
although Panshine made several mistakes. What he
had written himself, and what he had learnt by heart,

he played very well, but he could not play at sight correctly. Accordingly the second part of the sonata— a tolerably quick allegro—would not do at all. At the twentieth bar Panshine, who was a couple of bars behind, gave in, and pushed back his chair with a laugh.

" No! " he exclaimed, " I cannot play to-day. It is fortunate that Lemm cannot hear us; he would have had a fit."

Liza stood up, shut the piano, and then turned to Panshine.

" What shall we do then? " she asked.

" That question is so like you! You can never sit with folded hands for a moment. Well then, if you feel inclined, let's draw a little before it becomes quite dark. Perhaps another Muse—the Muse of painting —what's her name? I've forgotten——will be more propitious to me. Where is your album? I remember the landscape I was drawing in it was not finished."

Liza went into another room for the album, and Panshine, finding himself alone, took a cambric handkerchief out of his pocket, rubbed his nails and looked sideways at his hands. They were very white and well shaped; on the second finger of the left hand he wore a spiral gold ring.

Liza returned; Panshine seated himself by the window and opened the album.

" Ah! " he exclaimed. " I see you have begun to copy my landscape—and capitally—very good indeed— only—just give me the pencil—the shadows are not laid in black enough. Look here."

And Panshine added some long strokes with a vigorous touch. He always drew the same landscape—large dishevelled trees in the foreground, in the middle distance a plain, and on the horizon an indented chain of hills. Liza looked over his shoulder at his work.

" In drawing, as also in life in general," said Panshine, turning his head now to the right, now to the left, " lightness and daring—those are the first requisites."

At this moment Lemm entered the room, and, after

bowing gravely, was about to retire; but Panshine flung the album and pencil aside, and prevented him from leaving the room.

"Where are you going, dear Christoph Fedorovich? Won't you stay and take tea?"

"I am going home," said Lemm, in a surly voice; "my head aches."

"What nonsense! do remain. We will have a talk about Shakespeare."

"My head aches," repeated the old man.

"We tried to play Beethoven's sonata without you," continued Panshine, caressingly throwing his arm over the old man's shoulder and smiling sweetly; "but we didn't succeed in bringing it to a harmonious conclusion. Just imagine, I couldn't play two consecutive notes right."

"You had better have played your romance over again," replied Lemm; then, escaping from Panshine's hold, he went out of the room.

Liza ran after him, and caught him on the steps.

"Christophor Fedorovich, I want to speak to you," she said in German, as she led him across the short green grass to the gate. "I have done you a wrong—forgive me."

Lemm made no reply.

"I showed your cantata to Vladimir Nikolaevich; I was sure he would appreciate it, and, indeed, he was exceedingly pleased with it."

Lemm stopped still.

"It's no matter," he said in Russian, and then added in his native tongue,—"But he is utterly incapable of understanding it. How is it you don't see that? He is a *dilettante*—that is all."

"You are unjust towards him," replied Liza. "He understands everything, and can do almost everything himself."

"Yes, everything second-rate—poor goods, scamped work. But that pleases, and he pleases, and he is well content with that. Well, then, bravo!——But I am

303

not angry. I and that cantata, we are both old fools! I feel a little ashamed, but it's no matter."

" Forgive me, Christophor Fedorovich! " urged Liza anew.

" It's no matter, no matter," he repeated a second time in Russian. " You are a good girl.——Here is some one coming to pay you a visit. Good-bye. You are a very good girl."

And Lemm made his way with hasty steps to the gate, through which there was passing a gentleman who was a stranger to him, dressed in a grey paletot and a broad straw hat. Politely saluting him (he bowed to every new face in O., and always turned away his head from his acquaintances in the street—such was the rule he had adopted), Lemm went past him, and disappeared behind the wall.

The stranger gazed at him as he retired with surprise, then looked at Liza, and went straight up to her.

VII

" You won't remember me," he said, as he took off his hat, " but I recognised you, though it is seven years since I saw you last. You were a child then. I am Lavretsky. Is your mamma at home? Can I see her?"

" Mamma will be so glad," replied Liza. " She has heard of your arrival."

" Your name is Elizaveta, isn't it? " asked Lavretsky, as he mounted the steps leading up to the house.

" Yes."

" I remember you perfectly. Yours was even in those days one of the faces which one does not forget. I used to bring you sweetmeats then."

Liza blushed a little, and thought to herself, " What an odd man! " Lavretsky stopped for a minute in the hall.

Liza entered the drawing-room, in which Panshine's voice and laugh were making themselves heard. He was communicating some piece of town gossip to Maria Dmitrievna and Gedeonovsky, both of whom had by this time returned from the garden, and he was laughing loudly at his own story. At the name of Lavretsky, Maria Dmitrievna became nervous and turned pale, but went forward to receive him.

" How are you? how are you, my dear cousin? " she exclaimed, with an almost lachrymose voice, dwelling on each word she uttered. " How glad I am to see you! "

" How are you, my good cousin? " replied Lavretsky, with a friendly pressure of her outstretched hand. " Is all well with you? "

" Sit down, sit down, my dear Fedor Ivanovich. Oh, how delighted I am! But first let me introduce my daughter Liza."

305

"I have already introduced myself to Lizaveta Mikhailovna," interrupted Lavretsky.

"Monsieur Panshine — Sergius Petrovich Gedeonovsky. But do sit down. I look at you, and, really, I can scarcely trust my eyes. But tell me about your health; is it good?"

"I am quite well, as you can see. And you, too, cousin—if I can say so without bringing you bad luck [1] —you are none the worse for these seven years."

"When I think what a number of years it is since we last saw one another," musingly said Maria Dmitrievna. "Where do you come from now? Where have you left—that's to say, I meant"—she hurriedly corrected herself—"I meant to say, shall you stay with us long?"

"I come just now from Berlin," replied Lavretsky, "and to-morrow I shall go into the country—to stay there, in all probability, a long time."

"I suppose you are going to live at Lavriki?"

"No, not at Lavriki; but I have a small property about five-and-twenty versts from here, and I am going there."

"Is that the property which Glafira Petrovna left you?"

"Yes, that's it."

"But really, Fedor Ivanovich, you have such a charming house at Lavriki."

Lavretsky frowned a little.

"Yes—but I have a cottage on the other estate too; I don't require any more just now. That place is— most convenient for me at present."

Maria Dmitrievna became once more so embarrassed that she actually sat upright in her chair, and let her hands drop by her side. Panshine came to the rescue, and entered into conversation with Lavretsky. Maria Dmitrievna by degrees grew calm, leant back again

---

[1] A reference to the superstition of the " evil eye," still rife among the peasants in Russia. Though it has died out among the educated classes, yet the phrase, " not to cast an evil eye," is still made use of in conversation.

comfortably in her chair, and from time to time contributed a word or two to the conversation. But still she kept looking at her guest so pitifully, sighing so significantly, and shaking her head so sadly, that at last he lost all patience, and asked her, somewhat brusquely, if she was unwell.

"No, thank God!" answered Maria Dmitrievna; "but why do you ask?"

"Because I thought you did not seem quite yourself."

Maria Dmitrievna assumed a dignified and somewhat offended expression.

"If that's the way you take it," she thought, "it's a matter of perfect indifference to me; it's clear that everything slides off you like water off a goose. Any one else would have withered up with misery, but you've grown fat on it."

Maria Dmitrievna did not stand upon ceremony when she was only thinking to herself. When she spoke aloud she was more choice in her expressions.

And in reality Lavretsky did not look like a victim of destiny. His rosy-cheeked, thoroughly Russian face, with its large white forehead, somewhat thick nose, and long straight lips, seemed to speak of robust health and enduring vigour of constitution. He was powerfully built, and his light hair twined in curls, like a boy's, about his head. Only in his eyes, which were blue, rather prominent, and a little wanting in mobility, an expression might be remarked which it would be difficult to define. It might have been melancholy, or it might have been fatigue; and the ring of his voice seemed somewhat monotonous.

All this time Panshine was supporting the burden of the conversation. He brought it round to the advantages of sugar making, about which he had lately read two French pamphlets; their contents he now proceeded to disclose, speaking with an air of great modesty, but without saying a single word about the sources of his information.

"Why there's Fedia!" suddenly exclaimed the voice

of Marfa Timofeevna in the next room, the door of which
had been left half open. " Actually Fedia! " And the
old lady hastily entered the room. Lavretsky hadn't
had time to rise from his chair before she had caught him
in her arms. " Let me have a look at you," she exclaimed, holding him at a little distance from her. " Oh,
how well you are looking! You've grown a little older,
but you haven't altered a bit for the worse, that's a fact.
But what makes you kiss my hand, kiss my face if you
please, unless you don't like the look of my wrinkled
cheeks. I dare say you never asked after me, or whether
your aunt was alive or no. And yet it was my hands
received you when you first saw the light, you good-for-
nothing fellow! Ah, well, it's all one. But it was a
good idea of yours to come here. I say, my dear," she
suddenly exclaimed, turning to Maria Dmitrievna,
" have you offered him any refreshment? "

" I don't want anything," hastily said Lavretsky.

" Well, at all events, you will drink tea with us,
batyushka. Gracious heavens! A man comes, goodness
knows from how far off, and no one gives him so much
as a cup of tea. Liza, go and see after it quickly. I
remember he was a terrible glutton when he was a boy,
and even now, perhaps, he is fond of eating and drinking."

" Allow me to pay my respects, Marfa Timofeevna,"
said Panshine, coming up to the excited old lady, and
making her a low bow.

" Pray excuse me, my dear sir," replied Marfa Timofeevna, " I overlooked you in my joy. You're just like
your dear mother," she continued, turning anew to
Lavretsky, " only you always had your father's nose,
and you have it still. Well, shall you stay here
long? "

" I go away to-morrow, aunt."

" To where? "

" To my house at Vasilievskoe."

" To-morrow? "

" To-morrow."

" Well, if it must be to-morrow, so be it. God be with

you! You know what is best for yourself. Only mind you come and say good-bye." The old lady tapped him gently on the cheek. " I didn't suppose I should live to see you come back: not that I thought I was going to die—no, no; I have life enough left in me for ten years to come. All we Pestofs are long-lived—your late grandfather used to call us double-lived; but God alone could tell how long you were going to loiter abroad. Well, well! You are a fine fellow—a very fine fellow. I dare say you can still lift ten poods [1] with one hand, as you used to do. Your late father, if you'll excuse my saying so, was as nonsensical as he could be, but he did well in getting you that Swiss tutor. Do you remember the boxing matches you used to have with him? Gymnastics, wasn't it, you used to call them? But why should I go on cackling like this? I shall only prevent Monsieur Panshino (she never laid the accent on the first syllable of his name as she ought to have done) from favouring us with his opinions. On the whole we had much better go and have tea. Yes, let's go and have it on the terrace. We have magnificent cream—not like what they have in your Londons and Parises. Come away, come away; and you, Fediouchka, give me your arm. What a strong arm you have, to be sure! I shan't fall while you're by my side."

Every one rose and went out on the terrace, except Gedeonovsky, who slipped away stealthily. During the whole time Lavretsky was talking with the mistress of the house, with Panshine, and with Marfa Timofeevna, that old gentleman had been sitting in his corner, squeezing up his eyes and shooting out his lips, while he listened with the curiosity of a child to all that was being said. When he left, it was that he might hasten to spread through the town the news of the recent arrival.

Here is a picture of what was taking place at eleven o'clock that same evening in the Kalitines' house. Downstairs, on the threshold of the drawing-room,

[1] The pood weighs thirty-six pounds.

Panshine was taking leave of Liza and saying, as he held her hand in his—

" You know who it is that attracts me here ; you know why I am always coming to your house. Of what use are words when all is so clear ? "

Liza did not say a word in reply, she did not even smile. Slightly arching her eyebrows, and growing rather red, she kept her eyes fixed on the ground, but did not withdraw her hand. Upstairs, in Marfa Timofeevna's room, the light of the lamp which hung in the corner before the age-embrowned sacred pictures, fell on Lavretsky as he sat in an armchair, his elbows resting on his knees, his face hidden in his hands. In front of him stood the old lady, who from time to time silently passed her hand over his hair. He spent more than an hour with her after taking leave of the mistress of the house, he scarcely saying a word to his kind old friend and she not asking him any questions. And why should he have spoken ? what could she have asked ? She understood all so well, she so fully sympathised with all the feelings which filled his heart.

VIII

FEDOR IVANOVICH LAVRETSKY (we must ask our reader's permission to break off the thread of the story for a time) sprang from a noble family of long descent. The founder of the race migrated from Prussia during the reign of Basil the Blind,[1] and was favoured with a grant of two hundred *chetverts* [2] of land in the district of Biejetsk. Many of his descendants filled various official positions, and were appointed to governorships in distant places, under princes and influential personages, but none of them obtained any great amount of property, or arrived at a higher dignity than that of inspector of the Czar's table.

The richest and most influential of all the Lavretskys was Fedor Ivanovich's paternal great grandfather Andrei, a man who was harsh, insolent, shrewd, and crafty. Even up to the present day men have never ceased to talk about his despotic manners, his furious temper, his senseless prodigality, and his insatiable avarice. He was very tall and stout, his complexion was swarthy, and he wore no beard. He lisped, and he generally seemed half asleep. But the more quietly he spoke, the more did all around him tremble. He had found a wife not unlike himself. She had a round face, a yellow complexion, prominent eyes, and the nose of a hawk. A gipsy by descent, passionate and vindictive in temper, she refused to yield in anything to her husband, who all but brought her to her grave, and whom, although she had been eternally squabbling with him, she could not bear long to survive.

[1] In the fifteenth century.
[2] An old measure of land, variously estimated at from two to six acres.

311

Andrei's son, Peter, our Fedor's grandfather, did not take after his father. He was a simple country gentleman; rather odd, noisy in voice and slow in action, rough but not malicious, hospitable, and devoted to coursing. He was more than thirty years old when he inherited from his father two thousand souls,[1] all in excellent condition; but he soon began to squander his property, a part of which he disposed of by sale, and he spoilt his household. His large, warm, and dirty rooms were full of people of small degree, known and unknown, who swarmed in from all sides like cockroaches. All these visitors gorged themselves with whatever came in their way, drank their fill to intoxication, and carried off what they could, extolling and glorifying their affable host. As for their host, when he was out of humour with them, he called them scamps and parasites; but when deprived of their company, he soon found himself bored.

The wife of Peter Andreich was a quiet creature, whom he had taken from a neighbouring family in acquiescence with his father's choice and command. Her name was Anna Pavlovna. She never interfered in anything, received her guests cordially, and went out into society herself with pleasure—although " it was death " to her, to use her own phrase, to have to powder herself. " They put a felt cap on your head," she used to say in her old age; " they combed all your hair straight up on end, they smeared it with grease, they strewed it with flour, they stuck it full of iron pins; you couldn't wash it away afterwards. But to pay a visit without powdering was impossible. People would have taken offence. What a torment it was! " She liked to drive fast, and she was ready to play at cards from morning till evening. When her husband approached the card-table, she was always in the habit of covering with her hand the trumpery losses scored up against her; but she had made over to him, without reserve, all her dowry, all the money she had. She brought him two children—

[1] Male serfs.

a son named Ivan, our Fedor's father, and a daughter, Glafira.[1]

Ivan was not brought up at home, but in the house of an old and wealthy maiden aunt, Princess Kubensky. She styled him her heir (if it had not been for that, his father would not have let him go), dressed him like a doll, gave him teachers of every kind, and placed him under the care of a French tutor—an ex-abbé, a pupil of Jean Jacques Rousseau—a certain M. Courtin de Vaucelles, an adroit and subtle intriguer—" the very *fine fleur* of the emigration," as she expressed herself; and she ended by marrying this *fine fleur* when she was almost seventy years old. She transferred all her property to his name, and soon afterwards, rouged, perfumed with amber *à la Richelieu*, surrounded by negro boys, Italian greyhounds, and noisy parrots, she died, stretched on a crooked silken couch of the style of Louis the Fifteenth, with an enamelled snuff-box of Petitot's work in her hands—and died deserted by her husband. The insinuating M. Courtin had preferred to take himself and her money off to Paris.

Ivan was in his twentieth year when this unexpected blow struck him. We speak of the Princess's marriage, not her death. In his aunt's house, in which he had suddenly passed from the position of a wealthy heir to that of a hanger-on, he would not stay any longer. In Petersburg, the society in which he had grown up closed its doors upon him. For the lower ranks of the public service, and the laborious and obscure life they involved, he felt a strong repugnance. All this, it must be remembered, took place in the earliest part of the reign of the Emperor Alexander I.[2] He was obliged, greatly against his will, to return to his father's country house. Dirty, poor, and miserable did the paternal nest seem to him. The solitude and the dulness of a retired country life offended him at every step. He was devoured by ennui; besides, every one in the house, except his mother,

[1] The accent should be on the second syllable of this name.
[2] When corruption was the rule in the public service.

regarded him with unloving eyes. His father disliked his metropolitan habits, his dress-coats and shirt-frills, his books, his flute, his cleanliness—from which he justly argued that his son regarded him with a feeling of aversion. He was always grumbling at his son, and complaining of his conduct.

" Nothing we have here pleases him," he used to say. " He is so fastidious at table, he eats nothing. He cannot bear the air and the smell of the room. The sight of drunken people upsets him; and as to beating any one before him, you mustn't dare to do it. Then he won't enter the service; his health is delicate, forsooth! Bah! What an effeminate creature!—and all because his head is full of Voltaire! " The old man particularly disliked Voltaire, and also the " infidel " Diderot, although he had never read a word of their works. Reading was not in his line.

Peter Andreich was not mistaken. Both Diderot and Voltaire really were in his son's head; and not they alone. Rousseau and Raynal and Helvetius also, and many other similar writers, were in his head; but in his head only. Ivan Petrovich's former tutor, the retired abbé and encyclopædist, had satisfied himself with pouring all the collective wisdom of the eighteenth century over his pupil; and so the pupil existed, saturated with it. It held its own in him without mixing with his blood, without sinking into his mind, without resolving into fixed convictions. And would it be reasonable to ask for convictions from a youngster half a century ago, when we have not even yet acquired any?

Ivan Petrovich disconcerted the visitors also in his father's house. He was too proud to have anything to do with them; they feared him. With his sister Glafira, too, who was twelve years his senior, he did not at all agree. This Glafira was a strange being. Plain, deformed, meagre, with staring and severe eyes, and with thin, compressed lips, she, in her face and her voice, and in her angular and quick movements, resembled her grandmother, the gipsy, Andrei's wife. Obstinate, and

314

fond of power, she would not even hear of marriage. Ivan Petrovich's return home was by no means to her taste. So long as the Princess Kubensky kept him with her, Glafira had hoped to obtain at least half of her father's property; and in her avarice, as well as in other points, she resembled her grandmother. Besides this, Glafira was jealous of her brother. He had been educated so well; he spoke French so correctly, with a Parisian accent; and she scarcely knew how to say " *Bonjour,*" and " *Comment vous portez vous ?* " It is true that her parents were entirely ignorant of French, but that did not make things any better for her.

As to Ivan Petrovich, he did not know what to do with himself for vexation and ennui; he had not spent quite a year in the country, but even this time seemed to him like ten years. It was only with his mother that he was at ease in spirit; and for whole hours he used to sit in her low suite of rooms listening to the good lady's simple, unconnected talk, and stuffing himself with preserves. It happened that among Anna Pavlovna's maids there was a very pretty girl, named Malania. Intelligent and modest, with calm, sweet eyes, and finely-cut features, she pleased Ivan Petrovich from the very first, and he soon fell in love with her. He loved her timid gait, her modest replies, her gentle voice, her quiet smile. Every day she seemed to him more attractive than before. And she attached herself to Ivan Petrovich with the whole strength of her soul—as only Russian girls know how to devote themselves—and gave herself to him. In a country house no secret can be preserved long; in a short time almost every one knew of the young master's fondness for Malania. At last the news reached Peter Andreich himself. At another time it is probable that he would have paid very little attention to so unimportant an affair; but he had long nursed a grudge against his son, and he was delighted to have an opportunity of disgracing the philosophical exquisite from St. Petersburg. There ensued a storm, attended by noise and outcry. Malania was locked up in the store-room.[1] Ivan Petrovich was summoned into his father's presence. Anna Pavlovna also came running to the scene of confusion, and tried to appease her husband; but he would not listen to a word she said. Like a hawk, he pounced upon his son, charging him with immorality, atheism, and hypocrisy. He eagerly availed himself of so good an opportunity of discharging on him all his long-gathered spite against the Princess Kubensky, and overwhelmed him with insulting expressions.

At first Ivan Petrovich kept silence, and maintained his hold over himself; but when his father thought fit to threaten him with a disgraceful punishment, he could bear it no longer. "Ah!" he thought, "the infidel Diderot is going to be brought forward again. Well, then, I will put his teaching in action." And so with a quiet and even voice, although with a secret shuddering in all his limbs, he told his father that it was a mistake to accuse him of immorality; that he had no intention of justifying his fault, but that he was ready to make amends for it, and that all the more willingly, inasmuch as he felt himself superior to all prejudices; and, in fact —that he was ready to marry Malania. In uttering these words Ivan Petrovich undoubtedly attained the end he had in view. Peter Andreich was so confounded that he opened his eyes wide, and for a moment was struck dumb; but he immediately recovered his senses, and then and there, just as he was, wrapped in a dressing-gown trimmed with squirrels' fur, and with slippers on his bare feet, he rushed with clenched fists at his son, who, as if on purpose, had dressed his hair that day à la Titus, and had put on a blue dress-coat, quite new and made in the English fashion, tasselled boots, and dandified, tight-fitting buckskin pantaloons. Anna Pavlovna uttered a loud shriek, and hid her face in her hands; meanwhile her son ran right through the house, jumped into the courtyard, threw himself first into the kitchen garden and then into the flower garden, flew

[1] A sort of closet under the stairs.

across the park into the road, and ran and ran, without once looking back, until at last he ceased to hear behind him the sound of his father's heavy feet, the loud and broken cries with which his father sobbed out, " Stop, villain! Stop, or I will curse you! "

Ivan Petrovich took refuge in the house of a neighbour,[1] and his father returned home utterly exhausted, and bathed in perspiration. There he announced, almost before he had given himself time to recover breath, that he withdrew his blessing and his property from his son, whose stupid books he condemned to be burnt; and he gave orders to have the girl Malania sent, without delay, to a distant village. Some good people found out where Ivan Petrovich was, and told him everything. Full of shame and rage, he swore vengeance upon his father; and that very night, having lain in wait for the peasant's cart on which Malania was being sent away, he carried her off by force, galloped with her to the nearest town, and there married her. He was supplied with the necessary means by a neighbour, a hard-drinking, retired sailor, who was exceedingly good-natured, and a very great lover of all " noble histories," as he called them.

The next day Ivan Petrovich sent his father a letter, which was frigidly and ironically polite, and then betook himself to the estate of two of his second cousins— Dmitry Pestof, and his sister Marfa Timofeevna, with the latter of whom the reader is already acquainted. He told them everything that had happened, announced his intention of going to St. Petersburg to seek an appointment, and begged them to give shelter to his wife, even if only for a time. At the word " wife " he sobbed bitterly; and, in spite of his metropolitan education, and his philosophy, he humbly, like a thorough Russian peasant, knelt down at the feet of his relations, and even touched the floor with his forehead.

[1] Literally, " of a neighbouring *Odnodvorets*." That word signifies one who belongs by descent to the class of nobles and proprietors, but who has no serfs belonging to him, and is really a moujik, or peasant. Some villages are composed of inhabitants of this class, who are often intelligent, though uneducated.

The Pestofs, who were kind and compassionate people, willingly consented to his request. With them he spent three weeks, secretly expecting an answer from his father. But no answer came; no answer could come. Peter Andreich, when he received the news of the marriage, took to his bed, and gave orders that his son's name should never again be mentioned to him; but Ivan's mother, without her husband's knowledge, borrowed five hundred paper roubles from a neighbouring priest,[1] and sent them to her son with a little sacred picture for his wife. She was afraid of writing, but she told her messenger, a spare little peasant who could walk sixty versts in a day, to say to Ivan that he was not to fret too much, that, please God, all would yet go right, and his father's wrath would turn to kindness—that she too would have preferred a different daughter-in-law, but that evidently God had willed it as it was, and that she sent her parental benediction to Malania Sergievna. The spare little peasant had a rouble given him, asked leave to see the new mistress, whose gossip [2] he was, kissed her hand, and returned home.

So Ivan Petrovich betook himself to St. Petersburg with a light heart. An unknown future lay before him. Poverty might menace him; but he had broken with the hateful life in the country, and, above all, he had not fallen short of his instructors; he had really " put into action," and indeed done justice to, the doctrines of Rousseau, Diderot, and the " Declaration of the Rights of Man." The conviction of having accomplished a duty, a sense of pride and of triumph, filled his soul; and the fact of having to separate from his wife did not greatly alarm him; he would far sooner have been troubled by the necessity of having constantly to live with her. He had now to think of other affairs. One task was finished.

[1] Literally, " from the *Blagochinny*," an ecclesiastic who exercises supervision over a number of churches or parishes, a sort of Rural Dean.
[2] The word is used in its old meaning of " fellow-sponsor."

In St. Petersburg, contrary to his own expectations, he was successful. The Princess Kubensky—whom M. Courtin had already flung aside, but who had not yet contrived to die—in order that she might, at least to some extent, make amends for her conduct towards her nephew, recommended him to all her friends, and gave him five thousand roubles, almost all the money she had left, and a watch, with his crest wrought on its back surrounded by a wreath of Cupids.

Three months had not gone by before he received an appointment on the staff of the Russian embassy in London, whither he set sail (steamers were not even talked about then) in the first homeward bound English vessel he could find. A few months later he received a letter from Pestof. The kind-hearted gentleman congratulated him on the birth of a son, who had come into the world at the village of Pokrovskoe, on the 20th of August, 1807, and had been named Fedor, in honour of the holy martyr, Fedor Stratilates. On account of her extreme weakness, Malania Sergievna could add only a few lines. But even those few astonished Ivan Petrovich; he was not aware that Marfa Timofeevna had taught his wife to read and write.

It must not be supposed that Ivan Petrovich gave himself up for any length of time to the sweet emotion caused by paternal feeling. He was just then paying court to one of the celebrated Phrynes or Laises of the day—classical names were still in vogue at that time. The peace of Tilsit was only just concluded,[1] and every one was hastening to enjoy himself, every one was being swept round by a giddy whirlwind. The black eyes of a bold beauty had helped to turn his head also. He had very little money, but he played cards luckily, made friends, joined in all possible diversions—in a word, he sailed with all sail set.

[1] In consequence of which, the Russian embassy was withdrawn from London, and Ivan Petrovich probably went to Paris.

IX

FOR a long time the old Lavretsky could not forgive his
son for his marriage. If, at the end of six months, Ivan
Petrovich had appeared before him with contrite mien,
and had fallen at his feet, the old man would, perhaps,
have pardoned the offender — after having soundly
abused him, and given him a tap with his crutch by way
of frightening him. But Ivan Petrovich went on living
abroad, and, apparently, troubled himself but little
about his father. "Silence! don't dare to say another
word!" exclaimed Peter Andreich to his wife, every time
she tried to mollify him. "That puppy ought to be
always praying to God for me, since I have not laid my
curse upon him, the good-for-nothing fellow! Why, my
late father would have killed him with his own hands,
and he would have done well." All that Anna Pavlovna
could do was to cross herself stealthily when she heard
such terrible words as these. As to his son's wife, Peter
Andreich would not so much as hear of her at first; and
even when he had to answer a letter in which his
daughter-in-law was mentioned by Pestof, he ordered a
message to be sent to him to say that he did not know
of any one who could be his daughter-in-law, and that
it was contrary to the law to shelter runaway female
serfs, a fact of which he considered it a duty to warn him.
But afterwards, on learning the birth of his grandson, his
heart softened a little; he gave orders that inquiries
should be secretly made on his behalf about the mother's
health, and he sent her—but still, not as if it came from
himself—a small sum of money.

Before Fedor was a year old, his grandmother, Anna
Pavlovna, was struck down by a mortal complaint. A
few days before her death, when she could no longer rise
from her bed, she told her husband in the presence of

the priest, while her dying eyes swam with timid tears, that she wished to see her daughter-in-law, and to bid her farewell, and to bless her grandson. The old man, who was greatly moved, bade her set her mind at rest, and immediately sent his own carriage for his daughter-in-law, calling her, for the first time, Malania Sergievna.[1] Malania arrived with her boy, and with Marfa Timo-feevna, whom nothing would have induced to allow her to go alone, and who was determined not to allow her to meet with any harm. Half dead with fright, Malania Sergievna entered her father-in-law's study, a nurse carrying Fedia behind her. Peter Andreich looked at her in silence. She drew near and took his hand, on which her quivering lips could scarcely press a silent kiss.

" Well, noble lady," [2] he said at last,—" Good day to you; let's go to my wife's room."

He rose and bent over Fedia; the babe smiled and stretched out its tiny white hands towards him. The old man was touched.

" Ah, my orphaned one! " he said. " You have successfully pleaded your father's cause. I will not desert you, little bird."

As soon as Malania Sergievna entered Anna Pavlovna's bedroom, she fell on her knees near the door. Anna Pavlovna, having made her a sign to come to her bed-side, embraced her, and blessed her child. Then, turning towards her husband a face worn by cruel suffering, she would have spoken to him, but he prevented her.

" I know, I know what you want to ask," he said; " don't worry yourself. She shall remain with us, and for her sake I will forgive Vanka." [3]

Anna Pavlovna succeeded by a great effort in getting

[1] That is to say, no longer speaking of her as if she were still a servant.

[2] Literally, " thrashed-while-damp noblewoman," *i.e.* hastily ennobled. Much corn is thrashed in Russia before it has had time to get dry.

[3] A diminutive of Ivan, somewhat expressive of contempt. Vanya is the affectionate form.

hold of her husband's hand and pressing it to her lips. That same evening she died.

Peter Andreich kept his word. He let his son know that out of respect to his mother's last moments, and for the sake of the little Fedor, he gave him back his blessing, and would keep Malania Sergievna in his house. A couple of small rooms upstairs were accordingly given to Malania, and he presented her to his most important acquaintances, the one-eyed Brigadier Skurekhine and his wife. He also placed two maid-servants at her disposal, and a page to run her errands.

After Marfa Timofeevna had left her—who had conceived a perfect hatred for Glafira, and had quarrelled with her three times in the course of a single day—the poor woman at first found her position difficult and painful. But after a time she attained endurance, and grew accustomed to her father-in-law. He, on his part, grew accustomed to her, and became fond of her, though he scarcely ever spoke to her, although in his caresses themselves a certain involuntary contempt showed itself. But it was her sister-in-law who made Malania suffer the most. Even during her mother's lifetime, Glafira had gradually succeeded in getting the entire management of the house into her own hands. Every one, from her father downwards, yielded to her. Without her permission not even a lump of sugar was to be got. She would have preferred to die rather than to delegate her authority to another housewife—and such a housewife too! She had been even more irritated than Peter Andreich by her brother's marriage, so she determined to read the upstart a good lesson, and from the very first Malania Sergievna became her slave. And Malania, utterly without defence, weak in health, constantly a prey to trouble and alarm—how could she have striven against the proud and strong-willed Glafira? Not a day passed without Glafira reminding her of her former position, and praising her for not forgetting herself. Malania Sergievna would willingly have acquiesced in these remindings and praisings, however bitter they might be—but her child had been taken away from her. This drove her to despair. Under the pretext that she was not qualified to see after his education, she was scarcely ever allowed to go near him. Glafira undertook the task. The child passed entirely into her keeping.

In her sorrow, Malania Sergievna began to implore her husband in her letters to return quickly. Peter Andreich himself wished to see his son, but Ivan Petrovich merely sent letters in reply. He thanked his father for what had been done for his wife, and for the money which had been sent to himself, and he promised to come home soon—but he did not come.

At last the year 1812 recalled him from abroad. On seeing each other for the first time after a separation of six years, the father and the son met in a warm embrace, and did not say a single word in reference to their former quarrels. Nor was it a time for that. All Russia was rising against the foe, and they both felt that Russian blood flowed in their veins. Peter Andreich equipped a whole regiment of volunteers at his own expense. But the war ended; the danger passed away. Ivan Petrovich once more become bored, once more he was allured into the distance, into that world in which he had grown up, and in which he felt himself at home. Malania could not hold him back; she was valued at very little in his eyes. Even what she really had hoped had not been fulfilled. Like the rest, her husband thought that it was decidedly most expedient to confide Fedia's education to Glafira. Ivan's poor wife could not bear up against this blow, could not endure this second separation. Without a murmur, at the end of a few days, she quietly passed away.

In the course of her whole life she had never been able to resist anything; and so with her illness, also, she did not struggle. When she could no longer speak, and the shadows of death already lay on her face, her features still retained their old expression of patient perplexity, of unruffled and submissive sweetness. With her usual silent humility, she gazed at Glafira; and as Anna

323

Pavlovna on her deathbed had kissed the hand of Peter Andreich, so she pressed her lips to Glafira's hand, as she confided to Glafira's care her only child. So did this good and quiet being end her earthly career. Like a shrub torn from its native soil, and the next moment flung aside, its roots upturned to the sun, she withered and disappeared, leaving no trace behind, and no one to grieve for her. It is true that her maids regretted her, and so did Peter Andreich. The old man missed her kindly face, her silent presence. " Forgive—farewell—my quiet one! " he said, as he took leave of her for the last time, in the church. He wept as he threw a handful of earth into her grave.

He did not long survive her—not more than five years. In the winter of 1819 he died peacefully in Moscow, whither he had gone with Glafira and his grandson. In his will he desired to be buried by the side of Anna Pavlovna and " Malasha." [1]

Ivan Petrovich was at that time amusing himself in Paris, having retired from the service soon after the year 1815. On receiving the news of his father's death, he determined to return to Russia. The organisation of his property had to be considered. Besides, according to Glafira's letter, Fedia had finished his twelfth year; and the time had come for taking serious thought about his education.

[1] Diminutive of Malania.

X

IVAN PETROVICH returned to Russia an Anglomaniac. Short hair, starched frills, a pea-green, long-skirted coat with a number of little collars; a sour expression of countenance, something trenchant and at the same time careless in his demeanour, an utterance through the teeth, an abrupt wooden laugh, an absence of smile, a habit of conversing only on political or politico-economical subjects, a passion for under-done roast beef and port wine—everything in him breathed, so to speak, of Great Britain. He seemed entirely imbued by its spirit. But, strange to say, while becoming an Anglomaniac, Ivan Petrovich had also become a patriot,—at all events he called himself a patriot,—although he knew very little about Russia, he had not retained a single Russian habit, and he expressed himself in Russian oddly. In ordinary talk, his language was colourless and unwieldy, and absolutely bristled with Gallicisms. But the moment that the conversation turned upon serious topics, Ivan Petrovich immediately began to give utterance to such expressions as " to render manifest abnormal symptoms of enthusiasm," or " This is extravagantly inconsistent with the essential nature of circumstances," and so forth. He had brought with him some manuscript plans, intended to assist in the organisation and improvement of the empire. For he was greatly discontented with what he saw taking place. It was the absence of system which especially roused his indignation.

At his interview with his sister, he informed her in the first words he spoke that he meant to introduce radical reforms on his property, and that for the future all his affairs would be conducted on a new system. Glafira made no reply, but she clenched her teeth and thought, " What is to become of me then? " However, when

she had gone with her brother and her nephew to the
estate, her mind was soon set at ease. It is true that a
few changes were made in the house, and the hangers-on
and parasites were put to immediate flight. Among
their number suffered two old women, the one blind, the
other paralysed, and also a worn-out major of the
Ochakof [1] days, who, on account of his great voracity,
was fed upon nothing but black bread and lentiles. An
order was given also not to receive any of the former
visitors; they were replaced by a distant neighbour, a
certain blond and scrofulous baron, an exceedingly well
brought-up and remarkably dull man. New furniture
was sent from Moscow; spittoons, bells, and washhand
basins were introduced; the breakfast was served in a
novel fashion; foreign wines replaced the old national
spirits and liqueurs; new liveries were given to the
servants, and to the family coat of arms was added the
motto, "*In recto virtus.*"

In reality, however, the power of Glafira did not
diminish; all receipts and expenditures were settled,
as before, by her. A valet, who had been brought from
abroad, a native of Alsace, tried to compete with her,
and lost his place, in spite of the protection which his
master generally afforded him. In all that related to
housekeeping, and also to the administration of the
estate (for with these things too Glafira interfered)—in
spite of the intention often expressed by Ivan Petrovich
" to breathe new life into the chaos,"—all remained on
the old footing. Only the *obrok* [2] remained on the old
footing, and the *barshina* [3] became heavier, and the
peasants were forbidden to go straight to Ivan Petrovich.
The patriot already despised his fellow-citizens heartily.
Ivan Petrovich's system was applied in its full development only to Fedia. The boy's education really underwent " a radical reform." His father undertook the
sole direction of it himself.

[1] Ochakof is a town which was taken from the Turks by the
Russians in 1788.
[2] What the peasant paid his lord in money.
[3] What the peasant paid his lord in labour.

XI

UNTIL the return of Ivan Petrovich from abroad, Fedia remained, as we have already said, in the hands of Glafira Petrovna. He was not yet eight years old when his mother died. It was not every day that he had been allowed to see her, but he had become passionately attached to her. His recollections of her, especially of her pale and gentle face, her mournful eyes, and her timid caresses, were indelibly impressed upon his heart. It was but vaguely that he understood her position in the house, but he felt that between him and her there existed a barrier which she dared not and could not destroy. He felt shy of his father, who, on his part, never caressed him. His grandfather sometimes smoothed his hair and gave him his hand to kiss, but called him a savage, and thought him a fool. After Malania's death his aunt took him regularly in hand. Fedia feared her, feared her bright sharp eyes, her cutting voice; he never dared to make the slightest noise in her presence; if by chance he stirred ever so little on his chair, she would immediately exclaim in her hissing voice, "Where arc you going? sit still! "

On Sundays, after mass, he was allowed to play—that is to say, a thick book was given to him, a mysterious book, the work of a certain Maksimovich-Ambodik, bearing the title of *Symbols and Emblems*. In this book there were to be found about a thousand for the most part very puzzling pictures, with equally puzzling explanations in five languages. Cupid, represented with a naked and chubby body, played a great part in these pictures. To one of them, the title of which was *Saffron and the Rainbow*, was appended the explanation, " The effect of this is great." Opposite another, which represented " A Stork, flying with a violet in its beak,"

327

stood this motto, " To thee they are all known; " and " Cupid, and a bear licking its cub," was styled " Little by Little." Fedia used to pore over these pictures. He was familiar with them all even to their minutest details. Some of them—it was always the same ones—made him reflect, and excited his imagination: of other diversions he knew nothing.

When the time came for teaching him languages and music, Glafira Petrovna hired an old maid for a mere trifle, a Swede, whose eyes looked sideways, like a hare's, who spoke French and German more or less badly, played the piano so so, and pickled cucumbers to perfection. In the company of this governess, of his aunt, and of an old servant maid called Vasilievna, Fedia passed four whole years. Sometimes he would sit in a corner with his *Emblems*—there he would sit and sit. A scent of geraniums filled the low room, one tallow candle burnt dimly, the cricket chirped monotonously as if it were bored, the little clock ticked busily on the wall, a mouse scratched stealthily and gnawed behind the tapestry; and the three old maids, like the three Fates, knitted away silently and swiftly, the shadows of their hands now scampering along, now mysteriously quivering in the dusk; and strange, no less dusky, thoughts were being born in the child's mind.

No one would have called Fedia an interesting child. He was rather pale, but stout, badly built, and awkward —a regular moujik, to use the expression employed by Glafira Petrovna. The pallor would soon have vanished from his face if they had let him go out more into the fresh air. He learnt his lessons pretty well, though he was often idle. He never cried, but he sometimes evinced a savage obstinacy. At those times no one could do anything with him. Fedia did not love a single one of the persons by whom he was surrounded. Alas for that heart which has not loved in youth!

Such did Ivan Petrovich find him when he returned, and, without losing time, he at once began to apply his system to him.

"I want, above all, to make a man of him—*un homme*," he said to Glafira Petrovna, "and not only a man, but a Spartan." This plan he began to carry out by dressing his boy in Highland costume. The twelve-year-old little fellow had to go about with bare legs, and with a cock's feather in his cap. The Swedish governess was replaced by a young tutor from Switzerland, who was acquainted with all the niceties of gymnastics. Music was utterly forbidden, as an accomplishment unworthy of a man. Natural science, international law, and mathematics, as well as carpentry, which was selected in accordance with the advice of Jean Jacques Rousseau, and heraldry, which was introduced for the maintenance of chivalrous ideas—these were the subjects to which the future "man" had to give his attention. He had to get up at four in the morning and take a cold bath immediately, after which he had to run round a high pole at the end of a cord. He had one meal a day, consisting of one dish; he rode on horseback, and he shot with a cross-bow. On every fitting occasion he had to exercise himself, in imitation of his father, in gaining strength of will; and every evening he used to write, in a book reserved for that purpose, an account of how he had spent the day, and what were his ideas on the subject. Ivan Petrovich, on his side, wrote instructions for him in French, in which he styled him *mon fils*, and addressed him as *vous*. Fedia used to say "thou" to his father in Russian, but he did not dare to sit down in his presence.

The "system" muddled the boy's brains, confused his ideas, and cramped his mind; but, as far as his physical health was concerned, the new kind of life acted on him beneficially. At first he fell ill with a fever, but he soon recovered and became a fine fellow. His father grew proud of him, and styled him in his curious language "the child of nature, my creation." When Fedia reached the age of sixteen, Ivan Petrovich considered it a duty to inspire him in good time with contempt for the female sex—and so the young Spartan, with the first down beginning to appear upon his lips, timid in feeling, but with a body full of blood, and strength, and energy, already tried to seem careless, and cold, and rough.

Meanwhile time passed by. Ivan Petrovich spent the greater part of the year at Lavriki—that was the name of his chief hereditary estate; but in winter he used to go by himself to Moscow, where he put up at a hotel, attended his club assiduously, aired his eloquence freely, explained his plans in society, and more than ever gave himself out as an Anglomaniac, a grumbler, and a statesman. But the year 1825 came and brought with it much trouble.[1] Ivan Petrovich's intimate friends and acquaintances underwent a heavy tribulation. He made haste to betake himself far away into the country, and there he shut himself up in his house. Another year passed and Ivan Petrovich suddenly broke down, became feeble, and utterly gave way. His health having deserted him, the freethinker began to go to church, and to order prayers to be said for him;[2] the European began to steam himself in the Russian bath, to dine at two o'clock, to go to bed at nine, to be talked to sleep by the gossip of an old house-steward; the statesman burnt all his plans and all his correspondence, trembled before the governor, and treated the *Ispravnik*[3] with uneasy civility; the man of iron will whimpered and complained whenever he was troubled by a boil, or when his soup had got cold before he was served with it. Glafira again ruled supreme in the house; again did inspectors, overseers,[4] and simple peasants begin to go up the back staircase to the rooms occupied by the " old witch "— as she was called by the servants of the house.

[1] Arising from the conspiracy of the " Decembrists " and their attempts at a revolution, on the occasion of the death of Alexander I., and the accession of Nicholas to the throne.

[2] *Molebni :* prayers in which the name of the person who has paid for them is mentioned.

[3] Inspector of rural police.

[4] *Prikashchiki* and *Burmistrui :* two classes of overseers, the former dealing with economical matters only, the latter having to do with the administrative department also.

330

The change which had taken place in Ivan Petrovich
produced a strong impression on the mind of his son.
He had already entered on his nineteenth year, and he
had begun to think for himself, and to shake off the
weight of the hand which had been pressing him down.
Even before this he had remarked how different were
his father's deeds from his words, the wide and liberal
theories he professed from the hard and narrow des-
potism he practised; but he had not expected so abrupt
a transformation. In his old age the egotist revealed
himself in his full nature. The young Lavretsky was
just getting ready to go to Moscow, with a view to preparing himself for the university, when a new and unexpected misfortune fell on the head of Ivan Petrovich.
In the course of a single day the old man became blind,
hopelessly blind.

Distrusting the skill of Russian medical men, he did
all he could to get permission to travel abroad. It was
refused. Then, taking his son with him, he wandered
about Russia for three whole years trying one doctor
after another, incessantly journeying from place to place,
and, by his impatient fretfulness, driving his doctors,
his son, and his servants, to the verge of despair. Utterly
used up,[1] he returned to Lavriki a weeping and capricious infant. Days of bitterness ensued, in which all
suffered at his hands. He was quiet only while he was
feeding. Never had he eaten so much, nor so greedily.
At all other moments he allowed neither himself nor any
one else to be at peace. He prayed, grumbled at fate,
found fault with himself, with his system, with politics,
with all which he used to boast of, with all that he had
ever set up as a model for his son. He would declare
that he believed in nothing, and then he would betake
himself again to prayer; he could not bear a single
moment of solitude, and he compelled his servants constantly to sit near his bed day and night, and to entertain
him with stories, which he was in the habit of interrupt-

[1] Literally, " a regular rag."

ing by exclamations of, " You're all telling lies! " or,
" What utter nonsense! "

Glafira Petrovna had the largest share in all the
trouble he gave. He was absolutely unable to do without her; and until the very end she fulfilled all the
invalid's caprices, though sometimes she was unable to
reply immediately to what he said, for fear the tone of
her voice should betray the anger which was almost
choking her. So he creaked on for two years more, and
at length one day, in the beginning of the month of
May, he died. He had been carried out to the balcony,
and placed there in the sun. " Glasha! Glashka! broth,
broth, you old idi—," lisped his stammering tongue;
and then, without completing the last word, it became
silent for ever. Glafira, who had just snatched the cup
of broth from the hands of the major-domo, stopped
short, looked her brother in the face, very slowly crossed
herself, and went silently away. And his son, who
happened also to be on the spot, did not say a word
either, but he bent over the railing of the balcony, and
gazed for a long time into the garden, all green and
fragrant, all sparkling in the golden sunlight of spring.
He was twenty-three years old; how sadly, how swiftly
had those years passed by unmarked! Life opened out
before him now.

XII

AFTER his father's burial, having confided to the never-changing Glafira Petrovna the administration of his household, and the supervision of his agents, the young Lavretsky set out for Moscow, whither a vague but powerful longing attracted him. He knew in what his education had been defective, and he was determined to supply its deficiencies as far as was possible. In the course of the last five years he had read much, and he had seen a good deal with his own eyes. Many ideas has passed through his mind, many a professor might have envied him some of his knowledge; yet, at the same time, he was entirely ignorant of much that had long been familiar to every schoolboy. Lavretsky felt that he was not at his ease among his fellow-men; he had a secret inkling that he was an exceptional character. The Anglomaniac had played his son a cruel trick; his capricious education had borne its fruit. For many years he had implicitly obeyed his father; and when at last he had learned to value him aright, the effects of his father's teaching were already produced. Certain habits had become rooted in him. He did not know how to comport himself towards his fellow-men; at the age of twenty-three, with an eager longing after love in his bashful heart, he had not yet dared to look a woman in the face. With his clear and logical, but rathers luggish intellect, with his stubbornness, and his tendency to-wards inactivity and contemplation, he ought to have been flung at an early age into the whirl of life, instead of which he had been deliberately kept in seclusion. And now the magic circle was broken, but he remained standing on the same spot, cramped in mind and self-absorbed.

At his age it seemed a little ridiculous to put on the

uniform of a student,[1] but he did not fear ridicule.   His
Spartan education had at all events been so far useful,
insamuch as it had developed in him a contempt for the
world's gossiping.   So he donned a student's uniform
without being disconcerted, enrolling himself in the
faculty of physical and mathematical science.   His
robust figure, his ruddy face, his sprouting beard, his
taciturn manner, produced a singular impression on his
comrades.   They never suspected that under the rough
exterior of this man, who attended the lectures so regularly, driving up in a capacious rustic sledge, drawn by
a couple of horses, somewhat almost childlike was concealed.   They thought him an eccentric sort of pedant,
and they made no advances towards him, being able to
do very well without him.   And he, for his part, avoided
them.   During the first two years he passed at the
university, he became intimate with no one except the
student from whom he took lessons in Latin.   This
student, whose name was Mikhalevich, an enthusiast
and somewhat of a poet, grew warmly attached to
Lavretsky, and quite accidentally became the cause of
a serious change in his fortunes.

One evening when Lavretsky was at the theatre—he
never missed a single representation, for Mochalof was
then at the summit of his glory—he caught sight of a
young girl in a box on the first tier.   Never before had
his heart beaten so fast, though at that time no woman
ever passed before his stern eyes without sending its
pulses flying.   Leaning on the velvet border of the box,
the girl sat very still.   Youthful animation lighted up
every feature of her beautiful face; artistic feeling shone
in her lovely eyes, which looked out with a soft, attentive
gaze from underneath delicately pencilled eyebrows, in
the quick smile of her expressive lips, in the bearing of
her head, her arms, her neck.   As to her dress, it was
exquisite.   By her side sat a sallow, wrinkled woman
of five-and-forty, wearing a low dress and a black cap,

[1] The students at the Russian universities used to wear a
uniform, but they no longer do so.

with an unmeaning smile on her vacant face, to which she strove to give an aspect of attention. In the background of the box appeared an elderly man in a roomy coat, and with a high cravat. His small eyes had an expression of stupid conceit, modified by a kind of cringing suspicion; his moustache and whiskers were dyed, he had an immense meaningless forehead, and flabby cheeks: his whole appearance was that of a retired general.

Lavretsky kept his eyes fixed on the girl who had made such an impression on him. Suddenly the door of the box opened, and Mikhalevich entered. The appearance of the man who was almost his only acquaintance in all Moscow—his appearance in the company of the very girl who had absorbed his whole attention, seemed to Lavretsky strange and significant. As he continued looking at the box, he remarked that all its occupants treated Mikhalevich like an old friend. Lavretsky lost all interest in what was going on upon the stage; even Mochalof, although he was that evening " in the vein," did not produce his wonted impression upon him. During one very pathetic passage, Lavretsky looked almost involuntarily at the object of his admiration. She was leaning forward, a red glow colouring her cheeks. Her eyes were bent upon the stage, but gradually, under the influence of his fixed look, they turned and rested on him. All night long those eyes haunted him. At last, the carefully constructed dam was broken through. He shivered and he burnt by turns, and the very next day he went to see Mikhalevich. From him he learned that the name of the girl he admired so much was Varvara Pavlovna Korobine, that the elderly people who were with her in the box were her father and her mother, and that Mikhalevich had become acquainted with them the year before, during the period of his stay as tutor in Count N.'s family near Moscow. The enthusiast spoke of Varvara Pavlovna in the most eulogistic terms. " This girl, my brother," he exclaimed, in his peculiar, jerking kind of sing-song, " is an exceptional being, one endowed with genius, an artist in the true sense of the word, and besides all that, such an amiable creature." Perceiving from Lavretsky's questions how great an impression Varvara Pavlovna had made upon him, Mikhalevich, of his own accord, proposed to make him acquainted with her, adding that he was on the most familiar terms with them, that the general was not in the least haughty, and that the mother was as unintellectual as she well could be.

Lavretsky blushed, muttered something vague, and took himself off. For five whole days he fought against his timidity; on the sixth the young Spartan donned an entirely new uniform, and placed himself at the disposal of Mikhalevich, who, as an intimate friend of the family, contented himself with setting his hair straight —and the two companions set off together to visit the Korobines.

XIII

VARVARA PAVLOVNA's father, Pavel Petrovich Korobine, a retired major-general, had been on duty at St. Petersburg during almost the whole of his life. In his early years he had enjoyed the reputation of being an able dancer and driller, but as he was very poor he had to act as aide-de-camp to two or three generals of small renown in succession, one of whom gave him his daughter in marriage, together with a dowry of 25,000 roubles. Having made himself master of all the science of regulations and parades, even to their subtlest details, he "went on stretching the girth" until at last, after twenty years' service, he became a general, and obtained a regiment. At that point he might have reposed, and have quietly consolidated his fortune. He had indeed counted upon doing so, but he managed his affairs rather imprudently. It seems he had discovered a new method of speculating with the public money. The method turned out an excellent one, but he must needs practise quite unreasonable economy,[1] so information was laid against him, and a more than disagreeable, a ruinous scandal ensued. Somehow or other the general managed to get clear of the affair; but his career was stopped, and he was recommended to retire from active service. For about a couple of years he lingered on at St. Petersburg, in hopes that a snug civil appointment might fall to his lot; but no such appointment did fall to his lot. His daughter finished her education at the institute; his expenses increased day by day. So he determined, with suppressed indignation, to go to Moscow for economy's sake; and there, in the Old Stable Street, he hired a little house with an escutcheon seven feet high on the roof, and began to live as retired generals do in Moscow on an income of 2700 roubles a year.[2]

[1] In other words, he stole, but he neglected to bribe.
[2] Nearly £400, the roubles being " silver " ones. The difference in value between " silver " and " paper " roubles exists no longer.

337

LIZA

Moscow is a hospitable city, and ready to welcome any one who appears there, especially if he is a retired general. Pavel Petrovich's form, which, though heavy, was not devoid of martial bearing, began to appear in the drawing-rooms frequented by the best society of Moscow. The back of his head, bald, with the exception of a few tufts of dyed hair, and the stained ribbon of the Order of St. Anne, which he wore over a stock of the colour of a raven's wing, became familiar to all the young men of pale and wearied aspect who were wont to saunter moodily around the card tables while a dance was going on.

Pavel Petrovich understood how to hold his own in society. He said little, but always, as of old, spoke through the nose—except, of course, when he was talking to people of superior rank. He played at cards prudently, and when he was at home he ate with moderation. At a party he seemed to be feeding for six. Of his wife scarcely anything more can be said than that her name was Calliope Carlovna—that a tear always stood in her left eye, on the strength of which Calliope Carlovna, who to be sure was of German extraction, considered herself a woman of feeling—that she always seemed frightened about something—that she looked as if she never had enough to eat—and that she always wore a tight velvet dress, a cap, and bracelets of thin, dull metal.

As to Varvara Pavlovna, the general's only daughter, she was but seventeen years old when she left the institute in which she had been educated. While within its walls she was considered, if not the most beautiful, at all events the most intelligent, of the pupils, and the best musician, and before leaving it she obtained the Cipher.[1] She was not yet nineteen when Lavretsky saw her for the first time.

[1] The initial letter of the name of the empress, worn as a kind of decoration by the best pupils in the Imperial Institutes.

XIV

THE Spartan's legs trembled when Mikhalevich led him into the Korobines' not overwell furnished drawing-room, and introduced him to its occupants. But he overcame his timidity, and it soon disappeared. In General Korobine that kindliness which is common to all Russians was enhanced by the special affability which is peculiar to all persons whose fair fame has been a little soiled. As for the general's wife, she soon became as it were ignored by the whole party. But Varvara Pav-lovna was so calmly, so composedly gracious, that no one could be even for a moment in her presence without feeling himself at his ease. And at the same time from all her charming form, from her smiling eyes, from her faultlessly sloping shoulders, from the rose-tinged white-ness of her hands, from her elastic but at the same time as it were irresolute gait, from the very sound of her sweet and languorous voice — there breathed, like a delicate perfume, a subtle and incomprehensible charm —something which was at once tender and voluptuous and modest—something which it is difficult to express in words, which stirred the imagination and disturbed the mind, but disturbed it with sensations which were not akin to timidity.

Lavretsky introduced the subject of the theatre and the preceding night's performance; she immediately began to talk about Mochalof of her own accord, and did not confine herself to mere sighs and exclamations, but pronounced several criticisms on his acting, which were as remarkable for sound judgment as for womanly penetration. Mikhalevich mentioned music; she sat down to the piano without affectation, and played with precision several of Chopin's mazurkas, which were then only just coming into fashion. Dinner time came.

339

Lavretsky would have gone away, but they made him stop, and the general treated him at table with excellent Lafitte, which the footman had been hurriedly sent out to buy at Depre's.

It was late in the evening before Lavretsky returned home, and then he sat for a long time without undressing, covering his eyes with his hand, and yielding to the torpor of enchantment. It seemed to him that he had not till now understood what makes life worth having. All his resolutions and intentions, all the now valueless ideas of other days, had disappeared in a moment. His whole soul melted within him into one feeling, one desire; into the desire of happiness, of possession, of love, of the sweetness of a woman's love.

From that day he began to visit the Korobines frequently. After six months had passed, he proposed to Varvara Pavlovna, and his offer was accepted. Long, long before, even if it was not the night before Lavretsky's first visit, the general had asked Mikhalevich how many serfs[1] his friend had. Even Varvara Pavlovna, who had preserved her wonted composure and equanimity during the whole period of her young admirer's courtship, and even at the very moment of his declaration—even Varvara Pavlovna knew perfectly well that her betrothed was rich. And Calliope Carlovna thought to herself, " *Meine Tochter macht eine schöne Partie* "[2]—and bought herself a new cap.

---

[1] Literally, " souls," *i.e.* male peasants.
[2] My daughter is going to make a capital match.

XV

AND so his offer was accepted, but under certain conditions. In the first place, Lavretsky must immediately leave the university. Who could think of marrying a student? And what an extraordinary idea, a landed proprietor, a rich man, at twenty-six years of age, to be taking lessons like a schoolboy! In the second place, Varvara Pavlovna was to take upon herself the trouble of ordering and buying her trousseau. She even chose the presents the bridegroom was to give. She had very good taste, and a great deal of common sense, and she possessed a great liking for comfort, and no small skill in getting herself that comfort. Lavretsky was particularly struck by this talent when, immediately after the wedding, he and his wife set off for Lavriki, travelling in a convenient carriage which she had chosen herself. How carefully all their surroundings had been meditated over by Varvara Pavlovna! what prescience she had shown in providing them! What charming travelling contrivances made their appearance in the various convenient corners! what delicious toilet boxes! what excellent coffee machines! and how gracefully did Varvara Pavlovna herself make the coffee in the morning! But it must be confessed that Lavretsky was little fitted for critical observation just then. He revelled in his happiness, he was intoxicated by his good fortune, he abandoned himself to it like a child—he was, indeed, as innocent as a child, this young Hercules. Not in vain did a charmed influence attach itself to the whole presence of his young wife; not in vain did she promise to the imagination a secret treasure of unknown delights. She was even better than her promise.

When she arrived at Lavriki, which was in the very hottest part of the summer, the house seemed to her sombre and in bad order, the servants antiquated and ridiculous; but she did not think it necessary to say a word about this to her husband. If she had intended to settle at Lavriki, she would have altered everything there, beginning of course with the house; but the idea of staying in that out-of-the way corner never, even for an instant, came into her mind. She merely lodged in it, as she would have done in a tent, putting up with all its discomforts in the sweetest manner, and laughing at them pleasantly.

When Marfa Timofeevna came to see her old pupil, she produced a very favourable impression on Varvara Pavlovna. But Varvara was not at all to the old lady's liking. Nor did the young mistress of the house get on comfortably with Glafira Petrovna. She herself would have been content to leave Glafira in peace, but the general was anxious to get his hand into the management of his son-in-law's affairs. To see after the property of so near a relative, he said, was an occupation that even a general might adopt without disgrace. It is possible that Pavel Petrovich would not have disdained to occupy himself with the affairs of even an utter stranger.

Varvara Pavlovna carried out her plan of attack very skilfully. Although never putting herself forward, but being to all appearance thoroughly immersed in the bliss of the honeymoon, in the quiet life of the country, in music, and in books, she little by little worked upon Glafira, until that lady, one morning, burst into Lavretsky's study like a maniac, flung her bunch of keys on the table, and announced that she could no longer look after the affairs of the household, and that she did not wish to remain on the estate. As Lavretsky had been fitly prepared for the scene, he immediately gave his consent to her departure. This Glafira Petrovna had not expected. "Good," she said, and her brow grew dark. "I see that I am not wanted here. I know that I am expelled hence, driven away from the family nest. But, nephew, remember my words—nowhere will you be able

342

to build you a nest; your lot will be to wander about without ceasing. There is my parting legacy to you." That same day she went off to her own little property: a week later General Korobine arrived, and, with a pleasantly subdued air, took the whole management of the estate into his own hand.

In September Varvara Pavlovna carried off her husband to St. Petersburg. There the young couple spent two winters—migrating in the summer to Tsarskoe Selo. They lived in handsome, bright, admirably-furnished apartments; they made numerous acquaintances in the upper and even the highest circles of society; they went out a great deal and received frequently, giving very charming musical parties and dances. Varvara Pavlovna attracted visitors as a light does moths.

Such a distracting life did not greatly please Fedor Ivanovich. His wife wanted him to enter the service; but, partly in deference to his father's memory, partly in accordance with his own ideas, he would not do so, though he remained in St. Petersburg to please his wife. However, he soon found out that no one objected to his isolating himself, that it was not without an object that his study had been made the quietest and the most comfortable in the whole city, that his attentive wife was ever ready to encourage him in isolating himself; and from that time all went well. He again began to occupy himself with his as yet, as he thought, unfinished education. He entered upon a new course of reading; he even began the study of English. It was curious to see his powerful, broad-shouldered figure constantly bending over his writing-table, his full, ruddy, bearded face, half-hidden by the leaves of a dictionary or a copybook. His mornings were always spent over his work; later in the day he sat down to an excellent dinner—for Varvara Pavlovna always managed her household affairs admirably; and in the evening he entered an enchanted, perfumed, brilliant world, all peopled by young and joyous beings, the central point of their world being that extremely attentive manager of the household, his wife.

She made him happy with a son; but the poor child did not live long. It died in the spring; and in the summer, in accordance with the advice of the doctors, Lavretsky and his wife went the round of the foreign watering-places. Distraction was absolutely necessary for her after such a misfortune, and, besides, her health demanded a warmer climate. That summer and autumn they spent in Germany and Switzerland; and in the winter, as might be expected, they went to Paris.

In Paris Varvara Pavlovna bloomed like a rose; and there, just as quickly and as skilfully as she had done in St. Petersburg, she learnt how to build herself a snug little nest. She procured a very pretty set of apartments in one of the quiet but fashionable streets; she made her husband such a dressing-gown as he had never worn before; she secured an elegant lady's maid, an excellent cook, and an energetic footman; and she provided herself with an exquisite carriage and a charming cabinet piano. Before a week was over she could already cross a street, put on a shawl, open a parasol, and wear gloves, as well as the most pure-blooded of Parisian women.

She soon made acquaintances also. At first only Russians used to come to her house; then Frenchmen began to show themselves — amiable bachelors, of polished manners, exquisite in demeanour, and bearing high-sounding names. They all talked a great deal and very fast, they bowed gracefully, their eyes twinkled pleasantly. All of them possessed teeth which gleamed white between rosy lips; and how beautifully they smiled! Each of them brought his friends; and before long *La belle Madame de Lavretski* became well known from the *Chausée d'Antin* to the *Rue de Lille*. At that time—it was in 1836—the race of *feuilletonists* and journalists, which now swarms everywhere, numerous as the ants one sees when a hole is made in an ant-hill, had not yet succeeded in multiplying in numbers. Still, there used to appear in Varvara Pavlovna's drawing-room a certain M. Jules, a gentleman who bore a very bad character, whose appearance was unprepossessing, and whose manner was at once insolent and cringing—like that of all duellists and people who have been horse-whipped. Varvara disliked this M. Jules very much; but she received him because he wrote in several news-papers, and used to be constantly mentioning her, calling her sometimes Madame de L . . . tski, sometimes Madame de ——, *cette grande dame Russe si distinguée, qui demeure rue de P*——, and describing to the whole world, that is to say to some few hundreds of subscribers, who had nothing whatever to do with Madame de L . . . tski, how lovable and charming was that lady, *une vraie française par l'esprit*,—the French have no higher praise than this, —what an extraordinary musician she was, and how wonderfully she waltzed. (Varvara Pavlovna did really waltz so as to allure all hearts to the skirt of her light, floating robe.) In fact, he spread her fame abroad throughout the world; and this we know, whatever people may say, is pleasant.

Mademoiselle Mars had by that time quitted the stage, and Mademoiselle Rachel had not yet appeared there; but for all that Varvara Pavlovna none the less assiduously attended the theatres. She went into rap-tures about Italian music, and laughed over the ruins of Odry, yawned in a becoming manner at the legitimate drama, and cried at the sight of Madame Dorval's acting in some ultra-melodramatic piece. Above all, Liszt played at her house twice, and was so gracious, so un-affected! It was charming!

Amid such pleasurable sensations passed the winter, at the end of which Varvara Pavlovna was even pre-sented at court. As for Fedor Ivanovich, he was not exactly bored, but life began to weigh heavily on his shoulders at times—heavily because of its very empti-ness. He read the papers, he listened to the lectures at the *Sorbonne* and the *Collège de France*, he followed the debates in the chambers, he occupied himself in trans-lating a famous scientific work on irrigation. "I am not wasting my time," he thought; " all this is of use;

but next winter I really must return to Russia, and betake myself to active business." It would be hard to say if he had any clear idea of what were the special characteristics of that business, and only Heaven could tell whether he was likely to succeed in getting back to Russia in the winter. In the meanwhile he was intending to go with his wife to Baden. But an unexpected occurrence upset all his plans.

XVI

ONE day when he happened to go into Varvara Pavlovna's boudoir during her absence, Lavretsky saw a
carefully folded little piece of paper lying on the floor.
Half mechanically he picked it up and opened it—and
read the following lines written in French:—

" MY DEAR ANGEL BETTY,

" (I really cannot make up my mind to call you
Barbe or Varvara).   I have waited in vain for you at the
corner of the Boulevard.   Come to our rooms to-morrow
at half-past one.   That excellent husband of yours is
generally absorbed in his books at that time—we will
sing over again that song of your poet Pushkin which
you taught me, ' Old husband, cruel husband ! '   A
thousand kisses to your dear little hands and feet.   I
await you.   " ERNEST."

At first Lavretsky did not comprehend the meaning
of what he had read.   He read it a second time—and his
head swam, and the ground swayed beneath his feet
like the deck of a ship in a storm, and a half-stifled sound
issued from his lips that was neither quite a cry nor
quite a sob.

He was utterly confounded.   He had trusted his wife
so blindly; the possibility of deceit or of treachery on
her part had never entered into his mind.   This Ernest,
his wife's lover, was a pretty boy of about three-and-
twenty, with light hair, a turned-up nose, and a small
moustache—probably the most insignificant of all his
acquaintances.

Several minutes passed; a half hour passed.   Lavretsky still stood there, clenching the fatal note in his
hand, and gazing unmeaningly on the floor.   A sort of

347

dark whirlwind seemed to sweep round him, pale faces to glimmer through it.

A painful sensation of numbness had seized his heart. He felt as if he were falling, falling, falling—into a bottomless abyss.

The soft rustle of a silk dress roused him from his torpor by its familiar sound. Varvara Pavlovna came in hurriedly from out of doors. Lavretsky shuddered all over and rushed out of the room. He felt that at that moment he was ready to tear her to pieces, to strangle her with his own hands, at least to beat her all but to death in peasant fashion. Varvara Pavlovna, in her amizement, wanted to stop him. He just succeeded in whispering " Betty "—and then he fled from the house.

Lavretsky took a carriage and drove outside the barriers. All the rest of the day and the whole of the night he wandered about, constantly stopping and wringing his hands above his head. Sometimes he was frantic with rage, at others everything seemed to move him to laughter, even to a kind of mirth. When the morning dawned he felt half frozen, so he entered a wretched little surburban tavern, asked for a room, and sat down on a chair before the window. A convulsive fit of yawning seized him. By that time he was scarcely able to keep upright, and his bodily strength was utterly exhausted. Still he was not conscious of fatigue. But fatigue had its own way. He continued sitting there and gazing vacantly, but he comprehended nothing. He could not make out what had happened to him, why he found himself there, alone, in an empty, unknown room, with numbed limbs, with a sense of bitterness in his mouth, with a weight like that of a great stone on his heart. He could not understand what had induced her, his Varvara, to give herself to that Frenchman, and how, knowing herself to be false to him, she could have remained as calm as ever in his presence, as confiding and caressing as ever towards him. " I cannot make it out," whispered his dry lips. " And how can I be sure now that even at St. Petersburg——? " but he did not complete the question; a fresh gaping fit seized him, and his whole frame shrank and shivered. Sunny and sombre memories equally tormented him. He suddenly recollected how, a few days before, she had sat at the piano, when both he and Ernest were present, and had sung " Old husband, cruel husband! " He remembered the expression of her face, the strange brilliance of her eyes, and the colour in her cheeks—and he rose from his chair, longing to go to them and say, " You were wrong to play your tricks on me. My great grandfather used to hang his peasants on hooks by their ribs, and my grandfather was a peasant himself,"—and then kill them both. All of a sudden it would appear to him as if everything that had happened were a dream, even not so much as a dream, but just some absurd fancy; as if he had only to give himself a shake and take a look round—and he did look round; and as a hawk claws a captured bird, so did his misery strike deeper and deeper into his heart. What made things worse was that Lavretsky had hoped, in the course of a few months, to find himself once more a father. His past, his future, his whole life was poisoned.

At last he returned to Paris, went to a hotel, and sent Varvara Pavlovna M. Ernest's note with the following letter:—

" The scrap of paper which accompanies this will explain everything to you. I may as well tell you that you do not seem to have behaved in this matter with your usual tact. You, so careful a person, to drop such important papers (poor Lavretsky had been preparing this phrase, and fondling it, as it were, for several hours). I can see you no more, and I suppose that you too can have no wish for an interview with me. I assign you fifteen thousand roubles a year. I cannot give you more. Send your address to the steward of my estate. And now do what you like; live where you please. I wish you all prosperity. I want no answer."

Lavretsky told his wife that he wanted no answer; but he did expect, he even longed for an answer—an explanation of this strange, this incomprehensible affair. That same day Varvara Pavlovna sent him a long letter in French. It was the final blow. His last doubts vanished, and he even felt ashamed of having retained any doubts. Varvara Pavlovna did not attempt to justify herself. All that she wanted was to see him; she besought him not to condemn her irrevocably. The letter was cold and constrained, though marks of tears were to be seen on it here and there. Lavretsky smiled bitterly, and sent a message by the bearer, to the effect that the letter needed no reply.

Three days later he was no longer in Paris; but he went to Italy, not to Russia. He did not himself know why he chose Italy in particular. In reality, it was all the same to him where he went—so long as he did not go home. He sent word to his steward about his wife's allowance, ordering him, at the same time, to withdraw the whole management of the estate from General Korobine immediately, without waiting for any settlement of accounts, and to see to his Excellency's departure from Lavriki. He indulged in a vivid picture of the confusion of the expelled general, the useless airs which he would put on, and, in spite of his sorrow, he was conscious of a certain malicious satisfaction. At the same time he wrote to Glafira Petrovna, asking her to return to Lavriki, and drew up a power-of-attorney in her name. But Glafira Petrovna would not return to Lavriki; she even advertised in the newspapers that the power-of-attorney was cancelled,—a perfectly superfluous proceeding on her part.

Lavretsky hid himself in a little Italian town; but for a long time he could not help mentally following his wife's movements. He learnt from the newspapers that she had left Paris for Baden, as she had intended. Her name soon appeared in a short article signed by the M. Jules of whom we have already spoken. The perusal of that article produced a very unpleasant effect on

Lavretsky's mind. He detected in it, underneath the writer's usual sprightliness, a sort of tone of charitable commiseration. Next he learnt that a daughter had been born to him. Two months later he was informed by his steward that Varvara Pavlovna had drawn her first quarter's allowance. After that, scandalous reports about her began to arrive; then they became more and more frequent; at last a tragi-comic story, in which she played a very unenviable part, ran the round of all the journals and created a great sensation. Affairs had come to a climax. Varvara Pavlovna was now " a celebrity."

Lavretsky ceased to follow her movements. But it was long before he could master his own feelings. Sometimes he was seized by such a longing after his wife that he fancied he would have been ready to give everything he had—that he could, perhaps, even have forgiven her —if only he might once more have heard her caressing voice, have felt once more her hand in his. But time did not pass by in vain. He was not born for suffering. His healthy nature claimed its rights. Many things became intelligible for him. The very blow which had struck him seemed no longer to have come without warning. He understood his wife now. We can never fully understand persons with whom we are generally in close contact, until we have been separated from them. He was able to apply himself to business again, and to study, although now with much less than his former ardour; the scepticism for which both his education and his experience of life had paved the way, had taken lasting hold upon his mind. He became exceedingly indifferent to everything. Four years passed by, and he felt strong enough to return to his home, to meet his own people. Without having stopped either at St. Petersburg or at Moscow, he arrived at O., where we left him, and whither we now entreat the reader to return with us.

XVII

ABOUT ten o'clock in the morning, on the day after that of which we have already spoken, Lavretsky was going up the steps of the Kalitines' house, when he met Liza with her bonnet and gloves on.

" Where are you going? " he asked her.

" To church. To-day is Sunday."

" And so you go to church? "

Liza looked at him in silent wonder.

" I beg your pardon," said Lavretsky. " I—I did not mean to say that. I came to take leave of you. I shall start for my country-house in another hour."

" That isn't far from here, is it? " asked Liza.

" About five-and-twenty versts."

At this moment Lenochka appeared at the door, accompanied by a maid-servant.

" Mind you don't forget us," said Liza, and went down the steps.

" Don't forget me either. By the way," he continued, " you are going to church; say a prayer for me too, while you are there."

Liza stopped and turned towards him.

" Very well," she said, looking him full in the face. " I will pray for you too. Come, Lenochka."

Lavretsky found Maria Dmitrievna alone in the drawing-room, which was redolent of eau-de-cologne and peppermint. Her head ached, she said, and she had spent a restless night.

She received him with her usual languid amiability, and by degrees began to talk.

" Tell me," she asked him, " is not Vladimir Nikolaevich a very agreeable young man? "

" Who is Vladimir Nikolaevich? "

" Why Panshine, you know, who was here yesterday. He was immensely delighted with you. Between our-

selves I may mention, *mon cher cousin*, that he is perfectly infatuated with my Liza. Well, he is of good
family, he is getting on capitally in the service, he is
clever, and besides he is a chamberlain, and if such be
the will of God—I for my part, as a mother, shall be glad
of it. It is certainly a great responsibility; most certainly the happiness of children depends upon their
parents. But this much must be allowed. Up to the
present time, whether well or ill, I have done everything
myself, and entirely by myself. I have brought up my
children and taught them everything myself—and now
I have just written to Madame Bulous for a governess——"

Maria Dmitrievna launched out into a description of
her cares, her efforts, her maternal feelings. Lavretsky
listened to her in silence, and twirled his hat in his hands.
His cold, unsympathetic look at last disconcerted the
talkative lady.

" And what do you think of Liza ? " she asked.

" Lizaveta Mikhailovna is an exceedingly handsome
girl," replied Lavretsky. Then he got up, said good-bye,
and went to pay Marfa Timofeevna a visit. Maria
Dmitrievna looked after him with an expression of dissatisfaction, and thought to herself, " What a bear!
what a moujik ! Well, now I understand why his wife
couldn't remain faithful to him."

Marfa Timofeevna was sitting in her room, surrounded
by her court. This consisted of five beings, almost
equally dear to her heart—an educated bullfinch, to
which she had taken an affection because it could no
longer whistle or draw water, and which was afflicted
with a swollen neck; a quiet and exceedingly timid little
dog, called Roska; a bad-tempered cat, named Matros;
a dark-complexioned, lively little girl of nine, with very
large eyes and a sharp nose, whose name was Shurochka;[1]
and an elderly lady of about fifty-five, who wore a white
cap and a short, cinnamon-coloured *katsaveika* [2] over a

[1] One of the many diminutives of Alexandrina.
[2] A kind of jacket worn by women.

353

dark gown, and whose name was Nastasia Carpovna Ogarkof.

Shurochka was a fatherless and motherless girl, whose relations belonged to the lowest class of the bourgeoisie. Marfa Timofeevna had adopted her, as well as Roska, out of pity. She had found both the dog and the girl out in the streets. Both of them were thin and cold; the autumn rain had drenched them both. No one ever claimed Roska, and as to Shurockha, she was even gladly given up to Marfa Timofeevna by her uncle, a drunken shoemaker, who never had enough to eat himself, and could still less provide food for his niece, whom he used to hit over the head with his last.

As to Nastasia Carpovna, Marfa Timofeevna had made acquaintance with her on a pilgrimage, in a monastery. She went up to that old lady in church one day,— Nastasia Carpovna had pleased Marfa Timofeevna by praying, as the latter lady said, " in very good taste "— began to talk to her, and invited her home to a cup of tea. From that day she parted with her no more. Nastasia Carpovna, whose father had belonged to the class of poor gentry, was a widow without children. She was a woman of a very sweet and happy disposition; she had a round head, grey hair, and soft, white hands. Her face also was soft, and her features, including a somewhat comical snub nose, were heavy, but pleasant. She worshipped Marfa Timofeevna, who loved her dearly, although she teased her greatly about her susceptible heart. Nastasia Carpovna had a weakness for all young men, and never could help blushing like a girl at the most innocent joke. Her whole property consisted of twelve hundred paper roubles.[1] She lived at Marfa Timofeevna's expense, but on a footing of perfect equality with her. Marfa Timofeevna could not have endured anything like servility

" Ah, Fedia! " she began, as soon as she saw him. You didn't see my family last night. Please to admire them now; we are all met together for tea. This is our

[1] About £50.

354

second, our feast-day tea. You may embrace us all. Only Shurochka wouldn't let you, and the cat would scratch you. Is it to-day you go? "

" Yes," said Lavretsky, sitting down on a low chair. " I have just taken leave of Maria Dmitrievna. I saw Lizaveta Mikhailovna too."

" Call her Liza, my dear. Why should she be Mikhailovna for you? But do sit still, or you will break Shurochka's chair."

" She was on her way to church," continued Lavretsky. " Is she seriously inclined? "

" Yes, Fedia, very much so. More than you or I, Fedia."

" And do you mean to say you are not seriously inclined? " lisped Nastasia Carpovna. " If you have not gone to the early mass to-day, you will go to the later one."

" Not a bit of it. Thou shalt go alone. I've grown lazy, my mother," answered Marfa Timofeevna. " I am spoiling myself terribly with tea drinking."

She said *thou* to Nastasia Carpovna, although she lived on a footing of equality with her—but it was not for nothing that she was a Pestof. Three Pestofs occur in the Sinodik [1] of Ivan the Terrible. Marfa Timofeevna was perfectly well aware of the fact.

" Tell me, please," Lavretsky began again. " Maria Dmitrievna was talking to me just now about that— what's his name?—Panshine. What sort of man is he? "

" Good Lord! what a chatterbox she is! " grumbled Marfa Timofeevna. " I've no doubt she has communicated to you as a secret that he hangs about here as a suitor. She might have been contented to whisper about it with her *popovich*.[2] But no, it seems that is not enough for her. And yet there is nothing settled so far, thank God! but she's always chattering."

---

[1] *I.e.*, in the list of the nobles of his time, in the sixteenth century.

[2] The priest's son, *i.e.* Gedeonovsky.

" Why do you say, ' Thank God? ' " asked Lavretsky.

" Why, because this fine young man doesn't please me. And what is there in the matter to be delighted about, I should like to know? "

" Doesn't he please you? "

" No; he can't fascinate every one. It's enough for him that Nastasia Carpovna here is in love with him."

The poor widow was terribly disconcerted.

" How can you say so, Marfa Timofeevna? Do not you fear God? " she exclaimed, and a blush instantly suffused her face and neck.

" And certainly the rogue knows how to fascinate her," broke in Marfa Timofeevna. " He has given her a snuff-box. Fedia, ask her for a pinch of snuff. You will see what a splendid snuff-box it is. There is a hussar on horseback on the lid. You had much better not try to exculpate yourself, my mother."

Nastasia Carpovna could only wave her hands with a deprecatory air.

" Well, but about Liza? " asked Lavretsky. " Is he indifferent to her? "

" She seems to like him—and as to the rest, God knows. Another person's heart, you know, is a dark forest, and more especially a young girl's. Look at Shurochka there! Come and analyse hers. Why has she been hiding herself, but not going away, ever since you came in? "

Shurochka burst into a laugh she was unable to stifle, and ran out of the room. Lavretsky also rose from his seat.

" Yes," he said slowly; " one cannot fathom a girl's heart."

As he was going to take leave,

" Well; shall we see you soon? " asked Marfa Timofeevna.

" Perhaps, aunt. It's no great distance to where I'm going."

" Yes; you're going, no doubt, to Vasilievskoe. You won't live at Lavriki. Well, that's your affair. Only

356

go and kneel down at your mother's grave, and your grandmother's too, while you are there. You have picked up all kinds of wisdom abroad there, and perhaps, who can tell, they may feel, even in their graves, that you have come to visit them. And don't forget, Fedia, to have a service said for Glafira Petrovna too. Here is a rouble for you. Take it, take it please; it is I who wish to have the service performed for her. I didn't love her while she lived, but it must be confessed that she was a girl of character. She was clever. And then she didn't hurt you. And now go, and God be with you —else I shall tire you."

And Marfa Timofeevna embraced her nephew.

" And Liza shall not marry Panshine; don't make yourself uneasy about that. He isn't the sort of man she deserves for a husband."

" But I am not in the least uneasy about it," remarked Lavretsky as he retired.

XVIII

Four hours later he was on his way towards his home. His tarantass rolled swiftly along the soft cross-road. There had been no rain for a fortnight. The atmosphere was pervaded by a light fog of milky hue, which hid the distant forests from sight, while a smell of burning filled the air. A number of dusky clouds with blurred outlines stood out against a pale blue sky, and lingered, slowly drawn. A strongish wind swept by in an unbroken current, bearing no moisture with it, and not dispelling the great heat. His head leaning back on the cushions, his arms folded across his breast, Lavretsky gazed at the furrowed plains which opened fanwise before him, at the cytisus shrubs, at the crows and rooks which looked sideways at the passing carriage with dull suspicion, at the long ridges planted with mugwort, wormwood, and mountain ash. He gazed—and that vast level solitude, so fresh and so fertile, that expanse of verdure, and those sweeping slopes, the ravines studded with clumps of dwarfed oaks, the grey hamlets, the thinly-clad birch trees—all this Russian landscape, so long by him unseen, filled his mind with feelings which were sweet, but at the same time almost sad, and gave rise to a certain heaviness of heart, but one which was more akin to a pleasure than to a pain. His thoughts wandered slowly past, their forms as dark and ill-defined as those of the clouds, which also seemed vaguely wandering there on high. He thought of his childhood, of his mother, how they brought him to her on her deathbed, and how, pressing his head to her breast, she began to croon over him, but looked up at Glafira Petrovna and became silent. He thought of his father, at first robust, brazen-voiced, grumbling at everything—then blind, querulous, with white, uncared-for

beard. He remembered how one day at dinner, when
he had taken a little too much wine, the old man suddenly burst out laughing, and began to prate about his
conquests, winking his blind eyes the while, and growing
red in the face. He thought of Varvara Pavlovna—and
his face contracted involuntarily, like that of a man
who feels some sudden pain, and he gave his head an
impatient toss. Then his thoughts rested on Liza.
" There," he thought, " is a new life just beginning. A
good creature! I wonder what will become of her.
And she's pretty too, with her pale, fresh face, her so
serious eyes and lips, and that frank and guileless way
she has of looking at you. It's a pity she seems a little
enthusiastic. And her figure is good, and she moves
about lightly, and she has a quiet voice. I like her best
when she suddenly stands still, and listens attentively
and gravely, then becomes contemplative and shakes
her hair back. Yes, I agree, Panshine isn't worthy of
her. Yet what harm is there in him? However, as to
all that, why am I troubling my head about it? She
will follow the same road that all others have to follow.
I had better go to sleep." And Lavretsky closed his
eyes.

He could not sleep, but he sank into a traveller's
dreamy reverie. Just as before, pictures of bygone days
slowly rose and floated across his mind, blending with
each other, and becoming confused with other scenes.
Lavretsky began to think—heaven knows why—about
Sir Robert Peel; then about French history; lastly,
about the victory which he would have gained if he
had been a general. The firing and the shouting rang
in his ears. His head slipped on one side; he opened his
eyes—the same fields stretched before him, the same
level views met his eyes. The iron shoes of the outside
horses gleamed brightly by turns athwart the waving
dust, the driver's yellow[1] shirt swelled with the breeze.
" Here I am, returning virtuously to my birthplace,"
suddenly thought Lavretsky, and he called out, " Get

[1] Yellow, with red pieces let in under the armpits.

on there!" drew his cloak more closely around him, and pressed himself still nearer to the cushion. The tarantass gave a jerk. Lavretsky sat upright and opened his eyes wide. On the slope before him extended a small village. A little to the right was to be seen an old manor house of modest dimensions, its shutters closed, its portico awry. On one side stood a barn built of oak, small, but well preserved. The wide courtyard was entirely overgrown by nettles, as green and thick as hemp. This was Vasilievskoe.

The driver turned aside to the gate, and stopped his horses. Lavretsky's servant rose from his seat, ready to jump down, and shouted "Halloo!" A hoarse, dull barking arose in reply, but no dog made its appearance. The lackey again got ready to descend, and again cried "Halloo!" The feeble barking was repeated, and directly afterwards a man with snow-white hair, dressed in a nankeen caftan, ran into the yard from one of the corners. He looked at the tarantass, shielding his eyes from the sun, then suddenly struck both his hands upon his thighs, fidgeted about nervously for a moment, and finally ran to open the gates. The tarantass entered the courtyard, crushing the nettles under its wheels, and stopped before the portico. The white-headed old man, who was evidently of a very active turn, was already standing on the lowest step, his legs spread awkwardly apart. He unbuttoned the apron of the carriage, pulling up the leather with a jerk, and kissed his master's hand while assisting him to alight.

"Good day, good day, brother," said Lavretsky. "Your name is Anton, isn't it? So you're still alive?"

The old man bowed in silence, and then ran to fetch the keys. While he ran the driver sat motionless, leaning sideways and looking at the closed door, and Lavretsky's man-servant remained in the picturesque attitude in which he found himself after springing down to the ground, one of his arms resting on the box seat. The old man brought the keys and opened the door, lifting his elbows high the while and needlessly wriggling his body—then he stood on one side and again bowed down to his girdle.

" Here I am at home, actually returned! " thought Lavretsky, as he entered the little vestibule, while the shutters opened one after another with creak and rattle, and the light of day penetrated into the long-deserted rooms.

XIX

THE little house at which Lavretsky had arrived, and in which Glafira Petrovna had died two years before, had been built of solid pine timber in the preceding century. It looked very old, but it was good for another fifty years or more. Lavretsky walked through all the rooms, and, to the great disquiet of the faded old flies which clung to the cornices without moving, their backs covered with white dust, he had the windows thrown open everywhere. Since the death of Glafira Petrovna no one had opened them. Everything had remained precisely as it used to be in the house. In the drawing-room the little white sofas, with their thin legs, and their shining grey coverings, all worn and rumpled, vividly recalled to mind the times of Catharine. In that room also stood the famous armchair of the late proprietress, a chair with a high, straight back, in which, even in her old age, she used always to sit bolt upright. On the wall hung an old portrait of Fedor's great grandfather, Andrei Lavretsky. His dark, sallow countenance could scarcely be distinguished against the cracked and darkened background. His small, malicious eyes looked out morosely from beneath the heavy, apparently swollen eyelids. His black hair, worn without powder, rose up stiff as a brush above his heavy, wrinkled forehead. From the corner of the portrait hung a dusky wreath of *immortelles*. " Glafira Petrovna deigned to weave it herself," observed Anthony. In the bedroom stood a narrow bedstead, with curtains of some striped material, extremely old, but of very good quality. On the bed lay a heap of faded cushions and a thin, quilted counterpane; and above the bolster hung a picture of the Presentation of the Blessed Virgin in the Temple, the very picture which the old lady, when she lay dying, alone and forgotten, pressed for the last time with lips which were already beginning to grow cold. Near the window

362

stood a toilet table, inlaid with different kinds of wood and ornamented with plates of copper, supporting a crooked mirror in a frame of which the gilding had turned black. In a line with the bedroom was the oratory, a little room with bare walls; in the corner stood a heavy case for holding sacred pictures, and on the floor lay the scrap of carpet, worn threadbare and covered with droppings from wax candles, on which Glafira Petrovna used to prostrate herself when she prayed.

Anton went out with Lavretsky's servant to open the stable and coach-house doors. In his stead appeared an old woman, almost as old as himself, her hair covered by a handkerchief which came down to her very eyebrows. Her head shook and her eyes seemed dim, but they wore also an expression of zealous obedience, habitual and implicit, and at the same time of a kind of respectful condolence. She kissed Lavretsky's hand, and then remained near the door, awaiting his orders. He could not remember what her name was, nor even whether he had ever seen her before. It turned out that her name was Apraxia. Some forty years previously Glafira Petrovna had struck her off the list of the servants who lived in the house, and had ordered her to become a poultry maid. She seldom spoke, seemed half idiotic, and always wore a servile look. Besides this old couple, and three paunchy little children in long shirts, Anton's great grandchildren, there lived also in the seigniorial household an untaxable [1] moujik, who had only one arm. He cackled like a blackcock, and was fit for nothing. Of very little more use was the infirm old hound which had saluted Lavretsky's return by its barking. For ten whole years it had been fastened to a heavy chain, purchased by order of Glafira Petrovna, a burden under which it was now scarcely able to move.

Having examined the house, Lavretsky went out into the garden, and was well pleased with it. It was all

[1] One who had not received the usual grant of land from the community, and was not subject to rates like the rest.

overgrown with steppe grass, with dandelions, and with gooseberry and raspberry bushes; but there was plenty of shade in it, a number of old lime-trees growing there, of singularly large stature, with eccentrically ordered branches. They had been planted too close together, and a hundred years seemed to have elapsed since they were pruned. At the end of the garden was a small, clear lake, surrounded by a fringe of high, reddish-coloured rushes. The traces of a human life that is past soon disappear. Glafira's manor-house had not yet grown wild, but it seemed to have become already immersed in that quiet slumber which all that is earthly sleeps, whenever it is not affected by the restlessness of humanity.

Lavretsky also went through the village. The women looked at him from the doorways of their cottages, each resting her cheek upon her hand. The men bowed low from afar, the children ran out of sight, the dogs barked away at their ease. At last he felt hungry, but he did not expect his cook and the other servants till the evening. The waggon bringing provisions from Lavriki had not yet arrived. It was necessary to have recourse to Anton. The old man immediately made his arrangements. He caught an ancient fowl, and killed and plucked it. Apraxia slowly squeezed and washed it, scrubbing it as if it had been linen for the wash, before putting it into the stewpan. When at last it was ready, Anton laid the table, placing beside the dish a three-footed plated salt-cellar, blackened with age, and a cut-glass decanter, with a round glass stopper in its narrow neck. Then, in a kind of chant, he announced to Lavretsky that dinner was ready, and took his place behind his master's chair, a napkin wound around his right hand, and a kind of air of the past, like the odour of cypress-wood, hanging about him. Lavretsky tasted the broth, and took the fowl out of it. The bird's skin was covered all over with round blisters, a thick tendon ran up each leg, and the flesh was as tough as wood, and had a flavour like that which pervades a laundry. After dinner Lavretsky said that he would take tea if——

" I will bring it in a moment," broke in the old man, and he kept his promise. A few pinches of tea were found rolled up in a scrap of red paper. Also a small, but very zealous and noisy little *samovar* [1] was discovered, and some sugar in minute pieces, which looked as if they had been all but melted away. Lavretsky drank his tea out of a large cup. From his earliest childhood he remembered this cup, on which playing cards were painted, and from which only visitors were allowed to drink; and now he drank from it, like a visitor.

Towards the evening came the servants. Lavretsky did not like to sleep in his aunt's bed, so he had one made up for him in the dining-room. After putting out the candle, he lay for a long time looking around him, and thinking what were not joyous thoughts. He experienced the sensations which every one knows who has had to spend the night for the first time in a long uninhabited room. He fancied that the darkness which pressed in upon him from all sides could not accustom itself to the new tenant—that the very walls of the house were astonished at him. At last he sighed, pulled the counterpane well over him, and went to sleep. Anton remained on his legs long after every one else had gone to bed. For some time he spoke in a whisper to Apraxia, sighing low at intervals, and three times he crossed himself. The old servants had never expected that their master would settle down among them at Vasilievskoe, when he had such a fine estate, with a well-appointed manor-house close by. They did not suspect what was really the truth, that Lavriki was repugnant to its owner, that it aroused in his mind too painful recollections. After they had whispered to each other enough, Anton took a stick, and struck the watchman's board which had long hung silently by the barn. Then he lay down in the open yard, without troubling himself about any covering for his white head. The May night was calm and soothing, and the old man slept soundly.

[1] Urn.

XX

THE next day Lavretsky rose at a tolerably early hour, chatted with the *starosta*,[1] visited the rickyard, and had the chain taken off the yard dog, which just barked a little, but did not even come out of its kennel. Then, returning home, he fell into a sort of quiet reverie, from which he did not emerge all day. "Here I am, then, at the very bottom of the river!"[2] he said to himself more than once. He sat near the window without stirring, and seemed to listen to the flow of the quiet life which surrounded him, to the rare sounds which came from the village solitude. Behind the nettles some one was singing with a thin, feeble voice; a gnat seemed to be piping a second to it. The voice stopped, but the gnat still went on piping. Through the monotonous and obtrusive buzzing of the flies might be heard the humming of a large humble bee, which kept incessantly striking its head against the ceiling. A cock crowed in the street, hoarsely protracting its final note, a cart rattled past, a gate creaked in the village. "What?" suddenly screeched a woman's voice. "Ah, young lady!" said Anton to a little girl of two years old whom he was carrying in his arms. "Bring the *kvass* here," continued the same woman's voice. Then a death-like silence suddenly ensued.

Nothing stirred, not a sound was audible. The wind did not move the leaves. The swallows skimmed along the ground one after another without a cry, and their silent flight made a sad impression upon the heart of the looker on. "Here I am, then, at the bottom of the river," again thought Lavretsky. "And here life is

[1] The head of the village.
[2] A popular phrase, to express a life quiet as the depths of a river are.

always sluggish and still; whoever enters its circle must resign himself to his fate. Here there is no use in agitating oneself, no reason why one should give oneself trouble. He only will succeed here who traces his onward path as patiently as the plougher traces the furrow with his plough. And what strength there is in all around; what robust health dwells in the midst of this inactive stillness! There under the window climbs the large-leaved burdock from the thick grass. Above it the lovage extends its sappy stalk, while higher still the Virgin's tears hang out their rosy tendrils. Farther away in the fields shines the rye, and the oats are already in ear, and every leaf on its tree, every blade of grass on its stalk, stretches itself out to its full extent. On a woman's love my best years have been wasted! " (Lavretsky proceeded to think.) " Well, then, let the dulness here sober me and calm me down; let it educate me into being able to work like others without hurrying." And he again betook himself to listening to the silence, without expecting anything, and yet, at the same time, as if incessantly expecting something. The stillness embraced him on all sides; the sun went down quietly in a calm, blue sky, on which the clouds floated tranquilly, seeming as if they knew why and whither they were floating. In the other parts of the world, at that very moment, life was seething, noisily bestirring itself. Here the same life flowed silently along, like water over meadow grass. It was late in the evening before Lavretsky could tear himself away from the contemplation of this life so quietly welling forth—so tranquilly flowing past. Sorrow for the past melted away in his mind as the snow melts in spring; but, strange to say, never had the love of home exercised so strong or so profound an influence upon him.

XXI

In the course of a fortnight Lavretsky succeeded in setting Glafira's Petrovna's little house in order, and in trimming the courtyard and the garden. Its stable became stocked with horses; comfortable furniture was brought to it from Lavriki; and the town supplied it with wine, and with books and newspapers. In short, Lavretsky provided himself with everything he wanted, and began to lead a life which was neither exactly that of an ordinary landed proprietor, nor exactly that of a regular hermit. His days passed by in uniform regularity, but he never found them dull, although he had no visitors. He occupied himself assiduously and attentively with the management of his estate; he rode about the neighbourhood, and he read. But he read little. He preferred listening to old Anton's stories.

Lavretsky generally sat at the window, over a pipe and a cup of cold tea. Anton would stand at the door, his hands crossed behind his back, and would begin a deliberate narrative about old times, those fabulous times when oats and rye were sold, not by measure, but in large sacks, and for two or three roubles the sack; when on all sides, right up to the town, there stretched impenetrable forests and untouched steppes. "But now," grumbled the old man, over whose head eighty years had already passed, "everything has been so cut down and ploughed up that one can't drive anywhere." Anton would talk also at great length about his late mistress, Glafira Petrovna, saying how judicious and economical she was, how a certain gentleman, one of her young neighbours, had tried to gain her good graces for a time, and had begun to pay her frequent visits, and how in his honour she had deigned even to put on her gala-day cap with massacas ribbons, and her yellow dress made of *tru-tru-lévantine ;* but how, a little later, having become angry with her neighbour, that gentleman, on account of his indiscreet question, " I suppose, madam, you doubtless have a good sum of money in hand ? " she told her servants never to let him enter her house again—and how she then ordered that, after her death, everything, even to the smallest rag, should be handed over to Lavretsky. And, in reality, Lavretsky found his aunt's property quite intact, even down to the gala-day cap with the massacas ribbons, and the yellow dress of *tru-tru-lévantine.*

As to the old papers and curious documents on which Lavretsky had counted, he found nothing of the kind except one old volume in which his grandfather, Peter Andreich, had made various entries. In one place might be read, " Celebration in the city of St. Petersburg, of the Peace concluded with the Turkish Empire by his Excellency, Prince Alexander Alexandrovich Prozorovsky." In another, " Recipe of a decoction for the chest," with the remark, " This prescription was given the Generaless Prascovia Fedorovna Saltykof, by the Archpresbyter of the Life-beginning Trinity, Fedor Avksentevich." Sometimes there occurred a piece of political information, as follows:—

" About the French tigers there is somehow silence " —and close by, " In the *Moscow Gazette* there is an announcement of the decease of the First-Major Mikhail Petrovich Kolychef. Is not this the son of Peter Vasilievich Kolychef ? "

Lavretsky also found some old calendars and dreambooks, and the mystical work of M. Ambodik. Many a memory did the long-forgotten but familiar *Symbols and Emblems* recall to his mind. In the furthest recess of one of the drawers in Glafira's toilette-table, Lavretsky found a small packet, sealed with black wax, and tied with a narrow black ribbon. Inside the packet were two portraits lying face to face, the one, in pastel, of his father as a young man, with soft curls falling over his forehead, with long, languid eyes, and with a half-open mouth; the other an almost obliterated picture of a pale woman, in a white dress, with a white rose in her hand—his mother. Of herself Glafira never would allow a portrait to be taken.

"Although I did not then live in the house," Anton would say to Lavretsky, "yet I can remember your great grandfather, Andrei Afanasich. I was eighteen years old when he died. One day I met him in the garden—then my very thighs began to quake. But he didn't do anything, only asked me what my name was, and sent me to his bedroom for a pocket-handkerchief. He was truly a seigneur—every one must allow that; and he wouldn't allow that any one was better than himself. For I may tell you, your great grandfather had such a wonderful amulet—a monk from Mount Athos had given him that amulet—and that monk said to him, ' I give thee this, O Boyar, in return for thy hospitality. Wear it, and fear no judge.' Well, it's true, as is well known, that times were different then. What a seigneur wanted to do, that he did. If ever one of the gentry took it into his head to contradict him, he would just look at him, and say, ' Thou swimmest in shallow water ' [1]—that was a favourite phrase with him. And he lived, did your great grandfather of blessed memory, in small, wooden rooms. But what riches he left behind him! What silver, what stores of all kinds! All the cellars were crammed full of them. He was a real manager. That little decanter which you were pleased to praise was his. He used to drink brandy out of it. But just see! your grandfather, Peter Andreich, provided himself with a stone mansion, but he laid up no goods. Everything went badly with him, and he lived far worse than his father, and got himself no satisfaction, but spent all his money, and now there is nothing to remember him by—not so much as a silver spoon has come down to us from him; and for all that is left, one must thank Glafira Petrovna's care."

[1] Part of a Russian proverb.

" But is it true," interrupted Lavretsky, " that people used to call her an old witch? "

" But, then, who called her so? " replied Anton, with an air of discontent.

" But what is our mistress doing now, *batyushka* ? " the old man ventured to ask one day. " Where does she please to have her habitation? "

" I am separated from my wife," answered Lavretsky, with an effort. " Please don't ask me about her."

" I obey," sadly replied the old man.

At the end of three weeks Lavretsky rode over to O., and spent the evening at the Kalitines' house. He found Lemm there, and took a great liking to him. Although, thanks to his father, Lavretsky could not play any instrument, yet he was passionately fond of music—of classical, serious music, that is to say. Panshine was not at the Kalitines' that evening, for the governor had sent him somewhere into the country. Liza played unaccompanied, and that with great accuracy. Lemm grew lively and animated, rolled up a sheet of paper, and conducted the music. Maria Dmitrievna looked at him laughingly for a while, and then went off to bed. According to her, Beethoven was too agitating for her nerves.

At midnight Lavretsky saw Lemm home, and remained with him till three in the morning. Lemm talked a great deal. He stooped less than usual, his eyes opened wide and sparkled, his very hair remained pushed off from his brow. It was so long since any one had shown any sympathy with him, and Lavretsky was evidently interested in him, and questioned him carefully and attentively. This touched the old man. He ended by showing his music to his guest, and he played, and even sang, in his worn-out voice, some passages from his own works; among others, an entire ballad of Schiller's that he had set to music—that of Fridolin. Lavretsky was loud in its praise, made him repeat several parts, and, on going away, invited him to spend some days with him. Lemm, who was conducting him to the door, immediately consented, pressing his hand cordially. But when he found himself alone in the fresh, damp air, beneath the just-appearing dawn, he looked round, half-shut his eyes, bent himself together, and then crept back, like a culprit, to his bedroom. " *Ich bin wohl nicht klug* " (" I must be out of my wits "), he murmured, as he lay down in his short, hard bed.

He tried to make out that he was ill when, a few days later, Lavretsky's carriage came for him. But Lavretsky went up into his room, and persuaded him to go. Stronger than every other argument with him was the fact that Lavretsky had ordered a piano to be sent out to the country-house on purpose for him. The two companions went to the Kalitines' together, and spent the evening there, but not quite so pleasantly as on the previous occasion. Panshine was there, talking a great deal about his journey, and very amusingly mimicking the various proprietors he had met, and parodying their conversation. Lavretsky laughed, but Lemm refused to come out of his corner, where he remained in silence, noiselessly working his limbs like a spider, and wearing a dull and sulky look. It was not till he rose to take leave that he became at all animated. Even when sitting in the carriage, the old man at first seemed still unsociable and absorbed in his own thoughts. But the calm, warm air, the gentle breeze, the dim shadows, the scent of the grass and the birch-buds, the peaceful light of the moonless, starry sky, the rhythmical tramp and snorting of the horses, the mingled fascinations of the journey, of the spring, of the night—all entered into the soul of the poor German, and he began to talk with Lavretsky of his own accord.

XXII

HE began to talk about music, then about Liza, and then again about music. He seemed to pronounce his words more slowly when he spoke of Liza. Lavretsky turned the conversation to the subject of his compositions, and offered, half in jest, to write a libretto for him.

"Hm! a libretto!" answered Lemm. "No; that is beyond me. I no longer have the animation, the play of fancy, which are indispensable for an opera. Already my strength has deserted me. But if I could still do something, I should content myself with a romance. Of course I should like good words."

He became silent, and sat for a long time without moving, his eyes fixed on the sky.

"For instance," he said at length, "something in this way—'O stars, pure stars!'"

Lavretsky turned a little, and began to regard him attentively.

"'O stars, pure stars!'" repeated Lemm, "'you look alike on the just and the unjust. But only the innocent of heart'—or something of that kind—'understand you'—that is to say, no—'love you.' However, I am not a poet. What am I thinking about? But something of that kind—something lofty."

Lemm pushed his hat back from his forehead. Seen by the faint twilight of the clear night, his face seemed paler and younger.

"'And you know also,'" he continued, in a gradually lowered voice, "'you know those who love, who know how to love; for you are pure, you alone can console.' No; all that is not what I mean. I am not a poet. But something of that kind."

373

"I am sorry that I am not a poet either," remarked Lavretsky.

"Empty dreams!" continued Lemm, as he sank into the corner of the carriage. Then he shut his eyes as if he had made up his mind to go to sleep.

Several minutes passed. Lavretsky still listened.

"'Stars, pure stars . . . love,'" whispered the old man.

"Love!" repeated Lavretsky to himself. Then he fell into a reverie, and his heart grew heavy within him.

"You have set 'Fridolin' to charming music, Christophor Fedorovich," he said aloud after a time. "But what is your opinion? This Fridolin, after he had been brought into the presence of the countess by her husband, didn't he then immediately become her lover—eh?"

"You think so," answered Lemm, "because, most likely, experience——"

He stopped short, and turned away in confusion.

Lavretsky uttered a forced laugh. Then he too turned away from his companion, and began looking out along the road.

The stars had already begun to grow pale, and the sky to turn grey, when the carriage arrived before the steps of the little house at Vasilievskoe. Lavretsky conducted his guest to his allotted room, then went to his study, and sat down in front of the window. Out in the garden a nightingale was singing its last song before the dawn. Lavretsky remembered that at the Kalitines' also a nightingale had sung in the garden. He remembered also the quiet movement of Liza's eyes when, at its first notes, she had turned toward the dark casement. He began to think of her, and his heart grew calm.

"Pure maiden," he said, in a half-whisper, "pure stars," he added, with a smile, and then quietly lay down to sleep.

But Lemm sat for a long time on his bed, with a sheet of music on his knees. It seemed as if some sweet melody, yet unborn, were intending to visit him. He already underwent the feverish agitation, he already felt

374

the fatigue and the delight, of its vicinity; but it always eluded him.

" Neither poet nor musician! " he whispered at last; and his weary head sank heavily upon the pillow.

The next morning Lavretsky and his guest drank their tea in the garden, under an old lime-tree.

" Maestro," said Lavretsky, among other things, " you will soon have to compose a festal cantata."

" On what occasion? "

" Why, on that of M. Panshine's marriage with Liza. Didn't you observe what attention he paid her yesterday? All goes smoothly with them, evidently."

" That will never be! " exclaimed Lemm.

" Why? "

" Because it's impossible. However," he added, after pausing awhile, " in this world everything is possible. Especially in this country of yours—in Russia."

" Let us leave Russia out of the question for the present. But what do you see objectionable in that marriage? "

" Everything is objectionable—everything. Lizaveta Mikhailovna is a serious, true-hearted girl, with lofty sentiments. But he—he is, to describe him by one word, a *dil-le-tante*."

" But doesn't she love him? "

Lemm rose from his bench.

" No, she does not love him. That is to say, she is very pure of heart, and does not herself know the meaning of the words, ' to love.' Madame Von Kalitine tells her that he is an excellent young man; and she obeys Madame Von Kalitine because she is still quite a child, although she is now nineteen. She says her prayers every morning; she says her prayers every evening— and that is very praiseworthy. But she does not love him. She can love only what is noble. But he is not noble; that is to say, his soul is not noble."

Lemm uttered the whole of this speech fluently, and with animation, walking backwards and forwards with short steps in front of the tea-table, his eyes running along the ground meanwhile.

"Dearest Maestro!" suddenly exclaimed Lavretsky, "I think you are in love with my cousin yourself."

Lemm suddenly stopped short.

"Please do not jest with me in that way," he began, with faltering voice. "I am not out of my mind. I look forward to the dark grave, and not to a rosy future."

Lavretsky felt sorry for the old man, and begged his pardon. After breakfast Lemm played his cantata, and after dinner, at Lavretsky's own instigation, he again began to talk about Liza. Lavretsky listened to him attentively and with curiosity.

"What do you say to this, Christophor Fedorovitch?" he said at last. "Everything seems in order here now, and the garden is in full bloom. Why shouldn't I invite her to come here for the day, with her mother and my old aunt—eh? Will that be agreeable to you?"

Lemm bowed his head over his plate.

"Invite her," he said, in a scarcely audible voice.

"But we needn't ask Panshine."

"No, we needn't," answered the old man, with an almost childlike smile.

Two days later Lavretsky went into town and to the Kalitines'.

XXIII

HE found them all at home, but he did not tell them of his plan immediately. He wanted to speak to Liza alone first. Chance favoured him, and he was left alone with her in the drawing-room. They began to talk. As a general rule she was never shy with any one, and by this time she had succeeded in becoming accustomed to him. He listened to what she said, and as he looked at her face, he musingly repeated Lemm's words, and agreed with him. It sometimes happens that two persons who are already acquainted with each other, but not intimately, after the lapse of a few minutes suddenly become familiar friends—and the consciousness of this familiarity immediately expresses itself in their looks, in their gentle and kindly smiles, in their gestures themselves. And this happened now with Lavretsky and Liza. "Ah, so that's what you're like!" thought she, looking at him with friendly eyes. "Ah, so that's what you're like!" thought he also; and therefore he was not much surprised when she informed him, not without some little hesitation, that she had long wanted to say something to him, but that she was afraid of vexing him.

"Don't be afraid, speak out," he said, standing still in front of her.

Liza raised her clear eyes to his.

"You are so good," she began—and at the same time she thought, " yes, he is really good "—" I hope you will forgive me. I scarcely ought to have ventured to speak to you about it—but how could you—why did you separate from your wife? "

Lavretsky shuddered, then looked at Liza, and sat down by her side.

"My child," he began to say, " I beg you not to touch

upon that wound. Your touch is light, but—but in spite of all that, it will give me pain."

" I know," continued Liza, as if she had not heard him, " that she is guilty before you. I do not want to justify her. But how can they be separated whom God has joined together? "

" Our convictions on that score are widely different, Lizaveta Mikhailovna," said Lavretsky somewhat coldly. " We shall not be able to understand one another."

Liza grew pale. Her whole body shuddered slightly, but she was not silenced.

" You ought to forgive," she said quietly, " if you wish also to be forgiven."

" Forgive! " cried Lavretsky; " you ought first to know her for whom you plead. Forgive that woman, take her back to my house, her, that hollow, heartless creature! And who has told you that she wants to return to me? Why, she is completely satisfied with her position. But why should we talk of her? Her name ought never to be uttered by you. You are too pure, you are not in a position even to understand such a being."

" Why speak so bitterly? " said Liza, with an effort. The trembling of her hands began to be apparent. " You left her of your own accord, Fedor Ivanich."

" But I tell you," replied Lavretsky, with an involuntary burst of impatience, " you do not know the sort of creature she is."

" Then why did you marry her? " whispered Liza, with downcast eyes.

Lavretsky jumped up quickly from his chair.

" Why did I marry her? I was young and inexperienced then. I was taken in. A beautiful exterior fascinated me. I did not understand women; there was nothing I did understand. God grant you may make a happier marriage! But take my word for it, it is impossible to be certain about anything."

" I also may be unhappy," said Liza, her voice beginning to waver, " but then I shall have to be resigned.

I cannot express myself properly, but I mean to say that if we are not resigned——"

Lavretsky clenched his hands and stamped his foot.

"Don't be angry; please forgive me," hastily said Liza. At that moment Maria Dmitrievna came into the room. Liza stood up and was going away, when Lavretsky unexpectedly called after her:

"Stop a moment. I have a great favour to ask of your mother and you. It is that you will come and pay me a visit in my new home. I've got a piano, you know; Lemm is stopping with me; the lilacs are in bloom. You will get a breath of country air, and be able to return the same day. Do you consent?"

Liza looked at her mother, who immediately assumed an air of suffering. But Lavretsky did not give Madame Kalitine time to open her mouth. He instantly took both of her hands and kissed them, and Maria Dmitrievna, who always responded to winning ways, and had never for a moment expected such a piece of politeness from "the bear," felt herself touched, and gave her consent. While she was considering what day to appoint, Lavretsky went up to Liza and, still under the influence of emotion, whispered aside to her, "Thanks. You are a good girl. I am in the wrong." Then a colour came into her pale face, which lighted up with a quiet but joyous smile. Her eyes also smiled. Till that moment she had been afraid that she had offended him.

"M. Panshine can come with us, I suppose?" asked Maria Dmitrievna.

"Of course," replied Lavretsky. "But would it not be better for us to keep to our family circle?"

"But I think——" began Maria Dmitrievna, adding, however, "Well, just as you like."

It was settled that Lenochka and Shurochka should go. Marfa Timofeevna refused to take part in the excursion.

"It's a bore to me, my dear," she said, "to move my old bones; and there's nowhere, I suppose, in your house where I could pass the night; besides, I never can sleep in a strange bed. Let these young folks caper as they please."

Lavretsky had no other opportunity of speaking with Liza alone, but he kept looking at her in a manner that pleased her, and at the same time confused her a little. She felt very sorry for him. When he went away, he took leave of her with a warm pressure of the hand. She fell into a reverie as soon as she found herself alone.

On entering the drawing-room, after his return home,
Lavretsky met a tall, thin man, with a wrinkled but
animated face, untidy grey whiskers, a long, straight
nose, and small, inflamed eyes. This individual, who
was dressed in a shabby blue surtout, was Mikhalevich,
his former comrade at the university. At first Lavretsky did not recognise him, but he warmly embraced
him as soon as he had made himself known. The two
friends had not seen each other since the old Moscow
days. Then followed exclamations and questions.
Memories long lost to sight came out again into the light
of day. Smoking pipe after pipe in a hurried manner,
gulping down his tea, and waving his long hands in the
air, Mikhalevich related his adventures. There was
nothing very brilliant about them, and he could boast
of but little success in his various enterprises; but he
kept incessantly laughing a hoarse, nervous laugh. It
seemed that about a month previously he had obtained
a post in the private counting-house of a rich brandy-
farmer,[2] at about three hundred versts from O., and
having heard of Lavretsky's return from abroad, he had
turned out of his road, for the purpose of seeing his old
friend again. He spoke just as jerkingly as he used to
do in the days of youth, and he became as noisy and as
warm as he was in the habit of growing then. Lavretsky
began to speak about his own affairs, but Mikhalevich
stopped him, hastily stammering out, " I have heard
about it, brother; I have heard about it. Who could
have expected it? " and then immediately turned the
conversation on topics of general interest.

[1] Omitted in the French translation.
[2] One of the contractors who used to purchase the right of
supplying the people with brandy.

" I must go away again to-morrow, brother," he said.
" To-day, if you will allow it, we will sit up late. I want
to get a thoroughly good idea of what you are now, what
your intentions are and your convictions, what sort of
man you have become, what life has taught you " (Mikhalevich still made use of the phraseology current in the
year 1830). " As for me, brother, I have become
changed in many respects. The waters of life have
gone over my breast. Who was it said that? But in
what is important, what is substantial, I have not
changed. I believe, as I used to do, in the good, in the
true. And not only do I believe, but I feel certain now
—yes, I feel certain, certain. Listen; I make verses,
you know. There's no poetry in them, but there is
truth. I will read you my last piece. I have expressed
in it my most sincere convictions. Now listen."

Mikhalevich began to read his poem, which was rather
a long one. It ended with the following lines:—

" With my whole heart have I given myself up to new feelings;
    In spirit I have become like unto a child.
And I have burnt all that I used to worship,
    I worship all that I used to burn."

Mikhalevich all but wept as he pronounced these last
two verses. A slight twitching, the sign of a strong
emotion, affected his large lips; his plain face lighted
up. Lavretsky went on listening until at last the spirit
of contradiction was roused within him. He became
irritated by the Moscow student's enthusiasm, so perpetually on the boil, so continually ready for use. A
quarter of an hour had not elapsed before a dispute had
been kindled between the two friends, one of those endless disputes of which only Russians are capable. They
two, after a separation which had lasted for many years,
and those passed in two different worlds, neither of them
clearly understanding the other's thoughts, not even his
own, holding fast by words, and differing in words alone,
disputed about the most purely abstract ideas—and disputed exactly as if the matter had been one of life and

382

death to both of them. They shouted and cried aloud
to such an extent that every one in the house was disturbed, and poor Lemm, who had shut himself up in
his room the moment Mikhalevich arrived, felt utterly
perplexed, and even began to entertain some vague form
of fear.

"But after all this, what are you? *blasé!* "[1] cried
Mikhalevich at midnight.

"Does a *blasé* man ever look like me? " answered
Lavretsky. "He is always pale and sickly; but I, if
you like, will lift you off the ground with one hand."

"Well then, if not *blasé*, at least a sceptic,[2] and that
is still worse. But what right have you to be a sceptic?
Your life has not been a success, I admit. That wasn't
your fault. You were endowed with a soul full of affection, fit for passionate love, and you were kept away
from women by force. The first woman you came across
was sure to take you in."

"She took you in, too," morosely remarked Lavretsky.

"Granted, granted. In that I was the tool of fate.
But I'm talking nonsense. There's no such thing as fate.
My old habit of expressing myself inaccurately! But
what does that prove? "

"It proves this much, that I have been distorted from
childhood."

"Well, then, straighten yourself. That's the good of
being a man—one of the male sex. You haven't got to
borrow energy. But however that may be, it certainly
is possible, it certainly is allowable, to work upwards
from an isolated fact, so to speak, to a general law—to
an invariable rule."

"What rule? " said Lavretsky, interrupting him.
"I do not admit——"

"No, that is your rule, that is your rule," cried the
other, interrupting him in his turn.

[1] Literally, " disillusioned."
[2] He says in that original *Skyeptuik* instead of *Skeptik*, on
which the author remarks, " Mikhalevich's accent testified to
his birthplace having been in Little Russia."

"You are an egoist, that's what it is!" thundered Mikhalevich an hour later. "You wanted self-enjoyment; you wanted a happy life; you wanted to live only for yourself——"

"What is self-enjoyment?"

"—And everything has failed you; everything has given way under your feet."

"But what is self-enjoyment, I ask you?"

"—And it ought to give way. Because you looked for support there where it is impossible to find it; because you built your house on the quicksands——"

"Speak plainer, without metaphor, *because* I do not understand you."

"—Because—laugh away if you like—because there is no faith in you, no hearty warmth—and only a poor farthingsworth of intellect;[1] you are simply a pitiable creature, a behind-your-age disciple of Voltaire. That's what you are."

"Who? I a disciple of Voltaire?"

"Yes, just such a one as your father was; and you have never so much as suspected it."

"After that," exclaimed Lavretsky, "I have a right to say that you are a fanatic."

"Alas!" sorrowfully replied Mikhalevich, "unfortunately, I have not yet in any way deserved so grand a name——"

"I have found out now what to call you!" cried the self-same Mikhalevich at three o'clock in the morning. "You are not a sceptic, nor are you *blasé*, nor a disciple of Voltaire; you are a marmot,[2] and a culpable marmot; a marmot with a conscience, not a naïve marmot. Naïve marmots lie on the stove [3] and do nothing, because they can do nothing. They do not even think anything. But you are a thinking man, and yet you lie idly there. You could do something, and you do nothing. You lie on

---

[1] Literally, "intellect, in all merely a copeck intellect."

[2] A *baibak*, a sort of marmot or "prairie dog."

[3] The top of the stove forms the sleeping place in a Russian peasant's hut.

the top with full paunch and say, ' To lie idle—so must it be; because all that people ever do—is all vanity, mere nonsense that conduces to nothing.' "

" But what has shown you that I lie idle? " insisted Lavretsky. " Why do you suppose I have such ideas? "

"—And, besides this, all you people, all your brother-hood," continued Mikhalevich without stopping, " are deeply-read marmots. You all know where the German's shoe pinches him; you all know what faults Englishmen and Frenchmen have; and your miserable knowledge only serves to help you to justify your shameful laziness, your abominable idleness. There are some who even pride themselves on this, that ' I, forsooth, am a learned man. I lie idle, and they are fools to give themselves trouble.' Yes! even such persons as these do exist among us; not that I say this with reference to you; such persons as will spend all their life in a certain languor of ennui, and get accustomed to it, and exist in it like—like a mushroom in sour cream " (Mikhalevich could not help laughing at his own comparison). " Oh, that languor of ennui! it is the ruin of the Russian people. Throughout all time the wretched marmot is making up its mind to work——"

" But, after all, what are you scolding about? " cried Lavretsky in his turn. " To work, to do. You had better say what one should do, instead of scolding, O Demosthenes of Poltava." [1]

" Ah, yes, that's what you want! No, brother, I will not tell you that. Every one must teach himself that," replied Demosthenes in an ironical tone. " A proprietor, a noble, and not know what to do! You have no faith, or you would have known. No faith and no divina-tion." [2]

" At all events, let me draw breath for a moment, you fiend," prayed Lavretsky. " Let me take a look round me! "

[1] Poltava is the university town of Little Russia. It will be remembered that Mikhalevich is a Little Russian.
[2] *Otkrovenie*, discovery or revelation.

385

"Not a minute's breathing-time, not a second's," replied Mikhalevich, with a commanding gesture of the hand. "Not a single second. Death does not tarry, and life also ought not to tarry."

"And when and where have people taken it into their heads to make marmots of themselves?" he cried at four in the morning, in a voice that was now somewhat hoarse. "Why, here! Why, now! In Russia! When on every separate individual there lies a duty, a great responsibility, before God, before the nation, before himself! We sleep, but time goes by. We sleep——"

"Allow me to point out to you," observed Lavretsky, "that we do not at all sleep at present, but rather prevent other persons from sleeping. We stretch our throats like barndoor cocks. Listen, that one is crowing for the third time."

This sally made Mikhalevich laugh, and sobered him down. "Good-night," he said with a smile, and put away his pipe in its bag. "Good-night," said Lavretsky also. However, the friends still went on talking for more than an hour. But their voices did not rise high any longer, and their talk was quiet, sad, kindly talk.

Mikhalevich went away next day, in spite of all his host could do to detain him. Lavretsky did not succeed in persuading him to stay, but he got as much talk as he wanted out of him.

It turned out that Mikhalevich was utterly impecunious. Lavretsky had already been sorry to see in him, on the preceding evening, all the signs and characteristics of a poverty of long standing. His shoes were trodden down, his coat wanted a button behind, his hands were strangers to gloves, one or two bits of feather were sticking in his hair. When he arrived, he did not think of asking for a wash; and at supper he ate like a shark, tearing the meat to pieces with his fingers, and noisily gnawing the bones with his firm, discoloured teeth.

It turned out also that he had not thriven in the civil service, and that he had pinned all his hopes on the brandy-farmer, who had given him employment simply that he might have an " educated man " in his counting-house. In spite of all this, however, Mikhalevich had not lost courage, but kept on his way leading the life of a cynic, an idealist, and a poet; fervently caring for, and troubling himself about, the destinies of humanity and his special vocation in life—and giving very little heed to the question whether or no he would die of starvation.

Mikhalevich had never married; but he had fallen in love countless times, and he always wrote poetry about all his loves: with especial fervour did he sing about a mysterious, raven-haired " lady." It was rumoured, indeed, that this " lady " was nothing more than a Jewess, and one who had numerous friends among cavalry officers; but, after all, if one thinks the matter over, it is not one of much importance.

With Lemm, Mikhalevich did not get on well. His extremely loud way of talking, his rough manners, frightened the German, to whom they were entirely novel. One unfortunate man immediately and from afar recognises another, but in old age he is seldom willing to associate with him. Nor is that to be wondered at. He has nothing to share with him—not even hopes.

Before he left, Mikhalevich had another long talk with Lavretsky, to whom he predicted utter ruin if he did not rouse himself, and whom he entreated to occupy himself seriously with the question of the position of his serfs. He set himself up as a pattern for imitation, saying that he had been purified in the furnace of misfortune; and then he several times styled himself a happy man, comparing himself to a bird of the air, a lily of the valley.

" A dusky lily, at all events," remarked Lavretsky.

" Ah, brother, don't come the aristocrat," answered Mikhalevich good-humouredly; " but rather thank God that in your veins also there flows simple plebeian blood. But I see you are now in need of some pure, unearthly being, who might rouse you from your apathy."

387

"Thanks, brother," said Lavretsky; "I have had quite enough of those unearthly beings."

"Silence, cyneec!"[1] exclaimed Mikhalevich.

"Cynic," said Lavretsky, correcting him.

"Just so, cyneec," repeated the undisconcerted Mikhalevich.

Even when he had taken his seat in the tarantass, in which his flat and marvellously light portmanteau had been stowed away, he still went on talking. Enveloped in a kind of Spanish cloak, with a collar reddened by long use, and with lion's claws instead of hooks, he continued to pour forth his opinions on the destinies of Russia, waving his swarthy hand the while in the air, as if he were sowing the seeds of future prosperity. At last the horses set off.

"Remember my last three words!" he exclaimed, leaning almost entirely out of the carriage, and scarcely able to keep his balance. "Religion, Progress, Humanity! Farewell!" His head, on which his forage cap was pressed down to his eyes, disappeared from sight. Lavretsky was left alone at the door, where he remained gazing attentively along the road, until the carriage was out of sight. "And perhaps he is right," he thought, as he went back into the house. "Perhaps I am a marmot." Much of what Mikhalevich had said had succeeded in winning its way into his heart, although at the time he had contradicted him and disagreed with him. Let a man only be perfectly honest—no one can utterly gainsay him.

[1] He says *Tsuinuik* instead of *Tsinik*.

XXV

Two days later, Maria Dmitrievna arrived at Vasilievskoe, according to her promise, and all her young people with her. The little girls immediately ran into the garden, but Maria Dmitrievna languidly walked through the house, and languidly praised all she saw. She looked upon her visit to Lavretsky as a mark of great condescension, almost a benevolent action. She smiled affably when Anton and Apraxia came to kiss her hand, according to the old custom of household serfs, and in feeble accents she asked for tea.

To the great vexation of Anton, who had donned a pair of knitted white gloves, it was not he who handed the tea to the lady visitor, but Lavretsky's hired lackey, a fellow who, in the old man's opinion, had not a notion of etiquette. However, Anton had it all his own way at dinner. With firm step, he took up his position behind Madame Kalitine's chair, and he refused to give up his post to any one. The apparition of visitors at Vasilievskoe—a sight for so many years unknown there—both troubled and cheered the old man. It was a pleasure for him to see that his master was acquainted with persons of some standing in society.

Anton was not the only person who was agitated that day. Lemm was excited too. He had put on a shortish snuff-coloured coat with pointed tails, and had tied his cravat tight, he coughed incessantly, and made way for every one with kindly and affable mien. As for Lavretsky, he remarked with satisfaction that he remained on the same friendly footing with Liza as before. As soon as she arrived she cordially held out her hand to him.

After dinner, Lemm took a small roll of music-paper out of the tail-pocket of his coat, into which he had been

389

constantly putting his hand, and silently, with compressed lips, placed it on the piano. It contained a romance, which he had written the day before to some old-fashioned German words, in which mention was made of the stars. Liza immediately sat down to the piano, and interpreted the romance. Unfortunately the music turned out to be confused and unpleasantly constrained. It was evident that the composer had attempted to express some deep and passionate idea, but no result had been attained. The attempt remained an attempt, and nothing more. Both Lavretsky and Liza felt this, and Lemm was conscious of it too. Without saying a word, he put his romance back into his pocket; and, in reply to Liza's proposal to play it over again, he merely shook his head, and said, in a tone of meaning, " For the present — *basta !* " then bent his head, stooped his shoulders, and left the room.

Towards evening they all went out together to fish. In the little lake at the end of the garden there were numbers of carp and groundling. Madame Kalitine had an armchair set in the shade for her, near the edge of the water, and a carpet was spread out under her feet. Anton, as an old fisherman of great experience, offered her his services. Zealously did he fasten on the worms, slap them with his hand, and spit upon them, and then fling the line into the water himself, gracefully bending forwards the whole of his body. Maria Dmitrievna had already that day spoken about him to Fedor Ivanovich, using the following phrase of Institute-French:—" *Il n'y a plus maintenant de ces gens comme ça comme autrefois.*"

Lemm and the two little girls went on to the dam at the end of the lake. Lavretsky placed himself near Liza. The fish kept continually nibbling. Every minute a captured carp glistened in the air with its sometimes golden, sometimes silver, sides. The little girls kept up a ceaseless flow of joyful exclamations. Madame Kalitine herself two or three times uttered a plaintive cry. Lavretsky and Liza caught fewer fish than the others; probably because they paid less attention to their fishing, and let their floats drift up against the edge of the lake. The tall, reddish reeds murmured quietly around them; in front quietly shone the unruffled water, and the conversation they carried on was quiet too.

Liza stood on the little platform (placed there for the use of the washerwomen); Lavretsky sat on the bent stem of a willow. Liza wore a white dress, fastened round the waist by a broad, white ribbon. From one hand hung her straw hat; with the other she, not without some effort, supported her drooping fishing-rod. Lavretsky gazed at her pure, somewhat severe profile— at the hair turned back behind her ears—at her soft cheeks, the hue of which was like that of a young child's —and thought: " How charming you look, standing there by my lake! " Liza did not look at him, but kept her eyes fixed on the water, something which might be a smile lurking about their corners. Over both Lavretsky and Liza fell the shadow of a neighbouring lime-tree.

" Do you know," he began, " I have thought a great deal about our last conversation, and I have come to this conclusion, that you are exceedingly good."

" It certainly was not with that intention that I——" replied Liza, and became greatly confused.

" You are exceedingly good," repeated Lavretsky. " I am a rough-hewn man; but I feel that every one must love you. There is Lemm, for instance: he is simply in love with you."

Liza's eyebrows did not exactly frown, but they quivered. This always happened with her when she heard anything she did not like.

" I felt very sorry for him to-day, with his unsuccessful romance," continued Lavretsky. " To be young and to want knowledge—that is bearable. But to have grown old and to fail in strength—that is indeed heavy. And the worst of it is, that one doesn't know when one's strength has failed. To an old man such blows are hard to bear. Take care! you've a bite.—I hear," continued

Lavretsky, after a short pause, " that M. Panshine has written a very charming romance."

" Yes," replied Liza, " it is a small matter; but it isn't bad."

" But what is your opinion about him himself? " asked Lavretsky. " Is he a good musician? "

" I think he has a considerable musical faculty. But as yet he has not cultivated it as he ought."

" Just so. But is he a good man? "

Liza laughed aloud, and looked up quickly at Fedor Ivanovich.

" What a strange question! " she exclaimed, withdrawing her line from the water, and then throwing it a long way in again.

" Why strange? I ask you about him as one who has been away from here a long time—as a relation."

" As a relation? "

" Yes. I believe I am a sort of uncle of yours."

" Vladimir Nikolaevich has a good heart," said Liza. " He is clever. Mamma likes him very much."

" But you—do you like him? "

" He is a good man. Why shouldn't I like him? "

" Ah! " said Lavretsky, and became silent. A half-sad, half-mocking expression played upon his face. The fixed look with which he regarded her troubled Liza; but she went on smiling.

" Well, may God grant them happiness! " he murmured at last, as if to himself, and turned away his head.

Liza reddened.

" You are wrong, Fedor Ivanovich," she said; " you are wrong in thinking—— But don't you like Vladimir Ivanovich? " she asked suddenly.

" No."

" Why? "

" I think he has no heart."

The smile disappeared from Liza's lips.

" You are accustomed to judge people severely," she said, after a long silence.

" I don't think so. What right have I to judge others

392

severely, I should like to know, when I stand in need of indulgence myself? Or have you forgotten that it is only lazy people who do not mock me? But tell me," he added, " have you kept your promise? "

" What promise? "

" Have you prayed for me? "

" Yes, I have prayed for you; and I pray every day. But please do not talk lightly about that."

Lavretsky began to assure Liza that he had never dreamt of doing so—that he profoundly respected all convictions. After that he took to talking about religion, about its significance in the history of humanity, of the meaning of Christianity.

" One must be a Christian," said Liza, not without an effort, " not in order to recognise what is heavenly, or what is earthly, but because every one must die."

With an involuntary movement of surprise, Lavretsky raised his eyes to Liza's, and met her glance.

" What does that phrase of yours mean? " he said.

" It is not my phrase," she replied.

" Not yours? But why did you speak about death? "

" I don't know. I often think about it."

" Often? "

" Yes."

" One wouldn't say so, looking at you now. Your face seems so happy, so bright, and you smile——"

" Yes. I feel very happy now," replied Liza simply.

Lavretsky felt inclined to seize both her hands and press them warmly.

" Liza, Liza! " cried Madame Kalitine, " come here and see what a carp I have caught."

" Yes, mamma," answered Liza, and went to her.

But Lavretsky remained sitting on his willow stem.

" I talk to her just as if I still had an interest in life," he thought.

Liza had hung up her hat on a bough when she went away. It was with a strange and almost tender feeling that Lavretsky looked at the hat, and at its long, slightly rumpled ribbons.

393

Liza soon came back again and took up her former position on the platform.

"Why do you think that Vladimir Nikolaevich has no heart?" she asked, a few minutes afterwards.

"I have already told you that I may be mistaken. However, time will reveal all."

Liza became contemplative. Lavretsky began to talk about his mode of life at Vasilievskoe, about Mikhalevich, about Anton. He felt compelled to talk to Liza, to communicate to her all that went on in his heart. And she listened to him so attentively, with such kindly interest; the few remarks and answers she made appeared to him so sensible and so natural. He even told her so.

Liza was astonished. "Really?" she said. "As for me, I thought I was like my maid, Nastasia, and had no words 'of my own.' She said one day to her betrothed, 'You will be sure to be bored with me. You talk so beautifully to me about everything, but I have no words of my own.'"

"Heaven be praised!" thought Lavretsky.

XXVI

In the meantime the evening had arrived, and Maria Dmitrievna evinced a desire to return home. With some difficulty the little girls were torn away from the lake, and got ready for the journey. Lavretsky said he would accompany his guests half-way home, and ordered a horse to be saddled for him. After seeing Maria Dmitrievna into her carriage he looked about for Lemm; but the old man could nowhere be found. He had disappeared the moment the fishing was over. Anton slammed the carriage door to, with a strength remarkable at his age, and cried in a stern voice, "Drive on, coachman!" The carriage set off. Maria Dmitrievna and Liza occupied the back seats; the two girls and the maid sat in front.

The evening was warm and still, and the windows were open on both sides. Lavretsky rode close by the carriage on Liza's side, resting a hand on the door—he had thrown the reins on the neck of his easily trotting horse—and now and then exchanged two or three words with the young girl. The evening glow disappeared. Night came on, but the air seemed to grow even warmer than before. Maria Dmitrievna soon went to sleep; the little girls and the maid-servant slept also. Smoothly and rapidly the carriage rolled on. As Liza bent forwards the moon, which had only just made its appearance, lighted up her face, the fragrant night air breathed on her eyes and cheeks, and she felt herself happy. Her hand rested on the door of the carriage by the side of Lavretsky's. He too felt himself happy as he floated on in the calm warmth of the night, never moving his eyes away from the good young face, listening to the young voice, clear even in its whispers, which spoke simple, good words.

It even escaped his notice for a time that he had gone

more than half of the way. Then he would not disturb Madame Kalitine, but he pressed Liza's hand lightly and said, " We are friends now, are we not? " She nodded assent, and he pulled up his horse. The carriage rolled on its way quietly swinging and curtseying.

Lavretsky returned home at a walk. The magic of the summer night took possession of him. All that spread around him seemed so wonderfully strange, and yet at the same time so well known and so dear. Far and near all was still—and the eye could see very far, though it could not distinguish much of what it saw— but underneath that very stillness a young and flowering life made itself felt.

Lavretsky's horse walked on vigorously, swinging it- self steadily to right and left. Its great black shadow moved by its side. There was a sort of secret charm in the tramp of its hoofs, something strange and joyous in the noisy cry of the quails. The stars disappeared in a kind of luminous mist. The moon, not yet at its full, shone with steady lustre. Its light spread in a blue stream over the sky, and fell in a streak of vaporous gold on the thin clouds which went past close at hand.

The freshness of the air called a slight moisture into Lavretsky's eyes, passed caressingly over all his limbs, and flowed with free current into his chest. He was conscious of enjoying, and felt glad of that enjoyment. " Well, we will live on still; she has not entirely deprived us——" he did not say who, or of what. Then he began to think about Liza; that she could scarcely be in love with Panshine; that if he had met her under other cir- cumstances—God knows what might have come of it; that he understood Lemm's feelings about her now, although she had " no words of her own." And, more- over, that that was not true; for she had words of her own. " Do not speak lightly about that," recurred to Lavretsky's memory. For a long time he rode on with bent head, then he slowly drew himself up repeating,—

" And I have burnt all that I used to worship,
I worship all that I used to burn "—

396

then he suddenly struck his horse with his whip and galloped straight away home.

On alighting from his horse he gave a final look round, a thankful smile playing involuntarily on his lips. Night —silent, caressing night—lay on the hills and dales. From its fragrant depths afar—whether from heaven or from earth could not be told—there poured a soft and quiet warmth. Lavretsky wished a last farewell to Liza —and hastened up the steps.

The next day went by rather slowly, rain setting in early in the morning. Lemm looked askance, and compressed his lips even tighter and tighter, as if he had made a vow never to open them again. When Lavretsky lay down at night he took to bed with him a whole bundle of French newspapers, which had already lain unopened on his table for two or three weeks. He began carelessly to tear open their covers and to skim the contents of their columns, in which, for the matter of that, there was but little that was new. He was just on the point of throwing them aside, when he suddenly bounded out of bed as if something had stung him. In the *feuilleton* of one of the papers our former acquaintance, M. Jules, communicated to his readers a " painful piece of intelligence." " The fascinating, fair Muscovite," he wrote, " one of the queens of fashion, the ornament of Parisian *salons*, Madame de Lavretski," had died almost suddenly. And this news, unfortunately but too true, had just reached him, M. Jules. He was, so he continued, he might say, a friend of the deceased——

Lavretsky put on his clothes, went out into the garden, and walked up and down one of its alleys until the break of day.

At breakfast, next morning, Lemm asked Lavretsky to let him have horses in order to get back to town.

" It is time for me to return to business, that is to lessons," remarked the old man. " I am only wasting my time here uselessly."

Lavretsky did not reply at once. He seemed lost in a reverie.

"Very good," he said at last; "I will go with you myself."

Refusing the assistance of a servant, Lemm packed his little portmanteau, growing peevish the while and groaning over it, and then tore up and burnt some sheets of music paper. The carriage came to the door. As Lavretsky left his study he put in his pocket the copy of the newspaper he had read the night before. During the whole of the journey neither Lavretsky nor Lemm said much. Each of them was absorbed in his own thoughts, and each was glad that the other did not disturb him. And they parted rather coldly, an occurrence which, for the matter of that, often occurs among friends in Russia. Lavretsky drove the old man to his modest dwelling. Lemm took his portmanteau with him as he got out of the carriage, and, without stretching out his hand to his friend, he held the portmanteau before him with both hands, and, without even looking at him, said in Russian, " Farewell! " " Farewell! " echoed Lavretsky, and told the coachman to drive to his apartments; for he had taken lodgings in O.

After writing several letters, and making a hasty dinner, he went to the Kalitines'. There he found no one in the drawing-room but Panshine, who told him that Maria Dmitrievna would come directly, and immediately entered into conversation with him in the kindest and most affable manner. Until that day Panshine had treated Lavretsky, not with haughtiness exactly, but with condescension; but Liza, in describing her excursion of the day before, had spoken of Lavretsky as an excellent and clever man. That was enough; the " excellent " man must be captivated.

Panshine began by complimenting Lavretsky, giving him an account of the rapture with which, according to him, all the Kalitine family had spoken of Vasilievskoe; then, according to his custom, adroitly bringing the conversation round to himself, he began to speak of his occupations, of his views concerning life, the world, and the service; said a word or two about the future of

398

Russia, and about the necessity of holding the governors of provinces in hand; joked facetiously about himself in that respect, and added that he, among others, had been entrusted at St. Petersburg with the commission *de populariser l'idée du cadastre.* He spoke at tolerable length, and with careless assurance, solving all difficulties, and playing with the most important administrative and political questions as a juggler does with his balls. Such expressions as, " That is what I should do if I were the government," and " You, as an intelligent man, doubtless agree with me," were always at the tip of his tongue.

Lavretsky listened coldly to Panshine's eloquence. This handsome, clever, and unnecessarily elegant young man, with his serene smile, his polite voice, and his inquisitive eyes, was not to his liking. Panshine soon guessed, with the quick appreciation of the feelings of others which was peculiar to him, that he did not confer any special gratification on the person he was addressing, so he disappeared under cover of some plausible excuse, having made up his mind that Lavretsky might be an excellent man, but that he was unsympathetic, " *aigri,*" and, *en somme,* somewhat ridiculous.

Madame Kalitine arrived, accompanied by Gedeonovsky. Then came Marfa Timofeevna and Liza, and after them all the other members of the family. Afterwards, also, there arrived the lover of music, Madame Belenitsine, a thin little woman, with an almost childish little face, pretty but worn, a noisy black dress, a particoloured fan, and thick gold bracelets. With her came her husband, a corpulent man, with red cheeks, large hands and feet, white eyelashes, and a smile which never left his thick lips. His wife never spoke to him in society; and at home, in her tender moments, she used to call him " her sucking-pig."

Panshine returned; the room became animated and noisy. Such an assemblage of people was by no means agreeable to Lavretsky. He was especially annoyed by Madame Belenitsine, who kept perpetually staring at him through her eye-glass. If it had not been for Liza he would have gone away at once. He wanted to say a few words to her alone, but for a long time he could not obtain a fitting opportunity of doing so, and had to content himself with following her about with his eyes. It was with a secret joy that he did so. Never had her face seemed to him more noble and charming. She appeared to great advantage in the presence of Madame Belenitsine. That lady was incessantly fidgeting on her chair, working her narrow shoulders, laughing affectedly, and either all but closing her eyes or opening them unnaturally wide. Liza sat still, looked straight before her, and did not laugh at all.

Madame Kalitine sat down to cards with Marfa Timofeevna, Belenitsine, and Gedeonovsky, the latter of whom played very slowly, made continual mistakes, squeezed up his eyes, and mopped his face with his handkerchief. Panshine assumed an air of melancholy, and expressed himself tersely, sadly, and significantly—altogether after the fashion of an artist who has not yet had any opportunity of showing off—but in spite of the entreaties of Madame Belenitsine, who coquetted with him to a great extent, he would not consent to sing his romance. Lavretsky's presence embarrassed him.

Lavretsky himself spoke little, but the peculiar expression his face wore struck Liza as soon as he entered the room. She immediately felt that he had something to communicate to her; but, without knowing herself why, she was afraid of asking him any questions. At last, as she was passing into the next room to make the tea, she almost unconsciously looked towards him. He immediately followed her.

" What is the matter with you? " she asked, putting the teapot on the *samovar*.[1]

" You have remarked something, then? " he said.

" You are different to-day from what I have seen you before."

Lavretsky bent over the table.

[1] Urn.

" I wanted," he began, " to tell you a piece of news, but just now it is impossible. But read the part of this *feuilleton* which is marked in pencil," he added, giving her the copy of the newspaper he had brought with him. " Please keep the secret; I will come back to-morrow morning."

Liza was thoroughly amazed. At that moment Panshine appeared in the doorway. She put the newspaper in her pocket.

" Have you read Obermann,[1] Lizaveta Mikhailovna? " asked Panshine with a thoughtful air.

Liza replied vaguely as she passed out of the room, and then went upstairs. Lavretsky returned into the drawing-room and approached the card table. Marfa Timofeevna flushed, and, with her capstrings untied, began to complain to him of her partner Gedeonovsky, who, according to her, had not yet learnt his steps. " Card-playing," she said, " is evidently a very different thing from gossiping." Meanwhile Gedeonovsky never left off blinking and mopping himself with his handkerchief.

Presently Liza returned to the drawing-room and sat down in a corner. Lavretsky looked at her and she at him, and each experienced a painful sensation. He could read perplexity on her face, and a kind of secret reproach. Much as he wished it, he could not get a talk with her, and to remain in the same room with her as a mere visitor among other visitors was irksome to him, so he determined to go away.

When taking leave of her, he contrived to repeat that he would come next day, and he added that he counted on her friendship. " Come," she replied, with the same perplexed look still on her face.

After Lavretsky's departure, Panshine grew animated. He began to give advice to Gedeonovsky, and to make mock love to Madame Belenitsine, and at last he sang his romance. But when gazing at Liza, or talking to

[1] The sentimental romance of that name, written by E. Pivert de Sénancour.

her, he maintained the same air as before, one of deep meaning, with a touch of sadness in it.

All that night also, Lavretsky did not sleep. He was not unhappy, he was not agitated; on the contrary, he was perfectly calm; but he could not sleep. He was not even recalling the past. He simply looked at his present life. His heart beat firmly and equably, the hours flew by, he did not even think about sleeping. Only at times there came into his head the thought, "Surely this is not true, this is all nonsense." And then he would stop short, and presently let his head fall back and again betake himself to gazing into the stream of his life.

XXVII

MADAME KALITINE did not receive Lavretsky over cordially, when he paid her a visit next day. " Ah! he's making a custom of it," she thought. She was not of herself disposed to like him very much, and Panshine, who had got her thoroughly under his influence, had praised him the evening before in a very astutely disparaging manner. As she did not treat him as an honoured guest, nor think it necessary to trouble herself about one who was a relation, almost a member of the family circle, before half an hour had elapsed he went out into the garden. There he and Liza strolled along one of the alleys, while Lenochka and Shurochka played around the flower-plots at a little distance from them.

Liza was as quiet as usual, but more than usually pale. She took the folded leaf of the newspaper from her pocket, and handed it to Lavretsky.

" That is terrible news," she said.

Lavretsky made no reply.

" But, after all, perhaps it may not be true."

" That is why I asked you not to mention it to any one."

Liza walked on a little farther.

" Tell me," she began, " are not you sorry?—not at all sorry ? "

" I don't know myself what I feel," answered Lavretsky.

" But you loved her once ? "

" I did."

" Very much ? "

" Yes."

" And yet you are not sorry for her death ? "

" It is not only now that she has become dead for me."

" You are saying what is sinful. Don't be angry with

403

me. You have called me your friend. A friend may say anything. And it really seems terrible to me. The expression on your face yesterday was not good to see. Do you remember your complaining about her not long ago? And at that very time, perhaps, she was already no longer among the living. It is terrible. It is just as if it had been sent you as a punishment."

Lavretsky laughed bitterly.

" You think so?—at all events I am free now."

Liza shuddered.

" Do not speak so any more. What use is your freedom to you? You should not be thinking of that now, but of forgiveness——"

" I forgave her long ago," interrupted Lavretsky, with an impatient gesture.

" No, I don't mean that," answered Liza, reddening; " you have not understood me properly. It is you who ought to strive to get pardoned."

" Who is there to pardon me? "

" Who? Why God. Who can pardon us except God? "

Lavretsky grasped her hand.

" Ah! Lizaveta Mikhailovna! " he exclaimed, " believe me, I have already been punished enough—I have already expiated all, believe me."

" You cannot tell that," said Liza, in a low voice. " You forget. It was not long ago that you and I were talking, and you were not willing to forgive her."

Both of them walked along the alley for a time in silence.

" And about your daughter? " suddenly asked Liza, and then stopped short.

Lavretsky shuddered.

" Oh! don't disturb yourself about her. I have already sent off letters in all directions. The future of my daughter, as you—as you say—is assured. You need not trouble yourself on that score."

Liza smiled sadly.

" But you are right," continued Lavretsky. " What

404

am I to do with my freedom — what use is it to me?"

"When did you get this paper?" asked Liza, without answering his question.

"The day after your visit."

"And have not you—have not you even shed a tear?"

"No; I was thunderstruck. But whither should I look for tears? Should I cry over the past? Why, all mine has been, as it were, consumed with fire. Her fault did not actually destroy my happiness; it only proved to me that for me happiness had never really existed. What, then, had I to cry for? Besides—who knows?—perhaps I should have been more grieved if I had received this news a fortnight sooner."

"A fortnight!" replied Liza. "But what can have happened to make such a difference in that fortnight?"

Lavretsky made no reply at first, and Liza suddenly grew still redder than before.

"Yes, yes! you have guessed it!" unexpectedly cried Lavretsky. "In the course of that fortnight I have learnt what a woman's heart is like when it is pure and clear; and my past life seems even farther off from me than it used to be."

Liza became a little uncomfortable, and slowly turned to where Lenochka and Shurochka were in the flower-garden.

"But I am glad I showed you that newspaper," said Lavretsky, as he followed her. "I have grown accustomed to conceal nothing from you, and I hope you will confide in me equally in return."

"Do you really?" said Liza, stopping still. "In that case, I ought. But, no! it is impossible."

"What is it? Tell me—tell me!"

"I really think I ought not.—However," added Liza, turning to Lavretsky with a smile, "what is the good of a half-confidence? Do you know, I received a letter to-day?"

" From Panshine? "

" Yes, from him.   How did you guess that? "

" And he asks for your hand? "

" Yes," replied Liza, looking straight at Lavretsky with serious eyes.

Lavretsky, in his turn, looked seriously at Liza.

" Well, and what answer have you made him? " he said at last.

" I don't know what to answer," replied Liza, unfolding her arms, and letting them fall by her side.

" Why?   Do you like him? "

" Yes, I like him; I think he is a good man."

" That is just what you told me three days ago, and in the very same words.   But what I want to know is, do you love him—love him with that strong, passionate feeling which we usually call ' love '? "

" In the sense in which you understand the word— No."

" You are not in love with him? "

" No.   But is that necessary? "

" How do you mean? "

" Mamma likes him," continued Liza.   " He is good: I have no fault to find with him."

" But still you waver? "

" Yes—and, perhaps—you, your words are the cause of that.   Do you remember what you said the day before yesterday?   But all that is weakness——"

" Oh, my child! " suddenly exclaimed Lavretsky, and his voice trembled as he spoke, " don't be fatally wise— don't stigmatise as weakness the cry of your heart, unwilling to give itself away without love!   Do not take upon yourself so fearful a responsibility towards that man, whom you do not love, and yet to whom you would be about to belong."

" I shall only be obeying; I shall be taking nothing upon myself," began Liza.

" Obey your own heart, then.   It only will tell you the truth," said Lavretsky, interrupting her.   " Wisdom, experience—all that is mere vanity and vexation.   Do

LIZA

not deprive yourself of the best, the only real happiness upon earth.''

" And do you speak in that way, Fedor Ivanovich? You married for love yourself—and were you happy? "

Lavretsky clasped his hands above his head.

" Ah! do not talk about me. You cannot form any idea of what a young, inexperienced, absurdly brought-up boy may imagine to be love. However, why should one calumniate oneself? I told you just now I had never known happiness. No! I have been happy.''

" I think, Fedor Ivanovich," said Liza, lowering her voice—she always lowered her voice when she differed from the person she was speaking to; besides, she felt considerably agitated just then—" our happiness on earth does not depend upon ourselves——''

" It does depend upon ourselves—upon ourselves: " here he seized both her hands. Liza grew pale and looked at him earnestly, but almost with alarm—" at least if we do not ruin our own lives. For some people a love match may turn out unhappily, but not for you, with your calmness of temperament, with your serenity of soul. I do beseech you not to marry without love, merely from a feeling of duty, self-denial, or the like. All that is sheer infidelity, and moreover a matter of calculation—and worse still. Trust my words. I have a right to say this; a right for which I have paid dearly. And if your God——''

At that moment Lavretsky became aware that Lenochka and Shurochka were standing by Liza's side, and were staring at him with intense astonishment. He dropped Liza's hands, saying hastily, " Forgive me," and walked away towards the house.

" There is only one thing I have to ask you," he said, coming back to Liza. " Don't make up your mind directly, but wait a little, and think over what I have said to you. And even if you don't believe my words, but are determined to marry in accordance with the dictates of mere prudence—even in that case, M. Panshine is not the man you ought to marry. He must not

407

be your husband.   You will promise me not to be hasty, won't you?"

Liza wished to reply, but she could not utter a single word.   Not that she had decided on being "hasty"— but because her heart beat too strongly, and a feeling resembling that of fear impeded her breathing.

XXVIII

As Lavretsky was leaving the Kalitines' house he met
Panshine, with whom he exchanged a cold greeting.
Then he went home and shut himself up in his room.
The sensations he experienced were such as he had hardly
ever known before. Was it long ago that he was in a
condition of " peaceful torpor ? " Was it long ago that
he felt himself, as he had expressed it, " at the very
bottom of the river ? " What then had changed his
condition? What had brought him to the surface, to
the light of day? Was it the most ordinary and inevitable, though always unexpected, of occurrences—death?
Yes. But yet it was not so much his wife's death, his
own freedom, that he was thinking about, as this—what
answer will Liza give to Panshine?

He felt that in the course of the last three days he had
begun to look on Liza with different eyes. He remembered how, when he was returning home and thinking
of her in the silence of the night, he said to himself " If!
——" This " if," by which at that time he had referred
to the past, to the impossible, now applied to an actual
state of things, but not exactly such a one as he had then
supposed. Freedom by itself was little to him now.
" She will obey her mother," he thought. " She will
marry Panshine. But even if she refuses him—will it
not be just the same as far as I am concerned ? " Passing at that moment in front of a looking-glass, he just
glanced at his face in it, and then shrugged his shoulders.

Amid such thoughts as these the day passed swiftly by.
The evening arrived, and Lavretsky went to the Kalitines'. He walked fast until he drew near to the house,
but then he slackened his pace. Panshine's carriage was
standing before the door. " Well," thought Lavretsky,
as he entered the house, " I will not be selfish." No one

met him indoors, and all seemed quiet in the drawing-room. He opened the door, and found that Madame Kalitine was playing at piquet with Panshine. That gentleman bowed to him silently, while the lady of the house exclaimed, " Well, this is an unexpected pleasure," and slightly frowned. Lavretsky sat down beside her and began looking at her cards.

" So you can play piquet? " she asked, with a shade of secret vexation in her voice, and then remarked that she had thrown away a wrong card.

Panshine counted ninety, and began to take up the tricks calmly and politely, his countenance the while wearing a grave and dignified expression. It was thus, he thought, that diplomatists ought to play. It was thus, in all probability, that he used to play with some influential dignitary at St. Petersburg, whom he wished to impress with a favourable idea of his solidity and perspicacity. " One hundred and one, hundred and two, heart, hundred and three," said the measured tones of his voice, and Lavretsky could not tell which it expressed—dislike or assurance.

" Can't I see Marfa Timofeevna? " asked Lavretsky, observing that Panshine, with a still more dignified air than before, was about to shuffle the cards; not even a trace of the artist was visible in him now.

" I suppose so. She is upstairs in her room," answered Maria Dmitrievna. " You can ask for her."

Lavretsky went upstairs. He found Marfa Timofeevna also at cards. She was playing at *Durachki* with Nastasia Carpovna. Roska barked at him, but both the old ladies received him cordially. Marfa Timofeevna seemed in special good humour.

" Ah, Fedia! " she said, " do sit down, there's a good fellow. We shall have done our game directly. Will you have some preserves? Shurochka, give him the pot of strawberries. You won't have any? Well, then, sit there as you are. But as to smoking, you mustn't. I cannot abide your strong tobacco; besides, it would make Matros sneeze."

Lavretsky hastened to assure her that he had not the slightest desire to smoke.

" Have you been downstairs? " asked the old lady. " Whom did you find there? Is Panshine always hanging about there? But did you see Liza? No? She was to have come here. Why there she is—as soon as one mentions her."

Liza came into the room, caught sight of Lavretsky, and blushed.

" I have only come for a moment, Marfa Timofeevna," she was beginning.

" Why for a moment? " asked the old lady. " Why are all you young people so restless? You see I have a visitor there. Chat a little with him, amuse him."

Liza sat down on the edge of a chair, raised her eyes to Lavretsky, and felt at once that she could not do otherwise than let him know how her interview with Panshine had ended. But how was that to be managed? She felt at the same time confused and ashamed. Was it so short a time since she had become acquainted with that man, one who scarcely ever went to church even, and who bore the death of his wife so equably? and yet here she was already communicating her secrets to him. It was true that he took an interest in her; and that, on her side, she trusted him, and felt herself drawn towards him. But in spite of all this, she felt a certain kind of modest shame—as if a stranger had entered her pure maiden chamber.

Marfa Timofeevna came to her rescue.

" Well, if you will not amuse him," she said, " who is to amuse him, poor fellow? I am too old for him; he is too clever for me; and as to Nastasia Carpovna, he is too old for her. It's only boys she cares for."

" How can I amuse Fedor Ivanovich? " said Liza. " I would rather play him something on the piano, if he likes," she continued irresolutely.

" That's capital. You're a clever creature," replied Marfa Timofeevna. " Go downstairs, my dears. Come back again when you've done; but just now here I'm left the *durachka*,[1] so I'm savage. I must have my revenge."

Liza rose from her chair, and so did Lavretsky. As she was going downstairs, Liza stopped.

" What they say is true," she began. " The human heart is full of contradictions. Your example ought to have frightened me—ought to have made me distrust marrying for love, and yet I——"

" You've refused him? " said Lavretsky, interrupting her.

" No; but I have not accepted him either. I told him everything—all my feelings on the subject—and I asked him to wait a little. Are you satisfied? " she asked, with a sudden smile; and letting her hand skim lightly along the balustrade, she ran downstairs.

" What shall I play you? " she asked, as she opened the piano.

" Whatever you like." answered Lavretsky, taking a seat where he could look at her.

Liza began to play, and went on for some time without lifting her eyes from her fingers. At last she looked at Lavretsky, and stopped playing. The expression of his face seemed so strange and unusual to her.

" What is the matter? " she asked.

" Nothing," he replied. " All is well with me at present. I feel happy on your account; it makes me glad to look at you—do go on."

" I think," said Liza, a few minutes later, " if he had really loved me, he would not have written that letter; he ought to have felt that I could not answer him just now."

" That doesn't matter," said Lavretsky; " what does matter is that you do not love him."

" Stop! What is that you are saying? The image

[1] In the game of *durachki*, the player who remains the last is called the *durachok* or *durachka*, diminutive of *durak*, a fool. The game somewhat resembles our own " Old Bachelor " or " Old Maid."

of your dead wife is always haunting me, and I feel afraid of you."

"Doesn't my Liza play well, Woldemar?" Madame Kalitine was saying at this moment to Panshine.

"Yes," replied Panshine, "exceedingly well."

Madame Kalitine looked tenderly at her young partner; but he assumed a still more important and preoccupied look, and called fourteen kings.

XXIX

LAVRETSKY was no longer a very young man. He could not long delude himself as to the nature of the feeling with which Liza had inspired him. On that day he became finally convinced that he was in love with her. That conviction did not give him much pleasure.

" Is it possible," he thought, " that at five-and-thirty I have nothing else to do than to confide my heart a second time to a woman's keeping? But Liza is not like *her*. She would not have demanded humiliating sacrifices from me. She would not have led me astray from my occupations. She would have inspired me herself with a love for honourable hard work, and we should have gone forward together towards some noble end. Yes," he said, bringing his reflections to a close, " all that is very well. But the worst of it is that she will not go anywhere with me. It was not for nothing that she told me she felt afraid of me. And as to her not being in love with Panshine—that is but a poor consolation! "

Lavretsky went to Vasilievskoe; but he could not manage to spend even four days there—so wearisome did it seem to him. Moreover, he was tormented by suspense. The news which M. Jules had communicated required confirmation, and he had not yet received any letters. He returned to town, and passed the evening at the Kalitines'. He could easily see that Madame Kalitine had been set against him; but he succeeded in mollifying her a little by losing some fifteen roubles to her at piquet. He also contrived to get half an hour alone with Liza, in spite of her mother having recommended her, only the evening before, not to be too intimate with a man " *qui a un si grand ridicule.*"

He found a change in her. She seemed to have become more contemplative. She blamed him for stopping away; and she asked him if he would not go to church the next day—the next day being Sunday.

"Do come," she continued, before he had time to answer. "We will pray together for the repose of *her* soul." Then she added that she did not know what she ought to do—that she did not know whether she had any right to make Panshine wait longer for her decision.

"Why?" asked Lavretsky.

"Because," she replied, "I begin to suspect by this time what that decision will be."

Then she said that she had a headache, and went to her room, after irresolutely holding out the ends of her fingers to Lavretsky.

The next day Lavretsky went to morning service. Liza was already in the church when he entered. He remarked her, though she did not look towards him. She prayed fervently; her eyes shone with a quiet light; quietly she bowed and lifted her head.

He felt that she was praying for him also, and a strange emotion filled his soul. The people standing gravely around, the familiar faces, the harmonious chant, the odour of the incense, the long rays slanting through the windows, the very sombreness of the walls and arches—all appealed to his heart. It was long since he had been in church—long since he had turned his thoughts to God. And even now he did not utter any words of prayer—he did not even pray without words; but nevertheless, for a moment, if not in body, at least in mind, he bowed down and bent himself humbly to the ground. He remembered how, in the days of his childhood, he always used to pray in church till he felt on his forehead something like a kind of light touch. "That," he used then to think, "is my guardian angel, visiting me and pressing on me the seal of election." He looked at Liza. "It is you who have brought me here," he thought. "Touch me—touch my soul!" Meanwhile, she went on quietly praying. Her face seemed to him to be joyous, and once more he felt softened, and he asked, for another's soul, rest—for his own, pardon. They met outside in the porch, and she received him with a friendly look of serious happiness. The sun brightly lit up the fresh grass in the churchyard and the many-coloured dresses and kerchiefs of the women. The bells of the neighbouring churches sounded on high; the sparrows chirped on the walls. Lavretsky stood by, smiling and bare-headed; a light breeze played with his hair and Liza's, and with the ends of Liza's bonnet-strings. He seated Liza and her companion, Lenochka, in the carriage, gave away all the change he had about him to the beggars, and then strolled slowly home.

XXX

THE days which followed were days of heaviness for Lavretsky. He felt himself in a perpetual fever. Every morning he went to the post, and impatiently tore open his letters and newspapers; but in none of them did he find anything which could either confirm or contradict that rumour, on the truth of which he felt that so much now depended. At times he grew disgusted with himself. " What am I," he then would think, " who am waiting here, as a raven waits for blood, for certain intelligence of my wife's death? "

He went to the Kalitines' every day; but even there he was not more at his ease. The mistress of the house was evidently out of humour with him, and treated him with cold condescension. Panshine showed him exaggerated politeness; Lemm had become misanthropical, and scarcely even returned his greeting; and, worst of all, Liza seemed to avoid him. Whenever she happened to be left alone with him, she manifested symptoms of embarrassment, instead of the frank manner of former days. On such occasions she did not know what to say to him; and even he felt confused. In the course of a few days Liza had become changed from what he remembered her to have been. In her movements, in her voice, even in her laugh itself, a secret uneasiness manifested itself—something different from her former evenness of temper. Her mother, like a true egotist, did not suspect anything; but Marfa Timofeevna began to watch her favourite closely.

Lavretsky often blamed himself for having shown Liza the newspaper he had received; he could not help being conscious that there was something in his state of feeling which must be repugnant to a very delicate mind. He supposed, moreover, that the change which had

417

taken place in Liza arose from a struggle with herself, from her doubt as to what answer she should give to Panshine.

One day she returned him a book—one of Walter Scott's novels—which she had herself asked him for.

" Have you read it ? " he asked.

" No; I am not in a mood for books just now," she answered, and then was going away.

" Wait a minute," he said. " It is so long since I got a talk with you alone. You seem afraid of me. Is it so ? "

" Yes."

" But why ? "

" I don't know."

Lavretsky said nothing for a time.

" Tell me," he began again presently; " haven't you made up your mind yet ? "

" What do you mean ? " she replied, without lifting her eyes from the ground.

" Surely you understand me ? "

Liza suddenly reddened.

" Don't ask me about anything! " she exclaimed with animation. " I know nothing. I don't know myself."

And she went hastily away.

The next day Lavretsky arrived at the Kalitines' after dinner, and found all the preparations going on there for an evening-service. In a corner of the dining-room, a number of small icons [1] in golden frames, with tarnished little diamonds in the aureolas, were already placed against the wall on a square table, which was covered with a tablecloth of unspotted whiteness. An old servant, dressed in a grey coat and wearing shoes, traversed the whole room deliberately and noiselessly, placed two slender candlesticks with wax tapers in them before the icons, crossed himself, bowed, and silently left the room.

The drawing-room was dark and empty. Lavretsky went into the dining-room, and asked if it was any one's

[1] Sacred pictures.

418

name-day.[1]   He was told in a whisper that it was not, but that a service was to be performed in accordance with the request of Lizaveta Mikhailovna and Marfa Timofeevna.   The miracle-working picture was to have been brought, but it had gone to a sick person thirty versts off.

Soon afterwards the priest arrived with his acolytes—a middle-aged man, with a large bald spot on his head, who coughed loudly in the vestibule.   The ladies immediately came out of the boudoir in a row, and asked him for his blessing.   Lavretsky bowed to them in silence, and they as silently returned his greeting.   The priest remained a little longer where he was, then coughed again, and asked, in a low, deep voice—

" Do you wish me to begin? "

" Begin, reverend father," replied Maria Dmitrievna.

The priest began to robe.   An acolyte in a surplice humbly asked for a coal from the fire.   The scent of the incense began to spread around.   The footmen and the maid-servants came in from the ante-chamber and remained standing in a compact body at the door.   The dog Roska, which, as a general rule, never came downstairs from the upper storey, now suddenly made its appearance in the dining-room.   The servants tried to drive it out, but it got frightened, first ran about, and then lay down.   At last a footman got hold of it and carried it off.

The service began.   Lavretsky retired into a corner. His feelings were strange and almost painful.   He himself could not well define what it was that he felt.   Maria Dmitrievna stood in front of the rest, with an armchair behind her.   She crossed herself carelessly, languidly, like a great lady.   Sometimes she looked round, at others she suddenly raised her eyes towards the ceiling. The whole affair evidently bored her.

Marfa Timofeevna seemed preoccupied.   Nastasia

---

[1] A Russian keeps, not his birthday, but his name-day—that is, the day set apart by the church in honour of the saint after whom he is called.

Carpovna bowed down to the ground, and raised herself up again, with a sort of soft and modest sound. As for Liza, she did not stir from the spot where she was standing, she did not change her position upon it; from the concentrated expression of her face, it was evident that she was praying uninterruptedly and fervently.

At the end of the service she approached the crucifix, and kissed both it and the large red hand of the priest. Maria Dmitrievna invited him to take tea. He threw off his stole, assumed a sort of mundane air, and went into the drawing-room with the ladies. A conversation began, not of a very lively nature. The priest drank four cups of tea, wiping the bald part of his head the while with his handkerchief, stated among other things that the merchant Avoshnikof had given seven hundred roubles towards the gilding of the church's " cumpola," and favoured the company with an unfailing cure for freckles.

Lavretsky tried to get a seat near Liza, but she maintained her grave, almost austere air, and never once looked at him. She seemed intentionally to ignore him. A kind of serious, cold enthusiasm appeared to possess her. For some reason or other Lavretsky felt inclined to smile, and to utter words of jesting; but his heart was ill at ease, and at last he went away in a state of secret perplexity. There was something, he felt, in Liza's mind, which he could not understand.

On another occasion, as Lavretsky was sitting in the drawing-room, listening to the insinuating tones of Gedeonovsky's wearisome verbiage, he suddenly turned round, he knew not why, and caught the deep, attentive, inquiring look of Liza's eyes. That enigmatical look was directed towards him. The whole night long Lavretsky thought of it. His love was not like that of a boy, nor was it consistent with his age to sigh and to torment himself; and indeed it was not with a feeling of a merely passionate nature that Liza had inspired him. But love has its sufferings for every age—and he became perfectly acquainted with them.

XXXI

ONE day Lavretsky was as usual at the Kalitines'. An overpoweringly hot afternoon had been followed by such a beautiful evening that Madame Kalitine, notwithstanding her usual aversion to a draught, ordered all the windows and the doors leading into the garden to be opened. Moreover, she announced that she was not going to play cards, that it would be a sin to do so in such lovely weather, and that it was a duty to enjoy the beauties of nature.

Panshine was the only stranger present. Influenced by the evening, and feeling a flow of artistic emotion, but not wishing to sing in Lavretsky's presence, he threw himself into poetry. He read—and read well, only with too much consciousness, and with needlessly subtle distinctions—some of Lermontof's poems (Pushkin had not then succeeded in getting back into fashion). Suddenly, as if ashamed of his emotion, he began, in reference to the well-known *Duma*,[1] to blame and attack the new generation, not losing the opportunity which the subject afforded him of setting forth how, if the power lay in his hands, he would alter everything his own way.

" Russia," he said, " has lagged behind Europe, and must be driven up alongside of it. We are told that ours is a young country. That is all nonsense. Besides, we have no inventive power. Khomakof [2] himself admits that we have never invented so much as a mousetrap. Consequently we are obliged to imitate others, whether we like it or no.

" ' We are ill,' says Lermontof, and I agree with him. But we are ill because we have only half become Europeans. With that which has wounded us we must be

[1] For the poem so-called, see note at end of chapter.
[2] A poet, who was one of the leaders of the Slavophile party.

cured." (" *Le cadastre*," thought Lavretsky.) " Among us," he continued, " the best heads, *les meilleures têtes*, have long been convinced of this.   In reality, all peoples are alike;   only introduce good institutions, and the affair is settled.   To be sure, one may make some allowance for the existing life of the nation; that is our business, the business of people who are " (he all but said "statesmen ") " in the public service;   but, if need arises, don't be uneasy.   Those institutions will modify that life itself."

Maria Dmitrievna admiringly agreed with him. " What a clever man to have talking in my house! " she thought. Liza kept silence, leaning back in the recess of the window.   Lavretsky kept silence too.   Marfa Timofeevna, who was playing cards in a corner with her friend, grumbled something to herself.   Panshine walked up and down the room, speaking well, but with a sort of suppressed malice.   It seemed as if he was blaming, not so much a whole generation, as some individuals of his acquaintance.   A nightingale had made its home in a large lilac bush which stood in the Kalitines' garden, and the first notes of its even-song made themselves heard during the pauses in the eloquent harangue; the first stars began to kindle in the rose-stained sky above the motionless tops of the lime trees.   Presently Lavretsky rose and began to reply to Panshine.   A warm dispute soon commenced.

Lavretsky spoke in defence of the youth of Russia, and of the capacity of the country to suffice for itself.   He surrendered himself and his contemporaries, but he stood up for the new generation, and their wishes and convictions.   Panshine replied incisively and irritably, declared that clever people were bound to reform everything, and at length was carried away to such an extent that, forgetting his position as a chamberlain, and his proper line of action as a member of the civil service, he called Lavretsky a retrograde conservative, and alluded —very distantly it is true—to his false position in society. Lavretsky did not lose his temper, nor did he raise his voice; he remembered that Mikhalevich also had called him a retrograde, and, at the same time, a disciple of Voltaire; but he calmly beat Panshine on every point. He proved the impracticability of reforming by sudden bounds, and of introducing changes haughtily schemed on the heights of official self-complacency — changes which were not justified by an intimate acquaintance with the country, nor by a living faith in any ideal, not even in one of negation, and in illustration of this he adduced his own education. He demanded before everything else that the true spirit of the nation should be recognised, and that it should be looked up to with that humility without which no courage is possible, not even that wherewith to oppose falsehood. Finally he did not attempt to make any defence against what he considered a deserved reproach, that of giving way to a wasteful and inconsidcrate expenditure of both time and strength.

" All that is very fine! " at last exclaimed Panshine with vexation. " But here are you, just returned to Russia; what do you intend to do? "

" To cultivate the soil," replied Lavretsky; " and to cultivate it as well as possible."

" No doubt that is very praiseworthy," answered Panshine, " and I hear you have already had great success in that line; but you must admit that every one is not fitted for such an occupation——"

" *Une nature poétique*," said Marie Dmitrievna, " certainly cannot go cultivating the soil——*et puis*, it is your vocation, Vladimir Nikolaevich, to do everything *en grand*."

This was too much even for Panshine, who grew confused, and changed the conversation. He tried to turn it on the beauty of the starry heavens, on Schubert's music, but somehow his efforts did not prove successful. He ended by offering to play at piquet with Maria Dmitrievna. " What! on such an evening as this? " she feebly objected; but then she ordered the cards to be brought.

Panshine noisily tore open a new pack; and Liza and

Lavretsky, as if by mutual consent, both rose from their seats and placed themselves near Marfa Timofeevna. They both suddenly experienced a great feeling of happiness, mingled with a sense of mutual dread, which made them glad of the presence of a third person; at the same time, they both felt that the uneasiness from which they had suffered during the last few days had disappeared, and would return no more.

The old lady stealthily tapped Lavretsky on the cheek, screwed up her eyes with an air of pleasant malice, and shook her head repeatedly, saying in a whisper, " You've done for the genius—thanks! " Then all became still in the room. Nothing was to be heard but the faint crackling of the wax lights, and sometimes the fall of a hand on the table, or an exclamation on the score of points, and the song of the nightingale which, powerful, almost insolently loud, flowed in a great wave through the window, together with the dewy freshness of the night.

NOTE.—The following is a tolerably literal translation of the poem of Lermontof's to which allusion is made on p. 149, and which created no slight sensation when it first appeared, in the year 1838:—

A THOUGHT

Sorrowfully do I look upon the present generation! Its future seems either gloomy or meaningless, and meanwhile, whether under the burden of knowledge or of doubt, it grows old in idleness.

When scarcely out of the cradle, we reap the rich inheritance of the errors of our fathers, and the results of their tardy thoughts. Life soon grows wearisome for us, like a banquet at a stranger's festival, like a level road leading nowhere.

In the commencement of our career we fall away without a struggle, shamefully careless about right and wrong, shamefully timid in the face of danger.

So does a withered fruit which has prematurely ripened— attractive neither to the eye nor to the palate—hang like an alien orphan among blossoms; and the hour of their beauty is that of its fall.

Our intellect has dried up in the pursuit of fruitless science, while we have been concealing the purest of hopes from the knowledge of those who are near and dear to us, and stifling the noble utterance of such sentiments as are ridiculed by a mocking spirit.

We have scarcely tasted the cup of enjoyment, but for all that we have not husbanded our youthful strength. While we were always in dread of satiety, we have contrived to drain each joy of its best virtues.

No dreams of poetry, no creations of art, touch our hearts with a sweet rapture. We stingily hoard up within our breasts the last remnants of feeling—a treasure concealed by avarice, and which remains utterly unprofitable.

We love and we hate capriciously, sacrificing nothing either to our animosity or to our affection, a certain secret coldness possessing our souls, even while a fire is raging in our veins.

The sumptuous pleasures of our ancestors weary us, as well as their simple, childish diversions. Without enjoying happiness, without reaping glory, we hasten onwards to the grave, casting nought but mocking glances behind us.

A saturnine crowd, soon to be forgotten, we silently pass away from the world and leave no trace behind, without having handed down to the ages to come a single work of genius, or even a solitary thought laden with meaning.

And our descendants, regarding our memory with the severity of citizens called to sit in judgment on an affair concerning the state, will allude to us with the scathing irony of a ruined son, when he speaks of the father who has squandered away his patrimony.

XXXII

LIZA had not uttered a single word during the dispute between Lavretsky and Panshine, but she had followed it attentively, and had been on Lavretsky's side throughout. She cared very little about politics; but she was repelled by the self-sufficient tone of the worldly official, who had never shown himself in that light before, and his contempt for Russia offended her. It had never occurred to Liza to imagine that she was a patriot. But she was thoroughly at her ease with the Russian people. The Russian turn of mind pleased her. She would chat for hours, without thinking anything of it, with the chief of the village on her mother's estate, when he happened to come into town, and talk with him as if he were her equal, without any signs of seigneurial condescension. All this Lavretsky knew well. For his own part, he never would have cared to reply to Panshine; it was only for Liza's sake that he spoke.

They said nothing to each other, and even their eyes but rarely met. But they both felt that they had been drawn closer together that evening, they knew that they both had the same likes and dislikes. On one point only were they at variance; but Liza secretly hoped to bring him back to God. They sat down close by Marfa Timofeevna, and seemed to be following her game; nay, more, did actually follow it. But, meantime, their hearts grew full within them, and nothing escaped their senses—for them the nightingale sang softly, and the stars burnt, and the trees whispered, steeped in slumberous calm and lulled to rest by the warmth and softness of the summer night.

Lavretsky gave himself up to its wave of fascination, and his heart rejoiced within him. But no words can express the change that was being worked within the

426

pure soul of the maiden by his side. Even for herself it was a secret; let it remain, then, a secret for all others also. No one knows, no eye has seen or ever will see, how the grain which has been confided to the earth's bosom becomes instinct with vitality, and ripens into stirring, blossoming life.

Ten o'clock struck, and Marfa Timofeevna went upstairs to her room with Nastasia Carpovna. Lavretsky· and Liza walked about the room, stopped in front of the open door leading into the garden, looked first into the gloaming distance and then at each other—and smiled. It seemed as if they would so gladly have taken each other's hands and talked to their hearts' content.

They returned to Maria Dmitrievna and Panshine, whose game dragged itself out to an unusual length. At length the last " king " came to an end, and Madame Kalitine rose from her cushioned chair, sighing, and uttering sounds of weariness the while. Panshine took his hat, kissed her hand, remarked that nothing prevented more fortunate people from enjoying the night or going to sleep, but that he must sit up till morning over stupid papers, bowed coldly to Liza—with whom he was angry, for he had not expected that she would ask him to wait so long for an answer to his proposal—and retired. Lavretsky went away directly after him, following him to the gate, where he took leave of him. Panshine aroused his coachman, poking him in the neck with the end of his stick, seated himself in his droshky, and drove away. But Lavertsky did not feel inclined to go home, so he walked out of the town into the fields.

The night was still and clear, although there was no moon. For a long time Lavretsky wandered across the dewy grass. A narrow footpath lay in his way, and he followed it. It led him to a long hedge, in which there was a wicket gate. Without knowing why he did so, he tried to push it open; with a faint creak it did open, just as if it had been awaiting the touch of his hand. Lavretsky found himself in a garden, took a few steps along a lime-tree alley, and suddenly stopped short in utter amazement. He saw that he was in the Kalitines' garden.

A thick hazel bush close at hand flung a black patch of shadow on the ground. Into this he quickly passed, and there stood for some time without stirring from the spot, inwardly wondering and from time to time shrugging his shoulders. " This has not happened without some purpose," he thought.

Around all was still. From the house not the slightest sound reached him. He began cautiously to advance. At the corner of an alley all the house suddenly burst upon him with its dusky façade. In two windows only on the upper story were lights glimmering. In Liza's apartment a candle was burning behind the white blind, and in Marfa Timofeevna's bedroom glowed the red flame of the small lamp hanging in front of the sacred picture, on the gilded cover of which it was reflected in steady light. Down below the door leading on to the balcony gaped wide open.

Lavretsky sat down on a wooden bench, rested his head on his hand, and began looking at that door and at Liza's window. Midnight sounded in the town; in the house a little clock feebly struck twelve. The watchman beat the hour with quick strokes on his board. Lavretsky thought of nothing, expected nothing. It was pleasant to him to feel himself near Liza, to sit in her garden, and on the bench where she also often sat.

The light disappeared from Liza's room.

" A quiet night to you, dear girl," whispered Lavretsky, still sitting where he was without moving, and not taking his eyes off the darkened window.

Suddenly a light appeared at one of the windows of the lower story, crossed to another window, and then to a third. Some one was carrying a candle through the room. " Can it be Liza ? It cannot be," thought Lavretsky. He rose. A well-known face glimmered in the darkness, and Liza appeared in the drawing-room, wearing a white dress, her hair hanging loosely about her shoulders. Quietly approaching the table, she leant over it, put down the candle, and began looking for something. Then she turned towards the garden, and crossed to the open door; presently her light, slender, white-robed form stood still on the threshold.

A kind of shiver ran over Lavretsky's limbs, and the word " Liza! " escaped all but inaudibly from his lips.

She started, and then began to peer anxiously into the darkness.

" Liza! " said Lavretsky louder than before, and came out from the shadow of the alley.

Liza was startled. For a moment she bent forward; then she shrank back. She had recognised him. For the third time he called her, and held out his hands towards her. She passed out from the doorway and came into the garden.

" You! " she said. " You here! "

" I—I—— Come and hear what I have to say," whispered Lavretsky; and then, taking her hand, he led her to the bench.

She followed him without a word; but her pale face, her fixed look, and all her movements, testified her unutterable astonishment. Lavretsky made her sit down on the bench, and remained standing in front of her.

" I did not think of coming here," he began. " I was led here—— I—I—I love you," he ended by saying, feeling very nervous in spite of himself.

Liza slowly looked up at him. It seemed as if it had not been till that moment that she understood where she was, and what was happening to her. She would have risen, but she could not. Then she hid her face in her hands.

" Liza! " exclaimed Lavretsky; " Liza! " he repeated, and knelt down at her feet.

A slight shudder ran over her shoulders; she pressed the fingers of her white hands closer to her face.

" What is it ? " said Lavretsky. Then he heard a low sound of sobbing, and his heart sank within him. He understood the meaning of those tears.

429

" Can it be that you love me? " he whispered, with a caressing gesture of the hand.

" Stand up, stand up, Fedor Ivanovich," she at last succeeded in saying. " What are we doing? "

He rose from his knees, and sat down by her side on the bench. She was no longer crying, but her eyes, as she looked at him earnestly, were wet with tears.

" I am frightened! What are we doing? " she said again.

" I love you," he repeated. " I am ready to give my whole life for you."

She shuddered again, just as if something had stung her, then she raised her eyes to heaven.

" That is entirely in the hands of God," she replied.

" But you love me, Liza? We are going to be happy? "

She let fall her eyes. He softly drew her to himself, and her head sank upon his shoulder. He bent his head a little aside, and kissed her pale lips.

Half an hour later Lavretsky was again standing before the garden gate. He found it closed now, and was obliged to get over the fence. He returned into the town, and walked along its sleeping streets. His heart was full of happiness, intense and unexpected; all misgiving was dead within him. " Disappear, dark spirit of the Past! " he said to himself. " She.loves me. She will be mine."

Suddenly he seemed to hear strange triumphal sounds floating in the air above his head. He stopped. With greater grandeur than before the sounds went clanging forth. With strong, sonorous stream did they flow along—and in them, as it seemed to him, all his happiness spoke and sang. He looked round. The sounds came from the two upper windows of a small house.

" Lemm! " he exclaimed, and ran up to the door of the house. " Lemm, Lemm! " he repeated loudly.

The sounds died away, and the form of the old man, wrapped in a dressing-gown, with exposed chest and wildly floating hair, appeared at the window.

" Ha! it is you," he said, with an air of importance.

" Christophor Fedorovich, what wonderful music! For heaven's sake let me in! "

The old man did not say a word, but with a dignified motion of the hand he threw the key of the door out of the window into the street. Lavretsky hastily ran upstairs, entered the room, and was going to fling himself into Lemm's arms. But Lemm, with a gesture of command, pointed to a chair, and said sharply in his incorrect Russian, " Sit down and listen," then took his seat at the piano, looked round with a proud and severe glance, and began to play.

Lavretsky had heard nothing like it for a long time indeed. A sweet, passionate melody spoke to the heart with its very first notes. It seemed all thoroughly replete with sparkling light, fraught with inspiration, with beauty, and with joy. As it rose and sank it seemed to speak of all that is dear, and secret, and holy, on earth. It spoke too of a sorrow that can never end, and then it went to die away in the distant heaven.

Lavretsky had risen from his seat and remained standing, rooted to the spot, and pale with rapture. Those sounds entered very readily into his heart; for it had just been stirred into sensitiveness by the touch of a happy love, and they themselves were glowing with love.

" Play it again," he whispered, as soon as the last final chord had died away.

The old man looked at him with an eagle's glance, and said slowly, in his native tongue, striking his breast with his hand, " It is I who wrote that, for I am a great musician," and then he played once more his wonderful composition.

There were no lights in the room, but the rays of the rising moon entered obliquely through the window. The listening air seemed to tremble into music, and the poor little apartment looked like a sanctuary, while the silvery half-light gave to the head of the old man a noble and spiritual expression.

LIZA

Lavretsky came up to him and embraced him. At first Lemm did not respond to his embrace—even put him aside with his elbow. Then he remained rigid for some time, without moving any of his limbs, wearing the same severe, almost repellent, look as before, and only growling out twice, " Aha! " But at last a change came over him, his face grew calm, and his head was no longer thrown back. Then, in reply to Lavretsky's warm congratulations, he first smiled a little, and afterwards began to cry, sobbing faintly, like a child.

" It is wonderful," he said, " your coming just at this very moment. But I know everything—I know all about it."

" You know everything? " exclaimed Lavretsky in astonishment.

" You have heard what I said," replied Lemm. " Didn't you understand that I knew everything? "

Lavretsky did not get to sleep till the morning. All night long he remained sitting on the bed. Neither did Liza sleep. She was praying.

XXXIII

THE reader knows how Lavretsky had been brought up and educated. We will now say a few words about Liza's education. She was ten years old when her father died, who had troubled himself but little about her. Overwhelmed with business, constantly absorbed in the pursuit of adding to his income, a man of bilious temperament and a sour and impatient nature, he never grudged paying for the teachers and tutors, or for the dress and the other necessaries required by his children, but he could not bear " to nurse his squallers," according to his own expression—and, indeed, he never had any time for nursing them. He used to work, become absorbed in business, sleep a little, play cards on rare occasions, then work again. He often compared himself to a horse yoked to a threshing-machine. " My life has soon been spent," he said on his deathbed, a bitter smile contracting his lips

As to Maria Dmitrievna, she really troubled herself about Liza very little more than her husband did, for all that she had taken credit to herself, when speaking to Lavretsky, for having educated her children herself. She used to dress her like a doll, and when visitors were present, she would caress her and call her a good child and her darling, and that was all. Every continuous care troubled that indolent lady.

During her father's lifetime, Liza was left in the hands of a governess, a Mademoiselle Moreau, from Paris; but after his death she passed under the care of Marfa Timofeevna. That lady is already known to the reader. As for Mademoiselle Moreau, she was a very small woman, much wrinkled, having the manners of a bird, and the character of a bird also. In her youth she had led a very dissipated life; in her old age she retained only two passions—the love of dainties and the love of cards. When her appetite was satiated, and when she was not playing cards or talking nonsense, her countenance rapidly assumed an almost death-like expression. She would sit and gaze and breathe, but it was plain that there was not a single idea stirring in her mind. She could not even be called good; goodness is not an attribute of birds. In consequence either of her frivolous youth or of the air of Paris, which she had breathed from her childhood's days, there was rooted in her a kind of universal scepticism, which usually found expression in the words, " *Tout ça c'est des bêtises.*" She spoke an incorrect, but purely Parisian jargon, did not talk scandal, and had no caprices—what more could one expect from a governess? Over Liza she had but little influence. All the more powerful, then, was the influence exercised over the child by her nurse, Agafia Vlasievna.

That woman's story was a remarkable one. She sprang from a family of peasants, and was married at sixteen to a peasant; but she stood out in sharp relief against the mass of her peasant sisters. As a child, she had been spoilt by her father, who had been for twenty years the head of his commune, and who had made a good deal of money. She was singularly beautiful, and for grace and taste she was unsurpassed in the whole district, and she was intelligent, eloquent, and courageous. Her master, Dmitry Pestof, Madame Kalitine's father, a quiet and reserved man, saw her one day on the threshing-floor, had a talk with her, and fell passionately in love with her. Soon after this she became a widow. Pestof, although he was a married man, took her into his house, and had her dressed like one of the household. Agafia immediately made herself at home in her new position, just as if she had never led a different kind of life. Her complexion grew fairer, her figure became more rounded, and her arms, under their muslin sleeves, showed " white as wheat-flour," like those of a wealthy tradesman's wife. The *samovar* never quitted her table;

434

she would wear nothing but silks and velvets; she slept on feather-beds of down.

This happy life lasted five years; then Dmitry Pestof died. His widow, a lady of a kindly character, respected the memory of her late husband too much to wish to treat her rival with ignominy, especially as Agafia had never forgotten herself in her presence; but she married her to a herdsman, and sent her away from her sight.

Three years passed by. One hot summer day the lady happened to pay a visit to the cattle-yard. Agafia treated her to such a cool dish of rich cream, behaved herself so modestly, and looked so clean, so happy, so contented with everything, that her mistress informed her that she was pardoned, and allowed her to return into the house. Before six months had passed, the lady had become so attached to her, that she promoted her to the post of housekeeper, and confided all the domestic arrangements to her care. Thus Agafia came back into power, and again became fair and plump. Her mistress trusted her implicitly.

So passed five more years. Then misfortune came a second time on Agafia. Her husband, for whom she had obtained a place as footman, took to drink, began to absent himself from the house, and ended by stealing half a dozen of his mistress's silver spoons, and hiding them, till a fitting opportunity should arise for carrying them off, in his wife's box. The theft was found out. He was turned into a herdsman again, and Agafia fell into disgrace. She was not dismissed from the house, but she was degraded from the position of housekeeper to that of a needlewoman, and she was ordered to wear a handkerchief on her head instead of a cap. To every one's astonishment, Agafia bore the punishment inflicted on her with calm humility. By this time she was about thirty years old, all her children were dead, and her husband soon afterwards died also. The season for reflection had arrived for her, and she did reflect. She became very silent and very devout, never once letting matins or mass go unheeded by, and she gave away all her fine clothes. For fifteen years she led a quiet, grave, peaceful life, quarrelling with no one, giving way to all. If any one spoke to her harshly, she only bent her head and returned thanks for the lesson. Her mistress had forgiven her long ago, and had taken the ban off her—had even given her a cap off her own head to wear. But she herself refused to doff her handkerchief, and she would never consent to wear any but a sombre-coloured dress. After the death of her mistress she became even more quiet and more humble than before. It is easy to work upon a Russian's fears and to secure his attachment, but it is difficult to acquire his esteem; that he will not readily give, nor will he give it to every one. But the whole household esteemed Agafia. No one even so much as remembered her former faults: it was as if they had been buried in the grave with her old master.

When Kalitine married Maria Dmitrievna, he wanted to entrust the care of his household to Agafia; but she refused, "on account of temptation." He began to scold her, but she only bowed low and left the room. The shrewd Kalitine generally understood people; so he understood Agafia's character, and did not lose sight of her. When he settled in town, he appointed her, with her consent, to the post of nurse to Liza, who was then just beginning her fifth year.

At first Liza was frightened by the serious, even severe, face of her new nurse; but she soon became accustomed to her, and learned to love her warmly. The child was of a serious disposition herself. Her features called to mind Kalitine's regular and finely moulded face, but her eyes were not like those of her father; they shone with a quiet light, expressive of an earnest goodness that is rarely seen in children. She did not care about playing with dolls; she never laughed loudly nor long, and a feeling of self-respect always manifested itself in her conduct. It was not often that she fell into a reverie, but when she did so there was almost always good reason for it; then she would keep silence for a time, but generally ended by addressing to some person older than herself a question which showed that her mind had been working under the influence of a new impression. She very soon got over her childish lisp, and even before she was four years old she spoke with perfect distinctness. She was afraid of her father. As for her mother, she regarded her with a feeling which she could scarcely define, not being afraid of her, but not behaving towards her caressingly. As for that, she did not caress even her nurse, although she loved her with her whole heart. She and Agafia were never apart. It was curious to see them together. Agafia, all in black, with a dark handkerchief on her head, her face emaciated and of a wax-like transparency, but still beautiful and expressive, would sit erect on her chair, knitting stockings. At her feet Liza would be sitting on a little stool, also engaged in some work, or, her clear eyes uplifted with a serious expression, listening to what Agafia was telling her. Agafia never told her nursery tales. With a calm and even voice, she used to tell her about the life of the Blessed Virgin, or the lives of the hermits and people pleasing to God, or about the holy female martyrs. She would tell Liza how the saints lived in the deserts; how they worked out their salvation, enduring hunger and thirst; and how they did not fear kings, but confessed Christ; and how the birds of the air brought them food, and the wild beasts obeyed them; how from those spots where their blood had fallen flowers sprang up. (" Were they carnations? " once asked Liza, who was very fond of flowers.) Agafia spoke about these things to Liza seriously and humbly, as if she felt that it was not for her to pronounce such grand and holy words; and as Liza listened to her, the image of the Omnipresent, Omniscient God entered with a sweet influence into her very soul, filling her with a pure and reverent dread, and Christ seemed to her to be close to her, and to be a friend, almost, as it were, a relation. It was Agafia also who taught her to pray. Sometimes she awoke Liza at the early dawn, dressed her hastily, and

437

secretly conveyed her to matins. Liza would follow her on tiptoe, scarcely venturing to breathe. The cold, dim morning light, the raw air pervading the almost empty church, the very secrecy of those unexpected excursions, the cautious return home to bed—all that combination of the forbidden, the strange, the holy, thrilled the young girl, penetrated to the inmost depths of her being.

Agafia never blamed any one, and she never scolded Liza for any childish faults. When she was dissatisfied about anything, she merely kept silence, and Liza always understood that silence. With a child's quick instinct, she also knew well when Agafia was dissatisfied with others, whether it were with Maria Dmitrievna or with Kalitine himself.

For rather more than three years Agafia waited upon Liza. She was replaced by Mademoiselle Moreau; but the frivolous Frenchwoman, with her dry manner and her constant exclamation, *Tout ça c'est des bêtises !* could not expel from Liza's heart the recollection of her much-loved nurse. The seeds that had been sown had pushed their roots too far for that. After that Agafia, although she had ceased to attend Liza, remained for some time longer in the house, and often saw her pupil, and treated her as she had been used to do.

But when Marfa Timofeevna entered the Kalitines' house, Agafia did not get on well with her. The austere earnestness of the former " wearer of the coarse petti- coat " [1] did not please the impatient and self-willed old lady. Agafia obtained leave to go on a pilgrimage, and she never came back. Vague rumours asserted that she had retired into a schismatic convent. But the im- pression left by her on Liza's heart did not disappear. Just as before, the girl went to mass, as if she were going to a festival; and when in church prayed with en- thusiasm, with a kind of restrained and timid rapture, at which her mother secretly wondered not a little. Even Marfa Timofeevna, although she never put any

[1] The *Panovnitsa*, or wearer of the *Panovna*, a sort of petticoat made of a coarse stuff of motley hue.

constraint upon Liza, tried to induce her to moderate her zeal, and would not let her make so many prostrations. It was not a lady-like habit, she said.

Liza was a good scholar, that is, a persevering one; she was not gifted with a profound intellect, or with extraordinarily brilliant faculties, and nothing yielded to her without demanding from her no little exertion. She was a good pianist, but no one else, except Lemm, knew how much that accomplishment had cost her. She did not read much, and she had no " words of her own; " but she had ideas of her own, and she went her own way. In this matter, as well as in personal appearance, she may have taken after her father, for he never used to ask any one's advice as to what he should do.

And so she grew up, and so did her life pass, gently and tranquilly, until she had attained her nineteenth year. She was very charming, but she was not conscious of the fact. In all her movements, a natural, somewhat unconventional, grace revealed itself; in her voice there sounded the silver notes of early youth. The slightest pleasurable sensation would bring a fascinating smile to her lips, and add a deeper light, a kind of secret tenderness, to her already lustrous eyes. Kind and soft-hearted, thoroughly penetrated by a feeling of duty, and a fear of injuring any one in any way, she was attached to all whom she knew, but to no one person in particular. To God alone did she consecrate her love— loving Him with a timid, tender enthusiasm. Until Lavretsky came, no one had troubled the calmness of her inner life.

Such was Liza.

XXXIV

ABOUT the middle of the next day Lavretsky went to the Kalitines'. On his way there he met Panshine, who galloped past on horseback, his hat pulled low over his eyes. At the Kalitines', Lavretsky was not admitted, for the first time since he had made acquaintance with the family. Maria Dmitrievna was asleep, the footman declared; her head ached. Marfa Timofeevna and Lizaveta Mikhailovna were not at home.

Lavretsky walked round the outside of the garden in the vague hope of meeting Liza, but he saw no one. Two hours later he returned to the house, but received the same answer as before; moreover, the footman looked at him in a somewhat marked manner. Lavretsky thought it would be unbecoming to call three times in one day, so he determined to drive out to Vasilievskoe, where, moreover, he had business to transact.

On his way there he framed various plans, each one more charming than the rest. But on his arrival at his aunt's estate, sadness took hold of him. He entered into conversation with Anton; but the old man, as if purposely, would dwell on none but gloomy ideas. He told Lavretsky how Glafira Petrovna, just before her death, had bitten her own hand. And then, after an interval of silence, he added, with a sigh, " Every man, *barin batyushka*,[1] is destined to devour himself."

It was late in the day before Lavretsky set out on his return. The music he had heard the night before came back into his mind, and the image of Liza dawned on his heart in all its sweet serenity. He was touched by the thought that she loved him; and he arrived at his little house in the town, tranquillised and happy.

The first thing that struck him when he entered the

[1] Seigneur, father.

vestibule, was a smell of patchouli, a perfume he disliked exceedingly. He observed that a number of large trunks and boxes were standing there, and he thought there was a strange expression on the face of the servant who hastily came to meet him. He did not stop to analyse his impressions, but went straight into the drawing-room.

A lady, who wore a black silk dress with flounces, and whose pale face was half-hidden by a cambric handkerchief, rose from the sofa, took a few steps to meet him, bent her carefully-arranged and perfumed locks—and fell at his feet. Then, for the first time, he recognised her. That lady was his wife!

His breathing stopped. He leant against the wall.

" Do not drive me from you, Theodore! " she said in French; and her voice cut him to the heart like a knife. He looked at her without comprehending what he saw, and yet, at the same time, he involuntarily remarked that she had grown paler and stouter.

" Theodore! " she continued, lifting her eyes from time to time towards heaven, her exceedingly pretty fingers, tipped with polished nails of rosy hue, writhing the while in preconcerted agonies—" Theodore, I am guilty before you—deeply guilty. I will say more—I am a criminal; but hear what I have to say. I am tortured by remorse; I have become a burden to myself; I can bear my position no longer. Ever so many times I have thought of addressing you, but I was afraid of your anger. But I have determined to break every tie with the past——*puis, j'ai été si malade.* I was so ill," she added, passing her hand across her brow and cheek, " I took advantage of the report which was spread abroad of my death, and I left everything. Without stopping anywhere, I travelled day and night to come here quickly. For a long time I was in doubt whether to appear before you, my judge—*paraitre devant vous, mon juge ;* but at last I determined to go to you, remembering your constant goodness. I found out your address in Moscow. Believe me," she continued, quietly rising from the ground and seating herself upon the very edge of an armchair, " I often thought of death, and I could have found sufficient courage in my heart to deprive myself of life—ah! life is an intolerable burden to me now—but the thought of my child, of my little Ada, prevented me. She is here now; she is asleep in the next room, poor child. She is tired out. You will see her, won't you? She, at all events, is innocent before you; and so unfortunate—so unfortunate! " exclaimed Madame Lavretsky, and melted into tears.

Lavretsky regained his consciousness at last. He stood away from the wall, and turned towards the door.

" You are going away? " exclaimed his wife, in accents of despair. " Oh, that is cruel! without saying a single word to me—not even one of reproach! This contempt kills me; it is dreadful! "

Lavretsky stopped.

" What do you want me to say to you? " he said, in a hollow tone.

" Nothing—nothing! " she cried with animation. " I know that I have no right to demand anything. I am no fool, believe me. I don't hope, I don't dare to hope, for pardon. I only venture to entreat you to tell me what I ought to do, where I ought to live. I will obey your orders like a slave, whatever they may be."

" I have no orders to give," replied Lavretsky, in the same tone as before. " You know that all is over between us—and more than ever now. You can live where you like; and if your allowance is too small——"

" Ah, don't say such terrible things! " she said, interrupting him. " Forgive me, if only—if only for the sake of this angel."

And having uttered these words, Varvara Pavlovna suddenly rushed into the other room, and immediately returned with a very tastefully-dressed little girl in her arms. Thick flaxen curls fell about the pretty little rosy face and over the great black, sleepy eyes of the child, who smilingly blinked at the light, and held on to her mother's neck by a chubby little arm.

"*Ada, vois, c'est ton père,*" said Varvara Pavlovna, removing the curls from the child's eyes, and kissing her demonstratively. "*Prie-le avec moi.*"

"*C'est là, papa?*" the little girl lispingly began to stammer.

"*Oui, mon enfant, n'est-ce pas que tu l'aimes?*"

But the interview had become intolerable to Lavretsky.

"What melodrama is it just such a scene occurs in?" he muttered, and left the room.

Varvara Pavlovna remained standing where she was for some time, then she slightly shrugged her shoulders, took the little girl back into the other room, undressed her, and put her to bed. Then she took a book and sat down near the lamp. There she waited about an hour, but at last she went to bed herself.

"*Eh bien, madame?*" asked her maid,—a Frenchwoman whom she had brought with her from Paris,—as she unlaced her stays.

"*Eh bien,* Justine!" replied Varvara Pavlovna. "He has aged a great deal, but I think he is just as good as ever. Give me my gloves for the night, and get the grey dress, the high one, ready for to-morrow morning—and don't forget the mutton cutlets for Ada. To be sure it will be difficult to get them here, but we must try."

"*A la guerre comme à la guerre!*" replied Justine, and put out the light.

XXXV

For more than two hours Lavretsky wandered about the
streets. The night he had spent in the suburbs of Paris
came back into his mind. His heart seemed rent within
him, and his brain felt vacant and as it were numbed,
while the same set of evil, gloomy, mad thoughts went
ever circling in his mind. "She is alive; she is here,"
he whispered to himself with constantly recurring amazement. He felt that he had lost Liza. Wrath seemed to
suffocate him. The blow had too suddenly descended
upon him. How could he have so readily believed the
foolish gossip of a *feuilleton*, a mere scrap of paper? "But
if I had not believed it," he thought, "what would have
been the difference? I should not have known that Liza
loves me. She would not have known it herself." He
could not drive the thought of his wife out of his mind;
her form, her voice, her eyes haunted him. He cursed
himself, he cursed everything in the world.

Utterly tired out, he came to Lemm's house before the
dawn. For a long time he could not get the door opened;
at last the old man's nightcapped head appeared at the
window. Peevish and wrinkled, his face bore scarcely
any resemblance to that which, austerely inspired, had
looked royally down upon Lavretsky twenty-four hours
before, from all the height of its artistic grandeur.

"What do you want?" asked Lemm. "I cannot
play every night. I have taken a *tisane*."

But Lavretsky's face wore a strange expression which
could not escape notice. The old man shaded his eyes
with his hand, looked hard at his nocturnal visitor, and
let him in.

Lavretsky came into the room and dropped on a chair.
The old man remained standing before him, wrapping

444

the skirts of his motley old dressing-gown around him, stooping very much, and biting his lips.

" My wife has come," said Lavretsky, with drooping head; and then he suddenly burst into a fit of involuntary laughter.

Lemm's face expressed astonishment, but he preserved a grave silence, only wrapping his dressing-gown tighter around him.

" I suppose you don't know," continued Lavretsky. " I supposed—I saw in a newspaper that she was dead."

" O—h! Was it lately you saw that? " asked Lemm.

" Yes."

" O—h! " repeated the old man, raising his eyebrows, " and she has come here? "

" Yes. She is now in my house, and I—I am a most unfortunate man."

And he laughed again.

" You are a most unfortunate man," slowly repeated Lemm.

" Christophor Fedorovich," presently said Lavretsky, " will you undertake to deliver a note? "

" Hm! To whom, may I ask? "

" To Lizav—— "

" Ah! yes, yes, I understand. Very well. But when must the note be delivered? "

" To-morrow, as early as possible."

" Hm! I might send my cook, Katrin. No, I will go myself."

" And will you bring me back the answer? "

" I will."

Lemm sighed.

" Yes, my poor young friend," he said, " you certainly are—a most unfortunate young man."

Lavretsky wrote a few words to Liza, telling her of his wife's arrival, and begging her to make an appointment for an interview. Then he flung himself on the narrow sofa with his face to the wall. The old man also lay down on his bed, and there long tossed about, coughing and swallowing mouthfuls of his *tisane*.

445

The morning came; they both arose—strange were the looks they exchanged. Lavṛetsky would have liked to have killed himself just then. Katrin the cook brought them some bad coffee, and then, when eight o'clock struck, Lemm put on his hat and went out, saying that he was to have given a lesson at the Kalitines' at ten o'clock, but that he would find a fitting excuse for going there sooner.

Lavretsky again threw himself on the couch, and again a bitter laugh broke out from the depths of his heart. He thought of how his wife had driven him out of the house; he pictured to himself Liza's position, and then he shut his eyes, and wrung his hands above his head.

At length Lemm returned and brought him a scrap of paper, on which Liza had traced the following words in pencil: " We cannot see each other to-day; perhaps we may to-morrow evening. Farewell." Lavretsky thanked Lemm absently and stiffly, and then went home.

He found his wife at breakfast. Ada, with her hair all in curl-papers, and dressed in a short white frock with blue ribbons, was eating a mutton cutlet. Varvara Pavlovna rose from her seat the moment Lavretsky entered the room, and came towards him with an expression of humility on her face. He asked her to follow him into his study, and when there he shut the door and began to walk up and down the room. She sat down, folded her hands, and began to follow his movements with eyes which were still naturally beautiful, besides having their lids dyed a little.

For a long time Lavretsky could not begin what he had to say, feeling that he had not complete mastery over himself. As for his wife, he saw that she was not at all afraid of him, although she looked as if she might at any moment go off into a fainting fit.

" Listen, Madame," at last he began, breathing with difficulty, and at times setting his teeth hard. " There is no reason why we should be hypocritical towards each other. I do not believe in your repentance; but even if it were genuine, it would be impossible for me to rejoin you and live with you again."

Varvara Pavlovna bit her lips and half closed her eyes. " That's dislike," she thought. " It's all over. I'm not even a woman for him."

" Impossible," repeated Lavretsky, and buttoned his coat. " I don't know why you have been pleased to honour me by coming here. Most probably you are out of funds."

" Don't say that—you wound my feelings," whispered Varvara Pavlovna.

" However that may be, you are still, to my sorrow, my wife. I cannot drive you away, so this is what I propose. You can go to Lavriki—to-day if you like— and live there. There is an excellent house there, as you know. You shall have everything you can want, besides your allowance. Do you consent? "

Varvara Pavlovna raised her embroidered handkerchief to her face.

" I have already told you," she said, with a nervous twitching of her lips, " that I will agree to any arrangement you may please to make for me. At present I have only to ask you—will you at least allow me to thank you for your generosity? "

" No thanks, I beg of you—we shall do much better without them," hastily exclaimed Lavretsky. " Then," he added, approaching the door, " I may depend upon——"

" To-morrow I will be at Lavriki," replied Varvara Pavlovna, rising respectfully from her seat. " But Fedor Ivanich——" (She no longer familiarly called him Theodore.)

" What do you wish to say? "

" I am aware that I have not yet in any way deserved forgiveness. But may I hope that, at least, in time——"

" Ah, Varvara Pavlovna," cried Lavretsky, interrupting her, " you are a clever woman; but I, too, am not a fool. I know well that you have no need of forgiveness. Besides, I forgave you long ago; but there has always been a gulf between you and me."

"I shall know how to submit," answered Varvara Pavlovna, and bowed her head. "I have not forgotten my fault. I should not have wondered if I had learnt that you had even been glad to hear of my death," she added in a soft voice, with a slight wave of her hand towards the newspaper, which was lying on the table where Lavretsky had forgotten it.

Lavretsky shuddered. The *feuilleton* had a pencil mark against it. Varvara Pavlovna gazed at him with an expression of even greater humility than before on her face. She looked very handsome at that moment. Her grey dress, made by a Parisian milliner, fitted closely to her pliant figure, which seemed almost like that of a girl of seventeen. Her soft and slender neck, circled by a white collar, her bosom's gentle movement under the influence of her steady breathing, her arms and hands, on which she wore neither bracelets nor rings, her whole figure, from her lustrous hair to the tip of the scarcely visible *bottine*, all was so artistic!

Lavretsky eyed her with a look of hate, feeling hardly able to abstain from crying *brava*, hardly able to abstain from striking her down—and went away.

An hour later he was already on the road to Vasilievskoe, and two hours later Varvara Pavlovna ordered the best carriage on hire in the town to be got for her, put on a simple straw hat with a black veil, and a modest mantilla, left Justine in charge of Ada, and went to the Kalitines'. From the inquiries Justine had made, Madame Lavretsky had learnt that her husband was in the habit of going there every day.

448

XXXVI

THE day on which Lavretsky's wife arrived in O,—a sad day for him—was also a day of trial for Liza. Before she had had time to go downstairs and say good-morning to her mother, the sound of a horse's hoofs was heard underneath the window, and, with a secret feeling of alarm, she saw Panshine ride into the courtyard. " It is to get a definite answer that he has come so early," she thought; and she was not deceived. After taking a turn through the drawing-room, he proposed to go into the garden with her; and when there he asked her how his fate was to be decided.

Liza summoned up her courage, and told him that she could not be his wife. He listened to all she had to say, turning himself a little aside, with his hat pressed down over his eyes. Then, with perfect politeness, but in an altered tone, he asked her if that was her final decision, and whether he had not, in some way or other, been the cause of such a change in her ideas. Then he covered his eyes with his hand for a moment, breathed one quick sigh, and took his hand away from his face.

" I wanted not to follow the beaten track," he said sadly; " I wanted to choose a companion for myself, according to the dictates of my heart. But I see that is not to be. So farewell to my fancy! "

He made Liza a low bow, and went back into the house.

She hoped he would go away directly; but he went to her mother's boudoir, and remained an hour with her. As he was leaving the house, he said to Liza, " *Votre mère vous appelle : Adieu à jamais !* " then he got on his horse, and immediately set off at full gallop.

On going to her mother's room, Liza found her in tears. Panshine had told her about his failure.

"Why should you kill me? Why should you kill
me?" Thus did the mortified widow begin her complaint. "What better man do you want? Why is he
not fit to be your husband? A chamberlain! and so
disinterested! Why, at Petersburg he might marry any
of the maids of honour! And I—I had so longed for it.
And how long is it since you changed your mind about
him? Wherever has this cloud blown from?—for it
has never come of its own accord. Surely it isn't that
wiseacre? A pretty adviser you have found, if that's
the case!"

"And as for him, my poor, dear friend," continued
Maria Dmitrievna, "how respectful he was, how attentive, even in the midst of his sorrow! He has promised
not to desert me. Oh, I shall never be able to bear this!
Oh, my head is beginning to ache dreadfully! Send
Palashka here. You will kill me, if you don't think
better of it. Do you hear?" And then, after having
told Liza two or three times that she was ungrateful,
Maria Dmitrievna let her go away.

Liza went to her room. But before she had had a
moment's breathing-time after her scene with Panshine
and with her mother, another storm burst upon her,
and that from the quarter from which she least expected it.

Marfa Timofeevna suddenly came into her room, and
immediately shut the door after her. The old lady's
face was pale; her cap was all awry; her eyes were
flashing, her lips quivering. Liza was lost in astonishment. She had never seen her shrewd and steady aunt
in such a state before.

"Very good, young lady!" Marfa Timofeevna began
to whisper, with a broken and trembling voice. "Very
good! Only who taught you that, my mother——
Give me some water; I can't speak."

"Do be calm, aunt. What is the matter?" said Liza,
giving her a glass of water. "Why, I thought you
didn't like M. Panshine yourself."

Marfa Timofeevna pushed the glass away. "I can't

drink it. I should knock out my last teeth, if I tried. What has Panshine to do with it? Whatever have we to do with Panshine? Much better tell me who taught you to make appointments with people at night. Eh, my mother!"

Liza turned very pale.

"Don't try to deny it, please," continued Marfa Timofeevna. "Shurochka saw it all herself, and told me. I've had to forbid her chattering, but she never tells lies."

"I am not going to deny it, aunt," said Liza, in a scarcely audible voice.

"Ah, ah! Then it is so, my mother. You made an appointment with him, that old sinner, that remarkably sweet creature!"

"No."

"How was it, then?"

"I came down to the drawing-room to look for a book. He was out in the garden; and he called me."

"And you went? Very good, indeed! Perhaps you love him, then?"

"I do love him." said Liza quietly.

"Oh, my mothers! She does love him!" Here Marfa Timofeevna took off her cap. "She loves a married man! Eh? Loves him!"

"He had told me——" began Liza.

"What had he told you, this little hawk? Eh, what?"

"He had told me that his wife was dead."

Marfa Timofeevna made the sign of the cross. "The kingdom of heaven be to her," she whispered. "She was a frivolous woman. But don't let's think about that. So that's how it is. I see, he's a widower. Oh yes, he's going ahead. He has killed one wife, and now he's after a second. A nice sort of person he is, to be sure. But, niece, let me tell you this, in my young days things of this kind used to turn out very badly for girls. Don't be angry with me, my mother. It's only fools who are angry with the truth. I've even told them not to let him in to see me to-day. I love him, but I shall

451

never forgive him for this. So he is a widower! Give me some water. But as to your putting Panshine's nose out of joint, why I think you're a good girl for that. But don't go sitting out at night with men creatures. Don't make me wretched in my old age, and remember I'm not altogether given over to fondling. I can bite, too——A widower! "

Marfa Timofeevna went away, and Liza sat down in a corner, and cried a long time. Her heart was heavy within her. She had not deserved to be so humiliated. It was not in a joyous manner that love had made itself known to her. It was for the second time since yesterday morning that she was crying now. This new and unlooked-for feeling had only just sprung into life within her heart, and already how dearly had she had to pay for it, how roughly had other hands dealt with her treasured secret! She felt ashamed, and hurt, and unhappy; but neither doubt nor fear troubled her, and Lavretsky became only still dearer to her. She had hesitated so long as she was not sure of her own feelings; but after that interview, after that kiss——she could no longer hesitate. She knew now that she loved, and that she loved earnestly, honestly; she knew that her's was a firm attachment, one which would last for her whole life. As for threats, she did not fear them. She felt that this tie was one which no violence could break.

XXXVII

MARIA DMITRIEVNA was greatly embarrassed when she was informed that Madame Lavretsky was at the door. She did not even know whether she ought to receive her, being afraid of offending Lavretsky; but at last curiosity prevailed. "After all," she thought, "she is a relation, too." So she seated herself in an easy chair, and said to the footman, "Show her in."

A few minutes went by, then the door was thrown open, and Varvara Pavlovna, with a swift and almost noiseless step, came up to Maria Dmitrievna, and, without giving her time to rise from her chair, almost went down upon her knees before her.

"Thank you, aunt," she began in Russian, speaking softly, but in a tone of deep emotion. "Thank you; I had not even dared to hope that you would condescend so far. You are an angel of goodness."

Having said this, Varvara Pavlovna unexpectedly laid hold of one of Maria Dmitrievna's hands, gently pressed it between her pale-lilac Jouvin's gloves, and then lifted it respectfully to her pouting, rosy lips. Maria Dmitrievna was entirely carried away by the sight of such a handsome and exquisitely dressed woman almost at her feet, and did not know what position to assume. She felt half inclined to draw back her hand, half inclined to make her visitor sit down, and to say something affectionate to her. She ended by rising from her chair and kissing Varvara's smooth and perfumed forehead.

Varvara appeared to be totally overcome by that kiss.

"How do you do? *bonjour*," said Maria Dmitrievna. "I never imagined——however, I'm really delighted to see you. You will understand, my dear, it is not my business to be judge between a man and his wife."

" My husband is entirely in the right," said Varvara Pavlovna, interrupting her. " I alone am to blame."

" Those are very praiseworthy sentiments, very," said Maria Dmitrievna. " Is it long since you arrived? Have you seen him? But do sit down."

" I arrived yesterday," answered Varvara Pavlovna, sitting herself on a chair in an attitude expressive of humility. " I have seen my husband, and I have spoken with him."

" Ah! Well, and what did he say? "

" I was afraid that my coming so suddenly might make him angry," continued Varvara Pavlovna; " but he did not refuse to see me."

" That is to say, he has not—— Yes, yes, I understand," said Maria Dmitrievna. " It is only outwardly that he seems a little rough; his heart is really soft."

" Fedor Ivanovich has not pardoned me. He did not want to listen to me. But he has been good enough to let me have Lavriki to live in."

" Ah, a lovely place! "

" I shall set off there to-morrow, according to his desire. But I considered it a duty to pay you a visit first."

" I am very, very much obliged to you, my dear. One ought never to forget one's relations. But, do you know, I am astonished at your speaking Russian so well. C'est étonnant."

Varvara Pavlovna smiled.

" I have been too long abroad, Maria Dmitrievna, I am well aware of that. But my heart has always been Russian, and I have not forgotten my native land."

" Yes, yes. There's nothing like that. Your husband certainly didn't expect you in the least. Yes, trust my experience—la patrie avant tout. Oh! please let me! What a charming mantilla you have on! "

" Do you like it? " Varvara took it quickly off her shoulders. " It is very simple; one of Madame Baudran's."

" One can see that at a glance. How lovely, and in

what exquisite taste! I feel sure you've brought a number of charming things with you. How I should like to see them!"

"All my toilette is at your service, dearest aunt. I might show your maid something if you liked. I have brought a maid from Paris, a wonderful needlewoman."

"You are exceedingly good, my dear. But, really, I haven't the conscience——"

"Haven't the conscience!" repeated Varvara Pavlovna, in a reproachful tone. "If you wish to make me happy, you will dispose of me as if I belonged to you."

Maria Dmitrievna fairly gave way.

"*Vous êtes charmante,*" she said. "But why don't you take off your bonnet and gloves?"

"What! You allow me?" asked Varvara Pavlovna, gently clasping her hands with an air of deep emotion.

"Of course. You will dine with us, I hope. I—I will introduce my daughter to you." (Maria Dmitrievna felt embarrassed for a moment, but then, "Well, so be it," she thought.) "She happens not to be quite well to-day."

"Oh! *ma tante*, how kind you are!" exclaimed Varvara Pavlovna, lifting her handkerchief to her eyes.

At this moment the page announced Gedeonovsky's arrival, and the old gossip came in smiling, and bowing profoundly. Maria Dmitrievna introduced him to her visitor. At first he was somewhat abashed, but Varvara Pavlovna behaved to him with such coquettish respectfulness that his ears soon began to tingle, and amiable speeches and gossiping stories began to flow uninterruptedly from his lips.

Varvara Pavlovna listened to him, slightly smiling at times, then by degrees she too began to talk. She spoke in a modest way about Paris, about her travels, about Baden; she made Maria Dmitrievna laugh two or three times, and each time she uttered a gentle sigh afterwards, as if she were secretly reproaching herself for her unbecoming levity; she asked leave to bring Ada to the house; she took off her gloves, and with her smooth white hands she pointed out how and where flounces, ruches, lace, and so forth, were worn; she promised to bring a bottle of new English scent—the Victoria essence —and was as pleased as a child when Maria Dmitrievna consented to accept it as a present; and she melted into tears at the remembrance of the emotion she had experienced when she heard the first Russian bells.

" So profoundly did they sink into my very heart," she said.

At that moment Liza came into the room.

All that day, ever since the moment when, cold with dismay, Liza had read Lavretsky's note, she had been preparing herself for an interview with his wife. She foresaw that she would see her, and she determined not to avoid her, by way of inflicting upon herself a punishment for what she considered her culpable hopes. The unexpected crisis which had taken place in her fate had profoundly shaken her. In the course of about a couple of hours her face seemed to have grown thin. But she had not shed a single tear. " It is what you deserve," she said to herself, repressing, though not without difficulty, and at the cost of considerable agitation, certain bitter thoughts and evil impulses which frightened her as they arose in her mind. " Well, I must go," she thought, as soon as she heard of Madame Lavretsky's arrival, and she went.

She stood outside the drawing-room door for a long time before she could make up her mind to open it. At last, saying to herself, " I am guilty before her," she entered the room, and forced herself to look at her, even forced herself to smile. Varvara Pavlovna came forward to meet her as soon as she saw her come in, and made her a slight, but still a respectful salutation.

" Allow me to introduce myself," she began, in an insinuating tone. " Your mamma has been so indulgent towards me that I hope that you too will be—good to me."

The expression of Varvara Pavlovna's face as she uttered these last words, her cunning smile, her cold and, at the same time, loving look, the movements of her arms and shoulders, her very dress, her whole being, aroused such a feeling of repugnance in Liza's mind that she absolutely could not answer her, and only by a strong effort could succeed in holding out her hand to her. " This young lady dislikes me," thought Varvara Pavlovna, as she squeezed Liza's cold fingers, then, turning to Maria Dmitrievna, she said in a half whisper, " *Mais, elle est délicieuse !* "

Liza faintly reddened. In that exclamation she seemed to detect a tone of irony and insult. However, she determined not to trust to that impression, and she took her seat at her embroidery frame near the window.

Even there Varvara Pavlovna would not leave her in peace. She came to her, and began to praise her cleverness and taste. Liza's heart began to beat with painful force. Scarcely could she master her feelings, scarcely could she remain sitting quietly in her place. It seemed to her as if Varvara Pavlovna knew all and were mocking her with secret triumph. Fortunately for her, Gedeonovsky began to talk to Varvara and diverted her attention. Liza bent over her frame and watched her without being observed. " That woman," she thought, " was once loved by *him*." But then she immediately drove out of her mind even so much as the idea of Lavretsky. She felt her head gradually beginning to swim, and she was afraid of losing command over herself. Maria Dmitrievna began to talk about music.

" I have heard, my dear," she began, " that you are a wonderful *virtuosa.*"

" I haven't played for a long time," replied Varvara Pavlovna, but she immediately took her seat at the piano, and ran her fingers rapidly along the keys. " Do you wish me to play? "

" If you will do us that favour."

Varvara Pavlovna played in a masterly style a brilliant and difficult study by Herz. Her performance was marked by great power and rapidity.

" *A sylphide !* " exclaimed Gedeonovsky.

457

" It is wonderful! " declared Maria Dmitrievna. " I must confess you have fairly astonished me, Varvara Pavlovna," calling that lady by her name for the first time. " Why you might give concerts. We have a musician here, an old German, very learned and quite an original. He gives Liza lessons. You would simply make him go out of his mind."

" Is Lizaveta Mikhailovna also a musician? " asked Madame Lavretsky, turning her head a little towards her.

" Yes; she doesn't play badly, and she is very fond of music. But what does that signify in comparison with you? But we have a young man here besides. You really must make his acquaintance. He is a thorough artist in feeling, and he composes charmingly. He is the only person here who can fully appreciate you."

" A young man? " said Varvara Pavlovna. " What is he? Some poor fellow? "

" I beg your pardon. He is the leading cavalier here, and not here only—*et à Petersbourg*—a chamberlain, received in the best society. You surely must have heard of him—Vladimir Nikolaevich Panshine. He is here on government business—a future minister! "

" And an artist too? "

" An artist in feeling, and so amiable. You shall see him. He has been here a great deal for some time past. I asked him to come this evening. I *hope* he will come," added Maria Dmitrievna with a slight sigh and a bitter smile.

Liza understood the hidden meaning of that smile, but she had other things to think about then.

" And he's young? " repeated Varvara Pavlovna, lightly modulating from key to key.

" Twenty-eight years old—and a most pleasing exterior. *Un jeune homme accompli.*"

" A model young man, one may say," remarked Gedeonovsky.

Varvara Pavlovna suddenly began to play a noisy

458

waltz by Strauss, beginning with so loud and quick a
a trill that Gedeonovsky fairly started. Right in the
middle of the waltz she passed abruptly into a plaintive
air, and ended with the *Fra poco* out of *Lucia.* She had
suddenly remembered that joyful music was not in
keeping with her position.

Maria Dmitrievna was deeply touched by the air from
Lucia, in which great stress was laid upon the sentimental passages.

" What feeling! " she whispered to Gedeonovsky.

" *A Sylphide!* " repeated Gedeonovsky, lifting his
eyes towards heaven.

The dinner hour arrived. Marfa Timofeevna did not
come down from upstairs until the soup was already
placed on the table. She behaved very coldly to Varvara Pavlovna, answering her amiable speeches with
broken phrases, and never even looking at her. Varvara
soon perceived that there was no conversation to be got
out of that old lady, so she gave up talking to her. On
the other hand Madame Kalitine became still more
caressing in her behaviour toward her guest. She was
vexed by her aunt's rudeness.

After all, it was not only Varvara that the old lady
would not look at. She did not once look at Liza either,
although her eyes almost glowed with a meaning light.
Pale, almost yellow, there she sat, with compressed lips,
looking as if she were made of stone, and would eat
nothing.

As for Liza, she seemed calm, and was so in reality.
Her heart was quieter than it had been. A strange
callousness, the callousness of the condemned, had come
over her.

During dinner Varvara Pavlovna said little. She
seemed to have become timid again, and her face wore
an expression of modest melancholy. Gedeonovsky
was the only person who kept the conversation alive,
relating several of his stories, though from time to time
he looked timidly at Marfa Timofeevna, and coughed.
That cough always seized him whenever he was going tc

embellish the truth in her presence. But this time she did not meddle with him, never once interrupted him.

After dinner it turned out that Varvara Pavlovna was very fond of the game of preference. Madame Kalitine was so pleased at this that she felt quite touched and inwardly thought, " Why, what a fool Fedor Ivanovich must be! Fancy not having been able to comprehend such a woman! "

She sat down to cards with Varvara and Gedeonovsky; but Marfa Timofeevna carried off Liza to her room upstairs, saying that the girl " had no face left," and she was sure her head must be aching.

" Yes, her head aches terribly," said Madame Kalitine, addressing Varvara Pavlovna, and rolling her eyes. " I often have such headaches myself."

" Really! " answered Varvara Pavlovna.

Liza entered her aunt's room, and sank on a chair perfectly worn out. For a long time Marfa Timofeevna looked at her in silence, then she quietly knelt down before her, and began, still quite silently, to kiss her hands—first one, and then the other.

Liza bent forwards and reddened—then she began to cry; but she did not make her aunt rise, nor did she withdraw her hands from her. She felt that she had no right to withdraw them—had no right to prevent the old lady from expressing her sorrow, her sympathy—from asking to be pardoned for what had taken place the day before. And Marfa Timofeevna could not sufficiently kiss those poor, pale, nerveless hands; while silent tears poured down from her eyes and from Liza's too. And the cat, Matros, purred in the large chair by the side of the stocking and the ball of worsted; the long, thin flame of the little lamp feebly wavered in front of the holy picture; and in the next room, just the other side of the door, stood Nastasia Carpovna, and furtively wiped her eyes with a check pocket-handkerchief rolled up into a sort of ball.

XXXVIII

DOWNSTAIRS, meanwhile, the game of preference went on. Maria Dmitrievna was winning, and was in a very good humour. A servant entered, and announced Panshine's arrival. Maria Dmitrievna let fall her cards, and fidgeted in her chair. Varvara Pavlovna looked at her with a half-smile, and then turned her eyes towards the door.

Panshine appeared in a black dress-coat, buttoned all the way up, and wearing a high English shirt-collar. " It was painful for me to obey; but, you see, I have come; " that was what was expressed by his serious face, evidently just shaved for the occasion.

" Why, Vlademar! " exclaimed Maria Dmitrievna, " you used always to come in without being announced."

Panshine made no other reply than a look, and bowed politely to Maria Dmitrievna, but did not kiss her hand. She introduced him to Varvara Pavlovna. He drew back a pace, bowed to her with the same politeness and with an added expression of respectful grace, and then took a seat at the card-table. The game soon came to an end. Panshine asked after Lizaveta Mikhailovna, and expressed his regret at hearing that she was not quite well. Then he began to converse with Varvara Pavlovna, weighing every word carefully and emphasising it distinctly in true diplomatic style, and, when she spoke, respectfully hearing her answers to the end. But the seriousness of his diplomatic tone produced no effect upon Varvara Pavlovna, who would not have anything to do with it. On the contrary, she looked him full in the face with a sort of smiling earnestness, and in talking with him seemed thoroughly at her ease, while her delicate nostrils lightly quivered, as though with suppressed laughter.

Maria Dmitrievna began to extol Varvara's cleverness. Panshine bent his head politely, as far as his shirt-collar permitted him, declared that he had already been convinced of the exceptional nature of her talents, and all but brought round the conversation to the subject of Metternich himself. Varvara Pavlovna half-closed her velvety eyes, and, having said in a low voice, " But you are an artist also, *un confrère*," added still lower, " *Venez !* " and made a sign with her head in the direction of the piano. This single word, " *Venez !* " so abruptly spoken, utterly changed Panshine's appearance, as if by magic, in a single moment. His care-worn air disappeared, he began to smile, he became animated, he unbuttoned his coat, and, saying " I an artist! Not at all; but you, I hear, are an artist indeed," he followed Varvara Pavlovna to the piano.

" Tell him to sing the romance, ' How the moon floats,' " exclaimed Maria Dmitrievna.

" You sing? " asked Varvara Pavlovna, looking at him with a bright and rapid glance. " Sit down there."

Panshine began to excuse himself.

" Sit down," she repeated, tapping the back of the chair in a determined manner.

He sat down, coughed, pulled up his shirt-collar, and sang his romance.

" *Charmant*," said Varvara Pavlovna. " You sing admirably—*vous avez du style*. Sing it again."

She went round to the other side of the piano, and placed herself exactly opposite Panshine. He repeated his romance, giving a melodramatic variation to his voice. Varvara looked at him steadily, resting her elbows on the piano, with her white hands on a level with her lips. The song ended, " *Charmant ! Charmante idée*," she said, with the quiet confidence of a connoisseur. " Tell me, have you written anything for a woman's voice—a mezzo-soprano? "

" I scarcely write anything," answered Panshine. " I do so only now and then—between business-hours. But do you sing? "

"Oh, yes! do sing us something," said Maria Dmitrievna.

Varvara Pavlovna tossed her head, and pushed her hair back from her flushed cheeks. Then, addressing Panshine, she said—

"Our voices ought to go well together. Let us sing a duet. Do you know '*Son geloso*,' or '*La ci darem*,' or '*Mira la bianca luna?*'"

"I used to sing '*Mira la bianca luna*,'" answered Panshine; "but it was a long time ago. I have forgotten it now."

"Never mind, we will hum it over first by way of experiment. Let me come there."

Varvara Pavlovna sat down to the piano. Panshine stood by her side. They hummed over the duet, Varvara Pavlovna correcting him several times; then they sang it out aloud, and afterwards repeated it twice— "*Mira la bianca lu-u-una*." Varvara's voice had lost its freshness, but she managed it with great skill. At first Panshine was nervous, and sang rather false, but afterwards he experienced an artistic glow; and, if he did not sing faultlessly, at all events he shrugged his shoulders, swayed his body to and fro, and from time to time lifted his hand aloft, like a genuine vocalist.

Varvara Pavlovna afterwards played two or three little pieces by Thalberg, and coquettishly chanted a French song. Maria Dmitrievna did not know how to express her delight, and several times she felt inclined to send for Liza. Gedeonovsky, too, could not find words worthy of the occasion, and could only shake his head. Suddenly, however, and quite unexpectedly, he yawned, and only just contrived to hide his mouth with his hand. That yawn did not escape Varvara's notice. She suddenly turned her back upon the piano, saying, "*Assez de musique comme ça;* let us talk a little," and crossed her hands before her.

"*Oui, assez de musique*," gladly repeated Panshine, and began a conversation with her—a brisk and airy conversation, carried on in French. "Exactly as if it were in one of the best Paris drawing-rooms," thought Maria Dmitrievna, listening to their quick and supple talk.

Panshine felt completely happy. He smiled, and his eyes shone. At first, when he happened to meet Maria Dmitrievna's eyes, he would pass his hand across his face and frown and sigh abruptly, but after a time he entirely forgot her presence, and gave himself up unreservedly to the enjoyment of a half-fashionable, half-artistic chat.

Varvara Pavlovna proved herself a great philosopher. She had an answer ready for everything; she doubted nothing; she did not hesitate at anything. It was evident that she had talked often and much with all kinds of clever people. All her thoughts and feelings circled around Paris. When Panshine made literature the subject of the conversation, it turned out that she, like him, had read nothing but French books. George Sand irritated her; Balzac she esteemed, although he wearied her; to Eugene Sue and Scribe she ascribed a profound knowledge of the human heart; Dumas and Féval she adored. In reality, she preferred Paul de Kock to all the others; but, as may be supposed, she did not even mention his name. To tell the truth, literature did not interest her overmuch.

Varvara Pavlovna avoided with great skill everything that might, even remotely, allude to her own position. In all that she said, there was not even the slightest mention made of love; on the contrary, her language seemed rather to express an austere feeling with regard to the allurements of the passions, and to breathe the accents of disillusionment and resignation.

Panshine replied to her, but she refused to agree with him. Strange to say, however, at the very time when she was uttering words which conveyed what was frequently a harsh judgment, the accents of those very words were tender and caressing, and her eyes expressed —— What those charming eyes really expressed it would be hard to say, but it was something which had

464

no harshness about it, rather a mysterious sweetness. Panshine tried to make out their hidden meaning, tried to make his own eyes eloquent, but he was conscious that he failed. He acknowledged that Varvara Pavlovna, in her capacity as a real lioness from abroad, stood on a higher level than he; and, therefore, he was not altogether master of himself.

Varvara Pavlovna had a habit of every now and then just touching the sleeve of the person with whom she was conversing. These light touches greatly agitated Panshine. She had the faculty of easily becoming intimate with any one. Before a couple of hours had passed, it seemed to Panshine as if he had known her an age, and as if Liza—that very Liza whom he had loved so much, and to whom he had proposed the evening before—had vanished in a kind of fog.

Tea was brought; the conversation became even more free from restraint than before. Madame Kalitine rang for the page, and told him to ask Liza to come down if her headache was better. At the sound of Liza's name, Panshine began to talk about self-sacrifice, and to discuss the question as to which is the more capable of such sacrifice—man or woman. Maria Dmitrievna immediately became excited, began to affirm that the woman is the more capable, asserted that she could prove the fact in a few words, got confused over them, and ended with a sufficiently unfortunate comparison. Varvara Pavlovna took up a sheet of music, and half-screening her face with it, bent over towards Panshine, and said in a whisper, while she nibbled a biscuit, a quiet smile playing about her lips and her eyes, " *Elle n'a pas invente la poudre, la bonne dame.*"

Panshine was somewhat astonished, and a little alarmed by Varvara's audacity, but he did not detect the amount of contempt for himself that lay hid in that unexpected sally, and—forgetting all Maria Dmitrievna's kindness and her attachment towards him, forgetting the dinners she had given him, the money she had lent him— he replied (unhappy mortal that he was) in the same

465

tone, and with a similar smile, " *Je crois bien !* " and what is more he did not even say " *Je crois bien !* " but " *J'crois ben !* "

Varvara .Pavlovna gave him a friendly look, and rose from her seat. At that moment Liza entered the room. Marfa Timofeevna had tried to prevent her going, but in vain. Liza was resolved to endure her trial to the end. Varvara Pavlovna advanced to meet her, attended by Panshine, whose face again wore its former diplomatic expression.

" How are you now? " asked Varvara.

" I am better now, thank you," replied Liza.

" We have been passing the time with a little music," said Panshine. " It is a pity you did not hear Varvara Pavlovna. She sings charmingly, *en artiste consommée.*"

" Come here, *ma chère,*" said Madame Kalitine's voice.

With childlike obedience, Varvara immediately went to her, and sat down on a stool at her feet. Maria Dmitrievna had called her away, in order that she might leave her daughter alone with Panshine, if only for a moment. She still hoped in secret that Liza would change her mind. Besides this, an idea had come into her mind, which she wanted by all means to express.

" Do you know," she whispered to Varvara Pavlovna, " I want to try and reconcile you and your husband. I cannot promise to succeed, but I will try. He esteems me very much, you know."

Varvara slowly looked up at Maria Dmitrievna, and gracefully clasped her hands together.

" You would be my saviour, *ma tante,*" she said, with a sad voice. " I don't know how to thank you properly for all your kindness; but I am too guilty before Fedor Ivanovich. He cannot forgive me."

" But did you actually—in reality—? " began Maria Dmitrievna, with lively curiosity.

" Do not ask me," said Varvara, interrupting her, and then looked down. " I was young, light headed—— However, I don't wish to make excuses for myself."

" Well, in spite of all that, why not make the attempt?

Don't give way to despair," replied Maria Dmitrievna, and was going to tap her on the cheek, but looked at her, and was afraid. " She is modest and discreet," she thought, " but, for all that, a *lionne* still! "

" Are you unwell? " asked Panshine meanwhile.

" I am not quite well," replied Liza.

" I understand," he said, after rather a long silence, " Yes, I understand."

" What do you mean? "

" I understand," significantly repeated Panshine, who simply was at a loss for something to say.

Liza felt confused, but then she thought, " What does it matter? "

Meanwhile Panshine assumed an air of mystery and maintained silence, looking in a different direction with a grave expression on his face.

" Why I fancy it must be past eleven! " observed Maria Dmitrievna. Her guests understood the hint and began to take leave. Varvara was obliged to promise to come and dine to-morrow, and to bring Ada with her. Gedeonovsky, who had all but gone to sleep as he sat in a corner, offered to escort her home. Panshine bowed gravely to all the party; afterwards, as he stood on the steps after seeing Varvara into her carriage, he gave her hand a gentle pressure, and exclaimed, as she drove away, " *Au revoir !* " Gedeonovsky sat by her side in the carriage, and all the way home she amused herself by putting the tip of her little foot, as if by accident, on his foot. He felt abashed, and tried to make her complimentary speeches. She tittered, and made eyes at him when the light from the street lamps shone into the carriage. The waltz she had played rang in her ears and excited her. Wherever she might be she had only to imagine a ballroom and a blaze of light, and swift circling round to the sound of music, and her heart would burn within her, her eyes would glow with a strange lustre, a smile would wander around her lips, a kind of bacchanalian grace would seem to diffuse itself over her whole body.

LIZA

When they arrived at her house Varvara lightly bounded from the carriage, as only a *lionne* could bound, turned towards Gedeonovsky, and suddenly burst out laughing in his face.

"A charming creature," thought the councillor of state, as he made his way home to his lodgings, where his servant was waiting for him with a bottle of opodeldoc. "It's as well that I'm a steady man—— But why did she laugh?"

All that night long Marfa Timofeevna sat watching by Liza's bedside.

XXXIX

LAVRETSKY spent a day and a half at Vasilievskoe, wandering about the neighbourhood almost all the time. He could not remain long in any one place. His grief goaded him on. He experienced all the pangs of a ceaseless, impetuous, and impotent longing. He remembered the feeling which had come over him the day after his first arrival. He remembered the resolution he had formed then, and he felt angrily indignant with himself. What was it that had been able to wrest him aside from that which he had acknowledged as his duty, the single problem of his future life? The thirst after happiness—the old thirst after happiness. " It seems that Mikhalevich was right after all," he thought. " You wanted to find happiness in life once more," he said to himself. " You forgot that for happiness to visit a man even once is an undeserved favour, a steeping in luxury. Your happiness was incomplete — was false, you may say. Well, show what right you have to true and complete happiness! Look around you and see who is happy, who enjoys his life! There is a peasant going to the field to mow. It may be that he is satisfied with his lot. But what of that? Would you be willing to exchange lots with him? Remember your own mother. How exceedingly modest were her wishes, and yet what sort of a lot fell to her share! You seem to have only been boasting before Panshine, when you told him that you had come into Russia to till the soil. It was to run after the girls in your old age that you came. Tidings of freedom reached you, and you flung aside everything, forgot everything, ran like a child after a butterfly."

In the midst of his reflections the image of Liza constantly haunted him. By a violent effort he tried to

469

drive it away, and along with it another haunting face, other beautiful but ever malignant and hateful features.

Old Anton remarked that his master was not quite himself; and, after sighing several times behind the door, and several times on the threshold, he ventured to go up to him, and advised him to drink something hot. Lavretsky spoke to him harshly, and ordered him out of the room: afterwards he told the old man he was sorry he had done so; but this only made Anton sadder than he had been before.

Lavretsky could not stop in the drawing-room. He fancied that his great grandfather, Andrei, was looking out from his frame with contempt on his feeble descendant. " So much for you! You float in shallow water! " [1] the wry lips seemed to be saying to him. " Is it possible," he thought, " that I cannot gain mastery over myself; that I am going to yield to this——this trifling affair! " (Men who are seriously wounded in a battle always think their wounds " a mere trifle; " when a man can deceive himself no longer, it is time to give up living.) " Am I really a child? Well, yes. I have seen near at hand, I have almost grasped, the possibility of gaining a life-long happiness—and then it has suddenly disappeared. It is just the same in a lottery. Turn the wheel a little more, and the pauper would perhaps be rich. If it is not to be, it is not to be—and all is over. I will betake me to my work with set teeth, and I will force myself to be silent; and I shall succeed, for it is not for the first time that I take myself in hand. And why have I run away? Why do I stop here, vainly hiding my head, like an ostrich? Misfortune a terrible thing to look in the face! Nonsense! "

" Anton! " he called loudly, " let the tarantass be got ready immediately."

" Yes," he said to himself again. " I must compel myself to be silent; I must keep myself tightly in hand."

With such reflections as these Lavretsky sought to

[1] Part of a Russian proverb.

assuage his sorrow; but it remained as great and as bitter as before. Even Apraxia, who had outlived, not only her intelligence, but almost all her faculties, shook her head, and followed him with sad eyes as he started in the tarantass for the town. The horses galloped. He sat erect and motionless, and looked straight before him along the road.

XL

Liza had written to Lavretsky the night before, telling him to come and see her on this evening; but he went to his own house first. He did not find either his wife or his daughter there; and the servant told him that they had both gone to the Kalitines'! This piece of news both annoyed and enraged him. " Varvara Pavlovna seems to be determined not to let me live in peace," he thought, an angry feeling stirring in his heart. He began walking up and down the room, pushing away every moment, with hand or foot, one of the toys or books or feminine belongings which fell in his way. Then he called Justine, and told her to take away all that " rubbish."

" *Oui, monsieur*," she replied, with a grimace, and began to set the room in order, bending herself into graceful attitudes, and by each of her gestures making Lavretsky feel that she considered him an uncivilised bear. It was with a sensation of downright hatred that he watched the mocking expression of her faded, but still *piquante*, Parisian face, and looked at her white sleeves, her silk apron, and her little cap. At last he sent her away, and, after long hesitation, as Varvara Pavlovna did not return, he determined to go to the Kalitines', and pay a visit, not to Madame Kalitine (for nothing would have induced him to enter her drawing-room—that drawing-room in which his wife was), but to Marfa Timofeevna. He remembered that a back staircase, used by the maid-servants, led straight to her room.

Lavretsky carried out his plan. By a fortunate chance he met Shurochka in the courtyard, and she brought him to Marfa Timofeevna. He found the old lady, contrary to her usual custom, alone. She was without her cap, and was sitting in a corner of the room

LIZA

in a slouching attitude, her arms folded across her
breast. When she saw Lavretsky, she was much agitated, and jumping up hastily from her chair, she began
going here and there about the room, as if she were
looking for her cap.

" Ah! so you've come, then," she said, fussing about
and avoiding his eyes. " Well, good day to you!
Well, what's—what's to be done? Where were you
yesterday? Well, she has come. Well—yes. Well,
it must be—somehow or other."

Lavretsky sank upon a chair.

" Well, sit down, sit down," continued the old lady.
" Did you come straight upstairs? Yes, of course. Eh!
You came to see after me? Many thanks."

The old lady paused. Lavretsky did not know what
to say to her; but she understood him.

" Liza—yes; Liza was here just now," she continued,
tying and untying the strings of her work-bag. " She
isn't quite well. Shurochka, where are you? Come
here, my mother; cannot you sit still a moment? And
I have a headache myself. It must be that singing
which has given me it, and the music."

" What singing, aunt? "

" What! don't you know? They have already begun
—what do you call them?—duets down there. And all
in Italian—chi-chi and cha-cha—regular magpies. With
their long-drawn-out notes, one would think they were
going to draw one's very soul out. It's that Panshine,
and your wife too. And how quickly it was all arranged!
Quite without ceremony, just as if among near relations.
However, one must say that even a dog will try to find
itself a home somewhere. You needn't die outside if
folks don't chase you away from their houses."

" I certainly must confess I did not expect this,"
answered Lavretsky. " This must have required considerable daring."

" No, my dear, it isn't daring with her, it is calculation.
However, God be with her! They say you are going to
send her to Lavriki. Is that true? "

473

" Yes; I am going to make over that property to her."

" Has she asked you for money? "

" Not yet."

" Well, that request won't be long in coming. But —I haven't looked at you till now—are you well? "

" Quite well."

" Shurochka! " suddenly exclaimed the old lady. " Go and tell Lizaveta Mikhailovna—that is—no—ask her—— Is she down-stairs? "

" Yes."

" Well, yes. Ask her where she has put my book. She will know all about it."

" Very good."

The old lady commenced bustling about again, and began to open the drawers in her commode. Lavretsky remained quietly sitting on his chair.

Suddenly light steps were heard on the staircase—and Liza entered.

Lavretsky stood up and bowed. Liza remained near the door.

" Liza, Lizochka," hurriedly began Marfa Timofeevna, " where have you—where have you put my book? "

" What book, aunt? "

" Why, good gracious! that book. However, I didn't send for you—but it's all the same. What are you all doing downstairs? Here is Fedor Ivanovich come. How is your headache? "

" It's of no consequence."

" You always say, ' It's of no consequence.' What are you all doing down below?—having music again? "

" No—they are playing cards."

" Of course; she is ready for anything. Shurochka, I see you want to run out into the garden. Be off! "

" No, I don't, Marfa Timofeevna—— "

" No arguing, if you please. Be off. Nastasia Carpovna has gone into the garden by herself. Go and keep her company. You should show the old lady respect."

Shurochka left the room.

" But where is my cap? Wherever can it have got to? "

" Let me look for it," said Liza.

" Sit still, sit still! My own legs haven't dropped off yet. It certainly must be in my bedroom."

And Marfa Timofeevna went away, after casting a side-glance at Lavretsky. At first she left the door open, but suddenly she returned and shut it from the outside.

Liza leant back in her chair and silently hid her face in her hands.

Lavretsky remained standing where he was.

" This is how we have had to see each other! " he said at last.

Liza let her hands fall from before her face.

" Yes," she replied sadly, " we have soon been punished."

" Punished! " echoed Lavretsky. " For what have you, at all events, been punished? "

Liza looked up at him. Her eyes did not express either sorrow or anxiety; but they seemed to have become smaller and dimmer than they used to be. Her face was pale; even her slightly-parted lips had lost their colour.

Lavretsky's heart throbbed with pity and with love.

" You have written to me that all is over," he whispered. " Yes, all is over—before it had begun."

" All that must be forgotten," said Liza. " I am glad you have come. I was going to write to you; but it is better as it is. Only we must make the most of these few minutes. Each of us has a duty to fulfil. You, Fedor Ivanovich, must become reconciled with your wife."

" Liza! "

" I entreat you to let it be so. By this alone can expiation be made for——for all that has taken place. Think over it, and then you will not refuse my request."

" Liza! for God's sake! You ask what is impossible. I am ready to do everything you tell me; but to be reconciled with her *now !——* I consent to everything, I have forgotten everything; but I cannot do violence to my heart. Have some pity; this is cruel!"

"But I do not ask you to do what you say is impossible. Do not live with her, if you really cannot do so. But be reconciled with her," answered Liza, once more hiding her face in her hands. "Remember your daughter; and, besides, do it for my sake."

"Very good," said Lavretsky between his teeth. "Suppose I do this—in this I shall be fulfilling my duty; well, but you—in what does your duty consist?"

"That I know perfectly well."

Lavretsky suddenly shuddered.

"Surely you have not made up your mind to marry Panshine?" he asked.

"Oh, no!" replied Liza, with an almost imperceptible smile.

"Ah! Liza, Liza!" exclaimed Lavretsky, "how happy we might have been!"

Liza again looked up at him.

"Now even you must see, Fedor Ivanovich, that happiness does not depend upon ourselves, but upon God."

"Yes, because you——"

The door of the next room suddenly opened, and Marfa Timofeevna came in, holding her cap in her hand.

"I had trouble enough to find it," she said, standing between Liza and Lavretsky; "I had stuffed it away myself. Dear me, see what old age comes to! But, after all, youth is no better. Well, are you going to Lavriki with your wife?" she added, turning to Fedor Ivanovich.

"To Lavriki with her? I?—I don't know," he added, after a short pause.

"Won't you pay a visit downstairs?"

"Not to-day."

"Well, very good; do as you please. But you, Liza, ought to go downstairs, I think. Ah! my dears, I've forgotten to give any seed to my bullfinch too. Wait a minute; I will be back directly."

And Marfa Timofeevna ran out of the room, without ever having put on her cap.

Lavretsky quickly drew near to Liza.

"Liza," he began, with an imploring voice, "we are about to part for ever, and my heart is very heavy. Give me your hand at parting."

Liza raised her head. Her wearied, almost lustreless eyes looked at him steadily.

"No," she said, and drew back the hand she had half held out to him. "No, Lavretsky" (it was the first time that she called him by this name), "I will not give you my hand. Why should I? And now leave me, I beseech you. You know that I love you—Yes, I love you!" she added emphatically. "But no—no;" and she raised her handkerchief to her lips.

"At least, then, give me that handkerchief——"

The door creaked. The handkerchief glided down to Liza's knees. Lavretsky seized it before it had time to fall on the floor, and quickly hid it away in his pocket; then, as he turned round, he encountered the glance of Marfa Timofeevna's eyes.

"Lizochka, I think your mother is calling you," said the old lady.

Liza immediately got up from her chair, and left the room.

Marfa Timofeevna sat down again in her corner. Lavretsky was going to take leave of her.

"Fedia," she said, abruptly.

"What aunt?"

"Are you an honourable man?"

"What?"

"I ask you—Are you an honourable man?"

"I hope so."

"Hm! Well, then, give me your word that you are going to behave like an honourable man."

"Certainly. But why do you ask that?"

"I know why, perfectly well. And so do you, too, my

477

good friend.[1] As you are no fool, you will understand
why I ask you this, if you will only think over it a little.
But now, good-bye, my dear. Thank you for coming
to see me; but remember what I have said, Fedia; and
now give me a kiss. Ah, my dear, your burden is heavy
to bear, I know that. But no one finds his a light one.
There was a time when I used to envy the flies. There
are creatures, I thought, who live happily in the world.
But one night I heard a fly singing out under a spider's
claws. So, thought I, even they have their troubles.
What can be done, Fedia? But mind you never forget
what you have said to me. And now leave me—leave
me."

Lavretsky left by the back door, and had almost
reached the street, when a footman ran after him and
said, " Maria Dmitrievna told me to ask you to come
to her."

" Tell her I cannot come just now," began Lavretsky.

" She told me to ask you particularly," continued the
footman. " She told me to say that she was alone."

" Then her visitors have gone away? " asked Lavretsky.

" Yes," replied the footman, with something like a
grin on his face.

Lavretsky shrugged his shoulders, and followed him
into the house.

[1] Literally, "my foster father," or "my benefactor."

XLI

Maria Dmitrievna was alone in her boudoir. She was sitting in a large easy-chair, sniffing eau-de-cologne, with a little table by her side, on which was a glass containing orange-flower water. She was evidently excited, and seemed nervous about something.

Lavretsky came into the room.

" You wanted to see me," he said, bowing coldly.

" Yes," answered Maria Dmitrievna, and then she drank a little water. " I heard that you had gone straight upstairs to my aunt, so I told the servants to ask you to come and see me. I want to have a talk with you. Please sit down."

Maria Dmitrievna took breath. " You know that your wife has come," she continued.

" I am aware of that fact," said Lavretsky.

" Well—yes—that is—I meant to say she has been here, and I have received her. That is what I wanted to have an explanation about with you, Fedor Ivanich. I have deserved, I may say, general respect, thank God! and I wouldn't, for all the world, do anything unbecoming. But, although I saw beforehand that it would be disagreeable to you, Fedor Ivanich, yet I couldn't make up my mind to refuse her. She is a relation of mine—through you. Only put yourself into my position. What right had I to shut my door in her face? Surely you must agree with me."

" You are exciting yourself quite unnecessarily, Maria Dmitrievna," replied Lavretsky. " You have done what is perfectly right. I am not in the least angry. I never intended to deprive my wife of the power of seeing her acquaintances. I did not come to see you to-day simply because I did not wish to meet her. That was all."

479

"Ah! how glad I am to hear you say that, Fedor Ivanich!" exclaimed Maria Dmitrievna. "However, I always expected as much from your noble feelings. But as to my being excited, there's no wonder in that. I am a woman and a mother. And your wife—of course I cannot set myself up as a judge between you and her, I told her so herself; but she is such a charming person that no one can help being pleased with her."

Lavretsky smiled and twirled his hat in his hands.

"And there is something else that I wanted to say to you, Fedor Ivanich," continued Maria Dmitrievna, drawing a little nearer to him. "If you had only seen how modestly, how respectfully she behaved! Really it was perfectly touching. And if you had only heard how she spoke of you! 'I,' she said, 'am altogether guilty before him,' 'I,' she said, 'was not able to appreciate him.' 'He,' she said, 'is an angel, not a mere man.' I can assure you that's what she said—'an angel.' She is so penitent—I do solemnly declare I have never seen any one so penitent."

"But tell me, Maria Dmitrievna," said Lavretsky, "if I may be allowed to be so inquisitive. I hear that Varvara Pavlovna has been singing here. Was it in one of her penitent moments that she sang, or how——?"

"How can you talk like that and not feel ashamed of yourself? She played and sang simply to give me pleasure, and because I particularly entreated her, almost ordered her to do so. I saw that she was unhappy, so unhappy, and I thought how I could divert her a little; and besides that, I had heard that she had so much talent. Do show her some pity, Fedor Ivanich —she is utterly crushed—only ask Gedeonovsky— broken down entirely, *tout-a-fait*. How can you say such things of her?"

Lavretsky merely shrugged his shoulders.

"And besides, what a little angel your Adochka is! What a charming little creature! How pretty she is! and how good! and how well she speaks French! And she knows Russian too. She called me aunt in Russian.

And then as to shyness, you know, almost all children of her age are shy; but she is not at all so. It's wonderful how like you she is, Fedor Ivanich—eyes, eyebrows, in fact you all over—absolutely you. I don't usually like such young children, I must confess, but I am quite in love with your little daughter."

"Maria Dmitrievna," abruptly said Lavretsky, "allow me to inquire why you are saying all this to me?"

"Why?"—Maria Dmitrievna again had recourse to her eau-de-cologne and drank some water—"why I say this to you, Fedor Ivanich, is because—you see I am one of your relations, I take a deep interest in you. I know your heart is excellent. Mark my words, *mon cousin*—at all events I am a woman of experience, and I do not speak at random. Forgive, do forgive your wife!" (Maria Dmitrievna's eyes suddenly filled with tears.) "Only think—youth, inexperience, and perhaps also a bad example—hers was not the sort of mother to put her in the right way. Forgive her, Fedor Ivanich! She has been punished enough."

The tears flowed down Maria Dmitrievna's cheeks. She did not wipe them away; she was fond of weeping. Meanwhile Lavretsky sat as if on thorns. "Good God!" he thought, "what torture this is! What a day this has been for me!"

"You do not reply," Maria Dmitrievna recommenced: "how am I to understand you? Is it possible that you can be so cruel? No, I cannot believe that. I feel that my words have convinced you. Fedor Ivanich, God will reward you for your goodness! Now from my hands receive your wife!"

Lavretsky jumped up from his chair scarcely knowing what he was doing. Maria Dmitrievna had risen also, and had passed rapidly to the other side of the screen, from behind which she now brought out Madame Lavretsky. Pale, half lifeless, with downcast eyes, that lady seemed as if she had surrendered her whole power of thinking or willing for herself, and had given herself over entirely into the hands of Maria Dmitrievna.

LIZA

Lavretsky recoiled a pace.

"You have been there all this time!" he exclaimed.

"Don't blame her," Maria Dmitrievna hastened to say. "She wouldn't have stayed for anything; but I made her stay; I put her behind the screen. She declared that it would make you angrier than ever; but I wouldn't even listen to her. I know you better than she does. Take then from my hands your wife! Go to him, Varvara; have no fear; fall at your husband's feet" (here she gave Varvara's arm a pull), "and may my blessing——"

"Stop, Maria Dmitrievna!" interposed Lavretsky, in a voice shaking with emotion. "You seem to like sentimental scenes." (Lavretsky was not mistaken; from her earliest school-days Maria Dmitrievna had always been passionately fond of a touch of stage effect.) "They may amuse you, but to other people they may prove very unpleasant. However, I am not going to talk to you. In *this* scene you do not play the leading part."

"What is it *you* want from me, Madame?" he added, turning to his wife. "Have I not done for you all that I could? Do not tell me that it was not you who got up this scene. I should not believe you. You know that I cannot believe you. What is it you want? You are clever. You do nothing without an object. You must feel that to live with you, as I used formerly to live, is what I am not in a position to do—not because I am angry with you, but because I have become a different man. I told you that the very day you returned; and at that time you agreed with me in your own mind. But, perhaps, you wish to rehabilitate yourself in public opinion. Merely to live in my house is too little for you; you want to live with me under the same roof. Is it not so?"

"I want you to pardon me," replied Varvara Pavlovna, without lifting her eyes from the ground.

"She wants you to pardon her," repeated Maria Dmitrievna.

482

" And not for my own sake, but for Ada's," whispered Varvara.

" Not for her own take, but for your Ada's," repeated Maria Dmitrievna.

" Very good! That is what you want? " Lavretsky just managed to say. " Well, I consent even to that."

Varvara Pavlovna shot a quick glance at him. Maria Dmitrievna exclaimed, " Thank God! " again took Varvara by the arm, and again began, " Take, then, from my hands——"

" Stop, I tell you! " broke in Lavretsky. " I will consent to live with you, Varvara Pavlovna," he continued; " that is to say, I will take you to Lavriki, and live with you as long as I possibly can. Then I will go away; but I will visit you from time to time. You see, I do not wish to deceive you; only do not ask for more than that. You would laugh yourself, if I were to fulfil the wish of our respected relative, and press you to my heart—if I were to assure you that—that the past did not exist, that the felled tree would again produce leaves. But I see this plainly — one must submit. These words do not convey the same meaning to you as to me, but that does not matter. I repeat, I will live with you—or, no, I cannot promise that; but I will no longer avoid you; I will look on you as my wife again——"

" At all events, give her your hand on that," said Maria Dmitrievna, whose tears had dried up long ago.

" I have never yet deceived Varvara Pavlovna," answered Lavretsky. " She will believe me as it is. I will take her to Lavriki. But remember this, Varvara Pavlovna. Our treaty will be considered at an end, as soon as you give up stopping there. And now let me go away."

He bowed to both of the ladies, and went out quickly.

" Won't you take her with you? " Maria Dmitrievna called after him.

" Let him alone," said Varvara to her in a whisper, and then began to express her thanks to her, throwing her arms around her, kissing her hand, saying she had saved her.

Maria Dmitrievna condescended to accept her caresses, but in reality she was not contented with her; nor was she contented with Lavretsky, nor with the whole scene which she had taken so much pains to arrange. There had been nothing sentimental about it. According to her ideas Varvara Pavlovna ought to have thrown herself at her husband's feet.

"How was it you didn't understand what I meant?" she kept saying. "Surely I said to you, 'Down with you!'"

"It is better as it is, my dear aunt. Don't disturb yourself—all has turned out admirably," declared Varvara Pavlovna.

"Well, anyhow he is—as cold as ice," said Maria Dmitrievna. "It is true you didn't cry, but surely my tears flowed before his eyes. So he wants to shut you up at Lavriki. What! You won't be able to come out even to see me! All men are unfeeling," she ended by saying, and shook her head with an air of deep meaning.

"But at all events women can appreciate goodness and generosity," said Varvara Pavlovna. Then, slowly sinking on her knees, she threw her arms around Maria Dmitrievna's full waist, and hid her face in that lady's lap. That hidden face wore a smile, but Maria Dmitrievna's tears began to flow afresh.

As for Lavretsky, he returned home, shut himself up in his valet's room, flung himself on the couch, and lay there till the morning.

XLII

THE next day was Sunday. Lavretsky was not
awakened by the bells which clanged for early mass, for
he had not closed his eyes all night, but they reminded
him of another Sunday, when he went to church at Liza's
request. He rose in haste. A certain secret voice told
him that to-day also he would see her there. He left
the house quietly, telling the servant to say to Varvara
Pavlovna, who was still asleep, that he would be back to
dinner, and then, with long steps, he went where the
bell called him with its dreary uniformity of sound.

He arrived early; scarcely any one was yet in the
church. A reader was reciting the hours in the choir.
His voice, sometimes interrupted by a cough, sounded
monotonously, rising and falling by turns. Lavretsky
placed himself at a little distance from the door. The
worshippers arrived, one after another, stopped, crossed
themselves, and bowed in all directions. Their steps
resounded loudly through the silent and almost empty
space, and echoed along the vaulted roof. An infirm old
woman, wrapped in a threadbare hooded cloak, knelt by
Lavretsky's side and prayed fervently. Her toothless,
yellow, wrinkled face expressed intense emotion. Her
blood-shot eyes gazed upwards, without moving, on the
holy figures displayed upon the iconostasis. Her bony
hand kept incessantly coming out from under her cloak,
and making the sign of the cross—with a slow and sweeping gesture, and with steady pressure of the fingers on the
forehead and the body. A peasant with a morose and
thickly bearded face, his hair and clothes all in disorder,
came into the church, threw himself straight down on
his knees, and immediately began crossing and pros-
trating himself, throwing back his head and shaking it

after each inclination. So bitter a grief showed itself in his face and in all his gestures, that Lavretsky went up to him and asked him what was the matter. The peasant shrank back with an air of distrust; then, looking at him coldly, said in a hurried voice, " My son is dead," and again betook himself to his prostrations.

" What sorrow can they have too great to defy the consolations of the Church? " thought Lavretsky, and he tried to pray himself. But his heart seemed heavy and hardened, and his thoughts were afar off. He kept waiting for Liza; but Liza did not come. The church gradually filled with people, but he did not see Liza among them. Mass began, the deacon read the Gospel, the bell sounded for the final prayer. Lavretsky advanced a few steps, and suddenly he caught sight of Liza. She had come in before him, but he had not observed her till now. Standing in the space between the wall and the choir, to which she had pressed as close as possible, she never once looked round, never moved from her place. Lavretsky did not take his eyes off her till the service was quite finished; he was bidding her a last farewell. The congregation began to disperse, but she remained standing there. She seemed to be waiting for Lavretsky to go away. At last, however, she crossed herself for the last time, and went out without turning round. No one but a maid-servant was with her.

Lavretsky followed her out of the church, and came up with her in the street. She was walking very fast, her head drooping, her veil pulled low over her face.

" Good day, Lizaveta Mikhailovna," he said in a loud voice, with feigned indifference. " May I accompany you? "

She made no reply. He walked on by her side.

" Are you satisfied with me? " he asked, lowering his voice. " You have heard what took place yesterday, I suppose? "

" Yes, yes," she answered in a whisper; " that was very good; " and she quickened her pace.

486

" Then you are satisfied ? "

Liza only made a sign of assent.

" Fedor Ivanovich," she began, presently, in a calm but feeble voice, " I wanted to ask you something. Do not come any more to our house. Go away soon. We may see each other by-and-by—some day or other—a year hence, perhaps. But now, do this for my sake. In God's name, I beseech you, do what I ask! "

" I am ready to obey you in everything, Lizaveta Mikhailovna. But can it be that we must part thus? Is it possible that you will not say a single word to me ? "

" Fedor Ivanovich, you are walking here by my side. But you are already so far, far away from me; and not only you, but——"

" Go on, I entreat you! " exclaimed Lavretsky. " What do you mean ? "

" You will hear, perhaps—— But whatever it may be, forget—— No, do not forget me — remember me."

" I forget you! "

" Enough. Farewell. Please do not follow me."

" Liza——" began Lavretsky.

" Farewell, farewell! " she repeated, and then, drawing her veil still lower over her face, she went away, almost at a run.

Lavretsky looked after her for a time, and then walked down the street with drooping head. Presently he ran against Lemm, who also was walking along with his hat pulled low over his brows, and his eyes fixed on his feet.

They looked at each other for a time in silence.

" Well, what have you to say? " asked Lavretsky at last.

" What have I to say? " replied Lemm, in a surly voice. " I have nothing to say. ' All is dead and we are dead.' (' *Alles ist todt und wir sind todt.*') Do you go to the right ? "

" Yes."

487

" And I am going to the left. Good-bye."

On the following morning Lavretsky took his wife to
Lavriki. She went in front in a carriage with Ada and
Justine. He followed behind in a tarantass. During
the whole time of the journey, the little girl never stirred
from the carriage window. Everything astonished her:
the peasant men and women, the cottages, the wells, the
arches over the horses' necks, the little bells hanging
from them, and the numbers of rooks. Justine shared
her astonishment. Varvara Pavlovna kept laughing
at their remarks and exclamations. She was in excellent spirits; she had had an explanation with her
husband before leaving O.

" I understand your position," she had said to him;
and, from the expression of her quick eyes, he could see
that she did completely understand his position. " But
you will do me at least this justice—you will allow that
I am an easy person to live with. I shall not obtrude
myself on you, or annoy you. I only wished to ensure
Ada's future; I want nothing more."

" Yes, you have attained all your ends," said Lavretsky.

" There is only one thing I dream of now; to bury
myself for ever in seclusion. But I shall always remember your kindness——"

" There! enough of that! " said he, trying to stop her.

" And I shall know how to respect your tranquillity
and your independence," she continued, bringing her
preconcerted speech to a close.

Lavretsky bowed low. Varvara understood that her
husband silently thanked her.

The next day they arrived at Lavriki towards evening.
A week later Lavretsky went away to Moscow, having
left five thousand roubles at his wife's disposal; and the
day after Lavretsky's departure, Panshine appeared,
whom Varvara Pavlovna had entreated not to forget her
in her solitude. She received him in the most cordial
manner; and, till late that night, the lofty rooms of the

mansion and the very garden itself were enlivened by the sounds of music, and of song, and of joyous French talk.   Panshine spent three days with Varvara Pavlovna.   When saying farewell to her, and warmly pressing her beautiful hands, he promised to return very soon —and he kept his word.

XLIII

Liza had a little room of her own on the second floor of her mother's house—a bright, tidy room, with a bedstead with white curtains in it, a small writing-table, several flowerpots in the corners and in front of the windows, and fixed against the wall a set of bookshelves and a crucifix. It was called the nursery; Liza had been born in it.

After coming back from the church where Lavretsky had seen her, she set all her things in order with even more than usual care, dusted everything, examined all her papers and letters from her friends, and tied them up with pieces of ribbon, shut up all her drawers, and watered her flowers, giving each flower a caressing touch. And all this she did deliberately, quietly, with a kind of sweet and tranquil earnestness in the expression of her face. At last she stopped still in the middle of the room and looked slowly around her; then she approached the table over which hung the crucifix, fell on her knees, laid her head on her clasped hands, and remained for some time motionless. Presently Marfa Timofeevna entered the room and found her in that position. Liza did not perceive her arrival. The old lady went out of the room on tiptoe, and coughed loudly several times outside the door. Liza hastily rose and wiped her eyes, which shone with gathered but not fallen tears.

"So I see you have arranged your little cell afresh," said Marfa Timofeevna, bending low over a young rose-tree in one of the flower-pots. "How sweet this smells!"

Liza looked at her aunt with a meditative air.

"What was that word you used?" she whispered.

"What word—what?" sharply replied the old lady. "It is dreadful," she continued, suddenly pulling off her cap and sitting down on Liza's bed. " It is more than I can bear. This is the fourth day I ve been just as if I were boiling in a cauldron. I cannot any longer pretend I don't observe anything. I cannot bear to see you crying, to see how pale and withered you are growing. I cannot—I cannot."

" But what makes you say that, aunt? " said Liza. " There is nothing the matter with me, I——"

" Nothing? " exclaimed Marfa Timofeevna. " Tell that to some one else, not to me! Nothing! But who was on her knees just now? Whose eyelashes are still wet with tears? Nothing! Why, just look at yourself, what have you done to your face? where are your eyes gone? Nothing, indeed! As if I didn't know all! "

" Give me a little time, aunt. All this will pass away."

" Will pass away! Yes; but when? Good heavens! is it possible you have loved him so much? Why, he is quite an old fellow, Lizochka! Well, well! I don't deny he is a good man; will not bite; but what of that? We are all good people; the world isn't shut up in a corner, there will always be plenty of this sort of goodness."

" I can assure you all this will pass away—all this has already passed away."

" Listen to what I am going to tell you, Lizochka," suddenly said Marfa Timofeevna, making Liza sit down beside her on the bed, smoothing down the girl's hair, and setting her neckerchief straight while she spoke. " It seems to you, in the heat of the moment, as if it were impossible for your wound to be cured. Ah, my love, it is only death for which there is no cure. Only say to yourself, ' I won't give in—so much for him! ' and you will be surprised yourself to see how well and how quickly it will all pass away. Only have a little patience."

" Aunt," replied Liza, " it has already passed away All has passed away."

" Passed away! how passed away? Why your nose has actually grown peaky, and yet you say—' passed away.' Passed away indeed! "

" Yes, passed away, aunt—if only you are willing to help me," said Liza, with unexpected animation, and then threw her arms round Marfa Timofeevna's neck. " Dearest aunt, do be a friend to me, do help me, don't be angry with me, try to understand me——"

" But what is all this, what is all this, my mother? Don't frighten me, please. I shall cry out in another minute. Don't look at me like that: quick, tell me what is the meaning of all this! "

" I—I want——" Here Liza hid her face on Marfa Timofeevna's breast. " I want to go into a convent," she said in a low tone.

The old lady fairly bounded off the bed.

" Cross yourself, Lizochka! gather your senses together! what ever are you about? Heaven help you! " at last she stammered out. " Lie down and sleep a little, my darling. All this comes of your want of sleep, dearest."

Liza raised her head; her cheeks glowed.

" No, aunt," she said, " do not say that. I have prayed, I have asked God's advice, and I .have made up my mind. All is over. My life with you here is ended. Such lessons are not given to us without a purpose; besides, it is not for the first time that I think of it now. Happiness was not for me. Even when I did indulge in hopes of happiness, my heart shuddered within me. I know all, both my sins and those of others, and how papa made our money. I know all, and all that I must pray away, must pray away. I grieve to leave you, I grieve for mamma and for Lenochka; but there is no help for it. I feel that it is impossible for me to live here longer. I have already taken leave of everything, I have greeted everything in the house for the last time. Something calls me away. I am sad at heart, and I would fain hide myself away for ever. Please don't hinder me or try to dissuade

492

me; but do help me, or I shall have to go away by myself."

Marfa Timofeevna listened to her niece with horror.

" She is ill," she thought. " She is raving. We must send for a doctor; but for whom? Gedeonovsky praised some one the other day; but then he always lies—but perhaps he has actually told the truth this time."

But when she had become convinced that Liza was not ill, and was not raving—when to all her objections Liza had constantly made the same reply, Marfa Timofeevna was thoroughly alarmed, and became exceedingly sorrowful.

" But surely you don't know, my darling, what sort of life they lead in convents! " thus she began, in hopes of dissuading her. " Why they will feed you on yellow hemp oil, my own; they will dress you in coarse, very coarse clothing; they will make you go out in the cold; you will never be able to bear all this, Lizochka. All these ideas of yours are Agafia's doing. It is she who has driven you out of your senses. But then she began with living, and with living to her own satisfaction. Why shouldn't you live too? At all events, let me die in peace, and then do as you please. And who on earth has ever known any one go into a convent for the sake of such a one, for a goat's beard—God forgive me—for a man! Why, if you're so sad at heart, you should pay a visit to a convent, pray to a saint, order prayers to be said, but don't put the black veil on your head, my *batyushka*, my *matyushka*."

And Marfa Timofeevna cried bitterly.

Liza tried to console her, wiped the tears from her eyes, and cried herself, but maintained her purpose unshaken. In her despair, Marfa Timofeevna tried to turn threats to account, said she would reveal everything to Liza's mother; but that too had no effect. All that Liza would consent to do in consequence of the old lady's urgent entreaties was to put off the execution of her plan for a half year. In return Marfa Timofeevna was obliged to promise that, if Liza had not changed her

493

mind at the end of the six months, she would herself
assist in the matter, and would contrive to obtain
Madame Kalitine's consent.

As soon as the first cold weather arrived, in spite of
her promise to bury herself in seclusion, Varvara Pavlovna, who had provided herself with sufficient funds,
migrated to St. Petersburg. A modest but pretty set
of rooms had been found for her there by Panshine,
who had left the province of O. rather earlier than she
did. During the latter part of his stay in O., he had
completely lost Madame Kalitine's good graces. He
had suddenly given up visiting her, and indeed scarcely
stirred away from Lavriki. Varvara Pavlovna had
enslaved—literally enslaved him. No other word can
express the unbounded extent of the despotic sway she
exercised over him.

Lavretsky spent the winter in Moscow. In the
spring of the ensuing year the news reached him that
Liza had taken the veil in the B. convent, in one of the
most remote districts of Russia.

EPILOGUE

EIGHT years passed. The spring had come again——

But we will first of all say a few words about the fate of Mikhalevich, Panshine, and Madame Lavretsky, and then take leave of them for ever.

Mikhalevich, after much wandering to and fro, at last hit upon the business he was fitted for, and obtained the post of head inspector in one of the government educational institutes. His lot thoroughly satisfies him, and his pupils " adore " him, though at the same time they mimic him. Panshine has advanced high in the service, and already aims at becoming the head of a department. He stoops a little as he walks; it must be the weight of the Vladimir Cross which hangs from his neck, that bends him forward. In him the official decidedly preponderates over the artist now. His face, though still quite young, has grown yellow, his hair is thinner than it used to be, and he neither sings nor draws any longer. But he secretly occupies himself with literature. He has written a little comedy in the style of a " proverb; " and—as every one who writes now constantly brings on the stage some real person or some actual fact—he has introduced a coquette into it, and he reads it confidentially to a few ladies who are very kind to him. But he has never married, although he has had many excellent opportunities for doing so. For that Varvara Pavlovna is to blame.

As for her, she constantly inhabits Paris, just as she used to do. Lavretsky has opened a private account for her with his banker, and has paid a sufficient sum to ensure his being free from her—free from the possibility of being a second time unexpectedly visited by her. She has grown older and stouter, but she is still undoubtedly handsome, and always dresses in taste. Every one has

495

his ideal. Varvara Pavlovna has found hers—in the plays of M. Dumas *fils*. She assiduously frequents the theatres in which consumptive and sentimental Camelias appear on the boards; to be Madame Doche seems to her the height of human happiness. She once announced that she could not wish her daughter a happier fate. It may, however, be expected that destiny will save Mademoiselle Ada from that kind of happiness. From being a chubby, rosy child, she has changed into a pale, weak-chested girl, and her nerves are already unstrung. The number of Varvara Pavlovna's admirers has diminished, but they have not disappeared. Some of them she will, in all probability, retain to the end of her days. The most ardent of them in recent times has been a certain Zakurdalo-Skubyrnikof, a retired officer of the guard, a man of about thirty-eight years of age, wearing long moustaches, and possessing a singularly vigorous frame. The Frenchmen who frequent Madame Lavretsky's drawing-room call him *le gros taureau de l'Ukraine*. Varvara Pavlovna never invites him to her fashionable parties, but he is in full possession of her good graces.

And so—eight years had passed away. Again spring shone from heaven in radiant happiness. Again it smiled on earth and on man. Again, beneath its caress, all things began to love, to flower, to sing.

The town of O had changed but little in the course of these eight years, but Madame Kalitine's house had, as it were, grown young again. Its freshly-painted walls shone with a welcome whiteness, while the panes of its open windows flashed ruddy to the setting sun. Out of these windows there flowed into the street mirthful sounds of ringing youthful voices, of never-ceasing laughter. All the house seemed teeming with life and overflowing with irrepressible merriment. As for the former mistress of the house, she had been laid in the grave long ago. Maria Dmitrievna died two years after Liza took the veil. Nor did Marfa Timofeevna long survive her niece; they rest side by side in the cemetery

496

of the town. Nastasia Carpovna also was no longer
alive. During the course of several years the faithful
old lady used to go every day to pray at her friend's
grave. Then her time came, and her bones also were
laid in the mould.

But Maria Dmitrievna's house did not pass into the
hands of strangers, did not go out of her family—the
nest was not torn to pieces. Lenochka, who had grown
into a pretty and graceful girl; her betrothed, a flaxen-
locked officer of hussars; Maria Dmitrievna's son, who
had only recently married at St. Petersburg, and had
now arrived with his young bride to spend the spring in
O.; his wife's sister, a sixteen-year-old institute girl,
with clear eyes and rosy cheeks; and Shurochka, who
had also grown up and turned out pretty—these were
the young people who made the walls of the Kalitine
house resound with laughter and with talk. Everything
was altered in the house, everything had been made to
harmonise with its new inhabitants. Beardless young
servant lads, full of fun and laughter, had replaced the
grave old domestics of former days. A couple of setters
tore wildly about and jumped upon the couches, in the
rooms up and down which Roska, after it had grown fat,
used to waddle seriously. In the stable many horses
were stalled—clean-limbed canterers, smart trotters for
the centre of the *troika*, fiery gallopers with platted
manes for the side places, riding horses from the Don.
The hours for breakfast, dinner, and supper, were all
mixed up and confounded together. In the words of
the neighbours, " Such a state of things as never had
been known before " had taken place.

On the evening of which we are about to speak, the
inmates of the Kalitine house, of whom the eldest,
Lenochka's betrothed, was not more than four and
twenty, had taken to playing a game which was not of
a very complicated nature, but which seemed to be very
amusing to them, to judge by their happy laughter,—
that of running about the rooms, and trying to catch
each other. The dogs, too, ran about and barked; and

497

the canaries which hung up in cages before the windows, straining their throats in rivalry, heightened the general uproar by the piercing accents of their shrill singing. Just as this deafening amusement had reached its climax, a tarantass, all splashed with mud, drew up at the front gate, and a man about forty-five years old, wearing a travelling dress, got out of it and remained standing as if bewildered.

For some time he stood at the gate without moving, but gazing at the house with observant eyes; then he entered the courtyard by the wicket-gate, and slowly mounted the steps. He encountered no one in the vestibule; but suddenly the drawing-room door was flung open, and Shurochka, all rosy red, came running out of the room; and directly afterwards, with shrill cries, the whole of the youthful band rushed after her. Suddenly, at the sight of an unknown stranger, they stopped short, and became silent; but the bright eyes which were fixed on him still retained their friendly expression, the fresh young faces did not cease to smile. Then Maria Dmitrievna's son approached the visitor, and politely asked what he could do for him.

" I am Lavretsky," said the stranger.

A friendly cry of greeting answered him—not that all those young people were inordinately delighted at the arrival of a distant and almost forgotten relative, but simply because they were ready to rejoice and make a noise over every pleasurable occurrence. They all immediately surrounded Lavretsky. Lenochka, as his old acquaintance, was the first to name herself, assuring him that, if she had had a very little more time, she would most certainly have recognised him; and then she introduced all the rest of the company to him, giving them all, her betrothed included, their familiar forms of name. The whole party then went through the dining-room into the drawing-room. The paper on the walls of both rooms had been altered, but the furniture remained just as it used to be. Lavretsky recognised the piano. Even the embroidery-frame by the window remained exactly as it had been, and in the very same position as of old; and even seemed to have the same unfinished piece of work on it which had been there eight years before. They placed him in a large armchair, and sat down gravely around him. Questions, exclamations, anecdotes, followed swiftly one after another.

" What a long time it is since we saw you last! " naïvely remarked Lenochka; " and we haven't seen Varvara Pavlovna either."

" No wonder! " her brother hastily interrupted her— " I took you away to St. Petersburg; but Fedor Ivanich has lived all the time on his estate."

" Yes, and mamma too is dead, since then."

" And Marfa Timofeevna," said Shurochka.

" And Nastasia Carpovna," continued Lenochka, " and Monsieur Lemm."

" What? is Lemm dead too? " asked Lavretsky.

" Yes," answered young Kalitine. " He went away from here to Odessa. Some one is said to have persuaded him to go there, and there he died."

" You don't happen to know if he left any music behind? "

" I don't know, but I should scarcely think so."

A general silence ensued, and each one of the party looked at the others. A shade of sadness swept over all the youthful faces.

" But Matros is alive," suddenly cried Lenochka.

" And Gedeonovsky is alive," added her brother.

The name of Gedeonovsky at once called forth a merry laugh.

" Yes, he is still alive; and he tells stories just as he used to do," continued the young Kalitine—" only fancy! this madcap here " (pointing to his wife's sister, the institute girl) " put a quantity of pepper into his snuff-box yesterday."

" How he did sneeze! " exclaimed Lenochka—and irrepressible laughter again broke out on all sides.

" We had news of Liza the other day," said young

Kalitine. And again silence fell upon all the circle. " She is going on well—her health is gradually being restored now."

" Is she still in the same convent? " Lavretsky asked, not without an effort.

" Yes."

" Does she ever write to you? "

" No, never. We get news of her from other quarters."

A profound silence suddenly ensued. " An angel has noiselessly flown past," they all thought.

" Won't you go into the garden? " said Kalitine, addressing Lavretsky. " It is very pleasant now, although we have neglected it a little."

Lavretsky went into the garden, and the first thing he saw there was that very bench on which he and Liza had once passed a few happy moments—moments that never repeated themselves. It had grown black and warped, but still he recognised it, and that feeling took possession of his heart which is unequalled as well for sweetness as for bitterness—the feeling of lively regret for vanished youth, for once familiar happiness.

He walked by the side of the young people along the alleys. The lime-trees looked older than before, having grown a little taller during the last eight years, and casting a denser shade. All the underwood, also, had grown higher, and the raspberry bushes had spread vigorously, and the hazel copse was thickly tangled. From every side exhaled a fresh odour from the forest and the wood, from the grass and the lilacs.

" What a capital place for a game at Puss in the Corner! " suddenly cried Lenochka, as they entered upon a small grassy lawn surrounded by lime trees. " There are just five of us."

" But have you forgotten Fedor Ivanovich? " asked her brother; " or is it yourself you have not counted? "

Lenochka blushed a little.

" But would Fedor Ivanovich like—at his age——" she began stammering.

" Please play away," hastily interposed Lavretsky;

" don't pay any attention to me. I shall feel more comfortable if I know I am not boring you. And there is no necessity for your finding me something to do. We old people have a resource which you don't know yet, and which is better than any amusement—recollection."

The young people listened to Lavretsky with respectful, though slightly humorous politeness, just as if they were listening to a teacher who was reading them a lesson—then they all suddenly left him, and ran off to the lawn. One of them stood in the middle, the others occupied the four corners by the trees, and the game began.

But Lavretsky returned to the house, went into the dining-room, approached the piano, and touched one of the notes. It responded with a faint but clear sound, and a shudder thrilled his heart within him. With that note began the inspired melody, by means of which, on that most happy night long ago, Lemm, the dead Lemm, had thrown him into such raptures. Then Lavretsky passed into the drawing-room, and did not leave it for a long time.

In that room, in which he had seen Liza so often, her image floated more distinctly before him; the traces of her presence seemed to make themselves felt around him there. But his sorrow for her loss became painful and crushing; it bore with it none of the tranquillity which death inspires. Liza was still living somewhere, far away and lost to sight. He thought of her as he had known her in actual life; he could not recognise the girl he used to love in that pale, dim, ghostly form, half-hidden in a nun's dark robe, and surrounded by waving clouds of incense.

Nor would Lavretsky have been able to recognise himself, if he could have looked at himself as he in fancy was looking at Liza. In the course of those eight years his life had attained its final crisis—that crisis which many people never experience, but without which no man can be sure of maintaining his principles firm to the last.

501

LIZA

He had really given up thinking about his own happiness, about what would conduce to his own interests. He had become calm, and—why should we conceal the truth?—he had aged; and that not in face alone or frame, but he had aged in mind; for, indeed, not only is it difficult, but it is even hazardous to do what some people speak of—to preserve the heart young in bodily old age. Contentment, in old age, is deserved by him alone who has not lost his faith in what is good, his persevering strength of will, his desire for active employment. And Lavretsky did deserve to be contented; he had really become a good landlord; he had really learnt how to till the soil; and in that he laboured, he laboured not for himself alone, but he had, as far as in him lay the power, assured, and obtained guarantees for, the welfare of the peasantry on his estates.

Lavretsky went out of the house into the garden, and sat down on the bench he knew so well. There—on that loved spot, in sight of that house in which he had fruitlessly, and for the last time, stretched forth his hands towards that cup of promise in which foamed and sparkled the golden wine of enjoyment,—he, a lonely, homeless wanderer, while the joyous cries of that younger generation which had already forgotten him came flying to his ears, gazed steadily at his past life.

His heart became very sorrowful, but it was free now from any crushing sense of pain. He had nothing to be ashamed of; he had many sources of consolation. " Play on, young vigorous lives! " he thought—and his thoughts had no taint of bitterness in them—" the future awaits you, and your path of life in it will be comparatively easy for you. You will not be obliged, as we were, to seek out your path, to struggle, to fall, to rise again in utter darkness. We had to seek painfully by what means we might hold out to the end—and how many there were amongst us who did not hold out!—but your part is now to act, to work—and the blessing of old men like me shall be with you. For my part, after the day I have spent here, after the emotions I have here

502

experienced, nothing remains for me but to bid you a
last farewell; and, although sadly, yet without a tinge
of envy, without a single gloomy feeling, to say, in
sight of death, in sight of my awaiting God, ' Hail,
lonely old age!   Useless life, burn yourself out! ' "

Lavretsky rose up quietly, and quietly went away.
No one observed him, no one prevented him from going.
Louder than ever sounded the joyous cries in the garden,
behind the thick green walls of the lofty lime trees.
Lavretsky got into his tarantass, and told his coachman
to drive him home without hurrying the horses.

" And is that the end? " the unsatisfied reader may
perhaps ask.   " What became of Lavretsky afterwards?
and of Liza? "   But what can one say about people
who are still alive, but who have already quitted the
worldly stage?   Why should we turn back to them?
It is said that Lavretsky has visited the distant convent
in which Liza has hidden herself—and has seen her.   As
she crossed from choir to choir, she passed close by him
—passed onwards steadily, with the quick but silent
step of a nun, and did not look at him.   Only an almost
imperceptible tremor was seen to move the eyelashes
of the eye which was visible to him; only still lower did
she bend her emaciated face;   and the fingers of her
clasped hands, enlaced with her rosary, still more closely
compressed each other.

Of what did they both think?   what did they both
feel?   Who can know?   who shall tell?   Life has its
moments—has its feelings—to which we may be allowed
to allude, but on which it is not good to dwell.

*This book, designed by
William B. Taylor
is a production of
Edito-Service S.A., Geneva*

Printed in Switzerland